MOLDAVIAN MOON BOOK ONE

The Wolf's Torment

STEPHANIE BURKHART

Reviews for The Wolf's Torment

WINNER: GOLD, 2012 Reader's Favorite Contest, Fiction: Supernatural

4 Stars, LibriAmoreiMiei, "It's a paranormal novel compelling, full of suspense, adventurous and romantic."

4.5 Books, Book Bling, "This book has it all. What a treat."

5 Stars, The Crafty Cauldron, "Brilliantly written."

5 Stars, BTS Magazine, DEC 2013, Reviewer: Cassandra Graham, "It was a really good and suspenseful read. Pick up a copy. You'll definitely enjoy it."

Pen & Muse: "A complete werewolf story through and through, Burkhart does it again with an amazing cast of characters, entertaining dialogue and plot."

Long and Short, 4.5 Stars: Nominated for Long & Short's Book of the Week, NOV 2011. The Wolf's Torment is certainly more than a story about a werewolf. There is quite a bit of depth in this multifaceted story of a family's struggle with life, love and loss.

Reader's Favorites, 5 Stars: "The Wolf's Torment has it all, witches, werewolves, a vampire, princess and prince. This is paranormal romance at its finest.

5 Stars, Queen Tutt, Rhonda Tutt
(Abbreviated review)
Perfect Paranormal/ Fantasy with a Twist!

Wow! I absolutely loved this book. The secret lives of witches and were-wolves fill this story with a captivating romance and a twisted drama. I was totally glued to the pages and wanted it to last forever and wishing I had their magical spells to transport myself into their time period. The writing is beautifully smooth and visionary.

The characters are brilliantly built, and their chemistry will melt your heart. I loved Prince Mihai. He is a witch, and he knows it, but he has never practiced or even learned what talents he could obtain. He inherited his witch blood from his mother and the author's details of his mother's demise is tragic but is one of the first things that drew me into the story line, I couldn't put the book down – totally spellbinding.

Lady Theresa is a doll, she is so innocent and sweet, one would call her a daddy's girl even though she has older brother and sisters. She is very educated and naive of the witch and were-wolf world that surrounds her.

The story's plot line is perfect, and the climax unraveled all at once. This was an amazing story and I highly recommend this to all paranormal romance lovers. Excellent Read!

The Wolf's Torment: Moldavian Moon – Book One

[Revised Edition]
ISBN-13: 979-8-9891448-4-6

Cover Design by: Jenifer Ranieri
Interior Layout by: Laura Shinn Designs
http://laurashinn.yolasite.com

Author's website: http://StephanieBurkhart.com

~ * ~ * ~ * ~

Available online wherever ebooks and paperbacks are sold!

Night of Magic
Mr. Christmas Elf
Journey of the Heart
Arrow Through the Heart
Young Witchcraft
Christmas in Bayeux
A Polish Heart

~ * ~ * ~ * ~

2011 Dedication

For Dina Hickman, Michelle Simon, aka SkintheKat, and Kathy Kravitz. Thank you for all your help and inspiration.

2024 Dedication

To the creative higher self – seek the good in people.

~ * ~ * ~ * ~

Author's Note

As a matter of history, Romania was united as a nation in 1859. Carpathia and Transylvania were never principalities in their own right, and Moldavia's formal capital was Iasi, not Constanta. I have taken fictional liberties with the events that lead to Romanian unification to tell this story. This is, therefore, a work of fiction.

The Wolf's Torment

It's 1865 and Moldavia is a country nestled against the shores of the Black Sea. Lady Theresa travels from Austria to this country that's haunted by tales of vampires and werewolves. She's going to marry the Crown Prince, but she harbors her own unspoken secrets.

Prince Mihai has just returned to Moldavia to embrace his heritage – that he is a witch. He's intent on being a good husband and modernizing his county, but he must find a balance with his supernatural heritage. His best friend, Viktor, accompanies Mihai and marries Mihai's sister. In an unfortunate twist of fate, a werewolf bites Viktor.

Viktor's transformation threatens everyone around him, including his wife's safety and Mihai's happiness, but he's especially dangerous when he's near Theresa. Can Mihai save his family from Viktor's lies and deceptions?

Contents

The Wolf's Torment

Prologue

Constanta, Near the Black Sea
1855

The carriage slammed into a rut. It careened on its side, threatening to pitch over, but fortunately didn't. The driver cracked his leather whips, spurring on the horses. Mihai wasn't sure who was following them or why, he only knew they were after his Mama, whatever the cost.

He glanced out the side window of the carriage as it shook, hoping for a glimpse of his pursuers. Instead, he spied the setting sun casting golden shadows over the treetops of the surrounding woods. In the distance, torches blazed with tall flames as they lit up the turrets of his ancestral castle overlooking the Black Sea. He prayed they could make it far enough up the road to find the protection of his father's soldiers.

His mama withdrew from the rear window. "Mihai, come here."

He sprang into his mother's arms. She ran her hands over his thick, wavy hair and cupped his cheeks. "I know you're young, but you must be brave."

He stiffened his shoulders and held up his head. He was the Crown Prince of Moldavia, and he would not let his mother be hurt. "I am, Mama," he announced, knowing this was a grave situation. He just didn't know why.

"Mihai, you are just a boy."

"I'm old enough to protect you!" He was ten now. Why did she still think of him as a boy?

The carriage shook violently. It took another sharp turn and barely righted itself.

"She's close." Mihai's mother gripped his shoulders.

"Who is it, Mama?"

"My dear sweet son, I am not truly Alice deBusch, Princess of Weisgarten. My given name is Esmeralda Vacay, and I was raised Roma – a gypsy."

Mihai stared at her, confused. What did she mean? His father was the King of Moldavia. He would never marry a gypsy.

A loud pop thundered in his ears. The carriage jerked, stopped, then thrust forward, tumbling end over end before landing upside down. Mihai was cushioned in his mother's arms. He crawled out from under her, clutching her hand. "Mama!" He didn't feel very brave anymore.

She squeezed his hand back, gasping for breath as she attempted to get to her knees on the overturned ceiling of the carriage.

"I'm a gypsy witch, Mihai. Your father knew precisely who I was when we fell in love. He came up with the identity of Alice deBusch so we could marry," she continued between deep, hurried breaths.

"But witches are bad, Mama," Mihai said, recalling the tales and legends he had overheard from the servants in the castle.

"No, Mihai, not all witches are bad, believe that." She paused. "I have never used my power darkly. I did, however, incur the wrath of the witch who follows us because I wouldn't do her bidding, and I wouldn't do it because she is a dark witch." His mother ripped her skirt, tying it around her bleeding leg.

The carriage rattled as if a heavy stick had prodded it.

"Son, I am far too impulsive for my own good. Guard your heart, be strong yet—"

"Get out, Esmeralda! Get out and face me, cowardly snit."

Mihai hugged his mother again, unwilling to let her go.

She pushed the upside down door open and forced her way out of the carriage. He sat there, shaking with fear. After a deep breath, he dared to raise his head level to the window.

"I've finally found you, Esmeralda, hiding behind the skirts of a queen, no less. Well, I'll have from you now what you wouldn't give then."

Fear was replaced with courage, and Mihai scampered out of the carriage, his own neat, Venetian clothes now torn and dirty. He ran to his mother, who knelt before an old haggard woman. Their pursuer wore a dark cloak, and her face was lined with wrinkles. The knife in her hand glowed an eerie shade of obsidian fire. Her hateful eyes stabbed into the growing darkness, bent on revenge. A quick glance in the direction of the driver told Mihai that he was severely injured. He couldn't help them, and the two horses that were pulling the carriage were absent.

"Leave my Mama alone!" Mihai yelled.

His bold declaration only brought his mother's hand down on his shoulder. She squeezed it hard, making him flinch. Why did she do that? He was a prince. He had to save her.

"Be quiet, son!"

"Why, Esmeralda, you dared to spawn," said the old witch. "Well, no matter. If you don't pay your debt, I'll force your boy to pay it."

"Don't insult my son, Hecuba. He seeks to protect me, like any son would his mother."

"He's a pretty one, Esmeralda. Shall I have him pay for your cowardice?"

"No," his mother snapped. "I will not use my power to curse another living being."

"You owe me, snit. I did as your father wanted. He promised me your service. You were in no position to forsake your family's debt." Hecuba's voice was as cold as the night air.

Mihai swallowed. The witch's evil glare made him afraid. "I will not do evil on your behalf."

"Then I'll take what's owed to me – your son."

"No!"

Mihai's mother pushed him to the ground, and he took in a mouthful of dirt. Coughing and choking, he raised himself up on his elbows, the growing twilight now taking the place of the sunlight. He watched in horror as a powerful blast of lightning shot out from the old witch's knife, only to be parried quickly by his mother as she withdrew her own dagger from her torn skirts. Its bright white fire splayed the obsidian lightning just inches from his body.

He stayed on the ground, frozen. Cold sweat ran down his temple, but he was a prince, and a prince would show no weakness. His father had taught him that.

The old witch reached into the pocket of her cloak and withdrew a sharp pointed dart. His mama's eyes grew wide. Hecuba flung the dart directly at Mihai, but his mama directed her dagger's fire at it, knocking it away.

"I've had enough of this game, Esmeralda."

Mihai heard the old woman chant words he couldn't understand. His gaze cut to his mother. She stiffened her back. A dirty blue flame sliced the air, striking his mother in the chest.

Hecuba took a step forward. "Now, I will cancel out your debt to me, Esmeralda."

"No!" His mama slithered in front of Mihai, taking a second blast of blue flame.

Her eyes rolled back in her head, and blood dripped from the corner of her mouth. Drawing a deep breath, she scrunched up her body, summoning all that she could, and released a blast of her white energy, causing the old witch to fly off the ground, and strike her back against the hard bark of an oak tree. Hecuba slid down the trunk, her back awkwardly crooked against the wood. The roots then lunged out of the ground, fastening her wrists to the dirt.

"Mihai, son, I love you."

He couldn't stop his body from shaking. "I love you, too, Mama. Don't die!"

She turned to face him. He threw himself into her arms, his chest aching in pain.

"My father asked her for the gravest of sins – to kill another for revenge, promising his firstborn child into her service as repayment for the debt. I learned the ways of the witch as a young girl and when I came of age, I refused, leaving my family without honoring that debt. Shortly after that, I met your father. You understand, don't you?"

"I do! I do! Don't die, Mama! I love you!" He hugged her tighter, hoping that his hug would make her live.

"My death will pay the debt. Be a good king, Mihai. Don't be impulsive or reckless like me. Guard your heart. I could have made better choices," she gasped. "You must make better choices than me."

His lower lip trembled. What did she mean?

She jerked her hand forward, finding his. Her grasp was hard and icy. "It is too much for you. Go to your father and tell him what has happened. He will understand."

"Mama, don't die," Mihai sobbed.

"You are a witch, too, my son. It is in your blood as it is in mine."

"No, Mama!"

She hung her head and grew limp in his arms, the light in her eyes slowly fading. Deep inside his wounded heart, he knew his mother was dead. It was just too much to handle. Filled with rage, he grabbed his mother's dagger. It bled drops of white light onto the ground. He ran up to Hecuba, placing the blade against her neck.

The old witch's eyes snapped open, making Mihai jump

back.

She struggled to get up. “Think to kill me, snitty boy?”

Mihai steeled his shoulders.

“If you kill me, my coven will haunt your family forever.”

Mihai’s hand shook. “Shut up.”

“From a witch you were born,” Hecuba began. “Witch’s blood runs in you.”

“Shut up!”

“To witch a wife you’ll take.” Hecuba struggled against her bonds.

Mihai clenched the knife in his hand, his knuckles turning white.

“You’ll forever be in debt to a witch, sweet prince.”

Mihai lunged out, anger overcoming his fear of the witch. He sliced Hecuba’s neck just deep enough to draw blood. The sight of it unnerved him and he backed away, shaking. What was he going to do? Blackness surrounded him. The sounds of the night seemed to thunder in his ears. Owls hooted, hogs grunted as they skirted the wood line. His only hope were the flames from the torches on the castle’s turrets. He turned around and sprinted up the road, clenching his mother’s dagger. It seemed like he ran forever, with Delfin Castle coming into view by bits and pieces. When he finally ran up the steps and entered, he went directly to his father’s study and collapsed.

His father’s mouth twisted unpleasantly as Mihai told him how the old witch had found them in Constanta and given chase. His father reacted immediately, taking his best soldiers and racing down the road from which Mihai had just come. When his father returned less than an hour later, he carried his dead wife’s body in his arms.

Chapter One

Romania
1865

Mihai peered out the window of his train car, surveying the white snow that littered the Romanian countryside. Christmas was only a few days away. His heart was raw, aching, and he had no idea how to soothe it. He raked a hand through his hair, trying to brush away the uncomfortable tendrils of heartbreak that coiled through his body. Love was a cold beast and not one he wanted to encounter again anytime soon.

The door to the compartment opened and his best friend, Viktor Bacau, stepped inside. Thank God for Viktor. His friendship had made Mihai's call to duty easier to bear. Viktor was as tall as Mihai with a head of blond hair and blue eyes that reminded him of the depths of the Black Sea. What Mihai appreciated about his friend was his steady, even manner and his ability to make him laugh.

"We still have about two hours until we get to Bucharest," said Viktor.

Mihai leaned back in his seat. "My father will have a carriage waiting for us. It will take about half a day to get to Constanta."

Viktor clapped his hands and fell into his seat. "This voyage will never end. How long have we been traveling?"

"It's been two weeks since we left London."

"Well, at least we'll be home for the holidays."

"Do you mean it? You don't want to go to your home in Ukraine?"

"Chernivtsi? No. Fedir is there and I hardly think of him as my brother."

"But Chernivtsi is your home."

"It was my home. My parents have passed and you have treated me with the dignity and respect a brother should possess. Your home is my home now." Viktor's voice resonated with sincerity.

A smiled tugged at Mihai's lips. "Thank you. Your friendship means much to me. Can I count on your counsel and guidance as I assume my official duties?"

"Of course."

Mihai glanced out the window. The countryside appeared lonely and cold with snow clinging to the empty tree limbs. Snow also decorated wooden fences. It reminded him of his own chilled heart.

Viktor rubbed his chin. "Why so quiet?"

"It's nothing."

"You're thinking of Alexandra."

"I don't want to talk about her."

"No, you don't, so why are you thinking about her?" Viktor frowned. "You gave her the choice to come and she declined."

"I thought she loved me."

Viktor gave him a sympathetic smile. "Mihai, she didn't love you. You were a foreign prince who could offer her the attention she craved. Did you honestly think she would have come with you? She was a merchant's daughter."

Mihai's nostrils flared with mild anger. "She called Moldavia backward and uncultured."

"She did."

"And she had no desire to learn Romanian."

"No, she didn't. She played you, my friend."

"How could I have been such a fool?"

"She was very pretty."

"I should have looked past that. I should have made more of an effort to find out what was in her heart."

"Don't you have an arranged marriage?" Viktor wrinkled his brow.

Mihai sighed. "Yes." That was the last thing he wanted to think about.

"Well, why don't you give it a chance?"

"I'm not keen on marrying a woman I've never met."

"You might find your intended more agreeable to you."

"Can we talk about something else?" Mihai did not like being reminded of Alexandra and he was uncomfortable knowing that he'd soon be married to a woman he'd never seen before. The thought of getting involved with another woman so soon after Alexandra's rejection did not sit well with him, especially a woman who was picked for him.

"You know, the air is a little stale in here. Why don't we go get a pint?" Viktor suggested.

"That's a great idea."

They walked out into the hall. The floorboards creaked from the jarring motion of the train speeding down the tracks.

They arrived at the restaurant carriage and ordered beers and sandwiches. Viktor smiled once the waitress was gone, catching Mihai's attention. "I expect Moldavia is quite different from England. I get the impression your father isn't afraid to take risks."

"No, he's not. He's been a risk-taker all his life. Right now he's keen on modernizing the country. He's always doing something with his hands. Whittling wood, designing buildings on paper, and he's fascinated with trains. He wants to build a train station in Constanta and link the city to Bucharest. I think it's a brilliant idea. Constanta is a ruling city. It should have a train station."

"Do you think he's healthy enough?"

Mihai pinched the bridge of his nose. His father was another subject he didn't want to think about right now, either. "No, Doctor Stanza gave him six months to live. I'm going to have to get involved with the project right after the Christmas holidays."

"It sounds exciting," He paused and smiled. "I'm anxious to start my new life in Moldavia."

The waitress returned with their order and Mihai took a long sip of his drink. Viktor was the one constant in his rapidly changing life and he appreciated that.

Out of the corner of his eye, Mihai spied a grungy couple sitting in a booth on the opposite side of the train. The man stared at Viktor. He was older, around his father's age, with a rugged brow and greasy hair that might have been the same color as Viktor's if he had bothered to wash it. His blue eyes were as narrow as a snake's. The way he glared at Viktor sent an uneasy chill through his limbs.

The woman unnerved him even more. He'd seen that cold hazel gaze before, in his childhood, filled with hate and loathing, yet this woman was younger, around the man's age, with black curly hair. It couldn't be the same person. She sipped a cup of tea, her nostrils slightly flared. Mihai turned away sharply.

"Is something wrong?" asked Viktor.

"There's an odd couple sitting diagonally from us. The man is staring at you as if he knows you. Don't you feel it?"

Viktor shrugged his shoulders. "No." Then he turned around. The strange couple was gone. "There's no one."

"I didn't make it up. They made me feel uncomfortable."

"Well, they're gone now. I wouldn't worry about it," said Viktor.

Mihai said nothing. His senses had always been sharp. His mother once told him he had her senses – a witch's senses. He shivered at the thought. He'd read books since his mother's death, but had no practical knowledge of magic. Magic would not drag Moldavia kicking and screaming into the modern world, only technology would do that. While he didn't entirely shun his mother's inherited gifts, he had no desire to cultivate them. He didn't want the people of Moldavia to think their crown prince was a witch – a mystical being alive and haunting the land. That would give the myths and legends more reason to be believed.

Viktor checked his pocket watch. "Let's try to get a nap before we pull into Bucharest."

"Good idea." Mihai finished his drink and followed Viktor back to their compartment.

~ * ~

Bane slithered into the coach he shared with Hecuba on the train, heat and excitement rolling through his body. The blond-haired man was exquisite. His natural scent reeked of tiger lilies, a flower which grew around his native home in Ukraine. His nose continued to twitch as he sat down. Dalca's blessings were upon him.

Hecuba put her hands on her hips. "What's going on in that head of yours?"

"Oh, sit down, witch."

"I know that look, Bane."

He raised an eyebrow. "You do?"

"You want to make a wolf."

Bane chuckled, stretching out his long, lean legs on the floor. "The blond-haired man would make a magnificent wolf."

"I don't think it's a good idea."

"Why not?"

"Your recent choices have been made on impulse and they did not work out well."

"They were careless. It's not my fault their stupidity got them killed." Bane crossed his arms.

Hecuba kicked his legs to make room for herself and sat down across from him. “Don’t pout.”

“This one isn’t stupid, Hecuba. I want to make him the heir to the pack.”

“The Crown Prince of Moldavia is a witch. He could protect your target.”

“How rich! A prince for a friend.”

“That prince has Vacay blood. He could be a formidable opponent.”

Bane’s laugh filled the compartment. “Really? Well, the prince lacks courage.”

“How do you know? I’ve seen courage from him before – when he was young.”

“It’s in his posture – and his dull, little eyes.”

Hecuba rubbed her cheek. “Still, I wouldn’t underestimate him.” She paused, then glanced at Bane. “If you want my counsel, leave this one alone. He’ll only prove trouble. Timon should be enough for you.”

“No, I don’t want your counsel.” He paused. “Timon is too cruel and not clever enough. I must have another heir.”

Hecuba sighed.

“Send word to the pack at Mulfaltar we’ll be delayed. I want to follow that man to his final destination.”

“All right, I’ll do as you ask. I may be old, but I know trouble when I see it.”

“When are you due to age?” asked Bane.

“Two hours.”

“So soon?” He wrinkled his brow in concern. Hecuba’s de-aging potion usually lasted six hours, but now it appeared to last no longer than three.

“My body’s advanced years are rejecting the magic. When it completely rejects it, I’ll die.”

He clenched his fists. “You know how I feel about you. Can’t you stop it?”

“No. I can prolong it and delay it, but I can’t stop it.”

"Damn it, Hecuba, I can't live without you."

"Isn't two hundred years enough?" she asked, yawning.

"Not since I've been cursed to live as a wolf."

She stood and walked in front of him. He ran his gaze over her body. He loved her young form, how supple and vibrant it was. He couldn't imagine his life without this witch.

Chapter Two

Mihai's heart soared with pride as the royal carriage traveled down the snowy cobblestone streets of Constanta. Most of the buildings were wooden, but there were several brick buildings as well. As they passed the Parliament building, several passersby recognized the royal coach. They cheered and waved, driving the apprehension of his return away. He'd left a fifteen-year-old boy. Now he was returning a twenty-one year-old man, and it felt good to be home.

The coach ambled out of the main city and along a dirt road past several farms which would take them up a slight incline to Delfin Castle and his home.

Delfin Castle, the ancestral home of his Sigmaringen ancestors, rested on a hill overlooking the Black Sea. The royal land consisted of a section of coastline to the east and to the south there was a winery.

The carriage made good time. It entered the castle's courtyard and pulled up to the *porte-cochère*.

Mihai got out, ignoring the cold winter air that stung his cheeks, grateful for his heavy woolen overcoat, and stared up at his home. Nothing had changed. The castle was made of sturdy brick and limestone, brown in color, with four watch towers on the corners. The northeast corner was the highest tower, and it housed his telescope that he liked to use to peer at the night sky.

The southwest watch tower was the thinnest and at the top flew the flag of Moldavia. His father was home. Mihai drew in a deep breath. His emotions toward his father were deeply complex. He loved the man, but there were times Mihai felt his father had been too strict with him.

Viktor patted him on the back. "Are you ready?"

"Yes, of course."

They ascended the steps and walked up to the large wooden double doors. Two soldiers stood on either side. When Mihai stopped in front of them, they bowed.

"Your Grace."

"I'll go to my father's study and wait for him there."

"Yes, Your Grace."

One soldier opened the door, the other ran inside. Mihai followed him in with Viktor right behind. They took off their coats, handing them to a maid who hung them up in a nearby coatroom. Kerosene gas lamps hung on the walls, lighting the hallways and rooms.

Mihai walked through the entrance hall where a Christmas tree, at least ten feet tall, was decorated with silver balls and popcorn garland. He proceeded down the east hall toward his father's study, aware of the buzz in the castle. Excitement and happiness radiated from those around. It reminded him of how his mother used to enjoy a cup of hot chocolate after coming in from a cold winter day's events – warm and richly satisfying. Peace and satisfaction filled his heart.

He went to the study. Empty. Mihai frowned. A blaze roared in the fireplace, heating the room. Gas lamps burned on the walls.

Mihai investigated his father's bar, which was neatly disguised by two wooden doors on a bookshelf. He opened the doors and grinned at Viktor. "A drink?"

"How could I refuse?"

The door opened. "Mihai, you're home!"

"Sonia!"

His sister raced into the room and wrapped her arms around him, sharing a welcoming embrace. He smiled, delighted to see her again. How she had grown!

She placed her hands on his upper arms and stared into

his face. "My, you've gotten taller."

He promised to think of the happiness his homecoming brought instead of the bitter pill of Alexandra's refusal.

"So have you," she said.

Tall for a woman, his sister came up to his chin. Her long raven-black hair fell down past her shoulders. They both shared their father's ebony locks. Sonia, possessed amber-honey eyes, and high cheekbones, features reminiscent of their mother.

"It's good to see you again," said Mihai.

The sparkle in her expression filled the room with warmth. "The same, Brother. Father needs you. He may fuss a little, but he's glad to have you here. There's so much he wants to show you, but there's not much time."

"How is he?"

"He's been coughing more. His lungs rattle fiercely, and he's a bit more forgetful. Doctor Stanza gave him some laudanum a couple of hours ago."

Mihai frowned. Laudanum wasn't a good thing. It may take away the pain, but it took away a person's wits.

"Does the doctor know what's wrong with him yet?"

Sonia drew in an easy breath. "Not yet."

Viktor brought his fist up to his mouth and cleared his throat.

"Sonia, this is my good friend and confidante, Viktor Bacau. He's come with me from England and plans to stay here as my personal valet." Mihai put his hand on Sonia's shoulder and guided her around so she faced his friend.

Viktor bowed in front of her.

His sister's expression grew intense as she studied him.

Viktor smiled. "It's a pleasure to meet you, Your Grace."

Sonia giggled. "Oh, no, Mr. Bacau, no royal address for me in private, please."

"All right, Sonia..."

Sonia reached out and squeezed Viktor's hand, catching

his expression. They looked at each other, both of their gazes warming, and Mihai raised an eyebrow. Was Sonia attracted to his friend?

"May I call you Viktor?" she asked.

"Yes, of course."

Mihai turned around to the bar. "Is scotch acceptable?"

"Only if it's single malt," replied Sonia.

Mihai chuckled. Sonia had impeccable taste. He poured them each a glass, then raised his own. They followed. "Merry Christmas."

Everyone clinked glasses, smiling, and Mihai found small joy in being reunited with his sister again. The liquid coursed down his throat. The sadness of Alexandra's choice lessened. Oh, he had been ready to fight his father for her, demand to marry her, but she wanted to stay in England. She hadn't been worthy of his efforts. Love was a fickle beast he had no desire to entertain anytime soon. He drew in a deep breath, pushing thoughts of her away.

The door opened and his father walked in. He was slightly taller than Mihai, and he was too thin. The hair around his temples was graying and his green eyes lacked their usual spark. He wore his uniform, dark blue with a gold sash across his chest and several medals over his heart.

"Mihai, you're home!"

Mihai stood straighter and taller, steeling his spine, waiting for his father's tone to become strict. "Yes, Father. I'm home."

"Sonia, what a good sister you are to greet your brother." Mihai's father turned toward Viktor. "Who's this?"

"Viktor Bacau, my friend. He's agreed to be my personal valet."

Mihai's father looked Viktor up and down from head to toe. "He's tall."

A slight smile escaped the corners of Viktor's lips as he bowed. "Your Majesty."

"Oh, get up, boy."

Viktor stood up.

"So, you're my son's friend from England?"

"Yes, Your Majesty."

Mihai's father waved his hand in the air. "What did you study?"

"Journalism."

"That'll do. Mihai needs all the good advice he can get. See to it you give it to him."

"Of course."

Mihai pursed his lips to hold back a chuckle. His father had only gotten saltier since he'd been away. "Would you like a drink, Father?"

His father sat down on the couch that was adjacent to the fireplace. "Yes, of course, Sonia." He gestured for her to sit next to him. Viktor sat on the two-person sofa across from the couch. Mihai handed his father a drink and sat down next to Viktor.

Mihai never did care for change, but with his father sickly it was coming. He took a deep breath to steady himself. He hadn't expected to see his father so fragile. He would do his best to make his father happy in his last months.

"Christmas is a week away. You have two public engagements – escort your sister to the hospital along with our usual donation and go to Parliament, adjourning it for the holidays. After the holidays, the von Krackens are coming."

Mihai's left eyebrow raised a fraction. "The von Krackens?"

His father's eyes narrowed. "Your bride's family. Georg and I intend to announce the engagement in January."

"Oh."

"Don't look so business-like."

How did he appear? He hadn't given his arranged marriage much thought and he wasn't ready for another woman in his life.

"Sonia, you'll have to give him some etiquette lessons. I want him to make a good impression when they come."

"Father, really, I don't need—"

His father glared at him. "Georg's daughter is a fine young woman. I saw her last September. It's important to make a good impression with them. Her father is giving Moldavia several thousand *lei* for the building of a railroad from here to Bucharest."

Mihai pursed his lips, holding his tongue. "Yes, Father." The von Krackens sounded very generous.

The room grew silent. Mihai ran a hand through his hair and glanced at the window. His father's voice cut through the silence.

"You'll marry after Easter. Nothing will make me happier to know you're married, and if God is willing, I'll be around to see your child."

"Of course you will," said Mihai. What else could he say? One thing was for sure – his father was very keen on *this* marriage. There was no way he'd ever approve of Alexandra.

Mihai's father sipped the drink from his glass. "I'm realistic, boy. The proposal for the railroad is on my desk. Study it. Have your friend study it. I want you to present it to the Parliament after Christmas. I would like to see the project break ground as soon as the weather warms."

"I will."

"Once the railroad is complete, I want you to work with Mircea Moldoveanu, he just came to the throne in Carpathia, along with the other rulers of the Romanian principalities to bring about unification."

"Is that all? Get married, have a child, build a railroad,

and unify Romania?"

His father waved his hand in the air. "Don't sass me, boy. I know it's a lot, but I won't be around to do it. Sonia, your new friend, and your new wife will help."

Mihai mustered up a smile and nodded. "Yes, Father." This was his responsibility now. So why did it feel like the weight of the world was on his shoulders? He'd be good. He would do his best. But would it be enough?

~ * ~

Viktor sat next to Mihai, trying to avoid staring at Sonia. She was as beautiful as a wood nymph. Her figure was curving and regal, what he envisioned a princess to be, and her dress accented her firm uplifted breasts. When she squeezed his hand, he felt incredible strength in her slim fingers. Her amber eyes burned with a smoldering fire that pierced his defenses. Her high, exotic cheekbones spoke to her nobility and complemented her full, red, curved lips. Sonia's thick, dark hair tumbled carelessly down her back and he longed to run his fingers through such a luscious mane.

He struggled to tame his racing thoughts. Viktor had never seen such an alluring woman before, but she was his friend's sister. What would Mihai think of his lusty thoughts toward her?

The king stood. "I'm tired. I need to rest."

Everyone else stood as well.

"I'll see you all at breakfast tomorrow," said the king.

"Yes, Father," replied Mihai.

The king walked out. Mihai glanced at Viktor and Sonia. "I'm tired, too. I'll show you to your room, Viktor."

"There's no need. I'll show your friend to his room. You go and relax," said Sonia.

"Are you sure?" asked Mihai.

"Of course."

"Put him in the east wing on the bottom floor," said

Mihai.

"Give him a guest room?"

"Viktor and I will need our space."

Viktor chuckled. Yes, he adored his friend, but he would like to have his privacy.

"Good night, Sonia. Viktor."

"Good night," they both replied.

Mihai left. Viktor turned toward Sonia, hoping it wasn't too awkward.

"Do you have a lot of luggage?" she asked, sitting back down.

"Just one bag. I'll need to do some shopping."

She gestured for him to take the seat next to her. He smiled and did so, turning to face her, thrilled to have this time alone with her.

"There are several good tailors in Constanta and if the commission comes from the castle, they do quick work. I'll give you a list so you can go into town tomorrow. We must havc you looking like a valet."

"Thank you."

It grew a bit quiet. Viktor sipped his drink, his excitement churning into awkward knots. He hoped the drink would settle his anxiety. "So, ah, the king mentioned the hospital?"

"He's quite proud of it. He had architects from England help him design it. The construction was finished right before Mihai left. I work as a nurse there."

His lips parted in surprise. "You work?"

She paused and finished her drink. "Does that surprise you?"

"Why do you do it?"

"Because I want to. It's good, honest work that challenges me. I like helping others and I don't like to be idle. Mihai will inherit, of course, but Moldavia is my home and I would like to be able to help him."

"I admire you for that."

She placed her hand over his, sending warm tingles up his arm. "So, tell me about you. Why did you come here with Mihai instead of going to your own home?"

Despite her interest and genuine concern, Viktor grew uneasy. This was never an easy topic to discuss. He didn't like thinking about his family. Viktor withdrew his hand and raked it through his hair. The uncomfortable feeling settled in the pit of his stomach. He pursed his lips and steeled his shoulders, finding his strength.

"You don't have to tell me—"

Viktor held up his hand. "No, I want to. I'm from a town called Chernivtsi in Ukraine. The local count is beholden to the Russian aristocracy."

She nodded.

"My father was a decent man, but troubled at times. He was also the count and having to answer to the Russians wounded his pride." Viktor paused for breath. "My older brothers, Fedir and Alexi, received a local education, but my parents saw fit to send me to England where I met Mihai. I suspect my parents' favored me as a son, but my father died right before I left and my mother died while I was away. Fedir stopped sending my tuition when she died."

"I'm sorry."

"My brothers were barely civil to me growing up. I think they were aware of my parents' favoritism. I did not want to go home to that."

"How did you get through the university in England?'

"Mihai helped me out, giving me part of his spending money. I did freelance reporting to help my income. Mihai has been more of a brother to me than my own."

"Mihai has a good heart. He's very generous."

Viktor smiled. "Like your mother?"

"Yes, like our mother."

It grew silent again. Viktor furrowed his brow. "Well, I didn't mean to sound so depressing..."

"Not at all. Let's try not to dwell on that and let's look to the future. I much prefer being happy."

"Me, too."

She stood up. "Let me show you to your room."

"Where's yours?"

"Upstairs in the royal apartments. They're very nice, but lack one thing."

He raised a curious eyebrow as he stood up. "What?"

She smiled. "Privacy."

He grinned as he followed her out. He would definitely like to be alone with her. Perhaps it was a good thing his room would be on the bottom floor away from the royal apartments. All in due time. He didn't want to rush with her. For now, it was enough to acknowledge his attraction.

~ * ~

The sunlight filtered into Sonia's room. She walked over to her bureau, fresh from her bath and newly dressed for the day. Sitting down in front of the mirror, she brushed her hair. Her brother's friend, Viktor, was an attractive man. He had an unusual appearance, different from most of the men she'd seen. Tall, with blue eyes that sparkled like rare sapphires and an ingenuously appealing smile, his broad shoulders hinted of untapped power. His thick, blond curls gleamed like dark gold. The clean, light, pure look of him impressed her. She wanted to get to know him – and his room offered privacy should she choose to visit him. Her cheeks reddened at the thought. She couldn't believe she'd been so bold as to hint that to him last night.

A knock on the door shook her out of her musings.

"Come in."

Mihai entered wearing breeches tucked into riding boots and a simple white linen shirt with long sleeves. "Do you have a minute?"

She put the brush on her bureau and motioned for him to sit on her bed. "What, no 'good morning?' Where are your manners?"

Mihai flashed her a quick smile, but paced the length of her bed instead of sitting on it. Something had made him anxious.

"Good morning, Sonia."

"So, what has you full of vigor this early in the morning?" she asked.

"I had a dream last night."

"Do tell."

He stopped and looked directly at her, his eyes dancing with confusion. "Theresa came to me in a dream. She wanted to wish me a Merry Christmas."

Sonia raised an eyebrow. She knew he was sensitive at times to the emotions of those around him and his dreams could be exceptionally vivid. Their mother was a witch and they suspected these sensations were inherited from her.

"Say something," he said.

Sonia smiled, the imp in her unable to resist teasing him. "Did you wish her a Merry Christmas back?"

"Sonia, do not joke!"

"What do you want me to say?"

"I...I don't know. What's she like? Did you see her in September?"

"I did, and in fact, she sent you a gift for Christmas. It's under the tree. I sent her one back from you."

"What did you send her?"

"An ornament for her tree."

He clasped his hands in front of him. "Thank you for being so thoughtful."

"You're welcome, but why are you so anxious? It was just a dream."

His shoulders tensed and she suspected the dream unsettled him.

"Does she have auburn hair? Hazel eyes? Is she slender?"

"Yes."

"She's very pretty," said Mihai. It was more of a statement than a question.

"She has attractive features, I suppose."

"She's pleasant? Has a nice disposition?"

"Yes. Why are you asking me all this? What did your dream tell you?"

"It's our mother's blood working in me – isn't it? It's trying to tell me something."

"So...was the dream good or bad? It didn't sound harmful. Was it enlightening?"

"Theresa appears a lovely young woman and I fear I might have ruined things for her."

"How so? You've never met her."

"I had an affair with a woman in England. I loved her and I thought she loved me, but she refused to come to Moldavia. It...broke me. I don't think I can give another woman my heart – even if she is as alluring as the woman in my dreams."

Sonia steepled her fingers, hiding her disappointment behind them, surprised to learn of her brother's affair.

"Say something. I see the disappointment in your eyes."

"What can I say? Yes, I'm disappointed, but don't make any hasty decisions, especially based on a dream. Always be honest with Theresa when she arrives. Honesty will never fail you."

He nodded, and finally sat down on the bed, lowering his head into his hands. Sonia's heart went out to him. He rarely showed such vulnerability and even then only with her. She went to the bed and wrapped her arms around him.

"I know it's much, father's dying, your marriage, your added responsibilities, but you are the Crown Prince.

These are your burdens to bear."

He lifted his head and squared his broad shoulders. "You're right. I will focus on my duty."

"If you ever need to talk or a private moment, I'll be there for you."

He squeezed her hand and smiled. "Thank you. Perhaps you could research the power of the witch and these dreams I'm having. It's time I finally understood our mother's inheritance." He paused. "And it wouldn't hurt you to learn either."

"Perhaps I will," she hesitated. "I sense a change in the air and I can't put my finger on it. I'll see if I find her old journals."

"Thank you." He turned around and walked out, his head held high. Sonia had never explored the power of the witch either, but like Mihai, she was never interested in exploring it – until now.

Chapter Three

Theresa Isabella von Kracken nervously flittered her hand over her thick winter jacket. This was nerve-racking. Tonight was the night – she was going to meet the man in her dreams.

Her father sat across from her in the carriage. Her older sister, Beatrice, sat next to him. Her sister checked her appearance in a handheld mirror she withdrew from her small evening purse. Theresa's purse was just as small and she had no idea how her sister fit so much into it.

Theresa didn't feel like fussing much. Instead, she peered out the window. Old dirty snow lined the access road up to Delfin Castle and her groom's ancestral home. Small little knots twined in her stomach. She closed her eyes, trying to push the sensation away. She didn't want to be a wallflower. She wanted to be charming and witty like her sister always was.

Her thoughts drifted to her most recent dream. Mihai had saved her from a beast. What courage! Her dream prince had chiseled cheeks, which spoke of untapped strength. His eyes were malachite green, sizzling with heated emotions under long, dark lashes. His hard shoulders and broad chest hinted at a sculpted body. His lips were firm and sensual, begging to be kissed.

"Theresa, don't you dare fall asleep. We'll be there in a few minutes," said her father.

Her eyes snapped open.

"Oh, Father, who can blame her – it's as hot as an oven with that heating brick at our feet and these heavy coats," said Beatrice.

Theresa's father glared at Beatrice. "Should I open the window and let the winter air in?"

Beatrice wiggled her nose. She always did that when her father scolded her. Theresa just poked her tongue into her cheek and tried not to roll her eyes.

Some would say her family was a little odd, and at an early age, she had learned to tell no one of her dreams. Once, she told her sister, Victoria, of a dream when she was seven. Theresa saw Victoria's French teacher die in a boating accident. The following week, her family had learned that was precisely what had happened over the weekend. Victoria never said anything to her father, but Theresa could tell her sister had been upset by the prediction.

The carriage hit a rough, frost-covered patch and jostled them. Theresa's older siblings, Victoria and Edward, hadn't been able to come. She had heard her father engaged in a spirited debate with Edward that somebody had to watch over the family business, but Theresa never quite understood what the family business was. In fact, the entire west wing of her family's castle was guarded and locked. Theresa had never been in it. Her father claimed it held memories he'd sooner forget, but there were times, late at night, when Theresa could have sworn she heard loud banging noises and chanting from that part of the castle.

She peered out the window. Delfin Castle came into view. At the top of the hill, it stood overlooking the Black Sea. Moldavia's flag flew from the tallest and thinnest tower. The carriage pulled up to a circular drive in front of the impressive building and came to a halt. A footman opened the door. Theresa stepped out, the cold air stinging her cheeks. She looked at the massive wooden door and drew in a deep breath, steeling her courage. Damned if the knots in her stomach didn't go away. They only seemed to have gotten bigger. She'd have to ask Beatrice for some peppermint to calm her nerves. Bea always had something in her purse when someone wasn't feeling well.

Her father escorted them up the stairs. Torches were evenly spaced along the steps. As she walked into the entranceway, several tapestries hung on the stone walls, probably depicting scenes from Moldavia's history. A soldier took her coat, revealing her gold and lace engagement gown. Her father stayed at her side as they walked out of the entrance hall and past the grand staircase that led to the second floor. Lingering guests near the doorway to the ballroom made way for her, as if knowing her importance.

A butler approached them. Theresa's father whispered in his ear.

Her stomach did a flip-flop. Beatrice reached over and squeezed her hand. "I'm here," she whispered.

"Thank you." Theresa could always count on Beatrice.

The butler turned around and the noise grew to a hushed whisper.

"Introducing Austrian Duke, Georg von Kracken, and his daughters, Ladies Theresa and Beatrice."

All the eyes in the ballroom turned on Theresa. The weight of the silence fell onto her shoulders. Why did it feel like she had an itch on her nose that under no circumstances she should scratch right now, though she was tempted.

Her father placed his hand in the small of her back and escorted her right up to the Moldavian royal family. King Stelian stood in the middle, Princess Sonia was on his left, and Prince Mihai was to his right.

She lightly nipped at her lower lip with her teeth. Her dreams had done Prince Mihai no justice. He stood straight and tall, his stance emphasizing the force of his thighs and the slimness of his hips. His body was beautifully proportioned with dark, smoldering green eyes framing his handsome face. What firm lips he had. She tried hard not to stare at him, but his good looks held her attention.

Her father tapped her lightly against her back. Damn. She had to curtsey. Lowering her eyes, she did just that. Beatrice curtsied as well.

"King Stelian, Crown Prince Mihai, Princess Sonia, may I introduce you to my daughters, Theresa and Beatrice."

Theresa's gaze swept over Mihai. His red, rich lips curved into a smile and he took her hand, placing a delicate kiss on her knuckles. A pleasant wave of heat slid up her arm and she took a quick breath to steady herself.

"Lady Theresa, you are more beautiful in person than in a dream." Mihai's wonderfully deep voice warmed her to her toes.

"Thank you, Your Grace."

"Theresa, you and my son are going to be engaged by the end of the night. I insist you call him by his name," said King Stelian.

"Yes, Your Majesty."

King Stelian gestured toward the head dining table. "Come, let's eat. After dinner and some entertainment, Mihai will make your announcement."

Theresa's father nodded and smiled.

"Oh, and Georg, don't smoke around the priest. The smoke makes Father Gregori cough. You should hear him in church when he lights the incense."

Mihai offered his arm to her. She slid her hand into the crook of his elbow. A spark of flame jolted her. She looked into his smoldering eyes. He paused for a brief minute before the hint of a sly, sensual smile crossed his lips. Then he leaned over and whispered. "I'm just as nervous as you are."

"What do you do for the nerves? I usually take some peppermint."

"I never thought of it, but I'll ask Sonia if she can find some for us."

Theresa smiled and they proceeded to the head table.

~ * ~

Bane walked into the ballroom with a young Hecuba on his arm and none too soon. The guests were being seated for dinner. His nose twitched at the sickly sweet scent of roasted meat and rich desserts.

He'd kept his eye on the Prince's fair-haired man, but hadn't been able to make a move until now. The recent full moon saw him at the coven house in Mulfaltar, attending to pack duties.

Hecuba pursed her lips as she glanced at the head table. A waiter slid their food in front of them. Bane suppressed a gag reflex and drank out of his wine glass. At least the wine was decent.

Hecuba's eyes narrowed. Bane leaned toward her. They both wore the appropriate attire for the occasion, so he wondered what was bothering her. "What is it?" he whispered.

"The von Krackens are here," she replied in hushed tones.

He arched an eyebrow. "The witches?"

"The Austrian branch."

"Don't let them bother you. They won't cause trouble." Bane speared a potato and shoved it into his mouth. At least it was edible.

"The von Krackens are incredibly intuitive. They might realize I'm here if that brat of a prince doesn't first."

"He won't. You drank the potion. You're young now and you said he's done nothing with his gifts."

"There's too much power, too much spark of witchcraft in here." Hecuba put her hand on his forearm. "It is not a good night to bite him."

Bane's upper lip curled into a snarl. "I'll decide when to bite him and it will be tonight."

"The von Krackens' magic is just as powerful as mine, if not more, since they are truly young."

"Don't worry so, witch. It will be all right. Eat."

Hecuba frowned and cut her meat. They had spoken softly enough so as not to be overheard, but the other couples at the table stared at them as if they were lepers. Bane flashed them a smile, showing off his elongated incisors, and they looked away. Nosey snits. They should mind their own business. Yes, Bane would claim the prince's friend for his heir tonight.

~ * ~

Mihai had meant what he'd said – his intended was stunning. She was tall and slender and he liked how her golden dress scooped at the bust line revealing her gentle neck and an enticing 'v' in the hollow of her throat. Her hazel eyes dared to pierce his battlements. Loose tendrils of auburn hair fell down her back and he ached to run his fingers through them. No, he hadn't wanted to be attracted to her, but he was. The attraction unnerved him simply because it was there. It was raw and primal and burned through him like a raging fire – a much more intense feeling than he had felt for Alexandra, and yet he knew practically nothing about Theresa von Kracken. No, he had several dreams since sharing his first one with Sonia, and his intuition told him she had been open and honest.

Mihai sipped his wine. Dinner was almost finished. Theresa nibbled on her meal.

"So, Theresa, I understand you converted to Orthodoxy?"

"It's a beautiful religion, Mihai. I was glad to do it."

"Sonia said you were learning Romanian?"

"I'm near fluent now. It's only taken two months."

"Two months? That's very fast. Do you speak other languages?" He was surprised at her progress. Romanian was a tough language to learn. Picking it up in two months was practically unheard of.

"I speak English, French, and German."

"What else do you like to do?"

"I like to read."

"Oh? What?"

"I like to read of faraway places I'll never go. I find Sir Walter Scott very entertaining and I have a soft spot for any stories with pirates."

He chuckled. "I like Sir Walter Scott, too, but I try to avoid the pirates."

Theresa smiled.

Sonia stepped up in back of them and slid a small bag on the table between them. "Peppermint."

"Oh, thank you, Sonia. Where did you find it?" asked Theresa.

"Your sister gave it to me."

"Thank her for me."

Sonia nodded and walked off.

Mihai reached into the bag and handed a mint to Theresa. She plopped it into her mouth. He found the gesture refreshing. He popped a mint into his mouth, too.

"Did you enjoy your time in London?" she asked.

"Yes, I did." His jaw tightened with unease. He never wanted to mention London around her. It would only bring up those raw uneasy feelings he'd rather forget.

His father put a hand on his shoulder. "It's time to dance."

Mihai led Theresa out to the dance floor. They performed a waltz and he discovered Theresa had a natural grace, following his lead impeccably.

He flashed her a smile. Theresa was a perfect fit in his arms, and the suddenness of that realization drove two conflicting emotions through him – awkwardness because he wasn't expecting to enjoy her company and delight because he did. His father had chosen his bride well.

An aggressive tap on the shoulder stopped him mid-waltz.

"Shouldn't you introduce me?" asked Viktor.

Mihai fought against a frown. He would have liked to have had the dance with Theresa alone. Instead, he thought to mind his manners for now.

"Theresa, this is my best friend, Viktor Bacau."

She politely nodded.

"Do you mind finishing the dance with me?" asked Viktor.

Theresa looked at Mihai. Reluctantly, he gave her a slight nod.

"I'd be honored to," she said.

Mihai left her side and walked off the dance floor. Sonia was there as well, her gaze fixed on Viktor. Was she experiencing the same thing he was? Reluctance? A God-awful feeling watching him with someone else? Was that the stirrings of jealousy?

He leaned over. "Why are you frowning?"

"Why are you?"

"I'm not."

"You are."

Why was his sister so stubborn? "I suppose I'd rather be dancing with Theresa."

"Viktor's just being polite."

"I suspect you'd rather be dancing with him."

Sonia pursed her lips and gently rocked back and forth on her feet. She always did that when Mihai had struck a nerve.

"You and Viktor have spent a lot of time together recently," Mihai continued.

Sonia stopped rocking, surprise in her eyes. "Well, I enjoy his company."

"And I suspect he enjoys yours."

Sonia shot him a sharp look. "Don't tease me, Mihai."

"Tease you? How?"

"He's your friend. We're trying hard to keep our feelings away from—"

He gently touched her elbow. "Don't."

She arched an eyebrow. "Don't? What are you saying?"

"If you are attracted to him, and him to you, I give you my blessing," He paused. "If you're worried about his station and what father may say about it, he is the son of a Ukrainian nobleman."

"I know." She hesitated, and a slight smile replaced her defensiveness. "Wait - you mean it?"

"Of course. I want you to be happy."

"I want you to be happy, too. Promise me you'll give Theresa a chance."

Mihai nodded. He found Theresa refreshing, but he wanted to really get to know her before he allowed her to pierce his defenses further.

~ * ~

Theresa was impressed with Viktor's smooth dancing. Mihai's friend was every bit the gentleman – and just as tall and handsome. It was Viktor's blue eyes that disarmed her. They sparkled in the light, flecked with bits of gold.

"Mihai is very lucky," said Viktor. "Congratulations on your engagement."

"Thank you." She paused. "What should I call you when the dance is over? Mr. Bacau? My Lord?"

"I suppose I could command a title being the son of a Count, but I prefer not to use one. Simply call me Viktor."

"Where are you from? I don't detect a local accent."

"Ukraine."

"Ah."

“I know this may sound odd, but you glow with happiness.”

“What’s so odd about that?” she asked.

“It’s hard to explain. There’s a radiance about you that’s good and honest and pure. It’s what Mihai needs right now.”

“Thank you, Viktor. I hope we all can be good friends. I sense the same about you – you’ve known hardship, yet you are happy.”

“I am, and yes, we will all be friends.”

The dance ended and Viktor escorted Theresa back to Mihai, who smiled as they approached.

Her intuition was ablaze tonight. She enjoyed Viktor’s company. He glanced at Sonia and Theresa sensed that Viktor harbored deep feelings for the younger woman – more than friendship. Mihai’s sister had always been kind to her so she hoped it would work out for them.

Mihai was another matter. His smile expressed pleasure, yet there was a hesitancy as well. He’d been polite and kind in public, but she sensed when they were alone, his defenses might be a challenge for her to break through.

~ * ~

Beatrice sat at a table, making small talk with those around her, sipping her wine. Theresa danced with her intended, then danced with his friend. A glint of black light caught the corner of her eye and she spun in that direction.

Her mouth fell open and her eyes grew wide. Hecuba! That foul witch was here. Why? And she looked as young and as nubile as a twenty-year-old. Ironic considering the old bat was pushing 200. The man next to her seemed presentable, but his obsidian aura gave him away – he was a wolf.

She closed her mouth and took a long sip of her wine to quell her shock. If Hecuba was here, that meant the dirty, foul witch was up to no good. That did not bode well. So what was the old crone doing here, anyway?

Beatrice put her wine glass down, opened her evening purse and removed an anise pill. Casually, she used the rest of her wine to wash it down. Anise was excellent for truth telling and she needed every trick in her arsenal tonight. She didn't want that old bitty ruining her sister's night.

Beatrice glanced at the old crone. She'd used a potion to change her appearance, and it was beginning to show signs of fading. Really? So soon? Black light seeped through her changed aura's yellow glow. That must have been what caught her attention.

So why was the witch here? Beatrice slid out of her seat and stayed on the fringes of the crowd, keeping her eyes and her senses tuned to Hecuba and her wolf.

The wolf's golden gaze fell onto a blond haired man – Mihai's friend, and he licked his lips like he was about to partake in a feast. Beatrice narrowed her eyes. Blondie was standing next to the king's daughter. In fact, Mihai, Theresa, Sonia and Blondie were talking as if old friends. And Hecuba's wolf wanted a bite. Beatrice put her hands on her hips. Well, not tonight. That foul pair wasn't going to ruin anything tonight – especially her sister's special moment.

Beatrice checked her purse. Good. She had enough tricks to protect her sister's new friend, but this had the makings of a long-term problem. She was going to have to convince Papa to stay here for a bit. She'd tackle that later. Blondie walked off with Sonia and the disgusting duo went in hot pursuit. Time to sharpen her claws and spring into action.

~ * ~

Sonia smiled, unable to tame her joy as Viktor and Theresa approached. Her heart warmed with the knowledge that Mihai approved of her and Viktor as a couple. She had been hesitant to ask him for fear that he would disapprove. She should have known his heart had always been a generous one and that above all he wanted her happiness.

As for her father, Sonia suspected he would also give his approval. He had confided in Sonia that he wanted to see her settled. Sonia had extracted his promise that she would be allowed to choose her husband and he wouldn't refuse her.

"I promised Theresa we would all be good friends." Viktor clasped his hands behind his back.

"Yes, I want that as well," said Mihai.

"I know Lent will soon be upon us, but we should plan some activities," said Theresa.

"How about a trip to the winery?" Sonia placed a hand on Viktor's elbow.

Theresa smiled. "I'd love it."

"There's so much to show you." Sonia's hand lingered.

"Don't forget to include me in your plans," said Mihai, teasingly.

"How could I forget the Crown Prince of Moldavia," Sonia giggled.

Mihai playfully waved his finger at Sonia as he grinned.

"Viktor, come with me to get a drink." Sonia gestured toward a serving table.

He nodded and followed her to the nearest waiter, but she continued walking past him. Mihai had given her his blessing and she couldn't wait to tell Viktor – in private. She knew the castle well and knew where she could be alone with him. Sonia increased her pace, slipping out of the ballroom and down a dimly lit hall.

Viktor caught up to her and placed his hand against her lower back. "Where are you taking me?"

She grinned. "I have wonderful news."

He raised an eyebrow, but she said nothing as they walked up a staircase. This was usually used by the servants without being seen.

When they got to the second floor, Sonia grabbed his hand and led him to a nearby balcony, looking north toward the forest. She shut the glass French doors, pressed her body against his, and wrapped her hands around the nape of his neck. Then she brushed her lips against his, unable to tame the raging fire she felt for him. He embraced her, returning her kiss with equal abandon. Their mouths opened and closed with a hunger Sonia was unable to satisfy. Viktor's tongue traced her lips, coaxing them open, sending new spirals of ecstasy through her.

Drawing on all her strength, she placed her hands on Viktor's chest.

"Sonia, darling, I thought you enjoyed that."

"I did. I do. I have wonderful news."

His lips curved into a wicked smile. "What?"

"Mihai is happy for us. He approves. We don't have to sneak around anymore." For the past two weeks they had been stealing kisses and embraces, afraid to go beyond that for fear of Mihai's disapproval. They had talked about their childhood fears and small things, such as their favorite flowers and pies. He had even gone to the hospital several times with her, and she had shown him her favorite restaurants and stores in Constanta. They had snowball fights in the courtyard and made angels in the snow.

Viktor's eyes grew wide. "You're serious?"

"Yes."

His face beamed with happiness that Sonia shared. Never had a man made her so content.

Viktor cupped her cheek. "We must tell Mihai how we feel about each other. Both of us."

"Yes..."

A loud clack against the thick glass directed them to look toward the door. Goose bumps pricked Sonia's flesh. She swallowed a blast of fear and uncertainty flooded her senses. Who was the thin, greasy man outside the door with dark blue eyes and why did he look at her and Viktor with such desire?

Someone caught the unknown man's attention and he glanced away. Viktor embraced her, holding her close. A deep inner sense flared within Sonia. Her witching sense? Danger loomed very near to her. She shivered.

~ * ~

Beatrice followed Hecuba and the wolf down a hall toward the back of the castle as they raced after Blondie and Sonia. They went to the right, up a series of stairs to the second floor and then to a balcony. Sonia shut the French glass doors that separated the balcony and hall. Hecuba and the wolf paused.

Beatrice plucked a vial out of her purse. This was her own personal potion and very versatile. She threw the glass vial over the disgusting duo's head and it shattered on the glass doors.

"Witch's brew be true to your mistress's instruction – seal the door tight, keep out the dark light."

Hecuba turned around and snarled. Beatrice stepped out of the shadows, extending her fingers like a cat's sharp claw. The wolf tugged on the door. It wouldn't open.

"Damn Dalca! What now?" The wolf's nostrils distended in frustration.

"I suggest you both leave the castle now or I'll call for my father."

The old crone put a hand on the wolf's arm. "My potion is starting to lose its integrity."

The wolf looked to Hecuba, then at Beatrice, then back to Hecuba. Grey started to invade the dark curls of

Hecuba's hair. He pointed a thin, sinewy finger at Beatrice. "This isn't over, witch."

"Leave the royals alone. They are under my protection."

"You do not frighten me," said the wolf.

Beatrice snarled. "Leave, now!"

Hecuba tugged on the wolf's arm and he followed her as they departed the way they came.

Beatrice wiped her hand across her brow and relaxed. Blondie and Sonia looked through the glass, their expressions full of concern. Beatrice dug into her purse, sprinkled some anast dust into her palm and walked up to the balcony doors, opening them. After all, she cast the spell. She could break it.

"Lady Beatrice, what just happened?" asked Sonia.

Beatrice flashed the couple a smile to disarm them and then flung the anast dust in their faces. They coughed and rubbed their eyes, inhaling the dust. After a few seconds, their faces grew blank. Anast dust made one forget and Beatrice wanted that. She walked up to both of them, placing her fingers against their temples.

"You remember coming here, spending time together, and then after ten minutes, you go back down to the ballroom. You did not see me or anyone else."

They both nodded. Beatrice stepped away and raced down the stairs to the first floor. She needed to have a long talk with her father.

~ * ~

Mihai checked his pocket watch. Where was Sonia? Viktor? He wanted them here when he proposed to Theresa.

"Is something wrong?" Theresa rocked back and forth on her toes.

Mihai tucked his watch back into his pocket. "My father is glaring at me."

"Oh?"

"He wants me to propose."

Theresa's cheeks reddened. "Oh. Do you have any more peppermint?"

"No, I'm sorry."

Theresa's sister, Beatrice, appeared out of nowhere and handed Theresa a stick of candy. "Here you are."

"Where did you come from?"

Beatrice pointed to the hall. "I went to get more mints."

As she did so, Viktor and Sonia appeared. Mihai let out a small breath and smiled, clapping his hands. "I was waiting on them."

"What happens now?" Theresa let out a breath and visibly relaxed.

Mihai leaned close, enjoying the light fragrance of jasmine that lingered on her shoulder. "I'm going to ask you to marry me."

Theresa stood a little straighter and smoothed her hands over her dress. What a brave soul she was. He wished he could ask her in private without so many onlookers, but his father wanted a formal, public proposal, and Mihai would do what he must to please him.

A loud bell rang out and the crowd quieted. Mihai looked in the direction of the bell. His father was the one ringing it. When Mihai had the crowd's attention, his father gestured toward Mihai.

Mihai nodded his head and got down on one knee, holding her hands in his.

"Lady Theresa von Kracken, will you marry me?" His voice carried for all to hear.

"Yes, Prince Mihai, I will."

He stood up, reached into his pocket and presented a glistening four-carat, marquise-cut diamond. Several 'oh's' and 'ah's' filled the air. He slid the ring onto Theresa's finger and a wave of possessiveness overcame him. – a wave he'd never felt before, even with Alexandra.

Father Gregori, the Orthodox priest that would marry them, stepped forward as was Orthodox custom. He joined the couple's hands, then made the sign of the Orthodox cross over them, blessing them and giving the church's approval for them to marry.

Mihai bowed his head. He was uncertain of what the future held, but he now had a duty to be a good husband to this woman, and he pledged to do just that. He placed a delicate kiss on Theresa's knuckles. May God watch over him and his country and help him move it forward into the modern world. A loud cry of approval from the attendants filled the ballroom, yet a hint of uneasiness lingered in his bones.

Chapter Four

Beatrice knocked on her father's door. It was a little early in the morning, but it didn't matter. She had to talk to him about what happened the previous night. Her father's valet opened the door.

"Who is it?" Her father's question rang clear in the silence.

"Beatrice."

"Come in."

Beatrice walked in, arms crossed. "We need to talk, Father."

Her father was putting on his cufflinks.

Beatrice glared at the valet. "In private."

Her father nodded at the servant and he departed.

"What is it, Bea?"

"Hecuba was here last night - with a wolf."

Her father paused and a thoughtful expression crossed his face. "Ah. That explains the stench I smelled last night. What did Hecuba want?"

"They followed Princess Sonia and her companion, but I stopped them before they made their presence known."

He wrinkled his brow, concerned. "Did you use magic?"

"Yes, of course I did. How else do you think I foiled Hecuba and her wolf?"

"Did anyone see you?"

"I used the anast dust."

"Good."

"Good? We all know how foul Hecuba is, and who knows what that wolf wants. It's not safe to leave Theresa here without protection."

Her father turned up the corner of his lip in a scowl. "Theresa must not know the ways of magic."

"Why not? Isn't she of age? She's going to be married."

He pursed his lips, pausing to contemplate before narrowing his eyes and looking directly at her. Her father meant business now.

"Bea, what I'm about to tell you is a secret – only Edward knows. You must swear to secrecy."

She nodded. "I swear."

"I have the gift of divination, but I've only experienced it after the birth of each of you. When Theresa was born, I saw her future – she must be raised ignorant of the magic in her blood and her witching heritage – and I have seen to it she is."

Beatrice's eyes grew wide. "If she had magic now, she could protect herself."

Her father set his shoulders. "This is not easy for me to discuss. Theresa faces death if she ever dares to practice magic."

"Death?"

"Yes. And I have no desire to watch a child of mine die."

Beatrice pinched the bridge of her nose. Shock coursed through her veins. She had never liked keeping her abilities from Theresa, but at least now she understood why.

"You promised silence, Bea."

Beatrice crossed her arms and glared at him. "At least allow me to stay until the wedding. That will give me enough time to find out what Hecuba and the wolf want."

"That's not a good idea."

"Do you want them to interfere with Theresa's marriage?"

Her father rubbed his forefinger across his chin, and paused. A few minutes past. "You're right – we need to learn more. This wasn't foreseen, but it does not mean it's a complication. Tell Theresa I've allowed you to stay to help with the wedding arrangements. Keep your eyes open. Use magic only when you have to, and wisely."

Beatrice's delight triggered a smile.

He shook a finger at her. "Use the family's runes to reach me if you learn of Hecuba's plans – even if you see her. Alert me immediately so I can assess the situation."

"Yes, Father." Beatrice tried not to pout. If her father didn't trust her, why did he let her stay? He was always a cautious old coot. She was just as talented and as powerful as Edward and now was her chance to prove it.

"You can go, Bea. I want to finish dressing so I won't be late for breakfast."

Beatrice went up to her father, gave him a kiss on the cheek and left, happy to have some extra time to spend with her sister.

~ * ~

Mihai held the cravat in his hand and glared at it as he stood in front of his mirror. He hated wearing the thing, but it was the fashion in London. It was probably the one British custom he didn't want to bring back with him, much preferring to leave his collar loose around his neck.

There was a knock on his door. He glanced at the small, mechanical clock on the nightstand next to his bed. It was almost time to go down to breakfast.

He went to the door and opened it. "Sonia! Good morning."

She walked past him, clutching an old leather-bound book to her chest. "Good morning, Brother. Have a spare minute?"

"For you? Of course."

She held up her book. "I found it in the room with our mother's old things."

"What is it?"

"It's a history of witchcraft."

A little knot of apprehension tightened in his shoulder and he reached over to rub it. "What did you learn?"

"What didn't I learn? This is fascinating reading. I'm leaving this for you."

"Sonia, I have no time to read it."

She placed it on his nightstand next to the clock. "Make some time."

He crossed his arms. "Tell me. Please?"

"It's in the blood. There's an extra something – the book called it 'feron.' It augments the magnetic properties in the blood tenfold, allowing the witch to tap into the energy around them."

"It almost sounds scientific."

She continued. "There's a whole chapter dedicated to Piotr Dalca – the first witch and direct blood child of Marius Dalca – the human whose blood was mutated so horribly, he spawned the vampire and werewolves as well."

Mihai cocked his head. What Sonia told him fascinated him, but it also repulsed him. He had to know more. "What happened to Piotr Dalca?"

"He went insane."

"Are you serious?"

"He couldn't tame the power of the witch. Look, there's a whole chapter about dreams and the power of divination. You've said you've dreamed of Theresa?"

"Yes."

"When I returned from London." He rubbed his chin, lost in thought. "And at least three more times since then."

"Perhaps your blood knew your destiny."

It grew silent between them and Mihai turned away from Sonia as he brushed his hand across the nape of his neck. Was he destined for Theresa? He didn't want to think about it. Yes, he liked her, despite his distrust of love. That emotion was an uncaring beast, and he did not want to fall *in* love with Theresa – it would only ruin their budding friendship. Is that what he felt? Friendship for her? He did. And he would embrace it. He did like Theresa. She was clever and willing to accept his culture, his religion, and his language. And she was beautiful, a classic beauty that made his heart race. His preoccupation with Alexandra – was it an attempt to rebel against his father's wishes? Was it his floundering endeavors to deal with intuition and instincts that were driving him to his mate? Was it redirection because he didn't understand?

"Thank you, Sonia. I'll try to read some pages tonight."

She smiled and pointed at the cravat on his bureau. "Are you going to wear that?"

"No, I don't think so. It's too darn uncomfortable."

She giggled. "It looks uncomfortable."

He held out his arm to her and she slid her hand into the crook of his elbow. Together, they went downstairs for breakfast. It was going to be an interesting day, to say the least.

~ * ~

Theresa's favorite meal of the day was breakfast. She loved the flavor of the foods and a hot drink on a cold morning. Her first breakfast at Delfin Castle did not disappoint. Mihai asked her to try a dark roasted coffee and she did. To her surprise, she liked it.

Beatrice told her she was staying until the wedding and Theresa was thrilled with the news. She always enjoyed Beatrice's sense of fun and honest advice. Theresa smiled inwardly believing her time in Moldavia had gotten off to a wonderful start.

Mihai finished his coffee. "I'm sorry, but I have work to do. Perhaps you could take care of our wedding plans and after dinner—"

"Mihai, it's Theresa's first day here. Put work aside and deal with it tomorrow," said King Stelian. He glared at Mihai over the rim of his coffee cup.

"Yes, Father."

"Good."

Theresa studied the expressions passing between father and son. Mihai appeared very business-like, not betraying a stitch of his feelings, while the King's face reflected mild annoyance with his son.

Mihai glanced at Theresa. "Are you finished?"

There was only a nibble of her omelet left.

"Don't rush her, Mihai," said the King.

Theresa tried to hide her grin. Mihai's father noticed everything.

"Father—"

Theresa put her napkin on her plate and stood. "I'm finished, Your Majesty, thank you."

"You're welcome."

Mihai stood as well and walked over to Theresa. His expression was very even, and he didn't seem quite himself, or at least like the man she'd gotten to know last night, a little nervous yet sweetly attentive.

He gestured for her to walk through the door and he followed. Once they were in the hall, Theresa turned toward him. "What now?"

"We're going to the study."

Disappointment filled her. "To work?"

"Only for a little bit. I'll leave instructions for Viktor."

"Then what?"

"I thought I'd take you up to my tower."

"Tower?"

A knowing, secretive smile crossed his lips. "Let it be a surprise."

"All right."

They arrived at the study and Theresa followed him inside. He motioned for her to take the chair across from the desk. He sat behind it, shuffling through papers and making notes. Theresa glanced around the study. Most of the furniture was a dark cherry wood. There were two windows and thankfully the drapes were drawn open letting in the morning light. There were two walls full of shelves and books. How positively masculine. It needed something to give it a little personality. Maybe a painting? Or two?

She leaned forward. “Tell me, Mihai, who is your favorite painter?”

He stopped writing and looked up. “I like a variety of painters – de Vileger, van Ruisdael, van de Velde—”

“Dutch painters.”

A slow smile hinting of admiration crossed his face. “Yes, they are.”

She folded her fingers and placed them on the desk. “They painted maritime seascapes.”

The hint of a smile turned into a full-fledged grin. “Very good. How do you know of them?”

“I did study art. I like Dutch painters myself because they're so incredibly lifelike.”

He put the papers on the table. “Why did you ask me about the painters?”

“I thought this study could use a painting or two.”

“Perhaps.”

She pointed to his papers. “May I ask what's so important that you wanted to work on it?”

His smile slowly vanished. “It's very involved.”

“Can you tell me?”

He paused, as if searching for something, and then satisfied, pointed at the desk. “My father has given me several tasks to complete and none are easy. This one involves building a railroad from here to Bucharest.”

“That is quite a task, but a much needed one.”

“I'll have Viktor take this proposal to the Prime Minister today.”

Theresa thoughtfully pursed her lips, grateful Mihai had shared a bit of his work with her. She craved to know more so she could help, yet she sensed he didn't want to be pushed. She'd have to walk a careful line.

"You look lost in thought, Theresa."

"Well, I think the railroad is a good idea, but I have no idea what building one entails, and I want to be helpful to you."

"I'll tell you more about it later. Right now I'm securing funds and proposing raising taxes to finance it. It won't be a big raise since your father is helping. I want the Prime Minister's approval before we bring it to Parliament."

"I see."

He stood, putting the papers into a small box on the corner of his desk. "Viktor can take care of it this afternoon."

She nodded, happy to have his full attention now.

He crossed his arms, his expression guarded. "I can't always put this aside. I'm afraid this is going to take up a good amount of my time during our engagement. Can you be patient with me? I have to work fast because I want to break ground when it warms – before my father becomes any more ill."

"I understand." And she did, but patience was never easy with her.

"Come." He gestured to the door and she walked out. Mihai slipped in front of her and they took a hall that led towards the servants' area of the castle. Just before they reached the servants' living quarters, he opened a door that was disguised as part of the stone wall and went inside. A small table with a candle in a pewter holder stood near the door. Mihai lit it and closed the door. Theresa followed him as they ascended the stairs. Thank goodness her dress had a thick crinoline under it, keeping her fairly warm. The staircase was cold and made of stones, yet Theresa was thrilled to learn of this secret passage.

They climbed for several minutes. They must have been high up in the castle by now. Mihai passed two wooden doors in the staircase until coming to a third at the end of the staircase. He opened it and Theresa walked into a darkened room illuminated by a small sunbeam coming in through dirty glass doors. Mihai walked over to the fireplace, placed wood and kindling in it, and started a fire. While he did that, Theresa walked around the room.

It was compact, yet cozy. There was a shelf with blankets, pillows, books, maps, and writing tools. A huge telescope mounted onto a metal tripod rested in front of the glass doors.

The fire blazed to life and Mihai grabbed a blanket, throwing it in front of the fireplace. He motioned for Theresa to sit down and she did. Mihai sat next to her. His expression appeared intense, and then softened.

"I bet you're wondering why I brought you here."

"I am curious."

"Well, I would have preferred to show you the winery or even take you out on the royal yacht, but it's still winter and too cold for those things."

"I understand."

"This is my escape when I can't leave the castle."

She arched an eyebrow. "Oh?"

"I like to look at the stars. My mother acquired the telescope." He paused and pointed to a stack of papers on a nearby shelf. "Those are my homemade star charts."

"You're an amateur astronomer?"

"I am." He paused again, and drew in a breath. "I brought you here because this place is private and special to me, and I know we could talk without being spied on."

She giggled. "Us? Spied on?"

"In case you hadn't noticed, my father is very keen that I...like you."

"I did notice."

His expression stilled and grew serious. Granted, she was nervous too, but she tried not to show it so much.

"So, do you?" she asked.

"Do I what?"

"Like me?"

He rubbed his hand across the nape of his neck. "Well, I would like to learn more about you."

She appreciated his honesty. She wanted his approval, craved it, but she did want to earn it, and he was right – they hardly knew each other.

He clapped his hands and rubbed them nervously. "So...do you like wine?"

"Yes."

"Red or white?"

"I prefer reds."

"The winery makes a wonderful cabernet."

"I can't wait to try some."

"I'll have some served at dinner tonight. Is Beatrice your only sibling?"

"No, I have a brother, Edward, and another sister, Victoria."

"It must have been fun, having a house full of children."

"My father had his hands full. We were always teasing each other."

"I didn't tease Sonia much."

"Why not?"

"I never wanted her to get mad at me."

"She doesn't strike me as being the type to take something like that so personally," said Theresa.

"I know that now."

"Ah. Do you mind if I ask why your parents didn't have more children?"

He paused an extra second before speaking. "To be honest, I believe my mother suffered a miscarriage or two. Doctor Stanza wasn't able to determine what caused them. I think they would have liked to have had more children, but it wasn't in the stars." Mihai rubbed his hands together.

She reached out and squeezed his hand, offering comfort. From the look on his face, she could tell he was disappointed with his father, yet worried for him as well. "I'm sorry."

His gaze came up to study her face, and she felt a little of the tension in his body drain away from him.

"Thank you."

"Whatever support I can give you, tell me."

He nodded.

The air grew quiet again. She hated the silence. He didn't have to tell her his whole life's story right away. They both needed time to get used to their arrangement. She leaned back a little, using her hands to brace herself. "I noticed the water on the sea glows a bit. Why is that?"

"There's a high amount of plankton in the water."

"I thought the Black Sea was landlocked?"

"Not quite. The Bosphorus Straits near Constantinople open it up."

She smiled, sensing he was relaxing. "Tell me more."

"The water rises and falls with the phases of the moon."

"Really?"

"From my studies, I learned that after the last ice age, as the polar caps retreated, the Black Sea was too deep, so it retained all the properties of an ocean."

"How interesting." Romania piqued her curiosity. Theresa wanted to learn everything she could about it. In fact, sometime soon, she hoped to take a tour of her new country. What an adventure that would be!

"The sea also has dolphins, tuna, herring, and even anchovies. Do you like yachting?"

"I've never been, but would like to go."

"Why?"

Theresa noticed how his posture relaxed a little more and she found it encouraging. "I hardly ever left my castle. My father was very protective of me. The most adventure I had was in a book. Yachting sounds like it would be an adventure I would enjoy very much."

"We'll go as soon as it warms up. Do you have any idea where you would like to go for your honeymoon?"

She smiled as heat seeped into her cheeks. "I have too many places I'd like to visit. What do you suggest?"

"We could take the yacht to Constantinople."

"All right."

He wrinkled his brow. "That was almost too easy."

"I am very agreeable, but you'll find I do have my opinions."

"I look forward to taking you on several adventures – and hearing your opinions."

She smiled, glad that he was opening up with her.

"Can I ask you a question? You must promise to keep it between us," he said.

She nodded.

"Did you dream of me during Christmas?"

Her stomach tightened, a little anxious. "Yes, I dreamed of you."

"Did you wish me a Merry Christmas?"

"I did."

His face lit up. "So it's true – we've shared dreams."

She nodded her head, surprised he was so accepting of it. It had been unnerving at first, but after talking with Bea she accepted it.

"Do you know why that is?" he asked.

"No, I don't understand it, but I know what I feel."

"What do you feel?"

"Every experience in my dreams was real and true."

He nodded, agreeing with her. "I know why."

"Why?" She rubbed her chin with a finger.

"Again, I must have your confidence."

"Of course."

"My mother was a witch. I have inherited her gifts."

"And Sonia?" she asked.

"Both of us."

"I know nothing about witches."

Relief crossed his face. "I don't know much myself. My mother died when I was ten and I wasn't trained."

She accepted him at his word, his tone of voice full of conviction.

"What do you think about being a witch?"

"We've never really wanted to explore that side of us."

"Why not?"

He scrubbed the back of his head, a little uncomfortable, but remembered Sonia's words. Be honest. "Well, I think we've both been afraid. We didn't want other people to think we were different."

"I wouldn't say you were different, just unique."

"This doesn't bother you?" he asked.

"I may know nothing of witches or witchcraft, but it makes sense how we were able to share several dreams, and quite honestly, I liked the dreams we've shared."

He placed his hand over hers. A spark of warmth trailed up her arm. "I'm starting to learn more about witchcraft, so I hope you won't be afraid. I want to understand my gift – now."

She studied his expression. This was a deep-seated fear of his. He didn't want to possess these talents, but he was willing to learn more so he understood it and he wanted her to accept this about him. She sensed something deeper from his expression – he couldn't bear her rejection.

"I will never leave you," she said, softly.

A small smile graced his lips. Again, it grew quiet, but Theresa believed she had earned a certain degree of trust from him.

~ * ~

Viktor entered Mihai's study and checked the boxes on the desk. Mihai had left a note for him to take an envelope to the Prime Minister. Viktor sat down and read the proposal, verifying the numbers. Satisfied, he tucked the envelope into the breast pocket of his frock jacket and walked down the hall.

Sonia and Beatrice stood in the entranceway, putting on their winter coats.

"So, where are you ladies going?" he asked.

"I'm going to show Lady Beatrice the hospital where I nurse and then a couple of businesses we can use for Mihai's wedding," said Sonia. "Are you leaving as well?"

Viktor reached for his coat. "I have to go see the Prime Minister."

Beatrice fumbled in her purse. "Are you going alone?"

"It's quicker if I do."

She brought her hands to her nose as if she was going to sneeze and let out a big gasp. Dust from her hand flew over him. "Oh, I'm so sorry."

Viktor flecked specks of dust off his jacket. "What was that?"

"Just a little rouge that must have gotten on my hands. Are you all right?"

"I'm fine."

"Will you be back for dinner?" Sonia slid on her mittens.

He smiled at her, adoring how her eyes sparkled when he looked at her. "Of course. May I escort you ladies to your carriage?"

"Yes, you may."

Viktor escorted them to the stables where they parted ways. He rode his horse, Diablo, taking care to avoid frostbitten holes in the hard winter ground.

Sonia had appeared radiant just now. They were both thrilled to know Mihai had no objection to them as a couple. Secure in that knowledge, Viktor intended to visit a jeweler after he finished with the Prime Minister. He wanted to ask her to marry him.

Viktor rode Diablo into town. People were bundled up in winter coats as they walked down the streets. Viktor arrived at the Parliament building and dismounted, securing Diablo to a nearby hitching post.

An icy chill raced down his spine.

He turned around, on guard. Nothing. Across the street an old lady in a dull fur coat watched him with beady little eyes. He shivered. Something was wrong, he knew it. He spun to race up the stairs and ran into a hard, rock-like body, causing him to crash to the ground.

The man was tall and sinewy with cold blue eyes. He snapped open his mouth, revealing long, sharp fang-like incisors.

Fear raced through Viktor's limbs. "What do you want?"

The sinewy man leaned forward over Viktor's neck, teeth bared, then stopped. "By Dalca! Nistal root!"

Viktor saw it as his chance to escape. He leapt to his feet and raced past his attacker into the Parliament building, not stopping until he got to the Prime Minister's office. He leaned back against the door and breathed deeply. He had never seen that foul man before but his thin, gaunt features reminded him, eerily enough, of his brother Fedir. Viktor's heart calmed down. He didn't know what nistal root was, but he was grateful for it. Once he regained his composure, he knocked on the Prime Minister's door, ready to take care of his business for Mihai.

~ * ~

Sonia moved effortlessly through the castle until she reached Viktor's room. It was late. Most of the castle was quiet except for the night maids who were cleaning up the common areas and refilling the kerosene lamps.

She knocked on Viktor's door. He opened it only wide enough for her to slip into his room. He looked at her with fierce, intense eyes. Her body arched against his and she placed her hands around the nape of his neck. He wrapped his strong, muscular arms around her and pressed a slow, smoldering kiss against her lips. She returned the kiss with equal passion, reveling in the velvet warmth of his kiss. Her heart belonged to him. His lips seared a path down her neck.

"Viktor..."

"You feel delicious," he said.

"I love you." The words tumbled out of her mouth as her heated emotions swirled around her.

Viktor caressed her neck and looked into her eyes. His face burned with a desire she'd never seen before.

"Sonia." He paused, cupping her cheeks. "I love you, too."

Her heart leapt with happiness knowing this good, honest man felt the same way about her. "Oh, Viktor."

He dropped to one knee in front of her, holding her hand in his. "Sonia, will you marry me?"

Joy radiated through every part of her being. "Yes, Viktor, yes!"

He reached into his pocket and withdrew a ring. "Tomorrow, I'll go to your father and ask for his approval."

"He won't refuse."

"Are you certain?"

"Yes. He won't refuse my choice."

Viktor slid the ring on her finger. "It's beautiful. You're beautiful."

It was a two-carat diamond in a marquis cut. Sonia walked over to the bed and held her finger next to the kerosene gas lamp. "I love it, Viktor."

He sat down next to her, smiling, entwining his fingers through hers. "It pales in comparison next to you."

"I can't tell you how happy I am."

"When do you want to get married?"

"As soon as we can."

He chuckled. "Where?"

"Anywhere."

"Perhaps we should spend the night thinking about it," said Viktor.

"Perhaps..." Sonia's voice faded away as Viktor gently eased her down onto the bed and kissed her.

Chapter Five

Mihai secured the uncomfortable cravat around his neck. He was going to Parliament later on and he had to look like a gentleman.

He fumbled at the knot and groaned, letting it collapse. How he hated the damned thing! Sonia's book caught the corner of his eye and he recalled something he'd read last night. Witches preferred to use an athame to channel energy because the blade, while dull, was precise. Maybe he could channel his energy to have the cravat tie itself.

He held up his hand in front of the mirror and closed his eyes, stilling his body.

Thum-thum. Thum-thum. The steady beat of his heart filled his head. He used that as his anchor and allowed his body to feel. There – spiky tendrils of energy snaked down his arm and rested in his fingertips. His fingers hummed with a force he knew he had, but hadn't consciously felt before.

He opened his eyes and waved his fingers over the cravat.

It jumped.

Mihai gasped, losing his concentration, and the steady humming force dissipated. He'd been so close!

There was a knock on the door. He frowned. He'd have to wait till later to try again, but at least he knew he could do it now – just like his mother had.

He walked to the door and opened it. "Viktor, Sonia. Come in."

They walked in, both smiling.

"We have good news, Mihai," said Viktor.

"Oh?"

"Your father has given us permission to wed."

Mihai clapped his hands, delighted with the news. He was glad his sister had found happiness with his best friend. "Congratulations!"

Sonia offered her hand to Mihai, showing off her engagement ring. Mihai took her hand and marveled at the ring, happy for his sister. "Are you planning a spring wedding?"

"We'd rather not. We want to get married before Lent."

"Really? That starts next week. Father agreed to that?"

"We haven't told him our wedding plans yet," said Viktor.

Sonia withdrew her hand. "I know Father would want to give me a wedding worthy of a princess, but I want something more intimate and personal. Can you talk to him?"

"It's...so quick." Sonia didn't need to be so hasty with her wedding. She could have one as grand as the one planned for him. She was worthy of it.

Viktor stepped forward and placed his hand on Mihai's shoulder. "I love Sonia, Mihai. I was raised Orthodox. We were thinking of having a priest marry us here in the castle's chapel with you, your father, and the von Krackens. It would mean more to us to have you all there in such an intimate setting."

Mihai turned to Sonia. "Is this truly what you want?"

"Yes." The conviction in her eyes and in her voice convinced Mihai. His sister was very much in love with Viktor. And for a moment he was envious of that, wishing he could experience that type of love.

"Thank you," she replied.

"Where would you go for your honeymoon?" asked Mihai.

"I want to take Sonia to Odessa. It's beautiful there and I want to share my Ukrainian heritage with her."

Mihai nodded, moved by the pride and emotion in Viktor's voice.

"When would you leave?" he asked.

"As soon as we marry. We know you're busy working on Father's railroad project, so we would only take two weeks and return by the first of March," Sonia replied.

"You have my help, of course, and I'm sure Theresa and her sister would love to help you with the arrangements," said Mihai. "Once I talk to father."

Sonia wrapped her arms around Mihai and hugged him tightly. "Thank you."

He placed his hands on her shoulders. "For what?"

"For bringing Viktor here – for your approval – for—"

He held up a hand. "I just want you both to be happy."

"We will." Sonia paused. "Where's your cravat? Aren't you going to Parliament today?"

He pointed to the bureau. "It's winning."

"I'll help." She grabbed the piece of clothing and wrapped it around his neck, tying it up neatly.

"Sonia, why don't you find Beatrice and Theresa? I need to discuss the next phase of the railroad," said Viktor. "I'll meet up with you at breakfast."

"If you insist." She placed her hand on his arm and leaned up on her tip-toes, giving him a light kiss on the cheek. Viktor smiled at the gesture and they both watched her leave.

Mihai turned to his friend after Sonia had gone. "I don't want my sister to be hurt."

"No, never. I love her very much. All I want is her happiness."

"Good. I believe she returns those feelings."

"Really? How can you tell?"

"It's how her eyes sparkle when she looks at you."

A smile crossed Viktor's face. "I adore her."

Mihai checked his appearance in the mirror. Could he

have that with Theresa? Dare he?

"So, Viktor, what did you want to discuss? Was the Prime Minister upset with the proposal?"

"No, he thought it was fair. He'll put it to a vote next week."

"Excellent. Once it passes, we can ask for bids from construction companies. Have you told my father?"

"He's still in his room." Viktor's face clouded with concern.

"He didn't get up?"

"Dr. Stanza advised the staff to have breakfast served in his room."

"What's wrong?" asked Mihai. Concern and worry spiked through him.

"Coughing fits."

Mihai clenched a fist, he hated knowing his father was not feeling well.

"I'm sorry, Mihai."

"I'll stop in to see him before I leave for Parliament."

"I have something I want to tell you – something I'd like to keep between us for now.

Mihai arched an eyebrow. "Oh?"

"Yesterday a man attacked me. I hadn't seen him before. It was near Parliament."

"Were you hurt?"

"No, but he had abnormally long teeth – almost fang-like. I thought he was going to bite me."

Fear knotted in Mihai's limbs. "Only the dark beasts have fangs."

"You mean vampires?"

"And wolves. There are rumors that hang on the fringe of our accepted society here in Romania, however I've found there's a bit of truth in rumors. I've never seen a wolf or a vampire, but I've experienced enough to believe."

Viktor wrapped his arms around his chest. "This

disturbs me."

"I want you to keep a pistol and a knife with you at all times – for your protection."

Viktor nodded. "It's a good idea."

"Did you tell Sonia?"

"No, I didn't want to upset her."

"Perhaps you should consider postponing the wedding until the threat is over?"

"No. Sonia wants the wedding and so do I. I don't want to disappoint her."

He put a hand on Viktor's shoulder. "I don't want anything bad to happen to you."

"I'll do my best to stay safe."

Mihai glanced at his bureau, spying the book about witchcraft resting on it. Perhaps he could develop his power to help keep Viktor safe. He promised himself to read more until the book was done. At this moment, it seemed nothing mattered more to him than keeping Viktor out of harm's way. He had no choice. He had to master the witch's power and quickly.

Viktor checked his watch that hung on a chain from his pocket. "We need to get moving. I'm sure the ladies are waiting for us at the breakfast table."

"How rude of us to keep them waiting." Mihai gestured toward the door and followed Viktor as they left the room.

~ * ~

Theresa peeked into the maternity ward of the hospital. Sonia worked in this ward and, when needed, she also helped out in the triage room. The ward appeared clean, half-full with resting mothers, several babies and take-charge nurses. She was in awe of the medical knowledge the nurses possessed.

Beatrice put a hand on her shoulder. "What are you thinking?"

"This is amazing. People give their hearts so freely to

help," said Theresa.

"Remember that when you are queen. Always try to be generous and helpful."

"Like Sonia?"

Beatrice clasped her hands behind her back. "Yes. Sonia has won the people's hearts by embracing them and working alongside them as a nurse."

Beatrice was right. She would be the queen of this principality soon and she wanted to do something to earn the people's respect. But what? Should she take up nursing? She admired Sonia's resolve and strength to do it, but didn't know if it was for her.

Sonia approached them alongside an older lady who wore a nurse's smock. Her grey hair peeked out of her cap, but her brown eyes sparkled with youth.

"Lady Theresa, Lady Beatrice, this is the head nurse and my trainer, Mrs. Nocesti."

The nurse curtsied.

"It's a pleasure to meet you," said Theresa.

"We're very happy for you and the Princess, My Lady." Mrs. Nocesti smiled at all of them. "Princess Sonia works hard here and the other nurses will miss her while she's gone."

"I'll come back after my honeymoon, Mrs. Nocesti, but I wanted to let you know it would be about a month," said Sonia.

"We'll keep you and your fiancé in our prayers."

"Thank you."

Sonia hugged the older woman affectionately and the women walked down the hall toward the entrance.

"Where are we going next? The dressmaker or the florist?" asked Beatrice.

Sonia smiled. "The dressmaker, I think."

Theresa grinned. "I suppose I should make an appointment for my wedding."

"Yes, you must," said Beatrice. "I'll make sure you do."

They buttoned their coats and walked out. Viktor stood next to the carriage's driver, bundled up and warm, their official escort.

"How was it, ladies?" he asked.

"A pleasant visit. Mrs. Nocesti wishes us the best and expects me back in a month."

Viktor opened the carriage's door. "Where to next?"

"The dressmaker," said Sonia.

Theresa paused before the carriage. A three-story house caught her eye. It looked old and worn down, the paint cracking and the wood dull. Several icicles hung from ledges on the third and second stories. What surprised her, though, were the lively children playing in the front yard. Why were children at such a rundown house? She placed her hand on Viktor's arm "What is that?"

"It's an orphanage, I believe."

"Yes, it was established about fifteen years ago," said Sonia. "By my mother."

"It's so run down."

"It appears so," said Beatrice.

Theresa didn't understand it, but she felt compelled to visit the children. They were so small and trusting. They deserved better. She walked away from the carriage and toward the orphanage. Viktor quickly stepped up to keep pace with her. Beatrice and Sonia ran after her.

"Where are you going?" asked Viktor.

"I want to see the orphanage." Theresa moved with purpose, her stride steady and strong. The establishment must have fell into a state of disrepair after Mihai's mother died.

"Why?" Beatrice asked as she caught up to Theresa.

Theresa glanced at her sister. "I think I've found the best way I can to be helpful."

Beatrice flashed Theresa a smile.

Viktor opened the wooden gate for her and everyone walked in. The children stopped playing and stared at them. What a sight the four of them must have made - all dressed up in fancy clothes. Theresa walked up the steps and knocked on the door.

After a small delay, an older man opened the door. He wore a heavy woolen suit. "May I help you?"

"This is Lady Theresa von Kracken, Prince Mihai's fiancée," said Viktor.

The older man promptly bowed. "My Lady. I am Mr. Abel Kazha."

"Hello, Mr. Kazha."

"What brings you here today, My Lady?"

"I saw the house and the children and I was moved."

"The children have a way of doing that. Would you like some tea?"

Theresa glanced at Beatrice and Sonia. Both looked a little red in the cheeks. "Yes, thank you."

Mr. Kazha quickly left. Theresa walked around the entrance hall. The curtains were dirty and the wooden floors creaked.

"What are you thinking, Sister?" asked Beatrice.

"I think the children might need some help."

"That's very kind of you," said Sonia.

Mr. Kazha walked into the room. "The cook will bring out the tea in a few minutes. How can I help you?"

"Perhaps it is I who can help you. How many children are here?"

"Close to twenty and four babies."

Theresa clutched her hand to her chest. "Babies? How do they come to stay here?"

"For some, their mothers died in childbirth. Some got pregnant with a sailor who left, never to come back. Some of their parents were just too poor to keep them."

Her heart broke hearing the stories. She loved children.

Victoria had two – a girl and a boy, and Theresa had liked embroidering them clothes when Victoria was expecting. She read to her niece and nephew and played with them. Theresa looked forward to having her own children one day.

"What sad stories. Is there something I can do to help?" she asked.

"The entire building needs repairs."

"Write up the list. For now I'll make arrangements to have enough coal, food, and clothing sent until winter is over."

"My Lady, that's too generous," said Mr. Kazha.

"I want them to be comfortable. What about toys?"

"We only have a few."

Theresa looked at Viktor and Sonia. "Can we organize something?"

"When I was in London, they had toy drives for Christmas," said Viktor.

"That's a wonderful idea."

Sonia finished sipping her tea. "You should talk to Mihai. I think he'd like to help you with this."

Theresa's heart warmed with the thought Mihai would support her in this endeavor that she felt so concerned about. "I will."

"We'll all help," Viktor smiled at Sonia.

"Yes, we will," Sonia turned the smile.

Viktor glanced at his timepiece. "Unfortunately, we have much to do, ladies."

Theresa stood up and took Mr. Kazha's hands in hers. "Thank you for talking to me. I'll send someone from the castle soon."

"Thank you, My Lady." Mr. Kazha bowed and Theresa led her friends out of the orphanage and to their carriage. Her heart soared with happiness. She would have made a poor nurse. By extending her patronage to the orphanage, she would help these children and bring smiles to their faces.

~ * ~

Bane jammed his hands into the pockets of his heavy winter overcoat and watched as the royal coach ambled away from the orphanage with his fair-haired man.

Hecuba stepped out of the shadows. "He's not worth all this."

"If it wasn't for that nistal root, I would have bitten him the other day."

"It's obvious he has the von Krackens' protection. One of their witches travels with them."

"There will be a moment when he has no protection. I will be watching, and when that moment comes, he will be mine."

Power and strength flowed through his limbs. He knew if he was patient, he would have what he wanted, and he wanted the Prince's man so his pack would have a wolf worthy of being their leader when Bane died.

~ * ~

Everyone at the dinner table was full of energy. Though the king listened with apparent interest as Sonia talked about her wedding dress and the flowers they'd ordered, he seemed tired and Theresa watched his eyes droop. After the dinner, Mihai went to the study and took Viktor with him.

She was a little agitated with Mihai's apparent aloofness, which everyone explained away with excuses. Their favorite one was work. Well, it was time he took a break from his work. How could they get to know each other and plan a wedding if he didn't spend time with her? She went to the kitchen, picked out a bottle of wine – a bottle from his winery – and went to his study. She knocked on the door, determination running through her bones.

"Come in."

Theresa entered the room and Mihai closed an old leather-bound book. He put it on his desk. Viktor stood beside him. "Theresa, what a pleasant surprise," Mihai said.

"Good. If Viktor doesn't mind, I'd love to have your company for the rest of the evening."

"I don't mind at all."

"But, we have—" began Mihai.

"Can it wait?" asked Theresa.

Mihai paused and looked at Viktor. "We'll do it first thing after breakfast tomorrow."

Viktor nodded and left.

Mihai pointed to the bottle in her hand. "What did you have in mind?"

"This is from your winery. I wanted to share a bottle with you in the tower." She clung to her resolve.

His face softened. "You're right. We should spend some time together."

A smile tipped the corner of her mouth, pleased to see that she had cracked a few of his defenses. Mihai held out his hand, silently offering to carry the bottle. She gave it to him and followed him out of the study, through the hallway to their secret staircase that would take them to the tower. Her pulse pounded at the thought of being alone with him again.

~ * ~

Mihai's body thrummed with anticipation as he climbed the stairs. He had been avoiding Theresa because she stirred so many emotions inside him – emotions he didn't think he was capable of having since he'd left England, but he was capable of them and he couldn't avoid her. Hell, he was going to marry her in seven weeks. And there was a part of him that anxiously anticipated their wedding.

They entered the tower and he went to the fireplace,

starting the fire.

"Do you have an opener?" she asked.

He pointed to a shelf. "Over there. There are glasses, too."

She took care of the wine as he watched the logs flame to life. Satisfied, he laid out a blanket in front of the fire and Theresa sat down next to him, offering him a glass.

He took it and smiled, tilting his glass forward. "*Noroc!*" It was Romanian for cheers and meant good luck.

"*Noroc,*" she replied.

He drank her in. Her auburn hair took on its own warm glow in the firelight. Her hazel eyes sparkled like diamonds. She wore light flowery perfume that weakened him to her presence. His heart filled with tenderness and he tried to push away his regrets in neglecting her. "So, tell me about your day, Theresa."

"It was busy. Sonia took us to her hospital and I found an orphanage."

He arched a curious eyebrow. "You did?"

"It's near the hospital. Sonia said your mother used to patronize it before she died. I want to help."

He sipped his wine, recalling his visits to the orphanage with his mother when he was younger. Sadly, it had been neglected since her death. "How so?"

"I told Mr. Kazha I would help with supplies for the winter and Viktor mentioned having a toy drive so the children can have toys. When spring comes, I'd like to have repairs done to the building."

Mihai liked her ideas. The passion and enthusiasm in her voice for the project shined through. "Why do you want to help?"

"Because they're children. Don't you like children?" she sounded defensive.

Mihai reached out and placed his hand over hers. "I like children, Theresa. I want to fill the castle with our children."

Her hazel eyes pierced the distance between them, and he heard the quick intake of her breath, betraying her surprise. He couldn't believe he'd admitted something so personal to her.

"Oh," she replied.

"How do you feel about that?"

"Children should be wanted and loved. They should be cherished," she said.

"I agree. Now, tell me, what about the children moved you?"

"They were so helpless, depending on the charity of others. I just want to make it so they didn't need to beg. I want all of their needs to be cared for."

"All children should have that. You have my support, of course. I'll talk to Viktor and tell him to take the funds you need out of my private account."

She lowered her gaze. Why had she done that? Was she suddenly embarrassed? He moved closer and curved his fingers under her chin, warmth pulsing through him, and raised her head so they were eye to eye. He enjoyed touching her.

"Thank you," she whispered.

"Why did you look away?"

"Perhaps I overstepped my bounds. I didn't know—"

"No, of course not. What I have is yours. You're going to be my wife, and soon, queen of this principality. I think your patronage of the orphanage is noble and much needed. It reflects the kind heart you have. That kind of selflessness is what I hoped my wife would have in her heart."

Her hazel eyes betrayed her vulnerability. Touched, Mihai leaned forward and placed his lips against hers for a kiss. He was slow and thoughtful, measured, so as not to surprise her, but he could have easily taken it further between them. She kissed him back and his senses spun. Her lips were warm and pliant, hinting of the berries and currants from the wine. Slowly, he pulled away, his heart pounding. She was innocent, untouched, and he did not want to rush her. Her comfort was important to him.

Damn his blood.

She ran her fingers over her lips and looked directly at him. God, his heart hungered to kiss her again. He wanted her in his arms – he wanted to be inside her. That sudden revelation rocked him to the core of his being.

She lowered her fingers. "Why do you want to fill the castle with children?"

It was an honest question, deserving of an honest answer. "I was lonely growing up."

"You were? You had Sonia."

"Yes, but it wasn't quite the same. We would have liked more siblings to play with – to grow up with."

"I understand."

"Do you?"

"I was the youngest of four. I loved growing up with Edward, Victoria and Beatrice."

"Then you understand my desire?"

"I do."

He reached out and cupped her cheek, unable to hold himself back. "Thank you. You are...amazing, and I appreciate your support. I suppose I haven't told you how much your patience means to me, how you converted to Orthodoxy and learned my language."

She placed her hand over his. "I would do anything for you."

"Why?"

"Because of the dreams."

He withdrew his hand, guilt from his affair washing over him. "I'm sorry."

"Don't be."

He pulled away and reached for his wine. "I have a lot on my mind." It was an excuse, but he did have much to think about, and his fiancée was starting to make her way into his thoughts, distracting him more.

"You can tell me anything."

Could he? How deep did his trust go? "I worry for my father."

"His illness?"

"Yes. I don't like seeing him so unwell. He always liked to do things with his hands. Now he coughs so hard his lungs rattle and he's thinner than I remember."

"I can't imagine it's easy. He's very proud of us. It's in his eyes."

"He's done much to bring Moldavia forward. He built the hospital and modernized the docks. Now I need to finish the railroad he wanted."

"He's proud of you, regardless."

His father had been good to Moldavia. Mihai sipped his wine and pushed his anxieties as far away from him as he could, but they stayed with him on the fringes of his mind

She looked at the clock. "It's getting late."

"Let me escort you to your room. After Viktor and Sonia leave, I promise to put aside time to work on our wedding."

She stood and he watched her wipe out the glasses. She had made a major crack in his battered heart tonight.

Chapter Six

The castle's chapel was not attached to the main building. It sat approximately one hundred feet from the castle to the northeast, in the middle of an oak grove. Mihai briskly walked the distance from the castle to the chapel, Theresa at his side. She was Sonia's maid of honor and Mihai was Viktor's best man. He opened the heavy wooden door and Theresa went in first. Viktor was in the small vestibule with Father Gregori waiting for Sonia and her father.

Mihai took Theresa's fur coat and placed it on a nearby bench with his. He wore the formal uniform of the Crown Prince and Theresa wore a blue gown.

"Where's Beatrice?" asked Mihai.

"Waiting inside with the other guests," said Viktor

"Father should be here in five minutes with Sonia."

Viktor rubbed his hands together. "Good."

Theresa stood off to the side, holding a small bouquet of flowers. Mihai took his spot next to Viktor. An Orthodox wedding was full of rich symbolism, but it was a rigorous ceremony for all involved. The rings were exchanged in the vestibule. Then the couple followed the priest into the church to the altar. They went through the rigors of the mass, standing during the readings. During the consecration of the Eucharist, the couple knelt before the altar. Once everyone had received communion, the couple was crowned and walked around the altar three times. Mihai had always thought the ceremony was beautiful.

The door opened and his father entered with Sonia. He had lost a little more weight, but his eyes were sharp and focused. Mihai helped him remove his coat, and Theresa did the same for Sonia.

Mihai's father had ennobled Viktor just yesterday, making him the Count of Ovid.

Smiling her happiness, Sonia walked up to Viktor.

Father Gregori looked at Mihai's father. "Shall we begin?"

"Yes."

Father Gregori swept his gaze over everyone in the vestibule. "Is there anyone here who objects to the marriage of Viktor and Sonia?"

No one spoke.

"Lord Bacau, do you come here of your own free will to marry Princess Sonia?"

"Yes." Firm conviction resonated in his voice.

"Princess Sonia, do you come here of your own free will to marry Lord Bacau?"

"Yes."

Father Gregori looked at Mihai. He stepped forward, and as Orthodox custom dictated, exchanged the wedding rings between Viktor and Sonia three times. The last time, Viktor took the ring and placed it on Sonia's finger and she did the same to Viktor.

Moist happiness glimmered in Sonia's eyes. Father Gregori blessed the rings as Viktor and Sonia held hands. Mihai glanced at Theresa. She appeared very composed, but her eyes were damp as well.

Father Gregori motioned for them to walk into the chapel. Mihai and Theresa followed behind Viktor and Sonia.

Gold and white candles adorned the chapel. The heavy scent of frankincense lingered in the air.

Father Gregori presented Viktor and Sonia each with a candle as they reached the altar.

"Christ is the light of the world and will light your way through life as husband and wife."

Mihai stood by Viktor as prayers and the readings were said. The host was consecrated. Viktor and Sonia received communion. After everyone had received, Sonia gave Theresa her candle and picked up a crown off the altar. Viktor knelt before her and she crowned him. Mihai brought his fist up to his mouth, trying to combat his own tears of joy for his sister and friend. Viktor crowned Sonia. Both of them were crying. Father Gregori led them around the altar three times and then proclaimed them man and wife.

Viktor and Sonia walked out of the chapel, hand in hand. Mihai and Theresa followed behind. There would be a small reception in the castle's ballroom and then the wedded couple would leave for Odessa on the royal yacht.

~ * ~

Hecuba lingered on the fringes of the ballroom, watching the small gathering celebrate the wedding of Lord Bacau and Princess Sonia. She had taken her potion to look young two hours ago and wore a maid's outfit. It gave her the freedom she needed to troll the castle. The rumors around Constanta were the king's daughter was getting married. Hecuba didn't care for this development one bit. It would only complicate matters as Bane was determined to bite the man Hecuba had now learned was Viktor Bacau.

A butler stopped near the doors and motioned for two lesser male servants. "Have Lord Bacau and Princess Sonia's bags packed in the carriage now. The yacht leaves for Odessa at five."

They nodded and went up the stairs. Hecuba glanced at the mechanical clock resting on a small table near the ballroom entrance. She had to leave soon, but she'd been here long enough to find out Viktor's plans. Bane would be pleased. The full moon would occur in a few days, making his bite that much more potent. Quietly, she walked down the hall to the servants' wing and disappeared out a side door into the cold winter night. They had to book passage on the next boat to Odessa immediately.

~ * ~

Viktor heard his wife retch and ran into the water closet, just off the main suite from the yacht's main stateroom. Sonia had vomited into a chamber pot. He ran to her and grabbed a clean rag, wetting it in a nearby washbowl. Sonia collapsed against the wall, and Viktor wiped her face.

"Darling, I hate seeing you like this."

She looked up into his eyes, her cheeks pale. "It will pass."

He went to the faucet, and poured water into a cup. The yacht had been recently fitted with running water. Thank goodness for the recent advances in plumbing.

He peered at Sonia, his heart going out to her. The sea was fairly gentle right now with only a light wind. He had never thought to ask her if she suffered from motion sickness.

He sat down next to her and gave her the glass. She washed out her mouth, spitting into a small pot Viktor offered her.

"Better?" he asked.

"A little."

"This isn't quite how I'd hoped we'd start our honeymoon," he said.

She reached out and squeezed his hand in hers. "Don't worry so. I see it in your eyes."

"But I am."

"Don't be. This is natural."

He arched an eyebrow, curious over her choice of words. "Natural?"

She sighed and raked a hand through her hair. "Trust me."

"We were just married. You didn't say anything about

getting motion sickness before we left. We could have prepared for it. This isn't natural."

"Viktor—"

He stood. "I'm going to see what we have in the medicine cabinet for your stomach. Do you need some willow bark?"

"I don't need any medicine."

"What do you mean?" Anxiety spiked through him. What was wrong with his wife? And why was she so evasive with him?

She got to her feet, still pale, and took his hand in hers. "Let's go to the bed and sit down."

"Are you sure?"

"The queasiness has passed."

He allowed her to lead him to the bed in the stateroom, but he was still worried for her.

Sonia sat and he sat down next to her, cupping her cheek. He searched out her expressive eyes, more confused than ever. "Are you all right?"

"I didn't want to tell you like this."

"Tell me what? I'm not going to stop until you talk to me."

"Oh, Viktor. I wanted to be in your arms, basking in the afterglow of our lovemaking when I told you."

He narrowed his eyes, confused. Was she sick or not?

She squeezed his hands. "I believe I'm going to have a baby."

His eyes grew wide. "A baby? So soon? We were just married."

She smiled, happiness filling her expression. "And we've been sleeping together for weeks now."

Fear, anxiety, and joy, all in an odd mix, thrummed through his veins. A baby! He was going to be a father. It was sudden, unexpected, yet a wonderful surprise.

"Tell me you're all right with this news," she said.

Concern danced in her eyes and he wrapped his arms

around her waist, pulling him against her body. "I'm thrilled, Sonia, I am. I just didn't think it would happen so soon."

She placed her hands on his shoulders and her expression grew serious. "You're sure?"

"Yes."

"I'm not so convinced."

He tenderly kissed her temple. "Lie down next to me and let me hold you."

She relaxed and he guided her onto the bed, snuggling her close. He was going to be a father! He vowed in his heart that he would be a good one. He would take care of Sonia, treasure her, pamper her, and give his child the best of him.

~ * ~

Mihai walked into his study, surprised to find his father sitting in his chair and looking over his paperwork. It was late. There was a roaring fire in the fireplace. Viktor and Sonia had left in the yacht on their way to Odessa.

He paused in front of the desk. A bottle of brandy and two empty glasses were next to his father. "Did you need something?"

His father glanced up, smiling, yet his eyes were weary. "Everything appears in order. You're right on schedule with the railroad."

He was, and his father already knew it. So why was he in Mihai's study?

"While Viktor's gone, I've assigned my man, Anton Tybeski, to act as your valet. I want you to take advantage of his services so you can spend more time with Theresa."

Mihai pursed his lips, trying to contain his confusion. He wanted to work on the railroad and break ground on it in the spring. From his father's haggard appearance, he had only a few months. As for spending time with Theresa, the thought thrilled him. He couldn't deny she heated his blood. He knew he could trust her. Damn him, he didn't want Theresa to leave him, too – especially now that he was exploring the power of witchcraft, knowing she wasn't repulsed by it.

His father stood up and poured the brandy into the glasses, handing Mihai one.

"Don't over-think things, like you have a tendency to do, Son."

Mihai sipped his drink yet remained silent.

His father finished the drink and put the glass on the desk. "Theresa is a beautiful young woman – don't ruin it with her. Do you know why I approved of Sonia's wedding?"

"I was surprised you didn't insist on a more formal wedding."

"I wanted to see her married to the man she loved. Oh, I tried to feel out a marriage between her and Sorin Getzi, but Sonia told me while the young man was nice there was no spark." His father paused. "I told her if she ever did fall in love and the young man was a decent and honest one, I'd approve."

Mihai nodded, understanding his father's reasoning a little better.

King Stelian put his hand on Mihai's shoulder. "Lent starts tomorrow, but remember, you'll be married the weekend after Easter. Get to know Theresa."

"Why are you pushing this?"

"I want you settled before I die, Mihai – like your sister."

Mihai's eyes narrowed as he attempted to hold his mixed emotions in check. "I will be."

"Good."

There was a knock on the door. Mihai's father ambled to the door and opened it.

"Ah, Theresa, I was just leaving. Why don't you enjoy a nightcap with Mihai?"

"I will," she paused, smiling. "Good night, Your Majesty."

"Good night," he said, gruffly. Then he closed the door behind him.

Mihai drew in a deep breath. Theresa had changed into a more casual dress. It had a scooping neckline that revealed the 'v' in the hollow of her neck and hinted at her smooth cleavage. Her hair tumbled down her back in loose waves and her eyes sparkled like rare topaz gems in the firelight.

Mihai scrubbed the back of his neck, searching for his willpower. It danced precariously close to the edge of his control.

He leaned against the edge of his desk, his eyes riveted on her. "What brings you here?"

"The king summoned me."

"Is that all? I sense something else simmering below the surface."

"I was lonely."

Her voice was matter-of-fact, pricking at his faults, but damn if she wasn't beautiful in the firelight. The rest of his plans for the evening would have to wait.

He held up his glass. "Would you like a drink?"

"What is it?"

"Brandy."

She clapped her hands and a smile tipped the corner of her lips. "I've never tried it, but it smells like it would be an interesting adventure."

He chuckled at her lightheartedness and went to the hidden bar, disguised as a closed shelf in the library walls, and removed a clean glass. He poured the drink and gave it to her, his eyes sweeping over her face. He stilled his body, probing with his newly discovered senses. Her emotions were an open book.

She had indeed been lonely and she wanted him to touch her. She ached for it. She wanted him to drive the loneliness away. The thought of sharing a more intimate embrace with her was enticing, and knowing she was open to it encouraged him. He held up his drink and they clicked glasses, sipping the amber liquid.

She didn't gag or choke, but swallowed hard and narrowed her eyes. "What a crisp adventure. I do believe it's warming my stomach."

He chuckled and held out his hand. She gave him the glass. He put it on the desk, then leaned against it again.

A burning curious look came into her eyes.

"Come here." His voice was raw and husky.

She walked toward him slowly, her hips swaying. "What are you thinking?"

"I would like to be closer to you."

She stopped in front of him and he reached out grabbing her waist, pulling her closer, settling her between his legs. Her body pressed against his and she put her hands on his chest.

For an instant, an intensity stole into her expression, an intensity he hadn't spotted before. "I don't believe I've ever been this close to you," she said.

"No, I don't believe you have either, but I rather enjoy it. I hope you do as well."

"Lent starts tomorrow."

"What do you say we do a little sinning tonight so we have something to be penitent for?" he suggested.

Her face grew eager at the suggestion. Damn. His blood raced through his veins as his heart hammered in his chest. Desire for her overtook his senses. He had an intense awareness of her thrumming through his body.

"Such naughty thoughts, my Prince."

Desire smoldered in her eyes. He wanted to kindle that into a raging fire. For him alone.

He claimed her sweet lips, crushing her against his body. She slid her hands up his chest and clutched his shoulders. Her body tensed, needing release. He deepened the kiss, refusing to let her escape. God, no, he refused to let his woman out of his arms. Mihai traced the soft fullness of her lips and she parted her mouth for him. Lord, her mouth was soft and sweet and giving. His tongue explored the recesses of her mouth, coaxing her to explore his.

He needed her. He needed this. He'd wanted to hold her and kiss her just like this for days now, but he had held back, afraid of what would happen if he let her this close too soon. Her desire, eagerness, willingness to please him washed over him in the most intense blast of energy he'd ever felt.

Mihai pulled away slightly, and cupped her cheeks. "I felt you."

She peered at him intently, her hands fisting in his shirt. "Felt?"

"In my body. I can't explain it. I sensed your desire. It's so alive, so vibrant."

"I don't understand."

"Still your body for a minute. Maybe you can sense me?" he suggested.

She closed her eyes and concentrated. "I sense your attraction."

He swallowed, unnerved by how right she was. Theresa must possess an instinctual gift that was tuned precisely for him. Or was this his witch's blood reacting with an intensity he was unaware of until now?

She ran her finger over his lips. "Kiss me again."

If this was how a witch felt when they were intimate, then he never wanted to leave her arms. He leaned against her, ravishing her mouth, with keen awareness of their heightened senses.

He felt her head spinning in pleasure and he was delighted to know it was him giving her such feelings. His lips left hers, trailing kisses over her jaw and down her neck, and he kissed that sweet 'v' in the hollow of her neck.

She moaned.

It drove him mad.

He ran his fingers up her stomach and cupped her breasts.

A blast of intense delight ripped through her and he felt that pulse over his body and into his veins.

"Do you want me to stop?" he rasped.

"No."

He unlaced the stays of her dress, loosening the bodice and gently pushed the fabric down past her breasts, revealing her flimsy chemise. He ran his fingers over the fabric, flicking her nipples between his thumbs and forefingers, pebbling them.

She groaned as she placed her hands again on his shoulders. He didn't quite understand it, but she shared the pleasure she felt with him with a mere touch.

He growled, trying to keep his own rising needs at bay. He had to please her, make her desire for intimacy so acute that when they finally coupled, she would find no pain and only pleasure.

"Yes, it feels good." Her husky voice fueled his aching body. He tore the chemise, freeing her breasts, and lowered his lips to take a rock-hard nipple into his mouth.

"Oh, God, Oh, Mihai..."

He caressed her sensitive swollen nipples with his tongue, driving a blast of heat to his groan, which was yearning for her touch.

And he did want her to feel his erection. He wanted her to be proud of her handiwork. Damn it, he had no self-control. He had to try, he had to.

Let me please you...

It wasn't voiced, but a desire he felt coming from her.

She wanted to make him feel the same pleasure and physical excitement she was experiencing.

He placed his hands over hers and slid them over his body, down to his trousers, placing her hands over the fabric covering his thick erection. She ran her hands over him.

He pulled away, grinding his teeth. His desire to take her was overwhelming, but he couldn't. No, he couldn't – not yet.

She cupped his cheeks. "What's wrong?"

"I think that's enough for tonight." He held on to the thin rope of his self-control.

"Our religion does not prohibit an engaged couple from such caresses."

He was all too aware of the fact he could make love to her right now and his religion would approve of it. They were engaged, and engaged couples shared the same benefits married couples did.

"No, it doesn't, but I think it best if we let this encounter simmer in our minds so the next time is that much more pleasurable."

"Oh." She looked disappointed.

He couldn't stand the hurt in her expression. "I do not want to rush what's happening between us. God, I have more control than this."

Her eyes softened. "Well, Lent does start tomorrow."

Mihai ground his teeth again. He didn't think he could wait for his honeymoon to be intimate with her.

"Let me escort you to your room."

"All right."

He tied the stays of her dress, so her chest was covered. Then he put his hand in the small of her back, guiding her out of the study. He had never experienced such intensity, nor had he felt a woman's emotions before, but if their future encounters held the same promise of strong pleasure, then he would make her quite happy.

~ * ~

Bane watched from the rail of the ship as it approached Odessa. He had booked passage on a steam-powered boat as soon as Hecuba told him of his mark's destination. And his mark had a name – Viktor. How delicious.

Viktor was several hours ahead of him, but Bane was resourceful and confident in his abilities to finally get what he wanted.

The winter wind whipped against his face. Hecuba rested down below. The potions she used to transform her body were getting more and more painful. Black magic had devoured her body. She had lived long – 200 years, but that was because she drank his blood, allowing his ability of regeneration and longevity to assist her body. It was now failing her. If she lived another two years, he would be surprised. And maybe it was time to give up the beast. He was nothing without her, and maybe he could finally consider death – especially if he could train Viktor to be his heir. Timon wasn't worthy.

He ran a hand through his greasy hair. There was something about this Viktor that resonated deep in his bones. Something he couldn't place – only that the man's natural scent, that of tiger lilies, reminded him of home.

Odessa's port came into view. Bane enjoyed being a wolf, reveling in the supernatural power of his body. He was the leader of his pack, and due to his age, he had skills younger wolves did not possess. Bane closed his eyes, recalling his younger days. He was born in a small Ukrainian town – Chernivtsi, over 200 years ago, near the Romanian principality of Transylvania. How the times had changed.

Bane looked to the sky, always aware of the phase of the moon. Because he was so old and a leader, he could transform at will. Younger wolves would only transform on the full moon when the moon's eerie light was at its full power, igniting the wolf's blood in its human host.

Werewolves needed two things come the full moon – to eat and have sex. When it came to satisfying the awful hunger, only human flesh and blood would do. There was something in human blood that held the hunger in check until the next full moon. Pig's blood could be substituted if a wolf's appetite couldn't be properly attended to, but it lacked that special quality to be totally filling. A wolf had the potential to go insane if they drank pig's blood three moons in a row.

Then there was the insatiable desire to have sex. Only a witch could sate the wolf's heightened desires. Their energy was intuitive, feeling the wolf's emotions, calming him. A human woman could accommodate a wolf, but couldn't calm him – the sex would be rough and dangerous with a human. Most wolves hunted for food at night, rested, and then, during the day, when they were human, coupled with the witches.

The full moon would occur in Odessa, and while he hated to be away from his pack in Mulfaltar, he refused to let the opportunity of biting Viktor pass him by again. He'd left Timon in charge. Timon was crafty yet cold, but the other two wolves could hold their own with Timon, and the witches would be protected by the wolves. Still Timon was no leader, and Bane had to think about the future of his pack. Hecuba would die soon and when she did, Bane would join her. He did not want to leave the pack to Timon.

He smiled, recognizing the Potemkin Stairs. Oh, yes, he'd have his heir tonight.

Chapter Seven

Bane's boat docked in Odessa around three p.m. He knew of a rundown inn near the docks that never asked questions for the right price and he paid for a room on the second floor overlooking the harbor and cargo ship berths.

Hecuba set out her herbs and roots and prepared the potions she would need later in the night. While she did that, Bane trolled the other berths. He found the royal yacht of Moldavia in an upscale part of the harbor. The captain and two crew members were doing maintenance checks.

He looked toward the horizon. The sunset would be soon. He closed his eyes, focusing on his acute sense of smell. He did not detect the tiger lilies that reminded him of his mark – of Viktor. Could Viktor be a descendant of Andriy, Bane's son who wasn't tainted by wolf's blood? He would know for sure when he tasted his prey. He needed to get Hecuba and quickly. The daylight was fading fast and he had little time if he was going to lie in wait for his mark.

~ * ~

Viktor walked alongside a row of shops near the berth where their yacht was moored. Beside him, Sonia peered at the clothes and jewelry displayed in the windows. The gas company's men lit lamps as the sun dipped below the horizon.

The air was colder than he expected. He jammed his gloved hands into the pockets of his winter overcoat and palmed the small revolver Mihai had given him before they left.

Sonia paused in front of a window, admiring some gems.

A pungent, wild animal scent swept a chill down his spine. He spun around, drawing the gun.

The sinewy, greasy man from two weeks before stood in front of him baring his fang-like teeth.

Sonia turned around and immediately grabbed Viktor's arm. "What's going on? Viktor?"

"I don't know."

"Shoot me. It won't stop me," the man said.

"Leave me and my wife alone!" Viktor held the pistol tight in his hand, terrified to fire it.

"You wouldn't shoot me."

"Watch me. Leave. Now."

"Hecuba!"

A young woman appeared out of the shadows and placed a rag over Sonia's mouth. Sonia attempted to shove her captor away. Viktor lunged forward, trying to push the woman from his struggling wife, but the man grabbed him, knocking the pistol out of Viktor's hand.

Intense fear rushed down Viktor's spine. This man's grip was stone-hard.

Sonia collapsed to the ground, unconscious. Viktor couldn't break free. The woman approached him.

"Why?" Viktor cried.

"I need an heir."

Hecuba slipped the rag over his mouth and nose. A lightheaded sensation washed over him. He tried one last, desperate bid to escape from his captor's custody, then lost consciousness.

~ * ~

When Viktor awoke, his eyes took an extra minute to focus. He sat in a chair, his hands and legs bound by rope. He caught the stench of rotting food and urine coming in from the window that appeared to lead out to an alley. He gagged and a small bit of spittle came up. Viktor moved his head to the side, vomiting on the floor instead of himself.

Loud clanging noises and boat whistles rang in his ears from the nearby docks. Oh God, where was Sonia?

"He's awake, Bane." The speaker, a young, slender female with round firm breasts and dark curly hair, stood next to a wooden table cluttered with knives, a mortar, pestle, and various herbs.

The man who'd attacked him, presumably Bane, sat in a chair and grinned. "Good."

Viktor's heart raced, the heavy adrenaline of fear controlling its rapid pace. If only he could reach the dagger tucked into his boot.

He swept his gaze over the room and located Sonia on a bed, her hands tied to the headboard. Her mouth was gagged and her ankles were tied together. She was awake, but her eyes weren't focused. What had they done to her?

"She's fine. Hecuba gave her a small dose of laudanum. She's awake, but drugged," said the man.

"If you've hurt her—"

His captor held up his hands. "I am many things, but I will not harm a woman who is carrying a child."

Viktor grunted, frustrated that he couldn't free himself or his wife. Instead, he quickly surveyed the rest of the room, glancing out the window. The moon was close to full – a fat waxing gibbous. Next to the window was an iron fire escape. A small fire burned in the fireplace on the wall opposite the bed and in back of Hecuba's table.

His male assailant stared at him. His golden amber eyes were unnatural pinpricks of light in the room. Bane's lips curved into a smile.

"I will teach you well."

Viktor swallowed, trying to tame the fear that knotted in his stomach. "Release me and my wife right now."

"That I cannot do."

"Why not?"

"Bane has a need for an heir. Timon won't do." Hecuba's voice was raw and hoarse.

Viktor's fear spiked. Sweat dribbled down the nape of his neck. "No. It's a legend."

"The werewolf is real. Tonight I will taste your blood and give you mine. You will belong to me and become a member of my pack."

Viktor tugged against the ropes with his hands. "No!"

Bane stood up. "This is an honor."

Viktor grimaced. Bane was thin, but muscular. He possessed short, greasy yellow hair and haunting gold eyes that commanded power.

Bane walked behind Viktor and put his hands on Viktor's shoulders.

"Hecuba, give him a small dose of laudanum so it takes the edge of his fear away."

Hecuba grabbed a thin vial and approached Viktor. He refused to open his mouth. She pushed his forehead back with unexpected strength, parting his lips with her free hand.

The liquid ran down his throat. Viktor cringed.

Bane began to change. His aquiline nose lengthened, but stopped short of becoming a snout, retaining a man's nostrils. His eyes grew feral. His fangs elongated, his lips became thin. Hair grew over his flesh. A half-man, half-wolf stood over him.

Bane placed his hand on the side of Viktor's head, pushed it to the side, and plunged his fangs into his neck.

"Argh!"

All coherent thought left him. Viktor could only feel. Blood was taken from his body in a swiftness that made his head spin. His spiritual essence held onto his emaciated body by a slender tether. His exhausted limbs shuddered.

The wolf left his neck and went to Viktor's mouth. Viktor's teeth instinctively bit down on the wolf's engorged lips and Bane's blood trickled into his mouth. Viktor gagged as the dark liquid tumbled down his throat. The coppery taste clung to his lips. Scenes of a life lived flooded Viktor's vision – Bane's life. He was now connected to the wolf.

Bane stepped away and loosened the ropes around Viktor's wrists. Hecuba untied the knots from around his ankles and Viktor collapsed onto the floor.

Tainted blood tore through his veins. The moon's light fell on him. His blood temporarily froze in his body and then exploded in a rush. Adrenaline furiously pumped through every muscle and every limb. His heart pistoned as fast as a steam engine. Viktor's muscles grew long and sinewy. Fur covered his body. Pitiful gasps were stifled when his vocal chords stretched beyond their limits. Human thought left him and he stood on all fours face-to-face with an animal much like himself.

The other wolf sniffed him all over, branding him, then pushed him toward the window. Thought penetrated his brain, but he had no idea how to reply. Viktor understood feelings, and now that the pain of the blood exchange was over, his body tingled with unexpected pleasure.

"Do not worry. It takes time to master this wolfen body."

Viktor shook his head.

"Follow me. Your new body has needs."

His body did crave. What, he did not know, but he better follow the other wolf or he would go mad if he didn't calm the rush thrumming through his veins.

He loped after Bane down the iron steps outside the window. His limbs moved with an awkwardness he was not accustomed to.

"Keep running. It's good for your legs."

The voice in his head unsettled him, yet he knew it was Bane and this was how the wolves communicated, by projecting thoughts. It wasn't just an animal's body – it was more. He had a higher consciousness than a true wolf.

"I am Viktor."

Bane stopped. *"You talk."*

"Yes."

"Very good."

"I despise you."

"I thought you might. It doesn't matter. I will care for you. We run."

"Why are we running?"

"You need to exercise your new body and you need to eat."

Viktor followed Bane to the docks. They kept to inky shadows, hiding from humans. Viktor did not feel right. Fiery knots in his stomach practically overwhelmed him. His abnormal appetite threatened to drive him off the cliff of sanity. It didn't help that the smell of sea salt and the pungent odor of grease upset this sensitive lupine nose. His need to find physical satisfaction of his heightened senses drove him to follow Bane despite his disgust for the vile being.

A lone crewman stood on one of the ships. Bane howled. The crewman straightened and searched the docks. Fear hung in his eyes. Raw, primal fear.

Bane shot out of the shadows, running toward the ship.

"Good God!" The sailor reached for the gun in his belt. Bane raced up the plank between the ship and the dock and jumped on the sailor. Viktor ran behind him. Bane's sharp claws severed the sailor's hand and gun from his wrist. Blood poured out. He fell down, struck his head hard on the wooden planks, and closed his eyes.

The sailor was dead.

Bane lapped at the blood oozing from the sailor's wrist.

"Eat, Viktor."

Viktor's snout twitched. This wasn't right. It wasn't human to crave the sweet, coppery smell of blood.

"What's wrong with you, cub? Drink the blood before his mates find him."

"Why?"

"Only human blood can give your body what you need to stop the hunger."

Bane took Viktor by the neck with his sharp, cusped teeth and shoved Viktor's snout into the blood. That was all it took. Viktor lapped at the sweet tasting liquid.

Ecstasy replaced hunger. Viktor was sated. And he was also disgusted with himself. He had always hated violence. Fedir's abuse had done that to him. Now his body reviled in the aftermath of what Bane had done.

"Let's go. This need has been met."

Viktor shook his neck and head, trying rid himself of disgust. What he had done was wrong and reprehensible, and he felt like the foulest creature on Earth.

When they reached the inn, Viktor stopped in front of the iron staircase that would take him back to the room.

"What's wrong?"

"I hate you."

Bane bit him on the neck, just enough to push through the fur and grab him, forcing him up the steps.

"You are my flesh, cub, and you will do as I say."

The thought thundered in Viktor's head. An inner awareness told him they had not only shared blood, but something more – a biological connection? Ancestry, perhaps? Viktor didn't want to believe it. His body had changed now, and while Viktor was disgusted by the change, thank the Heavens he wasn't dead. He had to live – he had to be a husband to Sonia and a father to his child. They needed him to stay alive.

His will resigned, he shrugged off Bane and went up the stairs on his own feet. Viktor jumped through the window. Sonia lay on the bed, eyes closed.

Hecuba sat in a chair, playing with tarot cards. Viktor dropped down by the bed, his body feeling sluggish.

Bane glared at him with his yellow, feral eyes. *"Go to sleep, cub. We'll deal with your other needs in the morning."*

Viktor lay down at the foot of the bed and closed his eyes.

~ * ~

"Wake up, Viktor."

A hand shoved him, and Viktor's eyes fluttered open. A sunbeam came in through the window. He sat up, realizing he was naked – and his manhood was painfully erect.

Bane threw a pair of trousers at him. "Get dressed."

Viktor's body ached to release his seed, but he held the desire back with the power of his mind. Slowly, he got to his feet.

Bane wore trousers only. "You need to be with a woman – and not the one on the bed."

Viktor buttoned his pants as he turned to look at Sonia. The rhythmic rise and fall of her chest told him she was sleeping. "Why not? She's my wife. She's the only one I want to be with."

"She's with child. I don't want you to harm her."

"How could I harm her?"

"Her body is delicate – changing to meet the needs of the child she carries," Bane paused. "Your body is stronger and quicker. Sex could injure her in her condition. From now on, you need a witch who can instinctively accommodate you and react to you."

Viktor glared at Bane. "Sonia is a witch."

Bane looked to Hecuba. "Is she?"

Hecuba nodded. "Yes. I tested her blood while you were gone last night. Her ferons are in a heightened state of awareness and would protectivity lash out if we were any more aggressive with her."

"Ferons? Aggressive?" Viktor questioned.

"Her body will instinctively protect her from physical harm but the growing child is draining to her and every witch is different. You must look to her mother's pregnancies for clues as to how her pregnancy will progress. Her confinement might be easy or challenging," Hecuba said.

Viktor clenched his fists, anger riding through him like a powerful wave cresting on the Black Sea's shore. He lunged at the man in front of him, wrapping his hands around his neck. "How dare you do this to me!"

Bane grabbed Viktor's wrists, and with incredible strength, tore Viktor's hands away from his neck. The older man's eyes glowed as brilliantly as the sun.

"I dare because I need an heir – and you are my choice. You are my flesh – a direct descendant of my lineage."

Viktor stopped, stunned by Bane's words. "Impossible!"

"I tasted your blood. You are descended from my son, Andriy Bacau – who was untainted by the wolf's bite."

Viktor swallowed. He narrowed his eyes. "I don't believe you."

"Feel the truth in your blood. It's there. I will take care of you – meet your body's needs – teach you the ways of the wolf so when I die, you can take my place."

"I don't want this! I will not do what you tell me." Viktor could barely contain his fury at this presumptuous beast. He had felt the truth in his blood. The horror of what Bane had done to him seeped into his bones.

Bane's nostrils flared in anger and he went to the bed, pointing at Sonia.

"You will do precisely what I say or I will kill her family."

Viktor froze, standing stock-still. "Don't touch my wife!"

"Are we clear, cub? You will be obedient to me or this woman's family will be ruined."

Viktor nodded in agreement to Bane's wishes. He could not bear to think that harm would happen to Sonia's family because of him.

Bane took a step away from the bed. "Take her to your yacht and then return. Tomorrow you may join her. Today, you will stay with me and learn."

"I need a shirt."

Hecuba grabbed a garment off the table and flung it at him. Then she pointed to shoes near the bed. She was now old with lines and creases covering her face. Her hair was gray and brittle. Viktor fastened the buttons on his shirt and slid on his shoes.

"Your coat and hers are in the closet."

Viktor put on his overcoat and then went to the bed. Sonia was still unconscious. He slid her arms into her coat and picked her up in his arms. She was as light as a feather.

"You have an hour. If you are not back then, I will hunt you down," said Bane.

Viktor nodded and walked out the door, Sonia securely cradled in his arms.

As he walked out the inn's front door, he received several curious looks, but he ignored them, focused on his task – taking Sonia to the safety of their yacht.

His heart broke. He was a beast now and Sonia had been there. Damn it! How could this happen to them? What would happen now?

People continued to stare at him oddly as he walked through the harbor. Finally, he came to the berth where their yacht was docked.

Captain Calurisi waved at them from the rear of the boat. "Lord Bacau?"

"Put down the plank."

The captain raced to the side of the boat and did as he was told.

Viktor went directly to their stateroom and placed Sonia on the bed.

"Should I fetch a doctor?" asked the captain.

"Yes. I have to leave. Do whatever the doctor says. I will return tomorrow and then we can depart for Constanta. My wife is not to leave this yacht once she wakes up – for her safety, of course."

The captain nodded and departed.

Viktor sat down on the bed, pushed a stray strand of hair away from Sonia's face and hung his head, doing his best to stifle his tears of pain. And regret. And anger. His life and Sonia's would never be the same, but he would do what he needed to so as to ensure that she was kept safe and away from Bane. Reluctantly, he stood up and walked out, leaving her sleeping on the bed.

Chapter Eight

Mihai peeked out of the carriage's window. Theresa's carriage was in front of his as they traveled up the access road to Delfin Castle. He smiled at the thought.

Home. Yes, Delfin Castle was now her home and he was glad.

He pulled his gaze away from the window. Anton Tybeski sat across from him, clutching a briefcase. His new assistant was very efficient and Mihai appreciated his work habits.

"Mr. Tybeski, would you be willing to take on an additional task?"

"What is it, Your Grace?"

"My fiancée, Lady Theresa, has expressed an interest in patronizing the town's orphanage. I'd like you to meet with Mr. Kazha and be our liaison."

"I'd be honored."

"Good. First thing tomorrow, I'll give you authorization to take money out of my personal account so you can establish a separate account specifically for the orphanage. Meet with Mr. Kazha and determine the most urgent tasks to be done and report back to me or Lord Bacau. He will also be involved."

"Yes, Your Grace."

"I'm pleased with your work and I know you'll do Theresa and me proud."

"Yes, Your Grace."

"Good. See me immediately after breakfast tomorrow."

Tybeski nodded. He was maybe five years older than Mihai, thin build with dark hair, and his work ethic impressed him.

The carriage pulled up to the stables and the footman opened the door. Mihai stepped out. The air carried a bone-chilling cold. It hadn't snowed in days, but a thin layer of old snow covered the hard ground. Several icicles hung from the second-story ledge of the castle.

Thank goodness spring was only a month away.

"Prince Mihai! What a delightful surprise." That was Beatrice.

He turned around to find Theresa and Beatrice bundled up in warm coats and hats. Their cheeks were red from the chill.

"Hello, ladies."

"Hello, Mihai."

Beatrice bowed.

"So what were you ladies up to this afternoon?"

Theresa rubbed her mittens together. "We sent the wedding announcements out and Beatrice and I ordered our dresses."

"Well done. What else is there to do?"

"We need flowers, musicians, caterers, a daguerreotyper..."

"And rings," he added.

"Yes, and rings."

Her sweet expression warmed his heart. The thought of putting his ring on her finger humbled him.

"We'd love to have your thoughts on our plans," said Beatrice.

Mihai gestured toward the castle, walking next to Theresa. He wanted to get the women out of the cold. Tybeski walked behind him.

"Well, tomorrow Mr. Tybeski and I have a busy day. Parliament passed my tax, so I must send out notices requesting bids, and Mr. Tybeski will be working on our behalf for the orphanage."

Theresa stepped in front of him, grabbing his hands.

They were in front of the castle's steps. Her face sparkled with excitement. "That's wonderful! Thank you, Mihai."

"I'm glad you approve. After dinner I want you to come to my study."

She quirked an eyebrow.

"I want to tell you about the railroad."

"You want to work on the railroad bid, you mean." A frown marred the perfection of her smooth face.

"If I wanted to work, I wouldn't ask you to come to my study."

"I'm sorry," she said, gently.

"Oh, let's go inside, I'm freezing and I want a very warm cup of tea." Beatrice looked at Mihai. "And if you want Theresa to join you in the study, she needs a very warm cup of tea, too."

Mihai cast his gaze toward the door and gestured with his hand for the ladies to go ahead of him. Beatrice was a colorful one, but it was Theresa who heated his blood with her innocence, her sense of adventure, and her caring nature. It was Theresa who he wanted to be with tonight – alone.

~ * ~

Theresa walked down the hall toward Mihai's study, thrilled to finally receive an invitation from him. They were only a week into Lent, but each time she was with Mihai, his hesitation and reservations grew less. His kisses grew bolder, harder, full of passion, and the way he ran his hands over her body ignited a fire in the core of her being that she could hardly contain.

Then there was 'the feeling' between them. She didn't know what else to call it. When she and Mihai were kissing, touching, caressing, she could swear she felt his emotions, his passions, his desires, and that only heightened the sensual experiences between them.

And he felt her.

She guessed this had to be because he was a witch. The thought didn't unnerve her. She'd overheard her family on occasions talking about witches and their powers, and she always accepted the existence of witches because they did, but she never thought she'd meet a real witch, let alone marry one. She believed witches to be good, so she had no fear of Mihai or his talents.

She stopped in front of the study's door. She wanted to be good. Beatrice once told her good was boring, but Theresa never believed that. She was having fun. Mihai stimulated her like no other. He listened to her. He believed in her causes. She would be a good wife to him and a good mother to his children.

Yes, she resolved, she would be good. Her shoulders set, she knocked on the door.

"Come in."

She walked in, closing the door behind her. Mihai stood behind the desk, a map nailed up on the wall behind him. A bottle of brandy and two glasses rested on his desk.

"Hello, Theresa."

"Hello, Mihai."

He studied her with an intense gaze.

"Would you like a drink?"

She stopped in front of the desk. "Yes."

He lowered his lashes, half covering his eyes, and his expression grew focused. He raised his hand, and as he did so, a glass lifted off the desk. He pushed out with his hand and the glass floated through the air. Theresa caught it.

A soft gasp escaped her lips. "How did you do that?"

He smiled. "Magic."

"I didn't think you could do things like that."

"I've been practicing." He paused to sip his drink. "It's a channeling of energy which gets easier the more I practice. I can even use it to tie a cravat around my neck now."

She giggled at that. "I'm amazed, Mihai, simply amazed."

He opened the middle drawer of his desk and held up a small, dagger-like knife. The blade looked incredibly dull, but the silver on the blade sparkled in the firelight.

"What is that?" she asked.

"It was my mother's athame. I found it in her box of personal items my father had sent to an old room for storage."

"What does it do?"

"Channel energy. I think the material of it excites the ferons in my blood."

She arched an eyebrow. "Ferons?"

Mihai pointed to an old leather-bound book on his desk. "This is a book on witchcraft I've been reading and learning from."

"Ah."

His openness alternately thrilled yet frightened her. Yes, she believed, but she had no idea witches could be so powerful. What was she getting into?

Mihai regarded her with a speculative gaze and he put the athame on the book. "I didn't mean to overwhelm you. You seemed accepting of what I am."

"I am. I do." She sipped from her glass, then put it on his desk. "I just didn't know it involved all this."

He walked out from around his desk and stood in front of her. "I will never harm you. I will never use my magic to hurt you or others. Do you believe me?" The conviction in his voice tore through to her soul, and she knew in that moment he would never harm her. She nodded.

"Let me show you the map. I want you to know about my project," said Mihai.

She followed him to the wall, spying Constanta next to the Black Sea. Mihai pointed to a city on the other side of the map. "This is Bucharest. It's not a far distance and the actual construction should only take through the summer."

Theresa tugged her lower lip through her teeth. He smelled of spice and soap – fresh and clean. He turned to look at her, raking his seductive gaze over her dress.

She drew in a breath. "So, ah, tell me about the bids."

He put his hands on her shoulders and looked into her eyes. "I'll be soliciting for bids from now until the end of March. I hope to choose a company by the first and I want to start after we return from our honeymoon."

The intense desire he had for her flowed through his hands into her limbs.

"You think of everything."

"Let's go to the tower." Thick emotion made his voice husky. His malachite eyes riveted on her face, then moved over her body slowly. "I missed touching you today."

She flashed what she hoped was a secretive smile. "You did?"

"Very much, and now all I want is to be completely alone with you."

A thrill shot through her body. Most of their shared intimacy had taken place in the study, and while she liked that room, she adored the ambience of the tower.

He leaned over and brushed his lips against her ear, his breath warm and sensual. "I want to be near you. I want to be with you. I simply want you, Theresa, and I don't want to deny it any longer." The faint tremor in his voice was seductive, full of emotion. His body radiated a feral heat he could barely contain. A shiver of excitement rippled through her. To be alone with him. To be intimate with him. She ached for it.

Theresa gave him her hand and he led her out of the study, down the hall, and up the secret staircase to the tower.

He placed kindling on top of the logs and lit a fire while Theresa went to the telescope. She looked through it. Grey clouds were scattered between the stars. Her heart raced.

He placed his hands on her shoulders. His masculine chest pressed against her back.

"You are so beautiful, Theresa."

Her arms dropped to her sides and he trailed his hands down them, coming to rest on her hands.

"I've tried to be good – holding you at a distance, wanting to go slow so as not to startle you, but our kisses aren't enough. I want more. My body craves yours with such intensity I don't know how I can keep my head in front of other people."

Her heartbeat skyrocketed at his words.

"I feel your apprehension, Theresa."

"What if I disappoint you?"

"Never. You know it's more than just our caresses – I can sense your pleasure just as you sense mine."

The pit of her stomach churned. His closeness was so male, so bracing. His body tensed, needing release, and Heaven help her, she wanted to be the one to offer that release.

"Yes, I do want you, Mihai," she whispered.

She felt him step away, leaving her cold, but only for a moment. "Turn around."

She did so.

"Undress me."

His eyes betrayed his ardor. She reached up and removed his cravat, throwing it on the floor. He took several deep breaths, trying to calm his excitement. She smiled at being able to feel the emotions coming from him. She thrilled him. Her fingers pushed off the vest, undid the buttons on his shirt and revealed his hard, well-defined chest. A fine layer of dark, curling hair ran against the curve of his muscles, down his abdomen, and into his trousers. She bit her lip, marveling at his maleness – his exquisite physique.

"Do you like what you see?" he asked.

"Yes."

"Turn around."

She did so. He unfastened the stays in the back of her dress and pushed the fabric down her body past her hips. It crumpled to the floor. Mihai then removed her chemise. She gasped as he ran a hand down her back. She was hot, and the opening between her legs dampened.

He kissed the nape of her neck. The strong hardness of his lips moved over her skin.

She groaned, her head spinning from his touch.

He took her hand and guided her to the rug in front of the fireplace. Gently, he leaned her so her back was against the rug. His mouth covered hers, sending new spirals of ecstasy ripping through her. He kissed one breast as he fondled the other in his fingers, pebbling the nipple.

She lay panting, lost in the growing intimacy. He trailed sweet kisses down her body until he got to her stomach. One finger brushed against her damp femininity.

She moaned.

"You like that, don't you?"

"Yes." She closed her eyes, arching her hips, inviting him to take more.

He slid another finger into her and pure pleasure flooded her. Explosive.

"No, not yet, Theresa."

He removed his fingers, leaving a painful ache, only to replace them with his mouth.

"Oh, God..."

The room spun. His mouth was divine ecstasy between her legs. Theresa tumbled off a cliff into the throes of heated bliss. Her legs shook uncontrollably and Mihai placed his hands on her thighs, steadying her.

Slowly the wave passed and she raised her head to look at him.

"You are truly amazing," he said.

"Let me please you," she responded.

Mihai stood up and removed his shoes, unfastened the buttons of his trousers, and pushed them down his well-muscled thighs.

Theresa got to her knees in front of him, marveling at his thick erection. She placed a hand on his shaft and slid it alongside the skin. He cocked his head back and groaned, diving his fingers into her hair

"Theresa, oh, God, oh, Theresa..."

His maleness thrilled her. She ran her hand up and down his hard shaft, feeling his body pulse with uncontrolled desire.

He pulled back and met her gaze. She lay down and he braced himself over her. His erection pierced her outer barrier. She arched toward him and looked into his face. He was on the edge – his self control fraying, but every thrust was gentle and went a little deeper.

She whimpered. Her chest heaved and her hips arched into him. Mihai broke, thrusting deeply and powerfully, impaling her with his manhood. She cried out from the pain that was mixed with pleasure. He stirred within her, thrusting in rhythm, and she matched his pace.

His body quivered and his seed flooded within her. He lit up in a bright light. She released her body to him and they bathed in the light before Mihai collapsed next to her.

They lay on the rug as the fire warmed them.

"Did you see the light that surrounded our bodies?" she asked.

"Yes. It didn't upset you, did it?"

"Does it always happen?"

"No – I don't know, I suspect it's how my body responded to our coupling."

She propped herself on her elbows. "Because you're a witch?"

"Yes."

"Well, it was wonderful."

He smiled at her and ran a finger under the soft curve of her breast. "Do you have regrets?"

"Regrets?"

"That we didn't wait for our honeymoon?"

"No. I have no regrets," she replied.

He paused and his body tensed. It was slight, but Theresa felt the tension. Was he suddenly apprehensive?

"What's wrong?" she asked.

"I do have one regret."

She arched an eyebrow? "Oh?"

"Let me explain."

~ * ~

Mihai wrapped his arms tightly around her waist, letting her know with his physical presence he didn't want her to leave, and buried his face against the tender flesh of her neck.

"I loved a woman in England. Her name was Alexandra and I gave her my heart, but she...chose to stay in England, and I learned she had used me. Her rejection and true nature hurt me more than I can say."

"What... what are you saying?" Hurt splayed across her face.

"I regret having this affair."

"Oh." She stilled in his arms. What was she thinking?

"Theresa, I'm sorry—"

"Well, this wasn't quite what I expected."

"I wanted to be honest with you."

"We just made love, Mihai. I wasn't expecting to hear that."

He frowned. She had a point. It was a careless mistake on his part. While he did want her to know, he shouldn't have told her like this. He had ruined a very special moment for them. How could he be such a fool? What had gotten into him to confess such a thing after their lovemaking?

"I need my dress."

He couldn't think of anything else to do, scared he was going to lose her in that moment, and channeled every ounce of his feelings into his hands, warming her face. "I am sorry. I was careless. I didn't mean to hurt you."

She stared into his eyes, understanding filling them.

"Stay. Let's talk. Don't... go."

"I won't leave you, but I want to get dressed and go to my room. I have much to think about."

He nodded, relieved for that, and helped her put on the dress. There was no kiss goodbye, no tender caresses. She peered at him with round, hazel, doe-like eyes, confusion heavy in them, and walked down the stairs.

God, he was honest with her! He had to be. So why did he feel like he might lose her? That cut deeper than Alexandra's rejection ever had. He could never be so foolish again.

Chapter Nine

Sonia sat on the bridge of the yacht staring at her tea as Captain Calurisi studied charts of the Black Sea. She did not want to be alone and the Captain felt uncomfortable in her stateroom.

The sun was shining, but the air was cold and her heart ached. The past couple of days had been a blur due to the laudanum, but she understood enough. They had been kidnapped and Viktor had been bitten by a werewolf. Her loving, gentle, kind husband had been made into a beast. She was numb at the thought. They were in love. They were on their honeymoon. They were going to have a baby. What now?

She hated that foul couple. She hated what happened to her husband, but how could she be with a beast? She wrapped her arms around herself, cold, tired, and scared.

"You should eat, Your Grace. The doctor says you need to maintain your strength," said Captain Calurisi.

"I know."

A crewman came to the door, knocked and opened it. "Sir, Lord Bacau has returned."

Sonia ran to the window and looked down onto the dock. Viktor stood at the foot of the walkway next to the boat. He was dressed in dirty clothes, his hair was stringy and there were dark bags under his eyes.

His gaze locked onto hers. She shivered. His blue eyes had turned amber gold.

He walked up the plank onto the boat. No doubt he was going to their stateroom to clean up. She had to go there. They had to talk.

"Are you all right, Your Grace?" asked the captain.

She turned to face him, steeling her shoulders. "I'm fine. I'm going to talk to my husband."

He nodded and Sonia hustled out. Captain Calurisi understood something was wrong, but not the details. Sonia had no idea what she was going to say to Viktor. She paused in front of the stateroom door, drew in a breath, and knocked.

"Come in."

She walked in and closed the door behind her. Viktor was running water for a bath and wore only his trousers. He appeared tired. Haggard. Drained. His chest had lost a bit of its definition. Had he been starved the last two days?

Sonia stayed next to the door, nervously rubbing her fingers together. He scrubbed a wash rag over his face and looked at her.

His eyes had indeed changed. They were yellow. Frightening. Viktor put the rag down.

"How are you, Sonia?"

"Fine."

"And the baby?"

"I'm still with child."

Relief washed over his face. "Thank God."

Sonia set her chin and imposed an iron control on her emotions. She looked directly at her husband. "What are you?"

"You know what I am now." He eyes narrowed a little. "I cannot undo this horror. We must both learn to deal with it," He paused. "Say it."

A cold shiver ripped down her spine, but she knew she had to confront their future and not run away from it. "You are a werewolf."

He nodded.

"What now?"

He took a step toward her, his face softening. She took a step backward and hit the door. Viktor stopped.

"You don't have to be afraid of me."

She arched an eyebrow. "I don't know what to expect from you now."

Viktor sighed and raked a hand through his greasy hair. "I have orders to go to Mulfaltar for the next full moon to meet Bane's pack and deal with my needs."

"Your *needs*?" Her heart sank.

"They are not pleasant, Sonia."

"Do not spare me, Viktor. I'm your *wife* – I'm having your *child*. I want to know exactly what I'm dealing with."

He pursed his lips. "I must have human blood."

Her eyes widened. His bluntness stunned her. "You have to kill?"

"No, I don't, but I have to satisfy the craving which will be incredibly strong around the full moon."

She swallowed and rubbed her hands up and down her arms. "Is there more?"

His eyes clouded with regret and disgust. "I have to have sex – with a witch."

Her mouth opened, but no words came out. She was too stunned to speak. Viktor took slow, measured steps toward her. "I have been cautioned – it must be a with a witch, however, due to your condition, it is not wise. I could harm you or the child."

Sonia tried to say something, but no words came out. It felt like the wind had suddenly left the sails of her marriage and she'd fallen hard onto the deck and she didn't know how to pick herself up.

"I am not proud of what I have to do. I did not ask to be bitten – you know that! I was kidnapped and violated."

She brought her fist up to her chin. "You have to have sex...with someone else?"

"Yes. Someone who can feel my emotions and respond to my new heightened reflexes."

"Why?" Her voice cracked. She couldn't bear the thought of her husband in another woman's bed.

"I'm stronger, faster, and have more stamina than the average man. Only a trained witch with her ability to use magic can accommodate this need," he paused. "Maybe one day, once you've had the child, we can be intimate again, but as I've been told, your body is not your own and you have no formal training."

Tears trickled down her cheeks and his words resonated throughout every fiber of her being. Viktor invaded her space. She flinched, but held her ground. Viktor's hand shook as he wiped her tears with his thumb. The physical contact was gentle, not what Sonia expected from him.

God, this beast was her husband. She loved him regardless.

"Sonia, I love you, and I think I can be the husband you need me to be if you'll give me a chance. If you'll learn to live with the new me," He paused, "And I really want that chance."

She looked into his terrified eyes. A wave of confusion washed over her. She still loved him – deeply.

Viktor embraced her. Shocked, she tried to push him away, pounding on his chest. He grabbed her wrists, stopping her, his grip hard.

"Stop it! I love you, Sonia, I do! I want to be a husband to you and a father to our child. Don't turn me away. I couldn't bear it!"

Sonia collapsed in his arms and he guided her to the bed, sitting down next to her.

Her heartbeat slowed as he brushed her hair away from her face. Peace stole into her heart. "Mihai is a witch. He'll help you – us. I'll learn witchcraft. I will." It was not an easy admission for her.

Viktor nodded. "Yes, he told me of his identity."

"I'm my mother's daughter. I'll learn like Mihai. I'll learn to be a witch."

Viktor wrapped his arms around her and rested his chin on her shoulder. His body shook alongside hers. Mihai had to be able to help them both or she would lose her husband forever.

"Let me clean up. Then I'll order Captain Calurisi to leave for Constanta immediately," he paused. "If anyone asks, we'll tell them that we were violently assaulted by common thieves, but we will tell Mihai the truth."

"All right." Sonia disengaged from him and watched while he walked into the water closet. In many ways he was still much like the man she married, but she had no idea what he was going to become. She just prayed Mihai could help her – help them both.

~ * ~

Hecuba mixed some anast root with her chamomile tea and cupped the mug, slowly sipping it. The hot liquid warmed her insides. The anast root would make her body forget the pain.

Bane slammed his traveling bag shut and locked it. "Hurry up, Hecuba."

She sat down on a chair at the table, her head spinning. After transforming into her old body she always drank chamomile tea and anast so she could function.

It wasn't working.

Bane looked at her. "What's wrong?"

"The anast..."

He walked up to her and picked up the pouch, smelling it. "Bad roots."

"It's not working," she gasped. Hecuba collapsed to the floor.

Bane frowned. "By Dalca!" He dug into his pocket and took out a cannabis stick. "Smoke this."

Hecuba's hand shook with pain. She couldn't hold it. Bane lit the stick and put it to her lips. She inhaled, weakly, and the smoke cut the edge of her pain. After a few drags, her body calmed and her head still spun, not from pain, but from the high of the cannabis.

Bane sat next to her. "Was it bad roots?"

"No, my body rejected the anast."

"Dalca!"

Hecuba lay on her back on the floor, her old body lightly shaking, leathered and cracked with age. It wouldn't be long for her now.

~ * ~

Theresa sat at the breakfast table, staring at her tea mug. She had hardly slept last night. This morning her body was tired and achy.

She believed Mihai was honest – that he had an affair in England and that he regretted it, but how he could he confess to such thing after making love? She felt deflated in a way. Let down. Second best.

What was she to do now? She'd learned Romanian, converted her religion, and was determined to help the children at the local orphanage. She couldn't look at Mihai.

"Theresa, do you feel all right?"

Her head shot up at the king's voice. She swallowed, trying to hide her troubled spirit.

"I'm fine, Your Majesty."

He raised his bushy eyebrows, expressing doubt.

Beatrice, who sat next to her, placed a hand on her wrist. "You've been very quiet at breakfast today."

"I didn't sleep well."

"Theresa." Mihai's deep, rich voice cut through the thick air at the table. She raised her eyes and glanced at him.

His malachite eyes blazed with concern.

"Yes, Mihai?"

"Can you come to my study after breakfast?"

"Son, I thought you had to meet with Mr. Tybeski," said the king.

"I'll be late. My work with him involves a project I want to involve Theresa with and I need her input."

The king nodded. Beatrice flashed a pleasant, yet forced smile.

"Yes, Mihai, I'll meet you."

Beatrice clapped her hands. "Well, when you finish, you can find me in the library going through the botany books."

A small smile curved around Theresa's lips at her sister's words. Beatrice loved botany. She had her own garden of flowers, herbs, and roots at their castle in Austria. Beatrice had taught Theresa a lot about flowers and herbs and what kind of properties they had.

"Thank you, Bea."

Beatrice grinned.

Theresa nibbled on her crumpet, finished her tea, and ate half the blueberries on her plate. When she pushed her food away, indicating she was finished, Mihai stood up.

"Are you ready?"

She nodded. He waited for her by the door, opened it, and then followed her out. He was quiet, but walked next to her. When they got to the study, he closed the door and claimed her mouth, crushing her against him. His hungry lips were full of emotion. She sensed deep regret in him. The emotional exchange thrummed through her bones and she was aware he felt her emotions too – second best. Damn her body – it betrayed her, because even though she was second best, she wanted more from him. Then her inner strength kicked in and she placed her hands on his muscled chest and pushed him away. She would need all of her strength now.

"Don't do this – don't put distance between us."

"How could you say something like that last night? After all the conversations we've had, after all the time we've shared together, you couldn't have told me about your English dalliance at some other time? I'm beginning to wonder if I really know you – or if you really know me."

"I do apologize, Theresa. I wanted to be honest with you, but you're right. The time wasn't right."

She stepped backward, hanging her head into her hands. Even now she felt concern, deep emotions and a hint of disgust roiling off him. He did feel strongly for her. And if she was patient enough, perhaps she could drive the hurt away that his previous lover had left in his heart. Perhaps, they both needed time, but patience was never a strong quality for her. Damn it, she needed it now.

She thought she loved him, but perhaps she loved the idea of love. Could she find love with Mihai? She hoped so, but now, in this moment, she realized it was a powerful emotion, one that needed to be nurtured and matured. And despite his mistake, she couldn't help but wait to give them the chance to find that mature love she understood love to be now.

"Theresa." He reached out and placed his hand on her shoulder. She pushed it away.

Their eyes met. God, she wanted to run into his arms, but she had her pride, too.

"I want you to court me," she said.

"Court you?" He arched an eyebrow. "We are courting. We're engaged."

She flicked her hand in the air. "This is an arranged marriage, and what's so ironic is that I believe you do have strong feelings for me, and I, you, but we both need time to get used to each other."

"Yes, I agree."

"So prove to me how deep your feelings run. Court me. Take time out of your schedule to take me places and spend time with me. Get to know me better." She took a deep unsteady breath and stepped back.

He stood straight, stiffening. "I can do that."

"Can you?"

He drew in a deep, heavy breath. "Yes, I can. I will."

"Good. I have a condition."

He crossed his arms. "Oh?"

"I don't think we should make love again until we're married."

He scrunched up his nose. Was he bothered by that?

"I mean it – not until we're married."

He frowned. "All right, then, I agree, but I reserve the right to kiss you."

She saw no harm in that. "All right. I would consider that part of courting."

He stepped forward, dropping his crossed arms. "And may I touch you?"

She held up her hand. "Not below the waist."

"You know how to tease a man."

"Believe me, I don't. I'm not a flirt like Beatrice or a sultry vixen like Victoria. I just want to be courted."

"Then I will. I'll find you when I return this afternoon."

She nodded. He reached for her hand, kissing the knuckles, as he bowed. Then he turned around and left. She smiled, pleased to know Mihai was willing to show her with his deeds how he felt. Pride washed over her. That hadn't been easy, but she had to do it. She wanted Mihai to show her with deeds that she wasn't second best.

~ * ~

Mihai thrummed his fingers on his desk in the study, a mixed bouquet of flowers resting in the corner. Theresa would be here shortly. Martisor was the first of March and he wanted to know what type of flowers Theresa liked so he could acquire a meaningful bouquet for her.

Martisor was a Romanian holiday. The man was responsible for giving the women in his life a small gift – plants, shells, or flowers. The giving of such a gift was meant to bring good luck to the women who received them. The holiday also marked the end of winter and the arrival of spring, but realistically, spring would arrive at the end of the month.

Theresa opened the door and closed it behind her. Mihai got to his feet.

"Good evening, Theresa."

"Good evening. It smells like a garden in here. Where did you get the flowers?"

He smiled, delighted that she appeared at ease. "In a shop downtown. What kinds of flowers do you like?"

"My favorite is the rose."

"Really? Why?"

"It's very soothing to the touch and it has a very pretty scent. Soft. Seductive."

"Any other flowers in thc bouquet you like?"

"The carnations and gardenias. I also like edelweiss."

"Edelweiss?"

"It's a small white flower, very clean and crisp smelling. There are fields of it in the meadows near my father's castle."

"Ah." He clapped his hands. "We should decorate the castle in edelweiss and orchids."

"Orchids?"

"They were my mother's favorite. Sonia also adores them."

"I'll talk to Beatrice tomorrow and then discuss with you the flower arrangements for the wedding. Will you have the time?"

He plucked a rose out of the bouquet and handed it to her. "I'll make the time."

A loud knock on the door interrupted them. Mihai frowned his displeasure. "Come in."

Anton Tybeski walked in with windblown hair and red cheeks.

"What's wrong, Mr. Tybeski?"

"Lord Bacau and Princess Sonia are back."

"So soon?" Mihai's pulse spiked.

"Princess Sonia is visibly upset."

Mihai clenched his fists, trying to tame the rising anger and concern for his sister. Theresa stood beside him and placed her hand on his forearm. He felt her support.

Sonia came to the doorway. Her hair was disheveled and her eyes were red. "Mihai!" She ran to him and he wrapped his arms around her. Her body shook. A bit of a commotion echoed in the hall before Viktor came to the door.

"What's going on?" asked Mihai.

"We must talk," said Viktor. His voice was hard, edged in steel as he walked into the room.

Beatrice ran up to the door, her eyes wide, full of shock.

"Come in and shut the door," said Mihai.

Beatrice did as he instructed and walked directly to Theresa. Concern and worry laced her eyes. She knew something.

Viktor paused near the sofa. Mihai looked down at Sonia.

"Sonia, what's wrong?"

"His eyes are yellow," she whispered.

Mihai glanced at Viktor. He appeared thinner, his face more angular. Then he noticed his friend's eyes. They were no longer blue, but amber yellow.

"Viktor, what happened to you?"

Beatrice stepped forward. "Perhaps Mr. Tybeski should leave?"

"Do you know something, Beatrice?" asked Theresa.

"No. I only suggested it since he wasn't family."

Tybeski stepped up. "Do you want me to go, Your Grace?"

"Perhaps it's for the best."

Tybeski nodded and walked out. Now alone, Mihai escorted Sonia to the sofa and sat down next to her. Viktor stood behind the leather-bound chair adjacent to the sofa, bracing his hands on the headrest, keeping a certain distance between them.

"Sonia, tell me what happened."

"Viktor is a werewolf."

"What? Impossible!" Mihai got to his feet, a wave of nervous apprehension threading through him.

"It is possible, Mihai. A wolf named Bane violated me on our honeymoon. I have transformed," Viktor said quietly.

Mihai lunged at his friend, grabbing the right lapel of his frock jacket. His nostrils were distended with shock, coupled with fear. For him. For Sonia. For Moldavia.

"You were armed!"

"Mihai, no, don't harm him. He tried to fight them, but they overpowered him." Sonia got to her feet and clenched her fists against his chest. "You have to help him – you're a witch, after all. You have to teach me to help him."

Mihai took a step back, his body as tight as a bowstring. Yes, he was a witch, but he had no idea what to do. He was no teacher.

"I must go to Mulfaltar the next full moon and meet with my maker's pack," said Viktor.

Mihai slowly ran his gaze over Viktor. Sonia was right. His eyes were no longer soft and kind, but hard and edged.

"Are you a danger to Sonia?"

"There's more you should know, Mihai," Viktor replied.

"What?"

"Sonia is expecting a baby."

The room grew silent. Mihai turned to face his sister. An odd mix of fear and happiness swept through him.

Uncertainty thrummed in Theresa's expression. Beatrice stepped forward and clapped her hands. "Here's what I suggest – Viktor and Sonia should sleep in separate beds – for the baby's sake."

Viktor straightened his shoulders. "Yes, of course."

"Perhaps you can blame your early return on a faulty part of the yacht. You should act normal so the servants don't suspect anything," continued Beatrice.

"We have agreed to a story that we were assaulted and sustained injuries," Viktor replied.

"Yes, that's our story, but his beautiful eyes – they aren't blue anymore..." Sonia's voice faded off.

"His eyes do stand out," said Theresa.

Beatrice pursed her lips. Was she nervous? Why? Mihai suspected Beatrice knew something more.

"Yes, well, I'm sure there's a dye you can drop into his eyes to make them blue again. You should research it, Mihai – being a witch and all," Beatrice suggested.

Sonia stepped forward. "What happens now?"

"Do you love him?" asked Mihai.

"Yes, of course, but I can't bear—"

"To be near me," finished Viktor. His voice was bereft of emotion.

"No, that's not it. I can't bear what's happened to you," Sonia replied.

Mihai rubbed his hand against the nape of his neck. The situation was untenable. His best friend was now a werewolf! How could he harbor such a creature in the royal family? He had to. Sonia loved him. And he was still Viktor, wasn't he? The friend who approached life with honesty and a kind heart?

"Damn it!"

Mihai grabbed the vase of flowers off his desk and threw it to the floor. Everyone jumped at his sudden action, but it felt good to release a little of his pent-up anger.

Theresa stepped forward toward him, but he held up a hand. "Help Sonia to her room. Tomorrow, we'll have Doctor Stanza look at her and hire a mid-wife."

Theresa said nothing, but put her hand on Sonia's elbow and guided her out of the room.

"Viktor, let me consult my book. Go to your room. Wait for me there."

"You have to know I fought, Mihai. I did not want this. I don't want to be a wolf."

"I believe you."

"Do you? There's doubt in your eyes."

"Doubt? No, disgust. Disgust at the entire situation."

Viktor drew in a breath. "I'll be in my room."

Mihai watched his friend leave. Slowly, he turned to face Beatrice, his arms crossed. "What do you know – and how?"

Chapter Ten

Beatrice avoided the flowers on the floor and walked to the desk. She placed her fingertips gently on Mihai's leather-bound book.

"What I'm about to tell you must be kept from Theresa."

He raised an eyebrow. "I do not intend on keeping secrets from my fiancée."

"You must. I can help you with Viktor – and Sonia, but you first must promise to keep certain things from my sister."

Mihai narrowed his eyes, suspecting Beatrice had kept secrets from Theresa for years. And the thought of it appalled him. Didn't Beatrice feel disgust with herself? Or were her displays of affection all for appearances' sake? Was he even being fair to her?

"Do you want my help with Viktor and Sonia or not? Certainly you have the power to keep him in check, but not the knowledge."

Mihai glowered at her. "Do not attempt to pit me against my family."

"You will fail miserably if you go it alone. I can help, but you must keep secrets. It is your choice to make."

Mihai's jaw clenched with tension. Neither choice suited him. He was trying to prove to Theresa that his deep feelings meant something to him. How could he do it if he had to keep secrets from her? And yes, he was a witch, and he was growing more practiced at channeling energy, but he did not know what he needed to keep Viktor and Sonia safe.

"Fine, I will keep your secrets, Beatrice."

She looked at him with all seriousness. "Good. The first thing you need to know is that I'm a witch."

Mihai drew in a small breath. He thought she was going to tell him that, but the tone of her voice took him off guard.

"The von Krackens are a royal witching family. Our family business, as we refer to it in front of Theresa, includes establishing covens, teaching new witches, and disciplining any that violates our code."

"Is Theresa a witch?" The thought of it thrilled him and scared him as well.

Beatrice pursed her lips and put her hands on her hips, trapping his gaze with hers. "Yes, she is, but she doesn't know it and she's not to know it. She wasn't raised a witch and she does not think I am. It must be like that."

"Why?"

"My father possesses divination and saw this future for her. You must respect his wishes. He's the Duke of our witching realm."

Mihai nodded. "Fine. I'll respect his wishes, but only because he's the father of my intended. How about Sonia?"

"That's complicated."

He drew in a deep breath, knowing this wouldn't be easy for his sister. "How can I use my powers to help Viktor?"

"That is much more complicated. He's tasted human blood, so his eyes have become a golden yellow."

She withdrew a small bag from the pocket of her dress and placed it on the desk. Then she took a vial from the bag and shook it, whispering a chant. A spell, perhaps? The liquid contents turned blue.

"He must use this dye. Every morning when he wakes, have him put this in his eyes. It will make them blue again. His yellow wolf eyes will attract attention."

"You'll show me how to make it?"

"Yes."

"How dangerous is he?" Concern for his sister and family settled into his heart.

"Very. A wolf must have human blood and have intercourse during the full moon. If these needs are met, then he can act human during the rest of the month, but it is not easy. The feral nature takes much to control."

Mihai swallowed back a thick knot of disgust. "How does he acquire human blood? Does he kill?"

Beatrice nodded.

Mihai shivered at the thought. Viktor's nature had always been gentle. He could only imagine how being forced to kill would tear down the goodness of his soul. "And who does he have intercourse with?" He dreaded the answer.

Beatrice looked directly at him. "A trained witch. We can sense emotions and feelings during the act and adjust to the wolf's needs. For Dalca's sake – do not allow him to be intimate with his wife right now. Though she is a witch and can respond to him, the rough sex will no doubt harm her and possibly cause a miscarriage. Wait until she gives birth," Beatrice paused. "And she still needs training."

"Even now that he's changed? He can't touch her?"

"I would encourage that he touch her, but he should not be intimate with her. The child will hinder her body's ability to respond intuitively to his heightened and quickened senses."

Mihai nodded. This was not pleasant news, yet it explained the wonderful encounter he'd had with Theresa. Mihai rubbed his eyes with his palm. "Does he have to do these... things?"

"Yes. Let him go to the pack meeting. His needs will be met and then he'll come here and be who he is, but you must watch his moods. He will have a tendency to be more feral and aggressive. I'll train you and Sonia in herbs and potions to help you manage."

"All right."

"We'll have to be careful. I don't want Theresa to think I have an interest in you. We'll meet late at night for an hour – no longer. There's much for you and Sonia to learn."

Mihai drew in a deep breath. It was overwhelming, but he had to be strong. His kin – his country – depended on it, especially since he now harbored a werewolf in the bosom of the royal family – a creature so foul and detested many would think him crazy for doing it, and yet he would do it because he loved his friend.

Beatrice motioned toward the door. "Come. We need to talk to Sonia. I want to measure her ferons."

Mihai steeled his shoulders and followed Beatrice out the door. They ascended the stairs and went to Sonia's room. Mihai knocked.

"Come in."

He opened the door. Sonia sat in a chair overlooking the window, her eyes moist from crying.

"Mihai? Beatrice?"

"We've come to help," said Mihai.

Sonia stood up and buried herself in his arms.

Beatrice clasped her hands in front of her. "There are things you must know, Sonia, but there are also secrets to keep. You must promise to keep them."

Sonia nodded. "I will."

"First, you must know I am a witch."

Sonia gasped, withdrew from Mihai, and clutched her chin with her hand. "I would not have guessed."

Beatrice offered Sonia a smile. "It is easy for me to hide my identity."

"Is Theresa a witch?" asked Sonia.

"Yes – and that is one of the secrets you must keep. She was not raised a witch and has no training. This is something our father has decreed through divination. Mihai has also promised to keep this secret."

Sonia looked up at Mihai, searching his face. He nodded, confirming his promise to Beatrice. “I’ll tell you more later.”

Sonia turned to face Beatrice. “All right. I’ll do it.”

“Good. Now, I can help you and Mihai, but I must test the ferons in your blood to see how strong you have the power.”

“I know what ferons are. I’ve read my mother’s old book.”

Beatrice went to the sink and found two clean glasses. She added a little water into each, pulled out her bag, searched its contents and withdrew a pouch full of a course grain. She placed it into the water and the water turned blue. Then she removed a small case from her pockets. She popped it open and looked at Mihai. “Let me see your finger.”

He approached and held out his hand. She pricked it, drawing blood, and let a drop fall into one of the glasses. It turned deep purple.

Beatrice whistled. “The ferons are strong in your body. Men tend to have a higher concentration.”

“And Sonia?”

Beatrice for motioned for her to approach. She pricked Sonia’s finger and dripped a couple of drops of blood into the other glass. The water turned a light purple color. Beatrice pursed her lips.

“The ferons are present but weak in your body.”

“What does that mean?” asked Sonia.

“Well, there’s no doubt you’re a witch, but you aren’t as powerful as Mihai. Don’t take it to heart. Compared to my family, both Victoria and I don’t have as many ferons as the men so we make up for it by studying those things that can augment our ferons. I study botany and Victoria studies healing.”

Sonia clasped her hands. "But I can do things like Mihai?"

"Yes, but you'll need much more practice than him. You'll need to train twice as hard. You must resolve yourself to do it."

She steeled her shoulders. "I will. I'll do it."

"And you've some interest in healing?"

"I do."

"Good. I'll get with you tomorrow about arranging a schedule and a place to study. It will be no longer than an hour and then you'll have to study and practice on your own."

Mihai reached out to Sonia and clasped her hand, offering her his reassurance.

Chapter Eleven

Mihai had always enjoyed flowers, but as he and Sonia studied with Beatrice, he learned that flowers offered more than beauty and gentle scents. Flowers had various properties from healing to increased stamina – mentally and physically. He came to understand Theresa's attraction to the rose was instinctual, and most witches preferred taking baths in rose hips which they found naturally soothing to them.

He entered his father's study carrying his small bouquet of flowers. His father stood next to a small bar with Viktor beside him, pouring glasses of brandy. Several vases filled with flowers rested on his father's desk.

Both men were thin, but for different reasons. His father was sick. Viktor was a wolf. His father's complexion appeared a little jaundiced, another symptom that his body was weakening. Mihai's heart went out to him.

Viktor's eyes appeared blue, but there were no depths to them. There was no feeling. They were empty. Mihai feared his friend couldn't express himself through his eyes as he had before. At least now, Sonia could stand to look at her husband. Mihai's heart broke for the struggles Viktor and Sonia faced.

"Mihai, where did you go for your flowers? Spain?" asked his father, gruffly.

"Sorry. I was reviewing contract bids and time escaped me."

"Well, you're here now and that's what counts. The ladies should arrive shortly."

"Would you like a drink?" asked Viktor.

"Yes. Thank you."

Viktor gave him a glass of brandy. His friend's mind was just as sharp as before, but Viktor's reflexes had become very quick, almost jarring, yet he seemed to retain his even temper and kind-heartedness.

There was a knock on the door and the ladies entered, Sonia followed by Theresa and then Beatrice. Everyone exchanged polite hugs, but Sonia kept her hugs very light. Her cheeks were pale.

"Sonia, how are you feeling?" Viktor put his drink down, but wasn't quite sure what to do with his hands, first jamming them into his pockets before restlessly pulling them out and clasping them behind his back.

"I'm just tired, that's all." She sat down on the sofa. A tray of tea and small scones were laid out for the ladies. Beatrice sat down next to Sonia and steeped a chamomile tea bag. Beatrice palmed a small vial of powder from her pockets and sprinkled it into the cup. She was sly and quick with the motion, and Mihai had become used to seeing Beatrice use slight of hand tricks.

"This tea will help you," said Beatrice. "It's chamomile."

Sonia reached for the cup exchanging a knowing look with Beatrice. "Thank you."

Theresa sat down on the other side of Sonia and gently rubbed her back.

Mihai's father clapped his hands. "Well, I can't tell you enough how pleased I am that you and Viktor are expecting a child, but I want you to take care of yourself. You must stay well for the child. Your mother..." his voice trailed off.

Mihai arched an eyebrow. "What about mother?"

"I just don't want Sonia to have a challenging confinement. Your mother never had an easy time *enceinte*."

"I'll go to bed early tonight," Sonia replied.

"Sonia's in fine hands, Your Majesty. Dr. Stanza is quite capable and Mrs. Nocesti from the hospital has agreed to be her mid-wife," said Viktor. His voice broke with concern, but he didn't go to Sonia.

Mihai knew Sonia grew anxious at times when Viktor got too close to her, so Viktor had to do it in other ways and his eyes were no help. Mihai wondered if the incident was too fresh in her memory.

His father drew in a deep breath and he placed a fist over his heart to help steady his breathing. Then he looked up. "I want to wish all the women here a Martisor filled with good luck throughout the year. Spring will be upon us shortly. The Earth will soon be reborn. May you all—" He began coughing violently. He leaned over his desk, bracing his hands on the edge of it for support.

Mihai ran to him and held his shoulders. Viktor grabbed a handkerchief and placed it over the king's mouth, but not before several drops of blood dripped onto the desk. When he finally stopped coughing, Mihai looked at Viktor.

"Get Dr. Stanza," he said in a low voice.

Viktor quickly departed. Mihai helped his father to a nearby chair and the king sat down. He closed his eyes and took deep, labored breaths.

Theresa clutched Sonia's hand, offering support. Beatrice withdrew several small vials from the hidden pockets in her dress. She sniffed two before she found the one she wanted.

"What are you doing?" asked Theresa.

"The doctor, no doubt, will give him laudanum which will only dull his senses and take away the pain. I'm going to give him a little blood root."

"Blood root?" Sonia pursed her lips and a thoughtful look crossed her face. "Blood root is good for the lungs, right?"

"Yes, it is," said Theresa, soothingly. "It will help him. Trust me. It's only called blood root because the root is as red as blood."

Beatrice poured the powdered root into the king's glass, and gently shook it before giving it to Mihai. He put the glass to his father's lips and held it steady between the coughs. Several gulps of liquid made it down his throat. After another minute, his father stopped coughing and rested his head against the side of the chair.

Beatrice put her hand against the king's cheek. "He'll be fine now."

Mihai nodded.

"I don't feel like talking, Son. Hand out the flowers." His father's voice was weak and raspy.

Viktor walked in with Dr. Stanza. Beatrice looked away and let the doctor examine the king.

"Does it hurt?" asked Dr. Stanza.

"I ache."

Dr. Stanza withdrew a small flask. "Take a small sip. It's laudanum."

His father did so. Mihai clenched his hands into fists. Thank God the ailment hadn't taken his father's wits, but it was robbing him of his mobility, and it wasn't good that he was coughing up blood. It would only get worse.

Beatrice stepped up beside Mihai. "Relax," she whispered.

"Your father needs to rest. I'll take him to his room," said Dr. Stanza. He helped the king to his feet and supported him as they slowly walked out.

Mihai unclenched his fists. "We should continue as my father wanted and pass out the flowers."

"You don't think we should wait?" asked Sonia. "It wouldn't be a bad omen, would it?"

"No, it's what he would want. Viktor, can you help? I don't know what flowers he intended to give out."

Viktor plucked several flowers out of a vase. Sonia and Theresa received white roses. Beatrice, a yellow carnation. Then Viktor gave Sonia a bouquet of yellow and white roses from himself. Sonia brought them to her nose.

"Thank you, Viktor."

"You're welcome."

Mihai looked at them. They shared a tender expression. Mihai turned his focus to Viktor. His posture wasn't so rigid. His voice was soft. He stood across the coffee table from Sonia. This was encouraging.

Mihai withdrew two small seashells from his trousers pocket and gave them to Sonia and Beatrice. Then he gave Theresa a bouquet of red roses entwined with edelweiss. Theresa drew in a long breath, enjoying the scent.

"Where did you get the flowers? And the edelweiss?"

"There's a florist near the Parliament building who imports most of his flowers from Spain and the Mediterranean this time of year," said Mihai.

"Yes, I remember. Beatrice and I have been there."

"Well, he earned every penny. The flowers are wonderful," said Beatrice.

"Father didn't finish his blessing," said Sonia.

"All we can do is hope for the best, especially with the new challenges that face us," said Mihai.

Viktor smiled. "Yes – hope. We must have hope. I like that word."

An awkward silence fell over the room. Mihai couldn't help but wonder if it was a bad omen that the king, his father, hadn't finished his speech, as Sonia implied.

"Sonia, let me escort you to your room so you can rest," said Viktor.

Sonia nodded and stood up. Viktor walked beside her, keeping a polite distance as they left. Mihai wondered if it bothered Viktor to keep his distance from his sister. Their movements and gestures were hesitant and strained, yet Sonia never verbally protested Viktor's lack of closeness.

Beatrice caught his attention by clapping her hands. "I'm tired, too. I'll see you both tomorrow."

Mihai caught the slight nod of Beatrice's head and knew she would be available for a lesson late tonight. They usually met in his study around one a.m. While the tower would offer more assurances of privacy, he would not take her there. That was his special place with Theresa.

Theresa kissed Beatrice on the cheek. "Good night, Bea."

"Good night, Tea."

Both ladies smiled and Beatrice walked out, leaving Mihai alone with Theresa.

"I hope your father will recover in the morning." She sat on the sofa and Mihai joined her.

"I think the blood root will help. Thank you for being so supportive with Sonia. I saw it mentioned in my book. How did you know of it?"

"It's like I said, Bea and I studied in Austria. She enjoyed botany – I see she's showing Sonia about some plants. Bea has a knack for gardening. She even grows edelweiss in the gardens."

"You're lucky to have her for a sister. She cares for you very much."

"Thank you, but she doesn't appreciate art like I do." Theresa winked.

"Oh?"

"I ordered your wedding gift while I was in town today."

"You did? Does it have to do with art?"

"Perhaps. And that's all I'm going to tell you."

Mihai pursed his lips, trying to push back his disappointment with himself. He had to get her a gift. What could he get her? What would she like to have that she didn't have already? China? Silk? A slow smile grew across his lips. Yes, silk would do quite nicely.

"Why are you smiling like that?"

"Because the perfect gift just came to mind for you."

"I'm curious."

"It will be beautiful, and that's all I'll tell you."

She smiled. "I'm looking forward to it."

"Good."

The room grew silent. He sighed. He didn't want silence between them.

"How is Viktor?" she asked.

"Viktor? He appears to be managing fine. It's a bit disconcerting to see the speed he uses to accomplish his tasks, but I'm getting used to it. He's very worried about Sonia."

"It's almost unbelievable what happened to him."

"These beasts hide on the fringes of our society – smartly, I might add – and usually do not call attention to themselves – not like they did centuries ago. Because of this, most people see them as legends in an old history book and do not realize they are still a threat."

Theresa smiled blandly. "I worry for both of them."

Mihai laced his fingers through hers. "I'll do my best to help Viktor. If he leaves us for the full moon and returns back to us whole for the rest of the month, it will be enough for me."

"There's still a part of you that's apprehensive. I feel it."

"I'm trying to modernize this principality. My father wants me to work toward Romanian unification. Legends like this only harm the efforts I'm making."

"But you are a witch."

"A fact that must be kept secret from the world."

She nodded. "I do not care for secrets."

"Nor do I."

A heavy sigh escaped from her lips, and Mihai drew her against him, holding her tight. Her body comforted him. Damn it, if she didn't stir his blood. He glanced at the mechanical clock on his father's desk. Eight. There simply were not enough seconds in the day to accomplish everything that needed to be done. Hope. He had to have hope like Viktor had.

Chapter Twelve

Viktor stayed at Delfin Castle as long as he dared, then saddled his horse and departed for Mulfaltar. He hated leaving Sonia in her condition, and he did not know what to expect when he arrived at the cabin.

Sonia was well cared for despite having bouts of nausea and needing afternoon naps. She still had trouble eating anything with onions and she had lost weight. If only he could hold her and offer comfort. Words were not enough, but he feared if he did go to her, he would caress her, and it would lead to lovemaking. He couldn't bear the thought of having rough sex with Sonia and hurting her so she would lose their child. Even though Sonia had told him she was witch, Viktor knew he had to be careful with her because of her condition. The baby was the only thing keeping him sane. It, and the promise of Sonia's love after the birth, was the only thing giving him hope. He grasped the reins that much harder. He hated the thought that he couldn't be intimate with his wife. He loved her. How he wanted to share a bed with her! Well, it would be soon.

Mihai had been helpful, but his friend recently started showing up to breakfast with bags under his eyes. There was a lot of pressure on Mihai to keep the railroad project moving smoothly, plus he was planning a wedding, helping Viktor, and worried about his father. Mihai needed to rest. Maybe he could do that while Viktor was away. His friend did seem more knowledgeable in magic, despite his initial hesitation of embracing it. Sonia did as well. Viktor was grateful for that, and perhaps he could take something back to them from his pack meeting that would be useful to him.

Mulfaltar was fifteen miles from Constanta, about an hour on horseback located between Constanta and Bucharest. Bane wanted him to go to a log cabin in the woods outside the small town. He called it the pack house. The directions were easy to recall. In the distance, just past a set of barren trees, a thin curl of smoke rose from a chimney.

The sun was close to the horizon. They would lose daylight soon. For the past couple of days, his muscles had surged with power and quickness, making him edgy. He had a short temper, which he'd worked hard to hold in check. Mihai had given him a rose/chamomile drink that helped to some extent, but it wasn't as potent as the cannabis and opium that Bane used.

Now at the cabin, Viktor drew on the reins, stopping his horse. He tied it up to a nearby hitching post. Three other horses were there as well. A barn was nearby.

He went to the door and knocked. It flung open. A tall, thin man with yellow eyes and long brown hair smiled at him, revealing pristine white teeth.

"You must be Viktor. I'm Gascon. Bane said you were coming."

Viktor walked past Gascon into the cabin. He was in a large main room. The air was heavy with a sweet, rose-scented incense. A small hallway on the opposite side of the room led to another part of the cabin. A fire roared in the fireplace. There were two sofas both adjacent to the fireplace. A wooden table with attached benches rested next to a small side window. Two men sat at the table facing each other, rolling what appeared to look like weeds into paper.

Gascon pointed. "That's Nasguard and that one is Timon."

Nasguard's long, black hair was pulled back away from his face. He was tall, yes, but unlike Viktor and the other wolves, he wasn't thin with sinewy, emaciated muscles and an angular face. His muscles were thick and he looked like a muscular man.

Timon was like Viktor, thin, gaunt, yellow eyes and thin limbs. He sneered at Viktor and went back to rolling.

Viktor's eyes narrowed. Timon did not like him.

Gascon slapped a hand on Viktor's shoulder. "The witches brought cannabis, come help us roll it."

"When we're done, we'll take the horses to the stables," said Nasguard.

"Who tends to the horses?" Viktor asked.

"We do. In the morning," Nasguard replied.

Viktor nodded and followed Gascon to the table. They sat down next to Nasguard. Bane had given Viktor cannabis in Odessa. It lessened the pain of the transformation in his joints and muscles when he became human again. What he had liked about the cannabis was that it didn't linger and it didn't take away from his wits like opium did.

"The witches are in the back," said Nasguard.

Viktor nodded his acknowledgement and watched Gascon roll, studying his technique.

"Bane gave you a new witch," said Timon. Hostility simmered just below the tone of his voice.

"What does that mean?" Viktor crossed his arms.

"Alina's father owes Hecuba a debt. Alina is in debt to the old witch for a year, then she'll be released," explained Gascon.

Nasguard leaned toward Viktor and smiled. "She's very beautiful. Timon is jealous."

Timon glared at Nasguard. "I deserve Alina more than he does."

"Well, Bane did not choose Alina for you, so stop crying about it. Diana is a clever witch in her own right and has always satisfied you," replied Nasguard.

Timon grunted.

Viktor pursed his lips and rolled a cannabis stick. He found it distasteful to be with a woman not his wife, but in Odessa, he was practically overcome with the urge to couple with a woman. Hecuba repulsed him. If he had to be with another woman – a witch – then he prayed he could at least look at her.

"Come," said Nasguard. He pointed to Viktor and they took the horses to the stables.

The last vestiges of sunlight faded from the sky.

As they returned to the house, Nasguard began taking off his clothes.

"What are you doing?" asked Viktor. The wolf's casual actions unnerved him.

"Nasguard pays good money for his clothes so he takes them off. He doesn't want to rip them," said Gascon.

Bane walked into the room, wearing trousers only. "The moon will rise soon." He paused and clapped his hands. "Viktor! Excellent. I knew you would come."

Viktor tried to push away his disgust. Timon would see it as a weakness and Viktor did not want to appear weak in front of him.

"Where else would I go?" replied Viktor.

Bane sneered his pleasure.

Viktor felt a twinge of discomfort. The flow of blood in his veins increased. The transformation was close. Bane went to the door and opened it. "It's better if we go outside. The witches can prepare the cabin."

Viktor marched out of the door with the other wolves. Barely past the door, the full power of the moon's light bathed them. He fell to the ground. His arms and legs elongated. His face grew sharp, angular. His nose shifted; a snout appeared. The rush of the sudden adrenaline washed over his body. He was invincible. All-powerful. He could do anything.

"There are gypsies nearby." Timon's nose twitched.

"We hunt." Bane trotted forward.

Viktor trotted after his leader, eager to lessen the unnatural demand of his feral hunger.

~ * ~

Viktor rubbed his eyes and sat up. He was on a floor at the foot of a bed. He wrapped his arms around himself as revulsion raced down his spine from the night's earlier activities. While he had not killed the pack's prey, the sight of fangs sinking into flesh had been unbearable to watch and he had to turn away, unable to look. The scent of roses drew his attention to the room. A fire blazed in the fireplace. There were no windows. He heard movement and shifted his head. A woman stepped into his view from the side of the bed holding a chalice. She was tall with delicate features, an ethereal presence. She wore a thin chemise. He could make out the firm curves of her breasts and her darkened nipples through the fabric. Her hair was light brown with chestnut highlights, long, and tussled with curls. Her wide, walnut-hazel eyes sparkled in the firelight.

"Viktor?" She knelt before him. Her voice was as light as a feather.

"Yes."

She offered the chalice. "Drink this. Your hunger is sated, but your body still aches from the transformation."

"What is it?"

"Just a little brandy."

"No cannabis?" he asked.

"I do not care to smell cannabis while we couple."

He nodded and sipped the brandy. It did take the edge of the pain away, warming his insides. God, this woman was beautiful in an earthy, bewitching way. He was naked on the floor and his manhood was painfully erect. He craved her touch, but was uncertain how he should act with her.

"Your name is Alina?" he asked, just to start conversation.

"Yes."

He gave the chalice back to her and she stood. She walked over to a small table and poured some water into the chalice along with two vials containing powder. Why didn't the revulsion go away? Why did it linger despite Alina's attempts to put him at ease?

"What are you doing?"

She drank out of the chalice and then wiped it out. "Protecting my womb, so I don't become with child."

He stood. "Clever."

Feral urges surged within his body and he clenched his fists. If he had to be intimate with her, and God knows his body was aching for it, he wanted to know more about her.

Alina stood next to the table, her arms at her sides. "I'm sorry, I don't know what to expect."

"The wolves mentioned you were new. Who is your father?"

"Radu Brancoveanu. He is the Count of Wallachia."

"Wallachia? Really. Are your family witches?"

"Royal witches."

He drew in a breath, trying desperately to curb the rising urges within him. Physical need warred with emotional disgust. "How does a royal witch find herself in debt to Bane?"

"It's Hecuba, really. She runs the coven. When my father was younger and more foolish, he incurred the debt to Hecuba. I owe her a year's service in the coven and then I can leave."

"This isn't a nice place to be."

She paused, taking her lip between her teeth, almost contemplative.

"Is there something you want to tell me?" asked Viktor.

"Do you have a woman you care for?"

He looked away, ashamed. Guilt riddled his insides. The thought of sharing a bed with a woman other than Sonia tore at his soul. "Yes."

"I do, too. I mean, I have a man."

He softened, turning his head back to look at her, surprised to learn she cared for someone else as well. "Who is he?"

"Ioan Getzi, the son of Transylvania's count."

Viktor waved his hand in the air. "Does he know about this? What you have to do?"

"He knows I've gone to Hecuba's coven. I suspect he knows that this is part of a witch's duty, but he did not want to discuss it."

"He's not a witch?"

"No."

"My wife, Sonia, is a witch, but she hasn't been trained. Her mother left books so she's reading them."

Alina nodded sympathetically.

"She's with child." Viktor's voice sounded dull, but he hated that he had to come here – he had to betray Sonia.

Alina stepped directly in front of him and placed her hand over his heart. Viktor ground his teeth, his self-control about to collapse.

"Even though she's a witch, you must not be intimate with her – she's not trained after all, for the child's sake." Alina offered him a sad smile. "You need to wait until she gives birth."

"So I've been told, but I love her. Being here with you does not feel right."

She gave him a ghost of a smile. "Nor does it feel right for me."

He placed his hand over hers. "I can't deny what my body needs. It's racing even now."

"I feel it. I will feel your emotions, give you what your body needs, but make me a promise."

"What?"

"Never let the other wolves couple with me. It would only shame me that much more. Never give your permission for them to touch me."

"They have to ask me?"

"Yes."

"Why?"

"Because I am yours. The wolf controls the witch. I need you to protect me."

"I promise." He would not let Alina down. While Nasguard and Gascon seemed determined to do what they must, Timon was exceptionally feral and it would not surprise Viktor if Timon tried to harm Alina.

She grasped his shoulders. "Thank you."

His control shattered and he pushed her onto the bed.

Forgive me, Sonia.

~ * ~

The door to the library opened. Theresa looked up from her calendar. It was the twentieth of March. Her wedding preparations kept her busy in the mornings. In the afternoon she tried to spend time with Sonia or visit the children at the orphanage. When Mihai could, he would join her.

Beatrice walked over to her, carrying a tray of tea and scones.

Theresa yawned.

"Do you want me to steep your tea?" asked Beatrice.

"No, I'll do it."

Beatrice bit into her scone. "You look tired."

"I suppose. It hit me suddenly."

Beatrice narrowed her eyes and slowly raked her gaze over Theresa.

Theresa wrinkled her brow, mildly offended. "What are you doing, Bea?"

"Thinking."

"About what? The dresses will be delivered in a week and the daguerreotyper promised to come tomorrow to survey the grounds."

"Weren't you suddenly tired yesterday, too?"

Theresa sipped her tea. "I suppose so."

"Do your breasts tingle?"

"Bea!"

"Do they?"

Theresa wrinkled her brow. "A little."

Beatrice crossed her arms. "Are you late?"

"Late?"

"Are your courses late?"

Theresa put down the cup and stared at the calendar. Now that Beatrice had mentioned it, she was several days late. Her heart beat faster.

"You don't think—"

Beatrice regarded her with amusement. "Why you naughty little girl. I had no idea you and Mihai were sharing a bed."

Theresa glared at her sister. "We are not!"

"No?" Beatrice giggled.

"It was just once."

"Once is all it takes, Sister."

"Oh, Bea, I can't be... it's so sudden."

"Well, I think it is."

Theresa hung her head in her hands. A baby? So soon? She adored children, but she was hoping to have more time. Mihai would be thrilled to hear the news. The children at the orphanage adored him. They all wanted him on their sides when they had snowball fights.

Beatrice slid an arm around Theresa's shoulders. "Why are you so upset? Yes, it's early, but I'm sure the Prince will be delighted. He only has eyes for you."

Theresa raised her head. "We're still learning about each other." Beatrice gave her a handkerchief and Theresa wiped her eyes.

"Do you love him?" asked Beatrice.

Theresa paused. Love. That was such a loaded word. She felt a connection to Mihai from their time spent together. She had never entertained thoughts of being with another man, but love? She cared for him, but did he care for her the same way? She straightened her shoulders. "I suppose I do."

"Then everything will be all right. You have to talk to Mihai."

"I do?"

Beatrice stood. "Yes. You'll tell him tonight."

"I need time."

"For what? Tell the Prince tonight so the doctor can confirm it. Besides, I think you'll make the old king very happy. He's a bit gruff and salty, but he wants you and Mihai to find happiness."

Theresa smiled at that, agreeing with her sister. "I think the news would liven the king's spirits."

Beatrice wrapped Theresa into a warm, vibrant hug. Theresa felt her sister's happiness and reassurance down to her bones. Mihai would indeed be happy. Theresa was resolved to tell him. Tonight. In the tower.

~ * ~

Mihai stared out the window in his study, his arms crossed over his chest. A full moon had just risen over the trees. Viktor would probably be home in a day or two – and hopefully he would be like the Viktor he remembered.

Sonia missed him terribly. She'd gone to bed early tonight, tired from her days' activities. She hadn't been back to the hospital to nurse since returning from Odessa, but she was finding fulfillment helping Theresa, embroidering, and her secret lessons with Beatrice.

Mihai was learning much from Beatrice, too. His focus was better; the channeling of energy through his body was crisp and clean. He was learning about the different herbs, roots, and flowers, a couple of potions, and even a spell. Beatrice was now giving him lessons on how to see people on a higher frequency – to study their auras and discern moods and feelings.

He yawned. Theresa would be here soon. He was eager for her visit. He wanted to coordinate their schedules so they could go pick out rings.

He smiled at the thought. Rings meant commitment. A forever promise. Friendship forever.

The door opened. Mihai turned around. To his surprise, Beatrice walked in.

"Where's Theresa?"

Beatrice handed him a note. "There will be no lesson tonight."

Mihai unfolded the paper.

Meet me in the tower. Theresa.

"This is unusual." And it was. They hadn't been to the tower since the night they had made love. Had something changed?

"Perhaps. How do you feel about my sister?" Beatrice asked.

"I care for her."

"Just care?"

"Beatrice, please..."

She waved a finger in the air, raking her gaze over him. "Tsk, tsk. Don't hide from your feelings. You'll find much more satisfaction if you knowledge them."

"You're reading my aura, aren't you?"

"Very astute."

"Why?"

"Auras never lie, unlike words."

"What did you discover?"

Her expression grew serious. "Love is a wonderful feeling. Acknowledge it. Whatever is haunting you, let it go.

If you do not, you will only hurt yourself – and her."

"Thank you for the unsolicited advice."

Beatrice smiled. "You're welcome."

"Do you need an escort to your room?" he asked.

"I can find my room all by myself, thank you. Now, why don't you seek out my sister?"

Mihai gestured toward the door and they both walked out. He parted from her to move down the hall to the servants' quarters and entered the secret stairway to the tower. What could Theresa want? Was she sick? No, Beatrice would have scolded him if she was. Theresa had been very firm about sticking to their rules and he'd honored them, which, on occasion had been a severe test of his willpower. Their wedding was only a month away, but that was far too long for him. Mihai wanted to be intimate with her. Was that love? Is that what Beatrice was getting at? Did Theresa love him? Was there a difference between the physical desire he felt for her and love? What was love?

He clenched his fists, pushing down his uncertain thoughts, and opened the door to the tower.

A fire burned in the fireplace. Theresa sat in front of the flames, looking at his star charts.

"Theresa?"

She looked up, smiling tentatively. "Hello, Mihai. Come. Sit."

He feathered his eyes over her. Her aura was shining, much like it had after their…lovemaking.

"What brings you up here?" He joined her on the rug.

"You."

"Oh?" He sensed her nervousness.

She held up a chart. "It's very accurate. You know your night sky."

"I suspect you must be just as talented if you're impressed with my charts."

"My brother, Edward, loved the stars. I'd go stargazing with him. He was very patient considering he was eight years older than me."

"Beatrice wasn't a stargazer?"

"No. It bored her to tears. Victoria was interested in it, but she didn't have patience for it."

"Ah." He spied a bottle of wine on the table next to the door. "Do you want me to open it?"

"If you want some. Wine makes my stomach queasy these days."

"Why? Are you ill? I have to confess, I didn't think we'd be back to the tower until after we married."

"No, I'm not ill, but I might get ill."

"Might get ill? What's wrong, Theresa?"

She threaded her fingers through his. "I think I'm with child."

His mouth dropped open in surprise. He quickly closed it, not wanting to startle her. Joy and happiness rushed through him and he wrapped her into his arms. This was wonderful! Their night together had given them a child! It was quick, but it didn't matter. He wanted her to be the mother of his children. She was kind and gentle and the children at the orphanage adored it when she read them stories on her visits – especially the little ones. They would sit next to her vying for the precious space with winsome smiles and affectionate hugs. Alexandra would have made a poor queen.

He stiffened at the thought of Alexandra. How could he think of her at a time like this when Theresa had just given him the happiest news of his life?

Theresa swallowed, betraying her apprehension. "What's wrong?"

"Nothing. I'm thrilled with the news."

"Are you sure?"

"Yes, but I want the doctor to examine you tomorrow."

"All right." She glanced at the fire.

He pushed his uneasy thoughts away from his mind and focused on his joy, then smiled at her. "I'll reschedule my morning appointments and we'll have the doctor look at you after breakfast."

"That's fine."

He cupped her chin with his fingers, using a gentle touch. "Are you happy?"

She bit her lower lip with her teeth. Confusion danced in her eyes. The sensation of being overwhelmed skimmed over the pulse of her emotions, yet a small current of happiness flowed underneath.

"Theresa, are you happy?" he asked again.

"Yes."

"You don't sound very convincing."

"This is very sudden, Mihai. I didn't think it would happen our first time. I wanted to be married – and secure before—"

He curved his hands around her cheeks so his gaze met hers.

"We will be married and I promise you security. You are the only woman I want in my life. You must believe that," He paused, sensing she needed more. "I've enjoyed just spending time getting to know you. I like your curiosity and I appreciate how accepting you've been with the information that I'm a witch. You're very clever and," he hesitated," You throw a nasty snowball."

"I do?"

"All the children at the orphanage want to be on your team, not mine."

"That's not my experience."

It grew awkwardly silent between them and she drew in a small breath. "This child is so soon. We're still getting to know each other."

"Perhaps, but I'm quite content to know you're *enceinte*."

"You are?"

"I care for you for very much."

She nodded. He leaned toward her, brushing his lips against hers, slow and thoughtful, reassurance thrumming through his kiss into her.

She placed her hands on his shoulders. He anchored his hands into her auburn tresses. God, this was the only place he wanted to be – in her arms. There was nothing more exciting knowing she was having his child. He would be a good father – no, the best. Mihai would treasure this special little child for all the days of his life. This was the best gift Theresa could have ever given them for their wedding. He nuzzled the side of her neck, wanting her to feel the happiness inside him.

"Mihai..."

He stopped and rubbed his thumb against her cheek. "Yes?"

"You're happy? Truly happy about this?"

"Yes. Theresa, I..." he paused.

Her breath hitched. "What?"

"I believe I'm falling in love with you."

She smiled then and wrapped her arms around him. He felt her joy leap in her heart. "I believe I'm falling in love with you, too."

Chapter Thirteen

Mihai shuffled through the papers on his desk, signing some, writing notes on others. Tomorrow was Easter and he wanted to finish this work so he could enjoy the festivities. His wedding was now a week away and he couldn't wait to marry Theresa – especially since she was with child. He stopped and smiled, gazing out the window, basking in the warm sunbeam. He was going to be a father. The thought thrilled him to no end.

There was a knock on the door and it opened. Only Viktor or Anton Tybeski announced themselves as such. Mihai stood up and Mr. Tybeski walked in, clutching his ledger. Mr. Tybeski was a hard worker, quick and efficient. Mihai appreciated his work ethic and had begun to value his opinions.

Mihai smiled and clapped his hands. "What's the assessment on the repairs to the orphanage?"

"It's going to be a major project. Wood is rotting and there's mold in the basement. I considered constructing a new building, but the costs are even higher."

Mihai stroked his chin with a finger. "Do you have any recommendations?"

"I would like to remodel the building."

"How long do you estimate the repairs to take?"

"All summer. The earliest completion would be in September."

Mihai sighed. "I would like to save the building for sentimental reasons. My mother established it. Leave me your findings and I'll review them later."

Mr. Tybeski placed the ledger on Mihai's desk.

Again there was a knock on the door and Viktor walked

in. His whole face was spread into a smile, which was unusual these days. Viktor rarely smiled. He held up a thin piece of paper.

"Good news, Mihai."

"Oh?"

"The Mantooth Construction Company accepted your offer."

"Excellent! This calls for a drink. Stay and celebrate with us, Mr. Tybeski."

A small smile crossed Mr. Tybeski's lips. "How can I refuse, Your Grace?"

Mihai went to the wall and opened a small wooden compartment, revealing several bottles. He withdrew a couple of glasses and poured them each a shot of brandy. This was good news indeed.

Four companies had bid on the project. After carefully examining all the bids, Mihai offered the contract to Mantooth. They came from Germany, and the Germans had a good reputation for sturdy construction.

"Norco!" said Mihai.

"Norco!"

Everyone tipped glasses and drank.

"They'll be sending representatives to meet with you next week, as well as to Bucharest to talk to Count Brancoveanu," said Viktor.

Mihai put his glass down. "Next week?"

"According to this, if they start their work now, determine the route, materials needed, labor, a building for Constanta's train station, they can start on May first."

Mihai frowned.

"Is something wrong?" asked Viktor.

"I was hoping to enjoy my honeymoon."

"You can. The king can oversee the project and I'll be here as well."

"Aren't you leaving in a week to meet with...friends?"

Viktor snarled, and his aura flared red. Mihai felt resentment rolling off him in waves. He didn't care for his friend's silent display, but chose to ignore it.

"Mr. Tybeski, can you work with Viktor on this?"

"Of course, Your Grace."

"I'll cut my honeymoon short by a few days. That should help."

Viktor held up his hand, and his aura cooled, as he reigned in his emotions. "You shouldn't have to. We can manage. The king still has his wits."

"Theresa will understand, Viktor."

Viktor turned away, and while his eyes were unreadable, there was no mistaking his agitated aura. Why? Mihai meant no insult; he only acknowledged that Viktor would have to leave to take care of his needs. Beatrice was right. Viktor's moods had a tendency for more dramatic swings as the full moon grew closer. Still, it appeared that Viktor was managing them.

Mihai glanced at the clock on the corner of his desk. It was time for him to conclude the meeting.

"Well, gentlemen, my afternoon will be spent with the ladies. Mr. Tybeski, enjoy the time with your family. I'll send for you on Tuesday."

"The same to you, Your Grace." Mr. Tybeski bowed and left.

Viktor faced Mihai. "I know this is not a good time for the construction company to arrive, but I can handle it with the king's help."

Mihai arched an eyebrow. "You can? As it is, the full moon is the night before my wedding, and you won't be there for that. It's important you take care of your needs – for Sonia's sake."

"You deserve time alone with Theresa."

"She will understand. I'll make it up to her. It's important you leave us and take the days you need."

"I don't like going."

"It must be done."

Viktor frowned and glanced toward the window. Mihai saw Viktor's aura flash and felt twinges of disappointment as well as anxiety coming from Viktor. His friend was making the effort to tame his underlying feral nature. Mihai said nothing, only watched. It couldn't be easy for him, struggling with two opposite sides, one that feasted on the depravities of life and one that wanted to be good, kind, and loving.

Viktor clasped his hands behind his back. "The ladies are coloring eggs in the kitchen, aren't they?"

"Yes. We'll be taking some eggs and pies that our cook baked to the orphanage."

"It sounds like fun," said Viktor.

Mihai patted Viktor's shoulder affectionately. "It should be."

Viktor said nothing, but joined Mihai as he walked out of the study. The fresh aroma of blueberry and meat pies filled the air. It only got richer as they approached the kitchen.

The kitchen was full of activity. His father sat at a long, wooden table with Beatrice, Sonia and Theresa. Miss Pompeli was checking the ovens. She had two assistants, one boiling eggs and the other wrapping their gifts and cleaning.

Sonia's cheeks were pale, but she appeared excited to color eggs. Theresa appeared vibrant. Her cheeks were red and her hair shined in the light. She rarely suffered from morning sickness, unlike Sonia, who got sick often. Doctor Stanza was growing concerned. Sonia had lost five pounds since the start of her pregnancy.

Theresa put some onion skins in a bowl of hot water, turning it yellow.

"Viktor and I are here to help," said Mihai, smiling.

"It's about time you got here, Boy. It's important you dip the first eggs," said his father. He grabbed an egg and thrust it at Mihai. "You, too, Viktor."

Viktor turned to Mihai. "What's so important about the first eggs?"

"The man colors his first egg red and gives it to his children. It's good luck for them," said Mihai. He flashed Theresa a grin, full of pride.

Beatrice giggled.

"I'm sure you'll have a child one day, Bea," said Theresa.

Mihai plopped his egg into the red dye. Viktor's joined his.

Sonia pulled out a yellow egg.

Viktor sat down across from Sonia. "Aren't you supposed to give me a red egg back?"

She giggled softly. "No, silly. It's only for the men."

Mihai put an egg in the blue dye. Theresa put an egg in the green dye.

"Viktor, the next egg should be blue. It's meant to bring good luck to your marriage," said Mihai.

Viktor put an egg in the blue dye.

Beatrice giggled again. "Oh, what a silly superstition."

"You're just jealous because you have no one to give you an egg," Viktor replied.

Sonia smiled at Viktor. He reached out and squeezed her hand. Mihai knew that was the most they dared to do.

Mihai's father handed Beatrice a blue egg. Beatrice's eyes grew wide. "For me?"

"Father! Beatrice is half your age!" exclaimed Mihai.

"Oh, relax. I didn't want her to feel left out."

Beatrice flashed Mihai's father a wicked grin. "How naughty, Your Majesty."

Mihai's father chuckled.

Theresa plucked an egg out of the orange dye and dried it, giving it to Mihai. "For you."

"Why orange?"

"It's warm. It reminds me of you."

"I'm warm?"

She bit her lower lip with her teeth. "Very warm."

He chuckled. Was she recalling their act of lovemaking? He took out his red egg, dried it, and presented it to Theresa. She smiled.

Viktor removed his red egg, dried it, and handed it to Sonia. She didn't grab it well and accidently dropped it on the table.

It cracked.

Fear filled Sonia's eyes.

No one smiled. It grew quiet.

"Oh, give her another one, Viktor. Aren't you entitled to a second chance?" said Beatrice finally.

"A second chance?" whispered Viktor. His aura darkened and his expression betrayed one of mute wretchedness. Mihai cursed himself for wanting to color eggs. He could only imagine the horror going through his sister's mind.

Beatrice gave Viktor her blue egg. "Hand it to her. I don't need it. Give yourself a second chance."

Mihai suspected Beatrice had sprinkled some anast dust on the egg to take away the edge of fear both Viktor and Sonia must be feeling. He had a knack for noticing the slight of hand tricks Beatrice employed.

Viktor handed the egg to Sonia. She cupped it in both hands, a slow smile growing across her lips. The anast was working on her, too.

How Mihai's heart went out to his sister. She was clearly struggling with this pregnancy physically, and it didn't help matters that her intimacy with her husband, both physical and emotional, had been curbed because of Viktor's condition. It dawned on him to ask Dr. Stanza how their mother bore her pregnancies, especially after his father had mentioned his mother had challenging confinements. Maybe it could provide clues to help Sonia.

Miss Pompeli, the cook, put a fresh bowl of hard boiled eggs on the table.

Theresa stood. "I'm going to wash my hands."

As Mihai nodded his acknowledgement, Theresa swooned and lunged forward, right into the king's arms.

"Alice! Are you all right?"

Mihai froze. So did Sonia. Alice was his mother's name. He raked his eyes over his father's face. He looked lost in a memory. Beatrice helped Theresa to her feet as Mihai's father backed up.

"Tea, are you well?" asked Beatrice.

"Just a little faint. I fear I stood up too quickly. I'm fine now."

Mihai walked over to her, and placed a hand on her shoulder. "Are you sure?"

"Is Alice well?"

Again, his mother's name. Mihai disengaged from Theresa and took his father's arm, holding it tight.

"Who is Alice?" asked Viktor.

"It's my mother's name," said Sonia.

"Father, this is Theresa, my fiancée. We're to be married next week." Mihai's voice was thick with concern.

"Right. Theresa. Is she well?"

Theresa nodded.

"She was a little faint, that's all," said Beatrice.

"Faint?"

Mihai's heart broke. This was the first time he had a loss of memory. Should he tell his father of Theresa's condition? Right now, only Beatrice and Dr. Stanza knew. They wanted to make an official announcement after their wedding.

Orthodoxy allowed an engaged couple intimacy.

"Mihai, is Theresa well or not?"

"Father, she's with child."

Shock washed over his father's eyes before astonishment, pride, and happiness took their turns.

"Well, well, well – both you and Sonia! This warms my heart. Congratulations to you."

Theresa's cheeks turned red.

Sonia stood and hugged her. "It's wonderful news. I would have never known. You wear it well – better than I."

"Thank you, Sonia," said Theresa softly.

"Congratulations, Mihai," said Viktor quietly.

Beatrice clapped her hands. "It's wonderful news, isn't it?"

Mihai looked directly at Theresa. "It is."

She gave him that sweet, simple smile he adored and his heart tripped. His wedding day couldn't come soon enough.

Chapter Fourteen

Viktor guided his horse toward the pack house. Smoke billowed out the chimney. He hated coming here. Mihai's wedding was tomorrow and he would miss it. Viktor wanted to be Mihai's best man, but Mihai's father would take his place. Damn his cursed bite. He detested what Bane had done to him, yet without Bane, he couldn't tame the feral urges inside of him.

Sonia appeared healthier. Her stomach now had a small, round bulge to it. She was still slender, though. She had put on some weight, but not much. When he left her, she was in the throes of a painful headache. Sonia couldn't focus on her lessons with Mihai and Beatrice, which disappointed them both – Sonia because her heart ached to embraced witchcraft so she could help him, and Viktor because it was the promise of Sonia using witchcraft that might make him being a wolf more bearable.

Mrs. Nocesti and Theresa had volunteered to sit with her to make sure she drank all her willow bark tea. It infuriated him to no end that he couldn't be with his wife. Every time he looked into her eyes, the sadness grew. He hated coming to the pack house, yet he was forced to do it.

Viktor slowed his horse and dismounted. He couldn't stop thinking about being intimate with his wife – his clever, charming wife. Viktor hated Bane that much more, for taking that pleasure away from him. His misery was like a steel weight over his heart.

Viktor walked into the pack house. Gascon and Nasguard were rolling weed at the table. He joined them.

"Where's Timon?" Viktor asked.

"With Bane gathering wood for the cabin."

"The witches?"

"In back," said Gascon.

Nasguard stopped rolling and looked directly at Viktor. "I need to tell you something, Viktor."

Viktor raised his eyebrow. "Oh?"

"Timon wants Alina."

Viktor pursed his lips. "Well, he can't have her. I won't give permission."

Nasguard patted Viktor's shoulder. "It's good that you protect your witch. It is a trait I admire, but Timon is crafty and you must take care around him. He does not like you."

"I gathered he didn't."

Gascon stopped rolling his weed. "It's more than just hate, Viktor. Bane intends for you to take over the pack – that was something Timon thought would be his legacy."

"Ah."

Nasguard pointed a finger at Viktor. "Do not be a fool. Timon is not well-liked. He disapproves of my coupling with Delilah, the vampire princess from Sinisteri, and he tricked Gascon into sharing his witch. Both Diana and Maria receive bruises from his coupling. He cannot rein in his anger, or he refuses. I do not know, nor do I care, but I know this – he will use every trick in his arsenal to gain your permission to couple with Alina. You must be one step ahead of him. It pains Gascon and me to see our witches suffer from Timon's abuse."

"Can't you do something about it?" asked Viktor.

"It is against the rules to discipline Timon. It must come from Bane, and he has yet to do so."

"I appreciate your warning." Protectiveness surged within Viktor. He would not let any harm come to Alina. She was forced into coming to the pack house as well.

Nasguard nodded. He placed his hands on Viktor's shoulders and looked directly into his eyes. "Remember this – do not eat the heart – never eat the heart. You will lose your wits – much like one does when they drink too much alcohol. Just drink the blood."

"Timon will try to get me to eat the heart?"

"That's how he tricked me," said Gascon. He crossed his arms. "I ate the heart, and in the intoxication, he asked me if he could have Maria. I said yes."

Viktor nodded.

"When we are wolves, the temptation will be great to eat the heart. Use your human mind to remember what I told you. Don't give in to the temptation."

The door opened. Bane and Timon walked through carrying several logs for the fireplace. Nasguard and Gascon immediately went back to rolling.

"Ah, Viktor, you're here. Good." Bane's voice hinted at satisfaction.

"Bane." Viktor said, acknowledging him.

Timon grunted, and threw the logs he was carrying in front of the fireplace.

"Argh!" A loud high-pitched wail came from the back rooms.

Bane looked at the hall. "Hecuba!"

The wolves scrambled to their feet and Bane raced into the hallway.

Viktor turned to Nasguard. "Is something wrong with Hecuba?"

"She's old. Her body is rejecting her magic," said Nasguard.

"Enough!" said Timon. "He'll learn."

Viktor glared at Timon before pushing past him and running down the hall. He came to an abrupt stop in a door frame. Hecuba lay on a bed. Her old body shook uncontrollably. Bane gripped her hand. Diana poured a thick, red liquid down Hecuba's throat. The old witch gurgled, her eyes went to the back of her head, then her body stilled.

"Is she all right?" asked Viktor. The sight of Hecuba in pain, her old, leathered body out of control, unnerved him.

Bane looked directly at him, his nostrils flaring. "Get him out of here!"

Alina stepped forward, placed her hand on Viktor's arm, and escorted him out.

"Why must I leave?" The insult that Bane demanded he leave roiled through Viktor's chest.

Alina leaned close. "Bane does not want you to see his witch like this. It's a matter of pride to him."

"Pride?"

"Hecuba is very old, close to 200 years. She's used black magic to extend her life, but her body cannot contain it anymore," Alina whispered.

"Nasguard mentioned it. Is she dying?"

"Yes. Diana is uncertain, but believes it is coming sooner than Hecuba anticipates."

"What happens when she dies?"

"We don't know. Diana will probably take over the coven, but she'll be bound by Hecuba's commitments."

Bane walked out of the room, glaring at Viktor. "Enough. The moon is close. We need to go outside now."

Viktor said nothing, following behind Bane. Even now, he felt his pulse quickening. The change would come soon. A raw, primitive grief overwhelmed him.

~ * ~

Viktor was sated. He slowly backed into the forest. The hunger was gone.

"Viktor."

He turned to look at Timon. The wolf threw a piece of meat at him. Viktor licked his lips.

"Eat it."

Viktor stepped toward it, then stopped. *"What is it?"*

"Meat."

Viktor heard the echo of Nasguard's deep, baritone voice

in his head. Never eat the heart.

"I'm sated."

"Consider it a peace offering."

"No."

Timon snarled. Viktor didn't want peace on Timon's terms.

Bane walked between the two. *"Enough. It's time to go back to the pack house. Follow me."*

Viktor trotted behind Bane, grateful for Nasguard's warning. He stayed close to Bane. Leaves sprouted on the trees and the weather wasn't as unpleasant as it had been in winter. When they got to the pack house, Viktor went straight to the room reserved for him. Alina greeted him, rubbing his back. Viktor lay down on the rug at the foot of the bed and fell asleep.

A loud knock on the door woke him. He got to his feet, rubbing his eyes. Alina stood next to the bed, her arms wrapped around herself.

"Who is that?" Viktor asked.

"Timon."

"Why didn't you answer the door?"

"I'm afraid of him."

Thank God for Nasguard's warning. He took a step toward the door and then stopped. God? Why did he thank God? God did nothing to prevent him from becoming a wolf. No, he would never thank God again.

Viktor continued to the door and opened it. Timon stood in front of him, his eyes flaming with need.

"Leave," said Timon.

"No."

Timon's lips curved into an unnatural smile. "I am senior to you."

"This is my room. I will not leave and you are not invited in."

Timon's nostrils distended. "You must give me what I

want."

Anger flared through Viktor and he clenched his fists to calm himself. "I do not have to give you a thing. I know what you want. Just ask so I can refuse you."

"You will pay for your insolence, cub."

Viktor grabbed Timon's forearm. "Never call me 'cub' again. You did not make me. My name is Viktor."

Timon shrugged Viktor away and marched off. Viktor closed the door, turning to face Alina. She ran into his arms.

Viktor ran his hand over her thick, glossy hair. Alina reeked of fear. His heart went out to her. He never wanted to care too much for her, but right now, he would protect his witch with all he had. Viktor held her close until she stopped shaking and the fear subsided. He sighed heavily at the emotional toll coming to the pack house had on his soul.

~ * ~

April twentieth was a day Mihai would never forget. He stood in the entranceway of Saint Mikhal's Orthodox Church waiting for Theresa to arrive. He exhaled a long sigh of contentment.

His father walked to the small window next to the wooden door and peered out. He looked thin and gaunt in his uniform, and his hand trembled slightly, but he wasn't coughing and he hadn't had any more episodes of memory loss since the time he confused Theresa for Alice. Mihai had to admit that unnerved him very much.

"Her carriage is pulling up now, Son."

Mihai drew in a deep breath to steady his racing heart. He wore the military uniform of the Crown Prince. The church was full. Beatrice was Theresa's maid of honor. Sonia didn't feel comfortable in the wedding party. Her illness sapped her strength. She was sitting in the front row, waiting for them. His heart went out to her. It seemed that no matter how much she rested or how much she ate, she was ill in one way or another. She had stopped throwing up her food, thank goodness, but now his sister had headaches that left her practically immobile. Sonia devoured Beatrice's botany book, but with her headaches, it was difficult for her to direct energy in their lessons. She did much better at directing energy if she didn't have a headache.

The door opened and all eyes turned toward Theresa. She walked into the entranceway, her arm threaded through her father's. God, she was stunning. Her dress was pure white, and the bodice fell down past her collarbone, accentuating the full curve of her breasts. The sleeves of the dress tapered down to her wrists. The dress hugged her waist. Beatrice and Victoria, Theresa's oldest sister, held her white train. Theresa wore pearl earrings and a matching necklace.

Theresa's father presented her to Mihai, and for a precious moment, time seemed suspended between them. The bells stopped ringing.

Father Gregori greeted the couple. His purple and gold robe glittered in the candlelight.

Mihai smiled at Theresa. She returned the smile.

"Is there anyone who objects to the marriage of Prince Mihai and Lady Theresa?" asked Father Gregori.

The vestibule was silent.

"Prince Mihai, do you come here of your own free will to marry Lady Theresa?"

"Yes." He grasped Theresa's hand, reassuring her he did. Her lips curved into a smile.

Yes, I want this. I want to marry you. I pray you can feel my sincerity.

"Lady Theresa, do you come here of your own free will to marry Prince Mihai?"

"Yes," she replied.

His father, King Stelian, stepped forward and exchanged the wedding rings between the couple. The last time, Mihai slid his ring on Theresa's finger. When he looked up, Theresa's eyes were moist, the apprehension gone.

Father Gregori motioned for the couple to enter the church. They followed the priest down the aisle. Beatrice clung to Mihai's father, who Mihai suspected really clung to her. Victoria and Edward, Theresa's other siblings, followed Beatrice and the king. When they got to the altar, everyone took their places and the wedding mass began.

Father Gregori presented them each with a candle.

"Christ is the light of the world and will light your way through life as husband and wife."

The prayers and readings were said. He and Theresa took communion. She exchanged her candle for a crown from Beatrice. Mihai kissed the crown and knelt before Theresa, reverence in his heart. Tears streamed down her cheeks, and Theresa placed the crown on his head. Mihai tried to push aside the rush of guilt that blasted him. Why hadn't he waited for Theresa? He needed to stop feeling guilty about his time in England. England was far away and Theresa was his here and now.

He stood up, pushing those unwanted thoughts away and prayed Theresa had not felt them. He took the crown from his father and held it up before his bride. Theresa kissed it and knelt before him. Gently, he placed it on her head. Thank God, Theresa had been strong enough to perform the ceremony. He helped her to her feet and they followed Father Gregori around the altar three times. The final time, Father Gregori turned to face them.

"In the name of God, I pronounce you husband and wife, Crown Prince and Princess Mihai and Theresa Sigmaringen."

The bells began to ring, announcing his marriage, and his heart soared with pride – and joy.

~ * ~

Mihai helped Theresa into the royal carriage, holding her train as she stepped inside. A crowd of people surrounded the church, raising loud cheers to the royal couple. Once Mihai was inside, the driver took off. They were going to Delfin Castle for their reception. A daguerreotyper would be there to take pictures.

Mihai sat next to Theresa and placed his arm around her shoulders. "How do you feel?"

"Tired."

"If you feel faint or ill, tell me."

She rested her cheek against his chest.

He kissed the top of her head. "I'm happy we're married now."

She raised her head and looked at him. "Are you? I felt your guilt right before you crowned me."

He pursed his lips, wanting to measure his response. "I've always been honest with you, so let me assure you it was guilt over my affair in England. I wish it never happened."

"Truly?"

"Yes. I should have waited for you."

She raised her hand to his cheek. "Let it go."

He placed his hand over hers. "You're right. Theresa, I—" He stopped, moved by a wave of heavy emotion.

"You, what?"

"I'm happy to be married."

She buried her face against his neck, radiating an inner peace. "I am, too."

~ * ~

Mihai stayed close to Theresa. They took pictures in the castle gardens overlooking the Black Sea and another set in the entrance hall. Then they had dinner and shared a waltz. When Theresa grew tired, he sat down next to her, sometimes getting her a drink, other times just offering reassurance. He talked to her brother, Edward, and her sister, Victoria, who had brought her children. Theresa had such a vibrant family. That's what he wanted – his very own family, full of life and affection for each other.

Sonia joined Mihai and Theresa as they sat at a table next to the dance floor. Today had been a good day for his sister, but she had also drank a lot of willow bark tea throughout the day to keep the headaches away. Still, he didn't think she had the strength to endure the rigorous standing and kneeling as a bridesmaid and was glad she had watched from the front pew.

Sonia smiled. "I'm very happy for you both."

Mihai stood and hugged his sister. "You look well."

"Thank you. I feel well. It's a rare day for me."

"Theresa! Daughter!"

Theresa stood and grinned at hearing her father's voice. He walked over, arms extended, and she ran into his burly embrace.

He parted from her, gripping his hands on her upper arms. There was no mistaking the pride in his eyes. "You look wonderful."

"Papa! That must have been the fifth time you said that."

"Oh, let me be proud of my little girl. Now, when is your honeymoon?"

"We leave tomorrow morning."

"So soon?"

"Yes."

Theresa's father looked up from her and then at Mihai. "I must talk with your husband. You don't mind if I take him aside, do you?"

"You're not going to scold him, are you?"

A playful spark danced in her father's eyes. "No, I'm just going to threaten him. If he doesn't treat you right—"

"Oh, Papa! No threats."

Her father chuckled. Mihai gestured toward the door. "We can talk in the study."

"Papa—"

"It will be fine, Theresa. I had the same talk with Victoria's husband, and I'll have the same talk with Beatrice's husband when she marries."

Theresa sighed.

"I'll keep you company," said Sonia. "I'm sure my father had the same talk with Viktor."

"Thank you."

Mihai squeezed Theresa's hand and escorted her father outside of the ballroom. Edward and Victoria quietly joined them.

Theresa's father looked at him. "I asked them to join us."

When he opened the door to his study, Mihai found Beatrice sitting in a chair, waiting for them. He didn't know if he should be worried, insulted or flattered. Why did Theresa's whole family have to be here?

"Would you like a drink?" Mihai asked.

"No, I want to get right to business," said Theresa's father.

Mihai gestured for him to take the couch. Theresa's father sat down. Edward and Victoria sat next to him. Beatrice stayed in her chair. Mihai grabbed a spare chair from a corner and joined the circle.

Theresa's father steepled his fingers. "I often wondered about Esmeralda. She had such promise, but her father was reckless with her future."

"You knew my mother?"

"Yes, I knew Esmeralda Vacay."

Mihai's heart leapt. What luck! His bride's father had known his mother, but of course, he would – he was a witch.

"What do you mean, her father was reckless?"

"He wanted revenge for a minor insult and promised Esmeralda into service to Hecuba and her coven. Esmeralda refused to go and disappeared. I learned years later through Count Brancoveanu that she married into Moldavia's royal house."

"Hecuba?" questioned Mihai. The witch who killed his mother!

Theresa's father looked at him, his expression serious. "Hecuba isn't your problem. The wolf in your house is."

"Viktor." Mihai drew in a breath. Viktor wasn't the same man he knew in London. Mihai's heart went out to his friend as he struggled to hold onto his caring and kind nature.

"Beatrice told me what occurred and that you and your sister received lessons from her."

"She has been a good teacher."

"Good. You'll need to keep learning and practicing on your own. Beatrice must accompany us back to Austria. When I can, I'll spare her for a visit or two, but you must be diligent or the wolf will ruin your house."

"Viktor would do no such thing."

"Yes, he will. He is a wolf. He wants two things – blood and sex. This feral need will consume his human body, and when it does, he will plot against you, purposely hurt you, and eventually try to kill you."

"Nonsense."

Theresa's father snapped to his feet. "You indignant boy! Do not presume to dictate to me how Viktor will behave. I know the wolf mentality and every man succumbs to the feral nature."

Mihai stood as well, unsure of how to react, but convinced the elder witch was very serious and he needed to be serious as well. "Tell me what to do."

"I sense reluctant acceptance coming from you, but you must not be reluctant to act when the time comes. Not only that, but the situation is complicated by Theresa's ignorance."

"Why did you raise her not to know her talents?" asked Mihai.

"I foresaw her future at birth and it dictated she must be ignorant of her heritage. If she ever practices witchcraft, she faces death."

"Death?" A wave of apprehension threaded through him. He'd wanted to explore witchcraft with her. What did her father mean?

"Yes – death by evisceration. I saw it clearly."

Mihai fisted his hands at the thought.

"Now I've felt a subtle shift in energy around my daughter and Beatrice has confirmed it. Being in close proximity to you, a practicing witch, novice though you are, has ignited the ferons in her blood. She feels you, does she not? She reacts to you instinctively?"

"Yes, she does."

"Her body is alive with magic."

"She needs to be told," said Mihai. "She doesn't have to practice, but she should know what she is."

Theresa's father rubbed his finger against his chin. "Perhaps she can be told, but she must never practice, and for now I think it best she remain ignorant around the wolf or he might seek her out."

"He wouldn't seek her out – he's married."

"Your sister can't be the witch he needs her to be. He needs a healthy trained witch – one not with child. To that end, Lady Alina Brancoveanu has been assigned as his witch. She'll do her best, but eventually your friend will embrace the wolf, and not even Alina will be able to help him then."

"Won't Viktor discover Theresa is a witch?"

"He will in time. He is now sensitive to the emotions and feelings of those belonging to Dalcas' blood. Currently, he is focused on Alina. He will feel Theresa soon enough."

"What can I do to protect her?" asked Mihai.

"Watch him closely. When you suspect he has discovered my daughter's nature, I want to know immediately. We might not have a choice in telling Theresa what she is, but she can never *practice* magic. If there is a spell to be cast or a potion to be mixed, *you* must do it."

"Let me tell Theresa now."

Theresa's father waved his hand in the air. "No, not yet. Let me try to dream. I have to think of every outcome. I have to anticipate what will happen."

Mihai's shoulders tensed. He wanted to tell Theresa what she was, but he would honor her father's request for now.

"I also know my daughter is with child."

"Yes, she is," Mihai paused. "We've discussed Theresa – is Sonia in danger?"

Theresa's father pursed his lips and hesitated before drawing in a breath and speaking. "In a way, your sister is the lynchpin in this situation. If she survives the birth and embraces as well as excels at her training, Alina can be released from her duty and Sonia can assume it. If the emotional attachment is deep between your sister and the wolf, and she can accommodate and satisfy him, then his ability to tame his feral nature will allow him to live a decent life as your friend and her husband."

"That sounds like a lot of 'if's," Mihai replied.

"Indeed and neither of you desired to embrace your mother's gifts until now. You both have a lot to learn," Theresa's father rubbed his hands together. "Don't fool yourself. Both your sister and my daughter face danger." He paused, reached into his pocket, and handed Mihai a small pouch. "These are my own personal runes. Every two weeks use them to make a square and channel your energy through your athame. Call for me. I want an update as to the wolf's condition. The safety of both women is important to me."

"I will."

Edward, Victoria, and Beatrice also gave him a pouch of runes. "If you can't reach me, try us all. Edward and Victoria are quite powerful in their own right and capable of advising you. Beatrice will leave a potions book with you along with one about botany. Edward will leave you his notes on astrology, and Victoria will leave you her notes on tarot."

"I know nothing about astrology and tarot."

"You'll have to learn as much as you can on your own. Teach your sister when you can. Have her read the books we'll leave with you. When I can, I'll send Beatrice back to you."

Mihai drew in a deep breath, steeling his courage. He would miss Beatrice. He valued her guidance.

"Keep both women safe. I want to see Theresa's child carried to term. The loss of a child to a witch is felt tenfold with our heightened emotions. It could drive her into a depression, or Dalca be damned, madness. The same holds true for a male witch – and you, of all, must keep your wits about you."

"I will. Why do you swear by Dalca?"

"Because he's the father of us all."

"I promise you, I'll do my best."

"Good. See to it you do. Keep to our meetings and keep what we discussed inside this room."

Mihai nodded. "I will."

Theresa's father smiled and then clapped his hands. "I believe you will. Now, do you have a cigar to offer me?"

"Father! They stink!" protested Beatrice.

Mihai chuckled and reached for his box.

~ * ~

Theresa walked through the doors of Mihai's room and

paused. She had never been to his room before. Thank God they didn't have to go through that barbaric ritual of bedding down with a hundred witnesses. She couldn't bear it.

She had separate apartments next to his, and a secret door connected the rooms.

Mihai shut the door behind them. Candles burned throughout the chamber and a fire blazed in a fireplace across from the bed. The bed was wide, with a thick down cover. A window faced the Black Sea. The curtains hung to the side. Theresa saw a full moon glittering on the sea.

Mihai placed his hands on her shoulders. "How do you feel?"

"Overwhelmed."

He went to the nightstand and grabbed a wrapped box, handing it to her. "For you. It's my wedding gift."

A smile tipped the corner of her lips and she anxiously ripped the wrapping off the box. A fine rose-colored silk nightgown rested inside.

"It's beautiful, Mihai. The material is so soft, so fine. I adore it."

"Will you wear it tonight?"

Her cheeks heated. "Yes."

"Good. I can't wait to see you in it."

She coughed. Why was she embarrassed?

Theresa glanced around the room looking for a square package that should have been delivered earlier today.

"Is something wrong?" he asked.

Slowly, Theresa investigated the room. Nothing. Opening the closet, she discovered the package. "Here's your wedding gift."

Mihai grinned, picked up the package and brought it to the bed. Theresa couldn't help but smile as he unwrapped it. Her husband reminded her of Victoria's son at Christmas opening his gifts, capturing that same youthful exuberance.

"de Vilegar! How did you...?"

"Papa helped me acquire the painting."

"It will go above the mantle in my study."

"I hoped you would put it there."

Mihai rested the painting on a table next to the door. He closed the distance between them and cupped her cheek. She closed her eyes at his gentle touch, placing her hand over his. This was perfect.

"When you first entered the church today, my heart skipped a beat. You were so beautiful in that dress."

She opened her eyes. "Thank you."

"You did so much for me. You learned my language. You converted to my religion. Just now, you gave me a painting from one of my favorite artists," He paused. "I want you."

Her lips curved into a wide smile.

He pressed her close to his body, his mouth covering hers with hungry desire. He wanted her, and she gave into the rising sensuality between them. The thought of being intimate again with him warmed her to her bones.

He slipped behind her. His nimble fingers made quick work of the buttons and stays that held her dress up. With a quick, firm shove, he pushed the dress to the floor. Then he loosened her corset and slid it over her head. The only thing between them was her chemise.

He grasped her hips and brushed his mouth against her ear, his breath hot and eager. "I'm going to undress now. Don't turn around. When I touch you again, I want you to feel what I'm doing. Promise me no words. Use your feelings to communicate with me."

She nodded. An intense physical awareness of him flooded her senses. A shiver of anticipation rippled through her.

Mihai took a minute or two to undress. When he finished, he brushed the hair away from her nape and kissed her. Her blood coursed through her veins like an awakened river. His closeness was so male, so bracing, she wanted to give in to the hunger and beg for more.

Slowly, he ran a hand down the hollow of her back. He knelt, kissed her waist, and gently turned her so she faced him. He splayed gentle fingers over her stomach. Her skin was tight, but she wasn't showing – not yet.

"Our child..." he whispered, his voice dropping off. Theresa closed her eyes and moaned. Delight ran over her. Mihai's excitement and joy at her pregnancy struck her full force.

He kissed her stomach, trailing his sweet lips up her body, teasing the space between her breasts and her neck, until he claimed her mouth with a hot and urgent kiss.

He wants me, and I want him. Heaven help me, I want this man.

They collapsed onto the sheets, Mihai on top of her, his tongue caressing her sensitive, swollen nipples. Such sweet torture!

May he never stop.

A finger curved into her passage and he lightly stroked her.

She needed him inside her – now. Theresa grabbed his hand with hers. "Please, Mihai...please..."

Delight danced in his eyes and he pulled away, leaning his back against the headboard. She cocked her head. Wasn't he going to get on top of her? He pressed a finger to her lips. His erection stood steely and hard, eager for her.

He cupped her cheek and she realized he wanted her like this – her on top of him. She nodded. He couched her and drove himself inside. Mihai then grabbed her waist to hold her steady. She closed her eyes, arching her back, enjoying the thrill of his male hardness deep within her. She gasped in sweet agony as he rocked her, guiding her rhythm.

His pleasure was pure and explosive. He flooded her senses and shuddered with ecstasy inside her. The world around her spun and tendrils of intoxicating bliss spiraled throughout her body. With the mutual climax, the light that had shone the last time they'd made love ignited again, flooding the room before slowly fading away. She collapsed against his chest, the hot tide of his passion ebbing with the light. His feelings were deep – to the core of his being. He wrapped his arms around her.

Theresa basked in his embrace.

His lips brushed her ear. "You are mine." His voice was raw, edgy, yet filled with conviction.

Theresa hugged her arms around his waist.

Chapter Fifteen

Viktor led his horse into the livery, glad to be done with his trip to Mulfaltar. A stable boy took the animal's reins, and Viktor made his way toward the closest entrance. He felt sated in an odd way. Sated, yet the goose bumps pricked his arms.

He inhaled deeply, finding comfort in the familiar salty scent of the Black Sea. This was his home, and more than anything, he would fight for it – and his wife. He was a man, not a beast, and determined to show an iron will when it came to his control over his feral nature.

Viktor glanced toward the shore. Only one royal yacht was moored. Mihai must be on his honeymoon. There was work to be done, and the sooner Viktor got involved, the better.

He walked into the rear entrance and into the kitchen. Miss Pompeli hovered over the stove stirring a stockpot.

"Lord Bacau! What a pleasant surprise."

He smiled. "It smells wonderful. What are you cooking?"

"A simple chicken stew. It seems to help the king."

"How is my wife?"

"She's havin' a good day, my Lord."

"And the king?"

"He's been coughin' up blood again, but he won't take the laudanum. Says he wants his wits about him for the railroad business."

Viktor hesitated. He wanted to bathe, but perhaps he should check on the king first. "Thank you, Daciana. I look forward to dinner."

She nodded. Viktor departed and made his way toward the king's study. He heard Sonia's father coughing just as he got to the door and Viktor paused, drawing in a deep breath. The king treated Viktor as if Viktor were his own son and had wholeheartedly approved of his marriage to Sonia. Viktor was resolved not to let the king down. He knocked on the door.

"Enter."

Viktor walked in. Sonia's father stood in front of a map, his arms crossed. He smiled when he saw Viktor.

"It's good to have you back, Son."

"It's good to be back."

"How is your family?"

"Well." Viktor hated lying to the king. He couldn't be told the truth of Viktor's condition, so he had been told that Viktor went to visit his family in Ukraine.

"What are you looking at?" asked Viktor.

"This is a proposed route of the railroad. There is a matter of a small hill. They can set the track around the hill or blast through it. By going around the hill, it will add fifteen minutes to the travel time. To blast and clear the hill puts the project's finish in October."

"Is October feasible?"

"It will be close. The ground starts to frost over toward the end of the month."

Viktor rubbed his chin with a finger. He liked the idea of blasting and clearing the hill for the quicker route.

"Well, what say you?" asked the king.

"Go through the hill."

The king chuckled. "Yes, that's what I was thinking as well – but it will be up to you and Mihai to see to it the work is done in time."

Viktor arched an eyebrow. "Oh?"

"It won't be much longer, Son. I have weeks to live, if that."

Viktor swallowed, tucking his hands under his armpits. Everyone respected Sonia's father, despite his gruff ways.

He'd done much good for the principality, his main accomplishment being the construction of the docks in Constanta, making the city a viable seaport and bringing more trade to the Romanian principalities.

"Son, I think you're going to miss me."

"Yes. So will Sonia and Mihai."

The king gestured toward his drinking cabinet. Viktor accompanied him and the king poured them each some brandy.

"I've got regrets, Boy." The king paused, then sat down in the chair across from the sofa. Viktor sat on the sofa.

"I loved my wife and when I see Sonia look at you, I know she's found that same feeling." Again, the king the paused and drew in a breath that rattled his lungs. "Don't be foolish with my daughter's heart."

He nodded, touched by the sincerity in the king's rough voice.

"Where is Sonia?" asked Viktor.

"In the library with the mid-wife. My daughter's embroidery has never been good, so don't bring attention to it."

He stood. "I promise."

The king waved his hand, motioning toward the door. "Go. Tybeski will be here first thing tomorrow. I'll get his opinion, too. Spend time with your wife."

Viktor exited and went directly to the library. He did want to see Sonia, if anything, just to tell her he was back before he went to take a bath. He missed her, and while Alina met his physical needs, she wasn't his wife. He missed Sonia's smile, hearing her thoughts, listening to her voice. Sonia and the baby were his reason for living.

He opened the door and spied Sonia, along with Mrs. Nocesti, both embroidering as they sat next to the window that overlooked the gardens. There was a sad little look on her face and Viktor knew from their conversations that

Sonia missed being a nurse. Dr. Stanza might have encouraged her nursing if she was healthier. Working at the hospital was Sonia's passion and she missed it terribly.

His wife looked up and smiled. "Viktor! You're back."

He crossed the expanse of the library and held out his hand. She stood and squeezed it. It wasn't enough. Not for him.

"I've missed you, darling."

"I've missed you, too."

"How are you feeling today?"

"Tired, but fine."

Mrs. Nocesti coughed. Viktor turned to face her. The nurse got to her feet. "Her Grace had a headache when she woke up, but I sat with her and the willow bark tea cleared it up."

"I had a nice lunch. I even had seconds," said Sonia, smiling.

"Have you gained weight?"

"A couple of pounds."

"You still need to gain at least another five pounds by the end of the week," said Mrs. Nocesti.

"I will see to it my wife has seconds all week." Viktor looked at Mrs. Nocesti and gestured with his eyes for her to leave.

She stood still.

Viktor pursed his lips, pushing back a sudden blast of anger at the nurse for failing to understand his gesture. "Mrs. Nocesti, I'd like a private moment with my wife. Please."

"Your Grace?"

Sonia sought out Viktor's expression, then looked at the nurse. "It's fine, Mrs. Nocesti."

With quiet efficiency, the nurse crossed the room and left.

Sonia withdrew her hand and he clenched his fists,

imposing an iron will on his control.

"It's not enough to hold your hand. I love you. Let me do more than touch your hand." Viktor's voice was raw, yet firm.

Sonia took a step back. "Is that wise?"

"I can control the beast."

"Viktor, this pregnancy is hard enough on me. I can't help but wonder if something is wrong. I try to eat, I try to rest, but I'm not as well as Theresa is," she paused. "I've been reading my mother's books. She did not have easy pregnancies."

"The child is growing, Sonia. Have faith in that."

"I do."

He held out his hand again and moved slowly, reaching out to her. Her sweet amber honey eyes widened in concern.

"Please...let me touch you..." he kept his voice gentle.

Sonia stayed her ground and Viktor curved his hand around her cheek. She closed her eyes and covered his hand with hers. Oh, thank Dalca. She allowed this! He stood there for a minute, letting her get used to the touch.

"May I kiss you?" he asked.

Her eyes snapped open and she studied him intently. Applying a new skill, he wondered? He sensed her reaching out with her emotions, hesitant – tentative, not as confident as Alina, and yet he sensed she was deliberate using her senses. He didn't respond to her probe, unsure he might spook her.

"Yes, I would like that," she replied.

He cupped her other cheek and brought her mouth to his. Her lips tasted of honey and lemon, fueling a sense of urgency in him.

Sonia placed her hands on his chest and disengaged, gasping.

"What's wrong?"

"I couldn't breathe."

Viktor took a step back. From the way she took deep breaths, he could see he'd been too demanding with her, even in that loving gesture. Damn it! "I'm sorry."

She nodded and closed her eyes. His wife was fragile. Still, her assessment and kiss had been encouraging, and he would need to be extremely gentle with her in the future. Sonia sat in the nearest chair. He fisted his hands, trying to quell the rising emotions.

"Thank you for the kiss," he said.

"You're welcome."

"I'll be back," he said.

Sonia opened her eyes and nodded. "I'll be here."

He quickly departed and went to his room. Confusion raced through him. He had gotten used to Alina reaching out to him, soothing him, and here was Sonia...He'd never felt her before – not that like. Dare he hope?

~ * ~

It was a bright mid-May morning as the royal carriage rode through the streets of Constanta, receiving cheers from the citizens who lined the curbs. Mihai, Theresa, his father, Sonia and Viktor were on their way to a park that was near the Parliament building. The park would house the Constanta train station, and Mihai wished to start the construction ceremonies by digging out the first shovel of dirt along with his father.

Sadness welled up inside him when he thought of his father. His clothes no longer fit his gaunt frame and his navy blue uniform had to be resized for the ceremony. Mihai's uniform was similar, but red, symbolic of the crown prince. Both Theresa and Sonia wore a red dress, as was custom for the royal princesses.

The park was cordoned off into several sections situating the crowd toward the rear with the press reporters near the front. The carriage stopped in a designated spot near the park's opening. The cavalry squad that guarded the royal family cleared a path for them.

The king threaded his arm through the arm of the Sergeant of the Guards, Sergeant Nicholai Ceseanu, who helped him up onto a platform. Mihai followed, Theresa at his side.

Mihai's mind wandered back to the four days he and Theresa had spent in the coastal Bulgarian town of Varna on their honeymoon. Varna was well known for having some of the best spas on the Black Sea. They'd relaxed at the finest hotel, ate the local food, enjoyed time at the spas, and fished in the sea. He smiled as he recalled his wife's exuberance. Their time in Varna had been a wonderful adventure, as Theresa had put it, and she'd been disappointed to cut it short.

He promised her another adventurous vacation next summer after the baby was born and they were more settled. The railroad should be finished by then and he would be able to give her the attention she deserved.

The royal party walked up onto the steps. Viktor stayed close to Sonia. Her body had been gaining its strength and she was able to join them.

Two men in frock jackets waited for them. They both bowed. A third man stepped forward.

"I am Herr Zering, Herr Schelberg's interpreter, Your Majesty."

"It's a pleasure to meet you." Mihai's father's voice was hoarse and he gestured for Mihai to talk.

"I am Crown Prince Mihai and this is my wife, Princess Theresa." He paused and the men bowed.

"Theresa and I are fluent in German and English," said Mihai, speaking German.

Herr Schelberg smiled. He was older, balding, with grey hair around the temples.

"Ah, it's good to communicate without an interpreter, but Herr Zering travels with me always."

"Of course," said Mihai.

"I am the commandant of the construction company." He paused and pointed to his associate. "This is Herr Wursteg. He is my second and will oversee most of the work. We are honored that you chose our company to build your railroad."

Viktor walked up to Mihai, leaning close. "The press wants you to say a few words."

Mihai stepped up to the podium, a sense of pride thrumming through his veins. After all his hard work, the railroad was actually going to happen.

"Ladies and gentlemen, distinguished guests, Herr Schelberg, and Herr Wursteg, welcome to this historic occasion. Building a railroad from Constanta to Bucharest will not only make travel easier between the two cities, but will also help to unite a nation. My father and I are proud to watch this project come to pass." He paused and the crowd cheered. Flashes from bulbs went off, nearly blinding him.

Mihai looked at the Germans. Herr Wursteg held up a shovel. Germans were very efficient. Mihai motioned to the steps and the party on the platform followed him. He went to a spot of dirt marked with yellow chalk and Herr Wursteg presented him with the shovel.

Mihai turned to his father. "Do you want the first scoop of dirt?"

"You deserve it, Son."

Mihai nodded and looked at his wife, who had been so patient with him today. "Theresa, join me."

She stepped up beside him and together they scooped the first shovel of dirt. More light bulbs went off.

Out of the corner of his eye, he saw Viktor's clasp his hands tightly behind his back. Mihai closed his eyes briefly, reaching out like Beatrice had taught him. Viktor was upset he wasn't asked to help with the first scoop. Mihai glanced at his friend. Viktor looked calm now, as he stood next to Sonia, but his fists were clenched, his jaw tight, his eyes narrow.

Mihai noted that Viktor was becoming more practiced at reigning in his expressions. Yes, he was trying to tame the feral nature that simmered underneath and Mihai would give his friend every opportunity to do so.

"Viktor, Sonia, help me with the next scoop."

Viktor graciously crooked his arm and Sonia laced her hand through it. Mihai handed them the shovel and then stepped away, standing next to Theresa, noting that Sonia was growing more comfortable with Viktor's touch. Was she getting used to her abilities?

Chapter Sixteen

It had been two weeks since Mihai last spoke to Theresa's father and he had to talk to him tonight. Mihai held Theresa until she fell asleep. He hated leaving their bed, but it was the only time he could contact her father.

The air was warm. Stars sparkled in the sky; however the humidity was thick this time of year, almost unbearable. Quietly, he slid his trousers up his legs, put on his boots, and buttoned his shirt. Mihai moved with stealth through the halls until he got to his study. He unlocked the middle drawer of his desk and removed the pouch that contained Georg von Kracken's runes. Following his instructions, Mihai made a square with the runes and used his athame to channel his energy.

"Georg von Kracken." Mihai kept his voice low, but firm.

Slowly, the elder man's face appeared in the square. "Mihai, well done, Son. Do you have anything new to report?"

"Viktor goes to his meeting in two days."

"Have you observed any inner struggles?"

"He is moodier than usual and often goes for a ride in the afternoon. He claims it helps to clear his head."

"How is he when he returns?"

"Normal. Refreshed, in a way."

"It's possible he might be releasing his aggression. Try to accompany him on one of his rides."

"Wouldn't that appear obvious?"

"He would discover any attempt to spy on him and that would only fuel mistrust."

Mihai nodded his understanding.

"How is my daughter?"

"She's starting to show."

"And your sister?"

"She has good days and bad. Her weight gain is better, but the headaches can be excruciating to her."

"Does the wolf touch her?"

"No."

Georg's shimmery expression frowned. "It is either the child or her body. I want you to contact Victoria and tell her what you've observed regarding your sister. Victoria is well-trained in healing."

"Thank you."

"The wolf is a cunning beast, Son. Find out what he does on these rides."

"I will."

"Good-bye."

"Good-bye."

Mihai put the runes away. He walked to the window and crossed his arms, staring out onto the Black Sea. It seemed like the only time he spent with Theresa was when they went to bed. Overseeing the construction and taking on added responsibilities as his father's health declined were putting a demand on his schedule, and he was beginning to resent it.

Theresa had never really seen the land surrounding the castle. Perhaps he could take her on a picnic lunch to the winery? He smiled at the thought. Tomorrow he'd have Mr. Tybeski clear a day on his schedule so he could spend it with his wife.

~ * ~

It was early in the morning and the sun had yet to rise, but Viktor wanted to leave early to go to the pack house.

He had to see Sonia first.

Quietly, he entered her room. A gas lamp burned on her nightstand. Sonia slept in a silk gown that was almost see-through. She was incredibly slender, but her belly swelled with the gentle curve of their child. He sat down in a chair next to the bed and lightly ran his fingers over her hair.

"Sonia."

She stirred.

"Sonia," he said, louder.

She stretched her body and yawned. Her eyes fluttered open.

"Viktor?"

"Yes, darling."

"I'm surprised to see you."

He frowned, wanting to see his wife before he had to go to another woman.

"I'm leaving. I wanted to tell you good-bye."

Her expression evened. "I'll miss you."

"Perhaps I can take you for a picnic when I return? I discovered a beautiful spot on a cliff overlooking the sea."

"Alone?"

"Yes, alone. It has been three months since we've been separated by my condition. Haven't I proved to you that I won't harm you?"

She sat up slowly and studied him. Viktor felt her. The touch was gentle. Energy caressed his skin. He knew what was next and did not want her to go further. He was ashamed. He did not want her to find Alina. Viktor pictured a scene on his cliff overlooking the sea in his mind's eyes with Sonia on a bright sunny day. Slowly, she nodded in acknowledgement. A whisp of a smile danced across her lips. "I would like to have a restful day with you on your cliff."

"Then I'll make the arrangements," he replied.

"All right."

He leaned forward quickly. Sonia stilled. He had to be soft. Gentle. Tender. These emotions were slowly drifting away from him. He had to practice slowing his body in front of Sonia. He reached out, cupping her cheek with his hand, keeping the cliff in his thoughts. She relaxed a bit. Viktor stroked her jaw line gently with his thumb and drew close to her.

Their lips met in a tender caress. Viktor didn't linger. Knowing he must not press for more, he disengaged from her. A tear dribbled down her cheek. He couldn't let his heart break for her. That would show human weakness. No, he had to be strong.

"Good bye, Sonia."

"Good bye."

He stood and felt the lightness of her slip away. As he walked out the door, the image of the cliff evaporated.

~ * ~

Viktor arrived at the pack house and spotted a carriage along with a horse that was tied to one of the hitching posts. Curiosity got the better of him. Were the witches here?

He tied up his horse. A noise came from the cabin – the hard slap of a hand striking flesh. It chilled him to the bone. Viktor raced to the door and threw it open. Timon stood over Diana. She was on the floor, her cheek red.

"What's going on?" demanded Viktor.

Timon sneered at him. "It does not concern you."

Viktor crossed the expanse of the room and knelt next to Diana. Alina and Maria were huddled in a corner, fear splayed across their exotic features.

Viktor stood. "Do not hit her again."

"She's my witch."

"It doesn't matter if she's your witch or not. I won't stand for you hitting her."

"You aren't in charge."

Viktor grabbed Timon by the lapels of his frock jacket and shoved him against the wall. It felt good to release all his pent-up frustration.

"Show some respect to her! She gives you a service so you can manage your human form month to month. If it wasn't for her, you'd probably be dead now."

"She is a witch, nothing more."

"She is a woman. If I ever see you strike her again, I will make you feel the same pain she does."

"Viktor, put him down. Now." Bane stepped into the room from the hallway, arms crossed, nostrils flaring in anger.

Viktor released a cringing Timon, then he turned to face Bane. "Why do you allow it?"

Bane snarled, baring his teeth. "Diana is his witch to do with as he pleases."

"It's not right."

"We'll talk later. Timon, join me. Viktor, stay here and roll weed."

Viktor said nothing, only clenching his fists to try and contain his rage. Timon and Bane walked away—most likely to collect firewood. For once, Viktor was glad he had arrived at the pack house early. He did not like these meetings, but the witches deserved respect. Perhaps that was Timon's problem. He respected nothing.

"Thank you, Viktor."

He looked at Alina. Her eyes expressed gratitude.

"You're welcome."

Alina put her arm around Diana's shoulders, and the witches disappeared down the hall.

~ * ~

Viktor got out of the bed and slid on a pair of trousers. Alina stirred, but remained sleeping. His muscles ached like never before. The more transformations he went through, the more painful they were. He looked on the table near the fireplace. No cannabis. Quietly, he closed the door behind him and went to the kitchen. Bane sat at the table, eating a plate of eggs.

"How are you, Viktor?"

"My muscles ache."

"Where's your cannabis?"

Viktor shrugged his shoulders. He wouldn't have put it past Timon to have taken his cigarettes.

Bane pointed to several rolled cannabis cigarettes. "There."

Viktor sat down.

"If you're hungry, there are more eggs."

Viktor grabbed a cigarette and lit it. "Why do you let Timon hit his witch?"

Bane's eyes narrowed. "There is nothing to forbid it. I do not approve of his treatment of her, but he must choose to exercise restraint."

"He does not."

"It is his choice."

"You are the leader. You could tell him to stop."

"I do not have say over what a wolf does with his witch."

"That's bullshit."

"It is the rules. I know Timon lacks restraint, and I'm glad you see that. It is his downfall. I don't want him to take the pack when I die. I want you to take it."

"Me? I don't want it."

"But you have restraint and compassion. You do what you have to with little complaints. Those are the marks of a leader."

"Timon will never follow me."

"He must if you succeed me. Nasguard and Gascon will have no problem following you."

"What if I refuse?"

"Then you subject the witches to Timon's cruelty."

Viktor put the cigarette down and went to make a plate of eggs. "You look healthy enough to me."

"I will die soon."

Viktor sat at the table with his plate. "I thought the healing factor kept us alive indefinitely."

"It does heal your body from transformations and keeps you young, but it can't heal you from a knife wound or a gunshot – especially if silver is used. Now, Hecuba will die shortly, and when she does, I will die as well."

"I never understood why you had such an old witch."

Bane pushed his plate aside and looked at Viktor contemplatively. "You should know my story."

"Why?"

"As my heir."

Viktor shoved a forkful of eggs into his mouth. He had never wanted to know much about this supernatural curse for fear that the more he learned, the more he would become detached from his human life. And he didn't care to be Bane's heir either, but it seemed he had little choice in the matter. Viktor did not want the witches subservient to Timon.

"I was born in 1669, and upon my father's death, I became the sixteenth Count of Chernivtsi. I married a woman I did not care for out of duty. She bore me a son and died in childbirth. My son, Andriy, was fragile. I sought out a wet nurse for him and found Hecuba."

Viktor raised an eyebrow. "Really? How can a witch live so long?"

"Listen and don't interrupt. Hecuba's wolf at the time was Kracken. Hecuba was incredibly beautiful as a young woman and Kracken took away her chalice. She was forced to bear his children."

"Is there a problem with that?"

"Such offspring are undesirable. The spawn will be wolf or witch," he paused. "It is not pleasant to raise a wolf child. We kill most – out of mercy. Hecuba bore the children. Some lived. Some died."

"Wasn't Kracken furious?"

"Yes, he was, but he had no say in what Hecuba did with the children. I met her after she had given birth and abandoned a child at the local orphanage. She tried to feed Andriy, but said his lungs were weak and that he was going to die."

"He didn't?"

"Hecuba told me there was a way to save him and took me to Kracken. Kracken said Hecuba could do magic to save him, but it would require cursing Andriy to become a werewolf when he turned eighteen. I agreed to take on the curse instead."

"You cursed yourself?"

"Yes."

"How rich!"

"I did it to save my line and it worked. Andriy lived and you are proof of it. You have his blood – my blood – in your veins. That's how I knew you would be a good choice for my heir."

Viktor shivered at the thought of his heritage, but said nothing, not wanting to further probe Bane at this time. This required reflection when he was not under the moon's influence.

"So, it's true? Hecuba's dying because of her age?"

"Yes. I killed Kracken and took Hecuba for my witch. She drinks my blood to prolong her life, but her body is too old and can't tame the magic like it once could. She will die and I will follow because I will have no other witch but her."

"It's a gruesome tale, Bane." Viktor crossed his arms to hold his fear in check. Would Alina replace Sonia? Would he be forced to take his life once Alina died? He shivered at the thought.

Bane reached out and slapped Viktor across the cheek. "Ungrateful, cub."

Viktor stood. "Me? I did not ask for this. I would rather be sharing my wife's bed instead of sharing a bed with a woman I hardly know."

"Alina does not please you?"

Viktor tucked his hands under his armpits. He did not want anything bad to happen to Alina.

"She pleases me very much."

"Good. Go back to your witch and reflect on what I told you."

Viktor walked out, careful not to say another word. Whether he liked it or not, he must accept he was Bane's chosen heir – and that could not sit well with Timon.

~ * ~

The door to the library opened and Sonia walked in with Mrs. Nocesti. Theresa put aside the book she was reading and smiled, delighted to see Sonia. She looked well with a nice red blush to her cheeks.

"Theresa!"

Theresa stood and hugged Sonia. "What brings you to the library today?"

"Knitting." Sonia held up her bag filled with her sewing accoutrements.

"Mrs. Nocesti, do you mind bringing us some tea?" asked Theresa.

"Yes, Your Grace," said the nurse. She turned around and left.

Theresa motioned to the couch and Sonia sat down next to her.

"You look well, Sonia."

"I've been having more good days and less bad ones. I've even gained weight. Dr. Stanza says the weight gain is good and it's probably what has made me feel better."

Theresa squeezed Sonia's hand. "I'm glad."

"You look a little sad."

"I suppose I am."

Sonia arched an eyebrow. “Why?”

Theresa pursed her lips, unsure of how to approach her dissatisfaction. After a moment’s thought, she took a breath to steel her courage.

“Do you miss being a nurse?”

“Yes.” Sonia put her hands in her lap. “I miss it very much. It gave me a measure of happiness going to the hospital and helping others. I hope to go back after the baby’s born.”

“Nursing is a part of you, isn’t it?”

“It is. I miss everything about it.”

“What do you tell yourself to help you get over that?”

“That I’ll go back to it, but the whole situation with Viktor is complicated and I don’t quite know how I fit into his world anymore.”

“With him being a wolf?”

“I love him very much, but he’s changing. His quick gestures make me nervous, and even though he colors his eyes, he can’t hide the fact they’re cool, almost unfeeling. He tries so hard to be the man he was when we met, so I try my best to show my support.” Sonia drew in a breath. “I feel myself growing in magic, I just wish I felt more confident in my abilities. Focusing can be challenging when I don’t feel well, and I’m not sure I’m doing it right.”

“I’m proud of you even trying to learn. It sounds complicated – like you have to have a faith in the unknown. I get the impression faith and practice is essential.” Theresa smiled. “Are you happy to be expecting?”

“I am. Are you?”

“I am, but it was so sudden. I had hoped for more time to settle in, so to speak.”

“What do you mean?”

“I wanted to do more than just give my support to the orphanage. I had hoped to tour the principality and get to know the people." Her voice drifted off in an undercurrent of insecurity.

"Is something bothering you?"

Theresa pursed her lips. Could she trust Sonia? She had to. Beatrice was gone and Theresa desperately needed a confidante.

"I've dreamed of Mihai often, but I suspect I dreamed more of him than he did of me."

"He's told me he's dreamed of you as well. You've probably shared dreams because he's a witch."

"I accept that. He's the only man I've ever thought of, but our time together has not been much – he's in Parliament or overseeing some part of the railroad construction, or studying his witchcraft. I begrudge him none of it, and I know he cares for me, but it's left me...lonely." Theresa didn't care for the loneliness one bit. She grew up in a house full of activity.

Sonia hugged Theresa then drew back, looking into Theresa's eyes. "I'm lonely, too."

"What do we do about it? I feel so frustrated, practically confined to the castle, and only allowed to visit the orphanage with an escort, but I need more."

"That's how I feel as well. I need something more."

Mrs. Nocesti opened the door, returning with the tea. She set the tea service on the table in front of them. Sonia leaned over and steeped her tea. Theresa did the same. Mrs. Nocesti settled into a nearby chair.

"Say, what book were you reading when I came in?" asked Sonia.

"Beatrice left her tarot cards behind, so I thought I'd learn how to read them."

"I'm sure it's interesting."

"Yes, it is." Theresa paused and looked away. Tarot cards were amusing, but soon she'd want another outlet to occupy her time. Maybe she should try painting. The opportunity for several maritime seascapes was just outside her window.

Sonia squeezed Theresa's hand, and Theresa could have sworn she felt Sonia's emotion – a light ripple, similar to Mihai's but weaker. "This will pass. We'll have our children and our lives will be filled with activity and purpose again."

"You sound so hopeful."

"That's all I have left."

Theresa sat back, sipping her tea. Confiding in Sonia felt good, and maybe, just maybe, she could find something to tame the restlessness that had seeped into her life.

~ * ~

Mihai's carriage stopped in front of the castle. The footman opened the door and he stepped out. It was a warm afternoon and he wanted to dedicate an hour to his tarot studies. Now, if only he could find those cards Beatrice had left behind.

"Mihai!"

He looked in the direction of the voice and saw Sonia escorted by Mrs. Nocesti.

Smiling, he went to meet her. It warmed his heart to see his sister up and active.

"Sonia! You look well." Mihai embraced her.

She placed her hands on his upper arms and returned his smile. "It's good to see you home early. Why don't you walk with me a bit?"

He crooked his arm for her.

"I'll go inside," said Mrs. Nocesti.

Mihai watched the nurse depart. Slowly, he ambled down the dirt path into the gardens.

"You look full of life today, Sister."

"I feel full of life."

"You know, I couldn't bear it if something happened to you."

"I'm doing what I'm told, but when I have good days, like today, I get restless."

"You must take care."

"Of course, but I'm used to having a fuller life than this. I don't want to wander the castle halls – I'd rather be at the hospital."

He paused, then offered a small smile. "Yes, I sense your frustration."

"Then I must be doing something if you can feel it. I'm trying to reach out to Viktor in a similar way, intuitively, emotionally, but I don't know if I'm successful."

"Continue practicing You are doing it right, I assure you."

"Good. Now I understand how busy you've been, but Theresa is starting to feel lonely."

Mihai drew in an uneasy breath. He'd suspected his wife grew restless. Was he failing her? He couldn't bear the thought.

"You need to spend more time with her." Sonia's tone of voice had a strong suggestion of reproach to it.

His jaw tightened. Lord knows, he wanted to do just that. "I'm going to take her on a picnic."

"Good. She needs it. While we were talking in the library, Papa came in. He called her Alice again."

Mihai stopped, chilled to his bones. "Again? How did she react?"

"It unsettled her. It unsettled me."

Mihai's stomach knotted with dread. "I'm sorry. I'll talk to Theresa about it."

"Good."

"I don't want to lose him," Mihai confessed.

"Neither do I, but it will happen and soon. Prepare yourself."

Mihai raked a hand through his hair. Thank God Theresa was with him. He needed her to steady him. As soon as they went back to the castle, he'd find Mr. Tybeski and have him reschedule tomorrow's appointments. The picnic couldn't wait.

"We'll get through it, Mihai. We have each other."

He patted Sonia's arm, reassuring her as well as himself. "Yes, we will." He couldn't bear it if something happened to his sister, knowing his father was unwell. She seemed to be doing better, but still she had days that would drain her strength. He'd reach out to Victoria for her thoughts.

~ * ~

Theresa rode in an open carriage. Mihai sat across from her. They were on the way to the winery for a picnic lunch and she couldn't have been more thrilled.

Mihai's smile caught her attention. "My mother would bring Sonia and me here often for a picnic lunch."

"What do you remember the most?"

"Enjoying the time with her. She'd draw sketches on paper. Sonia and I would have to guess what they were. Sometimes they were very silly."

"Should I draw some sketches for you?"

"If you want."

"I've been thinking of taking some lessons."

"You have?"

"Perhaps I can paint a canvas for your library."

"What would you draw?"

"The view of the Black Sea from our tower."

He reached across the carriage and placed his hand over hers. She felt his excitement. "I would treasure it."

The carriage stopped in front of the winery. Theresa looked up. The building was made of brick and was two stories high. The façade was rather plain and two heavy wooden doors, cracked with age, gave entrance to the facility.

Mihai stepped out of the carriage first and then helped Theresa down. He held her hand, and when both her feet were on the ground, he pressed his fingers around her waist, feeling the small, yet tight bulge of her middle.

"Our child is growing well."

"It is."

An older gentleman, around the king's age, clapped his hands as he approached. "Prince Mihai! Princess Theresa! What a pleasure."

"Theresa, this is Mr. Vaslan, our winemaker."

Mr. Vaslan bowed.

"It's nice to meet you," said Theresa.

"We're going to have a picnic lunch in the gardens. Perhaps you could give us a tour when we finish?"

"I'd be honored."

Mihai reached for the basket and blanket still in the carriage. Theresa waited patiently. Mihai gestured toward a path of smoothed dirt that led around the building. They picked a spot near the gazebo and placed the blanket on the grass. Theresa sat next to him and removed their lunch from the basket.

It was a fine day. There were only two or three clouds in the cerulean sky and the water in the Black Sea glowed from an overabundance of plankton.

Theresa was glad that Miss Pompeli had packed them sparkling water. She didn't care to drink wine anymore. It upset her stomach.

Mihai poured them two glasses of water and presented her with her glass.

"A toast."

"To what?"

"To our child."

They clinked glasses and sipped their water. It warmed Theresa to know that Mihai thought of their baby and his voice always held reverence when he spoke of it. She unwrapped her sandwich.

"Do you want me to hire an art instructor to help with your painting?"

Theresa pursed her lips. She was debating that.

"I'll look into it later. I think I'll go to the orphanage tomorrow."

"Why?"

"I wanted to spend some time with the children."

"Make sure Mr. Tybeski or Sergeant Ceseanu goes with you."

"You should come."

"I wish I could. I have to meet with the Prime Minister."

Theresa sighed. Mihai leaned over and cupped her chin with his fingers. "I see the disappointment in your eyes."

"I understand you have a principality to run."

"I think of you often when I'm not with you."

"You do?"

He dropped his hand. "Yes. What do you do to pass the time when I'm not with you?"

"I'm not much of an embroiderer. Sonia's much better than I. I am trying to knit a blanket for the baby, but I lose focus often and Sonia has to help me with the stitches."

"When it grows closer to the baby being born, we'll go into Constanta to the best shops for the baby's clothes. You don't have to knit them."

"You would do that?"

"Oh, I suppose I could send the servants, but I want to buy our child its first set of clothes. I want to be a good father, Theresa."

She smiled at the tender conviction in his voice. "You will be."

"I think of my father – how I wanted his approval, his blessing, his attention, and I grow disappointed. I never felt like I had it completely. I want my child to know I will treasure him or her. They will know I approve of them and I love them unconditionally."

"They will."

"I wish this day would last forever," he said.

"So do I."

"Tell me more - what else do you do to pass the time when I'm not there?"

"I found Beatrice's tarot cards."

He tensed. "I intend to learn about tarot."

"Well, I've been reading books to teach myself how to read them."

"Oh."

"Perhaps, since my handsome husband is a witch, he could give me some personal instruction in tarot."

"I don't know much myself. I have to research it as well."

"We can do it together."

"Why are you so eager to learn about tarot?"

"Because I think it's interesting."

He paused. "Well, then, we can do it together."

She turned to face him, cupping his cheek. "You mean it?"

"Yes."

She kissed him. His lips were warm, hinting at the honey which was on their sandwiches.

He raised his mouth from hers and gazed into her eyes. "This is perfect."

"What's wrong, Mihai? I sense anxiety in you."

"My father is thinner. His memory loss occurs more frequent."

"It's unsettling at times. Especially when he calls me Alice."

"I'm so sorry."

"I think he'll pass soon, Mihai. You have to be ready for it."

"I'll be fine."

She cocked her head. "Will you?"

He grabbed her hands and squeezed. "As long as I have you by my side, I will be fine."

Mixed feelings surged through Theresa. She understood Mihai was effectively running the country. This consumed most of his time and it tested her patience. She wanted to spend more time with him. Picnics. Touring the countryside. Visiting the orphanage. It didn't matter what they did, just that they did it together. To nurture their love, they had to find more time together.

Chapter Seventeen

The June night air clung hot and sticky to Mihai's skin, but he ignored it, focused on his task. He sat the runes on his desk, channeling his energy through his athame. "Victoria von Kracken."

The air within the runes shimmered. Victoria's face came into view. "Prince Mihai. How are you?"

"Truth be told, I'm tired, and I have to go to Cernavodå tomorrow. Herr Wursteg has requested guidance on how to proceed regarding the tunnel."

"I won't keep you. Thank you for reaching out to me. I'm inclined to believe that there is something wrong with your sister's body and not the baby."

"Why do you say that?"

"The baby is growing like it should as evidenced by your sister's weight gain. Can you obtain a sample of your sister's hair?"

"Yes, but—"

"Good. I'll dispatch Beatrice immediately to meet you at Cernavodå. It will take her a good two days' travel, so be patient if she's late." She paused. "Do you mind if I ask a delicate question?"

"No, go ahead."

"Did your mother have problems *enceinte*?"

Mihai rubbed his chin, thinking of his mother. He wished his memories were stronger. "Perhaps. I believe she miscarried a child or two. My father might have made a mention about it a couple of weeks ago."

"Try to research it. Sonia may be like her mother when it comes to childbearing. It may give us clues as to what she's going through."

Mihai nodded. "Victoria, can I ask you another question?"

"Yes, of course."

"Theresa found the tarot cards Beatrice left for me. I've been showing her the cards. Is that acceptable?"

Worry furrowed across Victoria's brow. "You risk making her aware of her own abilities."

"Is it such a bad thing?"

"There is a fine line between knowing she's a witch and practicing the craft. I'll have Beatrice advise you."

Mihai let out a breath, accepting Victoria's guidance. He didn't want to give up his tarot studies with Theresa. He enjoyed spending the time with her.

"Once I have your sister's hair, I'll examine it for clues and send you a message. Hopefully, I can advise you as to how you can keep her healthy."

"Thank you, Victoria."

"Good-bye, Prince Mihai."

"Good-bye."

Mihai leaned back in his chair and raked his hand through his hair. Why did he feel so overwhelmed?

~ * ~

The royal carriage approached the orphanage. Theresa sat across from Sonia, and Mrs. Nocesti sat next to Sonia. Sonia's health issues had diminished once she started to gain weight and now she rarely had a headache. Theresa's pregnancy was also visible, but Sonia's was more pronounced, since she was several weeks further along.

Theresa was thrilled that their babies would be close in age. It would be nice to have two children in the castle at the same time and watch them grow up together.

She had managed to occupy her time in the past month, but there were still times when the loneliness permeated deep into her soul, and when it did, the most unsettling thoughts would assuage her – including the fact that Mihai did not love her. She reminded herself of their power to feel each other's emotions, and that helped to reassure her he did love her.

To occupy her time, she had taken to painting the view from the tower overlooking the Black Sea. She enjoyed the challenge, but would worry the staff if she stayed away too long. Only Sonia knew that Theresa went to the tower to paint.

Though Theresa enjoyed painting, tarot cards fascinated her. The book she found was enlightening and complemented what Mihai told her, but what she loved the most was the feel of the cards. She sensed undercurrents of energy between her hands and the cards, guiding her selections. It was like the cards were picking her. She also enjoyed the fact that it was time spent with Mihai. He had been nervous at first, but by their third meeting, he had come to enjoy the time as well, yet she knew he was cautious – over what, she couldn't guess.

She closed her eyes briefly, recalling their last tarot lesson in the tower and how it had led to a passionate encounter. Oh, she enjoyed her tarot lessons all too much.

The carriage stopped. Mr. Tybeski jumped down from his spot next to the driver, and opened the door.

"We're here, Your Grace."

"Thank you."

He politely held her hand as she stepped out and he did the same for Sonia. Viktor had gone with Mihai who had taken a trip to inspect the hill the construction company was blasting a tunnel through.

Theresa walked past the gate and up the stairs to the orphanage. Mr. Kazha opened the door surrounded by several children.

"Princess Theresa is here!" exclaimed a young boy.

"Princess Sonia is here, too!" said another child.

A young boy about four grabbed Theresa's hand. "Will you read to us?"

"Of course, Nicolae."

A young girl, Marcela, took Sonia's hand. "Will you sit next to me, Princess Sonia?"

"I will, indeed."

The children led Theresa and Sonia into the sitting room. Theresa sat down on a sofa and the children surrounded her. Sonia sat on the sofa across from Theresa with Mrs. Nocesti standing behind her. Marcela sat to the right of Sonia.

Nicolae gave Theresa a book. His eyes grew wide.

"What's wrong, little Nicolae?"

"Are you going to have a baby like Princess Sonia?"

"Yes, I am."

"Will he be a prince?"

"Or a princess," said Theresa.

"I'm going to draw you a picture, Princess Theresa," said another child, Alin. He left the room, only to return quickly with a piece of paper and a pencil.

Theresa smiled and opened the book, preparing to read. Thank goodness for these wonderful, warm children who had opened their hearts up to her. They picked her spirits up and gave her hope when her own energy ebbed. She couldn't feel more needed and appreciated than she did with them.

~ * ~

Mihai stood between Herr Wursteg and Viktor as they watched workmen clearing the debris from the hill that had just been blasted.

"The tunnel is there. We must smooth the walls, add protective steel beams for support, and lay track," said Herr Wursteg.

"Are you on schedule?" Mihai asked.

"Yes. If I can hire ten more men, I might even finish a

few days ahead."

Mihai turned to face Viktor. "Is it affordable?"

Viktor rubbed his chin with a finger. "I'd have to go over the expenses. It may take an hour or two."

"I suggest we stay overnight in Cernavodă. This should give you the time to go over your figures."

Viktor nodded.

Mihai turned toward Herr Wursteg. "You'll have your answer after breakfast tomorrow."

"Thank you, Your Grace."

Mihai motioned toward their carriage and Viktor walked next to him.

"It might be feasible, but would it be worth it to finish only a day or two ahead of time?" asked Viktor.

Mihai gave the driver of the carriage instructions and then joined Viktor inside.

"If we can save a week or more, I want to do it."

"All right." Viktor paused. An awkward silence filled the carriage. "Sonia's doing better."

"Yes, she is."

"How's Theresa?"

"Well. It's good to have you with me, Viktor."

A slight smile graced his friend's lips. "Feels like old times, doesn't it?"

"I don't want to lose your friendship. You know that."

"I do." Again, he paused. "I should go to Mulfaltar instead of going to Constanta with you tomorrow."

"I understand. The full moon is close."

The carriage arrived at the inn where they had made arrangements to stay. Mihai and Viktor shared dinner together, then retired to separate rooms. Exhausted, Mihai went to bed, sleep quickly overcoming him.

~ * ~

A knock on the door roused Mihai from his sleep. A gas lamp burned on the other side of the room. He got up, wrapped his robe around him and opened the door.

Beatrice stood in front of him.

“Where’s my guard?” he asked.

“I blew a little dust his way. He’s fast asleep at his post.”

She walked into his room and he closed the door behind her. “He’s not hurt, is he?”

“Oh, he’ll be fine. I’ll wake him before I leave.”

Satisfied with Beatrice’s answer, Mihai glanced at the brass clock on the nightstand. “It’s two in the morning.”

Beatrice sat down in the chair next to the window. “I’m tired, I assure you.”

“I’m sorry, Beatrice. I don’t have anything to offer you.”

“I don’t intend to stay. Let’s get to business. Do you have a sample of your sister’s hair?”

Mihai went to his travel bag and removed a woman’s hairbrush, handing it to Beatrice. She placed it in her purse.

“Thank you. I would have thought you’d have a whole entourage of guards and servants traveling with you.”

“I have the coachmen, three soldiers, and Viktor. Moldavia is a principality.”

“Just curious. You may be a principality, but you are going to be a king.”

“I don’t like to travel with a lot of servants. It slows me down.”

“You said Viktor was here?”

“He’s going to his pack house tomorrow.”

“Good to know. How’s his behavior?”

“I asked to go with him on his rides, but he’s refused. I don’t want to push.”

“You can’t respect his privacy in this case. You need to know what he does.”

Mihai crossed his arms. “What do you suggest? Since becoming a wolf, he is moodier and more reserved, but he’s done nothing to have me question his honesty or loyalty.”

"He's a wolf and wolves are cunning. He will use your friendship to take advantage of you."

"I'll be mindful."

"Now, what's this about you showing Theresa tarot?"

"She found your deck and decided she wanted to learn."

Disapproval danced in Beatrice's eyes. "I wish you would have been more careful. How skilled is she? Has she tried any readings?"

"No. She knows the major and minor arcana, and the Celtic Cross spread."

Beatrice nibbled her lower lip. "Damn, Mihai, when she's ready to read put her off. Do not let her read herself."

"Why not herself?"

"If she reads herself, our father is unsure if that will constitute as practicing. He doesn't want to chance it until his dreams give him clarification. Right now, it's safer for her if she's not made aware of her heritage. Where are the cards now?"

"I have them."

Relief washed over her face. "Good. Keep a tight rein on those cards."

"I will." He didn't like the idea of hiding Theresa's heritage from her, but if her family thought it was for her own safety, he would comply with it. There was nothing he wanted to do more than to tell her she was a witch like him.

~ * ~

Viktor ran next to Gascon under the light of the full moon. Their hunger sated, they were on their way to the pack house, Bane leading the way.

A raven squawked and circled overhead.

Nasguard stopped and howled. The raven answered him.

Bane paused.

"Why are we stopping?" Viktor projected his thoughts to Gascon.

"You'll see."

The raven flew lower, gracefully transforming into a woman who wore all black. The woman landed next to Nasguard, cupping his wolfen face in her hands.

Viktor looked at Gascon. *"What is she?"*

"A vampire. She's a royal vampire from the town of Sinisteri, high up in the Carpathian mountains."

Timon snarled, drawing Viktor's attention. Jealousy flared in his amber-gold eyes.

Bane trotted up to Timon and stood beside him.

Viktor turned to face Gascon. *"I don't understand. Are Nasguard and the vampire lovers?"*

"Yes. Nasguard's body is not like ours. His is denser, so he's not thin like us. Bane calls Nasguard's body a rare occurrence. Nasguard can control his body better than us. When the moon is about an hour from the horizon, he can become human and be intimate with her."

"Why doesn't she become a wolf if she can change shapes?"

"There's no pleasure in it. Certainly, you'd rather be with Alina in your human form?"

"You're right. The vampire won't harm us?"

"No."

"Timon doesn't like it."

"He wants her, considering he's Bane's first made, but she won't have him. Only Nasguard can please her."

"Gascon, Viktor, let's go." Bane's voice was loud and clear in their heads.

The vampire changed into a raven again and followed close to Nasguard. The pack house came into view. As they approached, Hecuba, opened the door, her eyes drooping. Timon turned unexpectedly and pounced at the raven, fangs extended. He was going to bite her!

Viktor sprang, thinking only to protect the vampire. He hit Timon in his right flank, causing him to miss the bird.

They struck the ground hard, Timon landing at an awkward angle on his front paw.

"Enough!" Bane's voice rang loud in his head. *"Timon you will stay outside until sunrise."*

The raven once again transformed into a woman and this time approached Viktor, cupping his face in her warm hands.

"I am Delilah. I thank you for your protection, but it is not needed. I will not let the wolf you call Timon hurt me."

"But why would he try?"

"He hopes to succeed in order to claim me, but I would never let it happen. I want only Nasguard."

Viktor nodded. Delilah withdrew her hands, leaving him chilled.

The wolves pranced into the house. Viktor glanced behind him. The hatred in Timon's eyes couldn't be mistaken as anything else than a warning. No matter. Viktor held his head up high, proud that he'd protected the vampire.

Chapter Eighteen

Theresa looked out the window. The stars sparkled like precious jewels without the moon in the late June sky. An odd chill ran down her spine, and she tightened the robe around her. Where the chill came from, she didn't know, but she thought it was strange for such a humid night.

The door opened. She turned around. Mihai closed the door behind him, and flashed her a smile full of boyish affection.

"Thank you for waiting," he said.

"You promised me a tarot lesson."

He produced the deck from his vest's pocket and then took the vest off, wearing only a simple, white linen shirt.

"So I did."

Theresa crossed the distance between them, taking the deck from his hand. He reached out and grabbed her wrist. "Not so fast. Tell me about the fool."

She teased her lower lip with her teeth. "Um...let's see...the fool is full of hope, ready for a new adventure. He possesses freedom to explore without preconceived notions. He's an idealist."

Mihai pulled her against him, pressing her against the length of his body, his eyes probing her soul. Her core heated.

"What if the fool is reversed?" he asked.

"The path he's on is fraught with danger. There might be delays or trouble."

"Very good." Mihai wrapped an arm around her waist and placed a hand on her growing round belly. "Why don't you pick a card now?"

She dropped the deck and placed her hands on his

shirt, curling her fingers into the fabric. "I don't want to talk about the fool or any other card."

"You don't?"

"Kiss me."

The touch of his lips on hers was delicious, warm and full of desire. He continued, searing a path down her neck.

She closed her eyes and groaned.

He recaptured her lips, more demanding this time. Heat pulsed through her. Mihai broke the kiss, took her hand, and guided her to the bed. They sat down facing each other.

"It seems we get less and less studying done," he said.

She swept her gaze over his face. "I missed you today."

He placed a finger on her chin. "I missed you, too."

"My painting is almost finished."

"I can't wait to see it."

"de Vilegar I'm not, but I am rather pleased with it."

"You are a tease."

She wrapped her arms around his neck. "Oh, really?"

He cupped her cheek, drawing her close, his lips tempting hers. "I want you."

She trailed her hands over his shoulders to the front of his shirt and began to unfasten the buttons, delighted by the intense smoldering desire in his eyes. Her body ached for his touch.

They both startled at the abrupt and heavy knock on the door.

"Ignore it," he said.

Theresa slid her hands under his unbuttoned shirt, running them over his hard chest.

The knock grew louder. "Prince Mihai."

Mihai gently grabbed her wrists, stilling her actions. "It's Mr. Tybeski. It might be important. The air hasn't felt right all evening."

Theresa pulled away, having sensed the same thing.

How could that be? She thought she could sense Mihai's emotions because he was a witch and she was his lover. How could she sense more?

Mihai stood up, buttoned his shirt, and went to the door and opened it.

Mr. Tybeski appeared serious. "Your Grace, Dr. Stanza is with your father. He wants you to come quickly."

Theresa stepped next to her husband. Her shoulders tensed.

"Is my father dying?"

Mr. Tybeski stared at the floor, then back up. "Dr. Stanza believes so."

Mihai lifted his chin. "Send for my sister and her husband."

Mr. Tybeski nodded and trotted down the hall. Theresa reached for Mihai's hand.

"I'm here." This would not be an easy moment for Mihai or her, but Theresa was determined to show her bravery and strength to her husband.

"Thank God."

~ * ~

Mihai took his wife's hand and squeezed it tightly, drawing strength from the gesture, as he led them down the hall to his father's apartments. Fear, worry, and apprehension coursed through his limbs. He knew this day would eventually come, but he didn't feel prepared. Thank God Theresa was with him. She wouldn't leave him to face such a hard moment alone.

He paused in front of his father's door. Theresa placed a hand on his elbow.

"Go in before it's too late," she said.

Mihai drew in a deep breath, summoning his courage, and put his hand on the knob. It was cold, like the unusual wind he'd felt before. He pushed the door open and entered. His father's death didn't just mean he was losing a parent. Moldavia was losing a king and gaining another. He had to be strong.

Dr. Stanza appeared tired and haggard, holding his father's trembling hand. The king's eyes were yellow, sunken, and his face gaunt. Mihai walked to the end of the bed, Theresa next to him.

"The Prince is here," said Dr. Stanza.

"Father!" Sonia cried.

Mihai turned around. Sonia stood at the door, Viktor's hands on her shoulders. Her eyes were red and she clutched a handkerchief.

"Sonia, come." Mihai gestured toward her to join him. Viktor stood next to her, stoic and silent, supporting her.

"My children, come closer. I can barely see you." A mere whisper had now replaced his father's strong voice.

Mihai took his sister's hand and guided her to Dr. Stanza. She tried to stifle her sobs. His father's heavy breathing filled the room.

Dr. Stanza withdrew his hand, allowing Mihai to place his hand over his father's. "I am here, Father."

"Sonia?"

She placed her hand over Mihai's. "I'm here, too."

"Mihai, be good to Moldavia. Sonia, watch out for your brother. Help him."

"I will."

"And son, talk to Mircea. Between the two of you, I believe you can unite our nation. Bring Wallachia and Transylvania to your talks. Romania will be stronger as one country and not a cluster of small ones."

"I will, Father." Mihai's stomach grew heavy. He drew in another deep breath to stifle a growing sob.

"Theresa?"

"Yes, Father?"

"Support my son in all he does. Be a good mother to his children."

"I will."

"Viktor?"

Viktor stepped forward, placing an arm around Sonia's shoulders.

"Keep my daughter safe from harm. I'm trusting you. You are her protector now."

"Yes, Your Majesty."

"Sonia, Theresa, be good to your children. I die happy knowing the Sigmaringens will continue."

"Oh, Father..." A tremor wracked Sonia's voice. Viktor tightened his arms around her.

Theresa curved her fingers around Mihai's forearm and squeezed. Mihai sensed her strength ebbing, her sadness growing.

"Mihai, Sonia, I do...love you...both..."

"Father—"

"Alice, sweet Alice..."

His father's gaze drifted toward the window. His chest stopped rising. Dr. Stanza closed the king's eyes.

The cool chill had dissipated.

Sonia wrapped her arms around Mihai's waist. "He's gone...gone..."

Mihai hugged her, running his hands over her hair, trying to comfort her. He looked over Sonia's head, finding Viktor's gaze. While his eyes were expressionless, sadness and concern lined his face.

"Let me stay with her tonight," said Viktor. "She needs me."

Mihai nodded his assent. He sensed no emotional turmoil from Viktor, only concern for Sonia's well being. Mihai trusted Viktor in this moment. He may be moodier and quick to make decisions, fast with his physical actions, but Sonia should be with her husband tonight.

Mihai looked at Theresa. Her eyes were moist. This wasn't easy for her, either. He reached over and plucked a handkerchief off Dr. Stanza's table, presenting it to her. She thanked him with her expression.

Mihai brought his hand up to his chin, unable to hold back his memories anymore: hiding under his father's desk when he was four, sitting next to Sonia on the second story balcony when he was eight, watching his parents dance together at a formal ball, his father's proud expression when he had seen him off at the Bucharest train station when Mihai went to London. Mihai's heart was raw and aching from the loss of his father.

"King Mihai, I need your guidance," said Dr. Stanza.

Mihai stiffened his back and glanced at Viktor. "Can you take Sonia to her room and have Mr. Tybeski come in?"

Viktor nodded, holding Sonia close. He left the room and Mr. Tybeski joined them.

"Your Majesty?"

It was silent for an awkward moment. Everyone looked at Mihai. Kingship was now upon him.

"Dr. Stanza, prepare my father's body to lie in state. Mr. Tybeski, I need you to begin the funeral preparations that we discussed."

"Yes, Your Majesty."

"The traditional mourning period is two weeks in Moldavia." Mihai's voice started to shake and he stiffened again as his composure started to wane. "In order to ensure a smooth transition, I want the coronation..." He couldn't continue. He hung his head and cupped his face.

Theresa embraced him. "Mihai, we can make arrangements for the coronation later."

He lifted his chin, his eyes misting. "Mr. Tybeski, I want the coronation to be held as soon as the two weeks of mourning are over."

"Yes, Your Majesty."

Mihai took a deep breath, calming his nerves. The pain of losing his father ran deep, ripping through his bones. He looked into Theresa's eyes. She was sad, but her strength pulsed over him, calming him more.

"Mr. Tybeski, one more thing."

"Yes?"

"I will go to Parliament at nine tomorrow to announce my father's passing. I want you to personally tell the Prime Minister, Mr. Niceneavu, and have him hold his confidences until tomorrow. See to it he assembles both houses."

Mr. Tybeski nodded.

"The queen and I are not to be interrupted for any reason tonight. I'll see you both for breakfast at seven. All of us have a busy day tomorrow."

"Yes, Your Majesty," Tybeski and Stanza said together.

"Theresa?" Mihai held out his hand. She took it and they left the room. It was silent as they made their way back to their apartments. Once alone, he walked to the window and looked out into the night sky. The stars shined brightly overhead due to the new moon. The waves in the Black Sea sparkled from the plankton. He found the scene soothing. His muscles relaxed a bit.

Theresa wrapped her arms around his chest and he felt the growing child in her womb next to him. It gave him comfort, and he wiped a small tear away from the corner of his eye. Gently, he placed his hands over hers.

"Thank you," he said.

"You're welcome."

It grew silent again.

Theresa drew in a breath. "I sense a torrent of emotion flooding through you – anxiety, uneasiness, fear – confusion."

"I didn't want to lose my father like this."

"I'm sorry." She paused. "I lost my mother when I was four. I remember an ache and missing her, but nothing like what I sense in you right now."

"I'm sorry, Theresa. How young to lose your mother."

"I wish I had known her like Victoria and Edward had."

"How did your father react?"

"He was devastated and vowed never to remarry."

"I like your father, Theresa. Your family is alive and vibrant. I want a family like that."

"So do I."

He closed his eyes, thinking of their family – healthy boys and little girls who had Theresa's fair hair, and it calmed him further. He turned around and took her hand, leading her to the bed. They sat down and faced each other.

"Each day gets more complicated, and now I'm king. I'm grateful you're here with me."

She ran a finger tenderly over his chin. "You don't make it easy for me."

He gripped her waist, guiding her down so they lay on the bed, Theresa safe in his arms.

"I adored my mother. Losing her was hard," said Mihai.

"It was a carriage accident, wasn't it?"

"That's what my father told others, but it was more. My mother was a witch who had run away from her duties. An old witch named Hecuba found her and killed her."

"That's awful!"

"My mother did not practice in front of Sonia or I, and that incident made me shun what I was."

"Why did you change your mind about embracing your witch heritage?"

"Because I can't deny what I am anymore. I am a witch like my mother, and I must learn to be a good one to help Viktor – and Sonia." A twinge of guilt twisted like a knot in the back of his neck. Mihai hated denying Theresa knowledge of her heritage.

"I will support you in everything you do."

"Thank you. You steady me. You give me...hope.

Determination. I will unite Romania, and God willing, our children will benefit."

"I sense a little of hope's light in you. Focus on that. Let it grow and give you strength. I don't want the sadness that's deep inside to overwhelm you."

He kissed her temple. "I'm sorry you're lonely. When I finish the railroad, nothing ever again will take my attention from you or our family. I promise to be the best husband and father I can be."

Theresa said nothing. She wrapped her arms around him and he felt her strength.

~ * ~

Sensing Sonia's emotions was different from sensing Alina's in that he had to really focus and concentrate, but he didn't need to sense her emotion to know his wife's heart ached from losing her father. He gently closed the door to her room behind them and led her to the bed. Sonia's eyes were red, but she had stopped crying. He sat down beside her and took her hand in his, mindful to be gentle in his actions.

"I'm sorry about your father."

"He liked you."

"He did. I don't really know why."

"He knew you made me happy."

"Your father was very proud of you, Sonia. I suspect he was decent in many things." Viktor rubbed his thumb over her knuckles.

She squeezed his hand and looked into his eyes. "Will you stay with me tonight?"

Sonia had never made such a request of him since he had been changed. He knew she loved him, but that love had been tempered by a healthy understanding of what he was and what he was capable of. She needed him now and nothing would please him more than to stay with her tonight – especially at her invitation.

He cupped her cheek, looking at her. "I will. I'll miss him, too."

"Hold me."

He put his arm around her, but she moved so she lay on her side. Viktor felt the bulge of their child between them.

"Is it uncomfortable to be on your back?"

"Yes. The baby is moving."

"It is?" His heart tripped at the thought. He'd hardly touched their child for fear of panicking his wife.

She took his hand and placed it over her womb. Fluttering movement tickled his palm. A wide smile grew across his lips. The baby was alive, wonderfully alive.

"It feels so healthy."

"Amazing, isn't it? Especially considering how sick I've been."

He closed his eyes and reached out with his senses, trying to feel her. Happiness and sadness warred within her.

"I sense happiness in you. Why?" he asked.

"Because you're here with me."

He stifled a curse. He loved *Sonia*. She was clever and kind with an open mind and heart – and despite what had happened to him, he did see the love she bore him in her eyes. But despite all this, he couldn't be intimate with her – out of fear of hurting her or their child.

He still cared for Sonia, loved her, but as she was now, she could never physically please him like Alina, and that revelation rocked him to the core of his being. What he had with Alina was primal, raw, yet completely satisfying to his body. He withdrew his hand, guilt washing over him.

"Is something wrong?"

"No, I just was thinking of how much we have in common."

"Why do I sense guilt?"

"It's nothing, Sonia. I can deal with it."

"Even though you are," she paused and closed her eyes briefly, "a wolf, I couldn't bear to lose you."

"Really?" A part of him was delighted to learn Sonia couldn't stand to lose him. They still held an emotional connection and that made him feel very human in this moment. Another part, however, realized it might be quite a long time before there could be a physical connection between them again and until then, he would have to continue seeing Alina. That felt like an arrow through his heart.

"You are my child's father, and every child deserves to have their father in their life."

"Like you had yours?"

"He wasn't perfect, but he tried hard to make us all happy. My father was always proud of me and my nursing. I will miss him."

She placed a hand over her eyes as tears slid down her cheeks.

Viktor reached into a pocket and withdrew a fresh handkerchief, giving it to her. He loved this woman. She was having his baby and the pregnancy had been hard on her physically, draining her strength and resolve, but he realized now a part of his soul no longer belonged to her. Alina owned it. And that scared him. He rested his chin next to her temple and closed his eyes, fighting back his own tears.

Chapter Nineteen

July
St. Mikhail's Church

Mihai surveyed the church as he sat on his throne to the rear and left of the altar. Theresa sat beside him in a regal red satin gown. The ermine and a layer of crinolines were removed to keep her comfortable during the coronation ceremony. A silver tiara graced with diamonds and sapphires adorned her brow. Theresa's tiara symbolized her status as the crown princess.

The Patriarch of Constantinople and the head of the Orthodox Faith walked around the altar, swinging a canter of frankincense. The sweet aroma filled the church.

In the front, Sonia sat next to Aaron Tybeski. Victoria and Beatrice von Kracken sat on the other side of Sonia. Mr. Tybeski was assigned as her escort since the full moon would occur tonight. It was not the best time for his coronation, but Mihai couldn't put it off, either. He flexed his fingers, releasing some of his tension. He wanted Viktor at the ceremony, but the demands of the principality dictated the coronation be carried out now. Why did Mihai feel like he'd lost a little part of his best friend forever? It pained Mihai to see Viktor leave every month. When he returned, Viktor appeared thinner and exhausted. They rarely laughed like they did in London.

He glanced at his sister. Her face was an odd mix of pride and sadness. She'd also lost a part of Viktor. How her heart must ache.

The Patriarch stopped in front of the altar and gave the canter to Father Gregori who assisted him.

"Prince Mihai, come forward."

This was the moment he feared, yet embraced. Mihai wore a formal military-styled uniform, his trousers tucked into his knee-high boots. On the jacket, the medals symbolizing his status as the crown prince flashed in the dim light. A dark royal blue cape draped over his shoulders, complementing the uniform.

Mihai walked over to the Patriarch and knelt, taking a lower step in front of the priest. This symbolized the Patriarch's authority as a representative of God.

"Prostrate yourself. Show your humility to God."

He did as he was instructed. The position was uncomfortable as he faced the wooden floor. The Patriarch prayed over him.

"Christ told the crowd: Render therefore unto Cesar the things which are Cesar's; and unto God the things that are God's." The Patriarch paused. "Prince Mihai, you are charged to render unto the people of Moldavia the things that are theirs - keep them safe, provide for their well being, and guide them as a nation for the better."

A choir of monks chanted 'amen.' After several long minutes in the uncomfortable position, the Patriarch spoke again.

"Prince Mihai, kneel."

Mihai knelt on both of his knees. The elder priest put a crown of gold on Mihai's head. "Oh, God, bless we beseech thee this crown, and so sanctify your servant, Mihai, upon whose head this day thou dost place it for a sign of royal majesty, that he may be filled by Your abundant grace with all princely virtues: through the King eternal, Jesus Christ, our Lord."

He stood and turned to face the church. He would be a leader like his father, building infrastructure. He would unite Romania as a nation and dedicate his life to his people.

"I hereby present to the people of Moldavia gathered here, your undoubted King: Mihai I, your king: wherefore all you who are come this day to do your homage and service. King Mihai, are you willing to do the same?"

"Yes, I am."

The Patriarch stepped off the top step to a lower one, so Mihai was now above him, and presented Mihai with his scepter and orb.

"God save King Mihai!" cried the crowd in the church.

Mihai turned and faced the Patriarch. The elder priest put his thumb in a cup of thick myrrh and blessed Mihai, by making the Sign of the Orthodox Cross on his forehead.

"You may now crown your Queen."

Father Gregori stepped up and took the scepter and orb from Mihai. The Patriarch handed Mihai a gold crown, smaller in size, adorned in rubies and diamonds. Mihai approached Theresa. She stood. Another priest assisting with the ceremony removed her tiara. Mihai held the crown over his wife's head.

"Theresa, with this crown, I make you Queen of Moldavia, to rule by my side, and to share your guidance and wisdom with me as given to you by God."

He placed the crown on her head, thankful it was her he was crowning, and not Alexandra. He winced at the thought and tried to push it aside, focusing on his happiness at crowning Theresa.

"I, Theresa, Queen of Moldavia, do become your counselor, guide, and faithful servant. Faith and truth I will bear onto you, to live and die, against all manner of peoples, so help me God."

He took her hand and they looked out onto the crowd in the church. His heart filled with pride as the roar of acceptance of him, as king, filled the air.

~ * ~

After the coronation ceremony, Mihai returned to Delfin

Castle with his family and the von Krackens. Miss Pompeli served a feast. After the evening meal, Mihai escorted the women to the library.

"Theresa, ladies, if you don't mind, I'll retire to my study and you can visit with each other."

Theresa smiled at him. "That would be fine."

"Mihai..." Sonia's voice had a light tremor to it and she lunged out, grabbing Beatrice's arm. Mihai rushed forward and took Sonia's other arm. "What's wrong?"

She blinked over and over. "I can't see you."

Mihai stiffened. His sister had excellent vision. What could be wrong with her?

"Help her to the sofa. Beatrice, go get some willow bark," said Victoria.

Beatrice departed and Theresa held Sonia's hand as Mihai guided her to the sofa. They sat down and Mihai held his sister close. Her breathing was deep. She cupped his cheeks and looked into his face. Her pupils consumed most of the irises, and as he watched, they slowly began to shrink to normal. Fear danced across her face.

"I can see you now. Oh, thank God, I can see!"

Victoria gently placed her hand on Sonia's shoulder. "Do you have a headache?"

"I feel one coming on."

Beatrice returned carrying a tray of tea. Victoria glanced at Beatrice. The gesture was very subtle, but Beatrice gave her sister a slight nod of the head. Satisfied with that, Victoria presented Sonia with the tea.

"Drink as much as you can. The willow bark will lessen the pain."

Sonia shared a slight, knowing smile with Beatrice and brought the cup to her lips.

"How long were you unable to see?" asked Mihai.

"A minute or two, no more." Sonia took another long sip of her drink.

Worry permeated his bones. Sonia had always been healthy and vital. What was happening to her and how could he stop it? She'd never lost her sight before. Was his sister dying? The thought rocked him.

Sonia finished her tea and handed her cup to Theresa. Worry also laced the lines of her face. Sonia cocked her head back and rested it against the sofa. Mihai squeezed his sister's hand. She relaxed, placed her head against Mihai's shoulder, and fell asleep.

"Will she be all right?" asked Theresa. "She's always had headaches."

Victoria gave her a reassuring smile. "She'll be fine tonight. The willow bark will ease the pain."

Theresa nodded, accepting Victoria's words.

"King Mihai—"

"Victoria, call me 'Mihai' when it's just us. You are family."

She smiled. "Should I send for a servant to carry your sister to her room?"

"No, I'll do it." He gathered Sonia into his arms.

"Beatrice, stay here with Theresa. We'll be back shortly," said Victoria.

"Oh, Beatrice, can you send for Mrs. Nocesti. I'd like her to attend Sonia while she sleeps," said Mihai.

Beatrice nodded. Theresa's expression betrayed concern. Mihai gave her a look of reassurance and left, Victoria at his side. They arrived at Sonia's room and Mihai placed his sister on the bed, holding her hand. Viktor should be here! A twinge of anger lanced through his chest. Viktor had missed both his coronation and his wedding. Mihai tried to tell himself that Viktor cared, and he was only doing what he had to, but a little part of his mind was not convinced. Every month it seemed Viktor lost a little piece of his soul to those wolves.

Mrs. Nocesti entered the room.

"What happened, Your Majesty?"

"Sonia lost vision for a bit. We gave her some willow bark. Can you watch over her?"

"Yes, Your Majesty."

Mihai placed a kiss on his sister's temple and departed, Victoria at his side.

"Let's go to your study. We need to talk."

Mihai gestured toward the opposite hall. When they got to the study, Mihai closed the door and locked it so they wouldn't be disturbed.

Victoria leaned against his desk. "I'm deeply worried for your sister."

Mihai crossed his arms and stood next to the sofa. "What else did Beatrice put in that drink?"

"A smidgen of mugthorn root to help her fall asleep. She also gave her a concentrated dose of willow bark to help with the headache. Sonia should effectively sleep it off."

Mugthorn had non-addictive properties. Mihai gave a small sigh of relief. "What's wrong with my sister?"

"I do have a theory. Was this loss of vision her first?"

"Yes."

"I examined the hair sample you gave Beatrice."

"What did you find?"

"I believe the baby is growing as it should, but your sister's body has high levels of proteins – too high."

"Protein? I learned about that in England. It is a biological component used to make up our bodies. Antoine Foureroy discovered it."

"Very good. I also read the current journals. Proteins act as building blocks, specifically, for our muscles, but they have other tasks as well. It's amazing how science complements our magic."

"What does this mean for Sonia? Why does she have high proteins in her body?"

"I'm not quite sure, but I was able to induce a trance

and look at your sister's internal body from the hair sample. You know a child grows in a woman's womb?"

"Yes."

"There is a protective barrier between the womb and your sister's body. It is weak and needs reinforcement. I believe proteins from the baby are entering your sister's body over the weak barrier and are causing Sonia's symptoms."

"What can we do?" Fear knotted inside him.

"We must modify her diet. I'll leave you a list of foods which will help your sister's body strengthen this barrier, but I believe it to be very weak. It will take a strict regime. I want her to eat more fish, vegetables, fruits, nuts, and milk. No coffee, and only willow bark tea for headaches. I will leave you with a high concentrate of willow bark pills for her to take."

"All right."

"When is your sister due?"

"October, I believe."

"Were you able to research any of your mother's pregnancies?"

"I spoke to Dr. Stanza. I thought she miscarried twice, but he confirmed three times - all in the fourth month. He said it was around the time of 'the quickening.'"

Victoria pursed her lips. "When the baby movements can be felt by the mother. The fact Sonia is past that is encouraging. Did he note anything about your mother's live births – you and your sister?"

"We came quick. He said my mother lost a lot of blood which concerned him, but he had been able to stop it before it became life threatening."

"Did he report headaches? Lack of weight gain? Vision loss?"

"Some headaches," Mihai paused. "She was often tired. He reported brain fog – my mother would grow confused at times. She slept often."

Victoria rubbed her chin with her hand. "I see similarities, which explains much. Now, if Sonia shows any signs of distress, put her on bed rest immediately and expect the child to come early. Her body will only get weaker as the child grows. She must stay true to the diet, and even then, I don't know how much it will help her."

Mihai frowned, frustrated. "Sonia's always been an active woman. It's heartbreaking to see her so inactive. It's hard for her to endure."

"She must. God forbid if she or the child die in birth. The wolf in her house would turn feral."

"The wolf has a name - Viktor - and he has managed just fine so far." Mihai's jaw tensed, defensive. Viktor may be a wolf and while he struggled with his moods, he would be here with Sonia if he could.

Her eyes lightly narrowed. "Viktor feels and senses emotions as you do. If he loses his wife or child, or both, I have no doubt his emotions will turn dark, and if they do, then Theresa or even Alina might be in danger."

"Alina? Count Brancoveanu's daughter?"

"Yes, she is his witch by our request. We must keep her safe as well."

"She's the one who helps him during his time away, correct?"

"Yes. The Branconveanus are loyal to us, but we do not want to see Alina harmed. She's sacrificed much in helping us with this matter."

Mihai let out a deep breath, cupping his chin with his fingers. Viktor was moody, but he'd never been violent, even in England. Viktor possessed a gentle soul. The thought of killing or even harming someone was abhorrent to him. But losing one's wife might be enough to drive a man insane. He didn't want to think of losing Theresa to birth. He would go mad.

"You must prepare just in case. Can you do a simple defensive spell?"

"No."

"I'll give Beatrice leave to stay a week, but no longer. She'll teach you some simple defensive and offensive spells. Practice them as often as you can and away from Theresa. If Sonia is healthy, include her in your practices. Continue to contact us through the runes."

"I will."

"We better find Theresa."

Mihai unlocked the door and escorted Victoria back to the library. He'd learned much since committing to the study of witchcraft. He felt comfortable with his knowledge of roots, and growing familiarity with the tarot cards. He could channel energy through objects, but not with force, and he could sense Theresa's moods, as well as Viktor's. Viktor had grown more shadowed, but Mihai felt Viktor's humanity guided his decisions. Viktor was still good.

They arrived at the library, but Beatrice was alone.

"Theresa's retired to her apartments."

"I'll join her. Good night, ladies."

"Good night, Mihai," they replied.

Mihai ascended the stairs and grabbed his nightclothes. Then he used the door that joined their suites and went into her apartment. Theresa was in bed, reading a book. A gas lamp burned on the nightstand.

"How's Sonia?" She put the book down.

"Sleeping. Victoria's suggested I modify her diet."

"Victoria's very good at healing. I think she would have made a good doctor if she wasn't a woman."

"I agree." Mihai undressed and put on his nightclothes.

"How does it feel to be a crowned king?"

He slid under the covers. Theresa dimmed the gas lamp and he drew her close.

"I feel like so many people are looking up to me to do the

right thing. I can't fail them."

"You won't." Soft reassurance ran through her voice.

"I'll send Mr. Tybeski to obtain a progress report from Herr Wursteg tomorrow. I don't want to leave right away. When Viktor returns, I'm going to send him to Polesti to meet with King Mircea of Carpathia. I want to arrange a meeting of the nobles for next month."

"Must you work on unification so soon?"

"I want to start talks before you have the baby. I want the Romanian nobles to know I'm serious."

"You need to relax."

He kissed her temple. "I won't, really, not until Sonia has her baby – and you have ours."

"Well, I guess I could paint another canvas."

"You finished?"

"Yes. I'll show it to you tomorrow."

He placed his hand over her heart. "I sense frustration coming from you."

"Perhaps. I don't just want to paint or read books. I want to explore and discover this land. I want to visit the children at the orphanage more than I do. I want to sponsor a school or university. I want to ride a horse again, and..."

"Our baby will come soon, and when it does, I'll see to it you can do all that and more."

"Thank you."

He held her close and gently stroked her soft hair. His wife needed to find something that would interest her, keep her occupied and give her purpose. He couldn't fault her for that. He hoped that soon she would find what she was looking for.

~ * ~

A knock on the door roused Viktor. Alina rubbed her eyes as she sat up in the bed. Viktor sensed urgency coming from the woman at the door.

"Who is it?" asked Alina.

The door opened just enough so the person could be heard. "Alina, it's Maria. Hecuba and Diana need us. Hurry."

Alina slid the covers off her body and reached for her dress. Viktor did the same, sliding a pair of trousers over his thin hips.

"Something is wrong," said Viktor.

"I feel it, too. Help me with the stays of my dress."

Viktor slipped behind Alina, cinched up the stays and tied them. Alina shook out her hair and put it in a quick ponytail. She smelled wonderful – like honeysuckle. It was a scent that was quickly becoming one of his favorites.

Alina looked quite tussled from their lovemaking. He paused. This was the first time he thought of their liaisons as lovemaking. It unnerved him.

"Viktor, hurry."

He cinched up the last tie. Alina splashed water on her face and opened the door. Viktor followed behind, determined to ensure no harm came to his witch.

Loud cries filled with agony emanated from Nasguard's room. Upon entering, Delilah lay on the floor, writhing in pain. Her face was pale and her eyes were bloodshot. Hecuba knelt beside her, examining her.

"Delilah's been poisoned," said Alina.

Timon stood next to the window. The shades were drawn, keeping the growing sunlight out. A sneer tipped his thin lips and his beady eyes danced with delight.

"It's garlic poisoning," said Hecuba.

Bane crossed his arms, standing over the older witch. "Can you help her?"

"Use candles only. Keep the room dark. Diana, I need a sapphire." Hecuba's voice was thin and brittle.

Diana stood up and raced out of the door.

Viktor put a hand on Alina's shoulder and looked at

Bane. "Will garlic kill her?"

"Yes. It's poison to her."

"How did she get it?" asked Viktor.

Nasguard stepped forward, swallowing hard. "She drank from the chalice. There had to have been garlic in it."

"By Dalca! Who would put garlic in a chalice?" demanded Bane.

Viktor looked at Timon. So did Nasguard. Both knew how he wanted Delilah for himself. Nasguard lunged at Timon and grabbed him by the throat, his nostrils flaring with anger. "Admit it – you poisoned her!"

Timon gasped for breath. "Yes."

"Put him down, Nasguard. We'll deal with him later." Bane fisted his hands. "Right now the witches must save the vampire."

Diana rushed in holding a sapphire pendant. Hecuba grabbed the pendant in her dry, fragile hands and placed it over the vampire's neck.

"Come forth garlic...into...the stone..."

Hecuba could barely get the last words out. The stone slipped out from her hands and fell onto the floor.

The old witch looked at Diana. "Help me. The garlic is deep."

Diana grabbed the stone and held it over the vampire's neck. Hecuba put her hand over Diana's.

"Come forth garlic into the stone." Both Diana and Hecuba said the words. Diana's voice was strong and healthy. Hecuba's was raspy and weak.

The old witch collapsed. Diana kept her focus on the stone, but grimaced, her neck muscles straining.

"Hecuba!" Bane thrust the candle at Viktor. He took Hecuba into his arms and placed her on the bed.

"Maria! Alina! Come!" cried Diana.

Alina and Maria rushed forward and joined Diana in the chant. Delilah's pale skin faded to a healthy pink. Diana stood up, clutching the sapphire. She stumbled. The stone fell to the floor, no longer blue but brown. Gascon lunged out and caught Diana. He placed an arm under her knees and cradled her in his arms.

"Is she all right?" asked Viktor.

"She is drained. Some of the poison seeped into her from the stone. Alina and I will care for her," said Maria.

"No. One of you care for Diana, the other attend to Hecuba," said Bane.

Maria and Alina exchanged awkward glances.

"I'll care for Hecuba," said Maria. She looked at Nasguard. "Delilah needs rest. Keep the curtains drawn. She's gone into the hibernation state that daylight brings her kind."

"How is she?" asked Nasguard.

"She'll live, but it took much effort on our part and the vampire is weak."

Relief washed across Nasguard's face. "Thank you. All of you."

Alina stepped up next to Gascon and looked at Nasguard. "Put the vampire under the bed to keep any accidental light from falling on her. I must go to the other room with Diana and Gascon."

Viktor helped Nasguard slide Delilah under the bed. Timon stood in the corner, arms crossed. Viktor shared a knowing glance with Nasguard. Timon had done this – out of anger or spite, or jealousy, perhaps all three, but they both knew Bane had to punish him now or Timon would continue his destructive behavior.

~ * ~

Viktor walked into Diana's room. Alina sat next to the bed drinking some tea. The sun was getting ready to set. Diana leaned her back against the headboard.

"How are you?" he asked.

Alina handed Diana a cup.

"I'm well. How is Hecuba?" asked Diana.

"Her recovery is slow. She'll need to stay here a few more days."

"The moon will be waning tonight. You wolves won't transform, but you should stay here the extra night," said Diana.

Viktor nodded. "Is Hecuba's time to die close?"

"Yes," said Diana. "You must take over, Viktor. Timon is ruthless."

Viktor straightened his spine. He hated the thought, but realized Timon would make everyone's life hell. He had to seriously consider it. He didn't want the witches and other wolves to suffer any more than they did already. Dalca, the thought was abhorrent to him, but Timon was heartless.

"How can you stay with him, Diana?"

"I don't have a choice, but I do have tricks that help keep me safe enough."

"Can you break the bond with him?"

"Only he can break it, and he won't reject me."

Viktor crossed his arms. "Can I ask another question?"

She nodded.

"Why did you use a sapphire?"

"It protects against poisoning. The stone is a natural channeling source to draw poison out of a body."

"That's good to know. I'm going to start wearing one. I'm glad you're feeling better."

She gave him a small smile. "You're a good wolf, Viktor, but always watch your back around Timon."

Viktor pursed his lips. If Timon had taught him anything, it was to always be on guard for his next attack.

Viktor stood. "Alina, can you join me?"

"Shortly."

"I'll be in our room." Viktor exited. His heart was in knots. He didn't want to get involved any deeper in the pack than he was, but at every turn, Timon dragged him further into the world of wolves and witches with his behavior.

Viktor shut the door to his room and drew in a deep breath. His body ached. He needed cannabis. His heart squeezed in anguish. He lunged out and placed his hands on the wall next to the door as he hung his head.

No more! By Dalca, he didn't think he could bear anymore.

The door opened. Viktor knew it was Alina by her scent, but he didn't have it in him to raise his head and look at her. He didn't want her to see him weak – near defeat and with despair coursing through his veins. She said nothing only placed a hand on his shoulder. He found the gesture comforting.

Chapter Twenty

August, 1866

Mihai stood in front of his desk in his study and looked up on the wall where Theresa's portrait of the Black Sea hung. The lines were sharp and the craftsmanship was very neat. He admired the portrait, not only because it depicted the Black Sea that he loved, but also because his wife had painted it for him. Theresa was incredibly talented. She had recently started a canvas depicting the winery, and he couldn't wait to see it.

The door opened and Sonia walked in. "You wanted to see me?"

Mihai turned around and offered his sister a tender smile. "What did you have for breakfast?"

"Milk, sausages, and bread. Really, Mihai—"

"I see your complexion has gotten better with this new diet. I want you to stay on it while I'm away."

"It gets boring. One can only eat so much tuna."

"Viktor and I will be gone for close to a week. Mrs. Nocesti has strict instructions to keep feeding you tuna."

Sonia pouted. Mihai smiled. It was good to see her healthy again. He pointed to the table next to the couch. "Do you see that spoon with the tea service?"

She raised an eyebrow. "Yes."

"Throw it at me."

"I am not going to throw a spoon at you."

"Do it. I need the practice."

Hesitantly, she picked up the utensil and aimed. He stood with his hands by his side. Beatrice had taught him a simple defensive spell before she left. He couldn't risk practicing with Theresa. He didn't want to lie to her about who taught it to him.

Sonia flung the spoon at him. Quickly, he brought his hand up, making a wide arc charged with energy. "Stop!"

The spoon hit the arc and fell to the floor. The goal was to place the arc of energy in the trajectory of the object being thrown. Sonia's eyes grew wide.

"Amazing!"

"I'm learning to channel my energy outward. I find it requires much more focus and concentration."

"Why did you say 'stop?'"

"I have to invoke a spell to tell the energy what to do. It can be as simple as stop, or more challenging depending on the complexity of what you want to do."

She joined him and squeezed his hands. "I'm proud of you. I know this hasn't been easy for you to accept."

"Thank you. I want you to try it."

"Me?'

"Yes. Hold out your palm so it touches mine. Do you feel the energy?"

Sonia did as he instructed, closing her eyes. A mild rush of heat filled her palm.

"The heat – it's the energy?"

"Yes, my ferons are stimulating yours, for lack of a better way of saying it. Now, step back."

Sonia did so, her gaze completely focused on him. He picked up the spoon and prepared to throw it.

"Remember make the arc and tell the energy what to do."

Sonia nodded.

Mihai gently tossed the spoon.

Sonia made a wide arc with her hand. "Stop!"

The spoon hit the arc of energy and fell to the floor. A wide smile grew across her face.

"I did it, Mihai! I did it!"

He wrapped her in his arms and hugged her, as pride swelled throughout him.

The door opened and Viktor walked in, Theresa at his side, her arm crooked in his. She laughed at him, and he smiled at her.

Mihai stiffened. Viktor looked thoroughly at ease and relaxed in Theresa's presence.

A wolf needs a witch. Mihai didn't want the wolf in his house giving his wife too much attention. Especially since Theresa could react instinctively to his moods. Sonia needed to be one reacting instinctively to Viktor's moods.

"What's so funny?" Sonia approached Viktor and Theresa.

Mihai straightened his back and put a hand on Sonia's shoulder, trying to rein in the mix of fear and anxiety within him.

"We were talking about the children at the orphanage," said Viktor.

Theresa removed her hand from Viktor, but continued smiling. "One little boy, Danat, has a bit of a problem with his enunciation. I am now Queen Pisa instead of Queen Theresa."

Sonia chuckled. "Like the Leaning Tower of Pisa?"

"Yes," replied Theresa.

"Oh, bless him, he's only four!" Sonia replied.

"How are the renovations coming along?" asked Mihai, seriously.

Theresa cocked her head, confusion evident in her eyes. He could tell she was reading his mood.

"They're almost complete. The construction workers have taken two rooms on the third floor and are converting them into classrooms," said Viktor.

"Viktor's just told me Mr. Kazha is interviewing teachers for the children. There's going to be two. One for the young ones and another for the children over eight," said Theresa.

Mihai forced a smile. He was genuinely happy to hear the news, but he had been out of touch with the project since he'd been working on arranging a meeting with the other Romanian nobles.

What bothered him was that Viktor had worked hard on arranging the meeting as well, even traveling to Polesti and Bucharest yet he had found time to help Theresa with the orphanage. And he had to take time out of every month to deal with his wolfen curse. Mihai had barely given the orphanage a thought. He was too focused on the railroad and the meeting with the nobles.

He'd ignored his wife's desires to help the children at the orphanage and Viktor had not. Curse him! Not only that, this may be the moment Theresa's father had mentioned. Viktor's recent attention to Theresa, the fact he appeared relaxed in her presence – had he figured out what Theresa was? Or was Mihai misinterpreting the moment?

"Mihai, is something wrong?" The rare smile disappeared from Viktor's face.

"No, no, I fear I've neglected something, and it's something only I can fix."

"Can I help you with it while you're away?" asked Theresa.

He could tell from the expression in her eyes that she didn't know what to make of his mood.

"No, I'll take care of it when I return."

Viktor glanced at his pocket watch. "We need to leave soon. Count Brancoveanu is expecting us before nightfall."

"Are the carriages ready?" asked Mihai.

"Yes."

Sonia walked over to Viktor and reached for his hand. "I'll miss you."

"I'll miss you, too, Sonia. I won't return right away. The full moon coincides with the end of the week and I'll have to go to the pack house."

“I understand.” Sadness washed over Sonia’s eyes.

“I’m sorry.” Viktor wrapped his arms around Sonia and placed a kiss on her temple. “Thank you for understanding. Be safe.”

Mihai watched the scene unfold with interest as he gestured for Theresa to accompany him to the other side of the room to give his sister some privacy. Viktor and Sonia acted comfortable with their embrace. Was it instinctive reacting? Would he hold her too tight or be too rough with her? She didn’t act like he would. Had they stolen secret moments together? Had Sonia’s own abilities grown to the point were she was more comfortable around Viktor? How concerned should he be?

“Mihai, you’re staring.”

Theresa’s whispered voice broke him out of his deep thoughts.

“I’m sorry. I hate to leave, but this is the best time to travel to Bucharest and meet with the rest of the nobles – while the weather is warm and easy to travel in.” Mihai spoke softly so his voice wouldn’t carry.

She laid a hand on his arm and looked into his eyes. “Something else is bothering you. There’s an undercurrent of uneasiness surging within you.” Theresa also spoke softly.

He grasped her shoulders. “Yes, there is, but I have to work this out on my own. Tell me, how much time did you spend with Viktor this week?”

“Several hours.” She paused, a slow awareness dawning in her eyes. “Are you worried?”

“Yes. No. I don’t know,” he said quietly.

“Don’t be. Viktor was very polite and helpful. Nothing inappropriate occurred.”

He drew in a deep breath. Where did Viktor get the stamina and energy for all he’d done these past couple of weeks?

"I'll be gone close to a week. If you need anything—"

"I'll ask Mr. Tybeski."

"You can trust him – or Sergeant Ceseanu."

"I know."

He cupped her cheek and lightly kissed her. It wasn't easy pushing aside the uneasy feeling slowly cresting through him. It lingered, despite her reassurances.

He pulled away and glanced at the mechanical clock on a nearby table.

"Viktor, we need to go."

Viktor stepped away from Sonia and followed Mihai out of the study.

~ * ~

Mihai's carriage ambled across the bridge over the Dâmbovita River and approached Curtea Veche, the castle where the Count of Wallachia lived. The sun sat low in the sky. Mihai was pleased they made it before sunset.

"Sonia looks better. The change in her diet has helped," said Viktor.

"I'm glad. I'm worried for her."

Concern splayed across Viktor's expression. "I don't know what I would do if I lost her. She's been amazing..."

"It must be hard for the two of you – dealing with your condition."

"She's growing more comfortable with me. She's more confident when she touches me. I think she's more aware of her abilities and that's because of you. I can't thank you enough. I may not be able to act like a true husband, at least not yet, but I have hope that when the baby comes we can be a family."

"It's good to hear. I'm also growing stronger as a witch and I'll do whatever I can to help. My sister loves you very much and I want to see both of you happy."

Viktor nodded. Mihai sensed a general feeling of hope coming from his friend.

"How do you find the energy to help me and the orphanage?"

Viktor shrugged. "I like helping at the orphanage. I find it rewarding."

"How so?"

"The children are very genuine and Theresa adores them. Her presence is soothing to me."

"Why?"

Viktor's brows drew downward in a frown. He crossed his arms. "I don't know. I can't explain it. She puts me at ease, especially when we spend time at the orphanage with the children. I like her company." Viktor paused. "Are you concerned?"

Mihai pursed his lips. Viktor was reacting to Theresa, but he hadn't determined she was a witch yet – thank God. "I suppose a part of me is."

"You have no reason to be."

"I know. I'm sorry."

Viktor glanced out the window.

Mihai was curious. Was Viktor avoiding Mihai? Was this instinctive reacting?

Slowly, Viktor turned to face him. "I understand. It's all right."

It grew silent. The carriage turned down a dirt path toward the royal palace, Curtea Veche. It was in the heart of Bucharest and the gardens bordered the river. Mihai knew it had been in the Brancoveanu family for centuries, having been built by Vlad the Impaler. It was no taller than two stories and it had only one tower on the south side, constructed of stone and brick. There were several wings and it reminded Mihai more of a fortress than a castle. The gardens were in full bloom and the trees were lush with greenery. The scent of lavender lined among the entrance path tickled his nose. The scent reminded him of his mother, who had adored lavender.

Count Brancoveanu's flag flew above the entranceway along with the Carpathian and Transylvanian flags. He was the last to arrive.

The footman opened the door. Mihai stepped out and Viktor followed him. A soldier approached, a sergeant from his insignia, and bowed.

"Rise," said Mihai.

"Your Majesty, I am Sergeant Basov, in charge of the Count's guard. My men will see to it your horses are taken to the livery and your bags are taken to your room. Count Brancoveanu will receive you in his study."

"Thank you."

Mihai followed the soldier into the castle and through the halls, which were lit with gas lamps. Servants bustled about. Energy and excitement charged the air. The soldier led them to the study. Upon entering, an older man, around his father's age, rose from his seat. An attractive younger woman with a thick mane of light brown hair stood next to the Count. He bowed, she curtsicd.

"Count Brancoveanu," said Mihai. He knew the older man's first name was Radu, but didn't want to strike up informality with him just yet.

The elder man smiled and stood. "King Mihai, I think the last time I saw you, you were but a boy. Allow me to introduce my daughter and heir, Alina."

He bowed in front of her. "Lady Alina."

The name seemed familiar. Victoria had mentioned her. She was Viktor's witch. Mihai gestured toward Viktor. "This is Lord Bacau, my brother-in-law and personal valet. He's instrumental to me in these talks."

Viktor's mouth had dropped slightly open. Then he squared his shoulders, composing himself.

Lady Alina stepped forward and offered her hand. "Lord Bacau."

He bent over and grasped her hand. "Lady Alina."

Mihai glanced at the two. A familiarity danced in their eyes.

"It is a pleasure to make your acquaintance," said Alina.

Viktor took a step backward, but his gaze never left her.

Count Brancoveanu clapped his hands. "Would you like some brandy?"

"Yes, it would be nice after our trip," said Mihai. He sat on the sofa, Viktor next to him.

The count exchanged a glance with his daughter, who went to the small bar next to the desk and poured the drinks. He then sat down in a leather chair across from Mihai.

"Mircea is upstairs, settling in. Iancu is here with his boys, Sorin and Ioan. We'll be ready to start tomorrow. For the sake of simplicity, I think we can refer to each other by our given names. Is that acceptable to you?" asked Count Brancoveanu.

"That's fine."

Alina handed everyone a drink and sat down in a leather chair adjacent to her father.

"I would like my daughter to attend as well since she is my heir."

"I have no issue with that." Mihai sipped his drink.

"How was your journey?"

"Pleasant. We paralleled the railroad route. The tunnel is complete and the project is set to finish in early October."

Radu smiled. "Excellent! This is good news. I am sorry to hear about your father. He was a good man. He had a grand vision to unite us, and who knows, perhaps if he'd lived longer, he would have fulfilled it."

"Thank you, Radu. I'm excited to continue my father's work."

"How is your wife? In good health?"

"Our child is due in early November."

The older man smiled. "I see you wasted no time."

"I wish she could have traveled with me so you could have met her."

"We'll have more opportunities, I'm sure. Dinner will be served at seven. Afterwards, we can retire here for a nightcap or you can retire for the evening."

Mihai stood. "Thank you. I look forward to dinner."

Radu got to his feet as well. "Come, I'll personally show you to your rooms. Alina, join us."

She exchanged another familiar glance with Viktor. Perhaps Mihai should talk to her so he could fully understand the nature of what she did for him as a witch.

~ * ~

Viktor walked into his room, across from Mihai's in the guest wing. It was late and the moon was a waxing gibbous, just past the half phase. He crossed his arms, his emotions swirling around him like wild waves slamming onto a reef.

He hadn't planned to see Alina, but he should have known she would be here. She'd been honest with him about who she was. Alina was just as beautiful outside of the pack house. He wanted to see her tonight.

Dare he? Why was he even contemplating this? It wasn't that he had fallen out of love with Sonia, he hadn't, but he couldn't be intimate with her, especially with her difficult confinement, and that wore on his psyche.

Making love with Alina was a thrill. His sense of touch was heightened when he held her. Alina's mind gently soothed his aching, raw soul and her body was incredibly responsive to his.

He had to see her tonight.

Quietly, yet quickly, he slid out of his room and caught the honeysuckle scent that was distinctively Alina's.

A man was with her. His scent was musky, laced with a peppery spice.

He followed her scent down the hall. Two people – Alina and the man – were on a balcony overlooking the gardens. She was in his arms, her hands braced on the nape of his neck. Viktor hid in the shadows, his hands clenched as he tried to tame his unnatural jealousy.

"My God, Alina, you feel wonderful."

"I missed you, Ioan."

He kissed her neck, nipping at her flesh. Viktor suppressed a growl.

"How much longer must we wait? I want to ask your father to marry me."

"Another six months," said Alina.

The man's lips claimed hers. Viktor ground his teeth, fighting the urge to slam Ioan into the balcony's railing.

"Oh, Ioan..."

"Let me come to your bed, tonight. You know I love you."

She stepped back and placed a hand on his chest. "I can't. We must wait."

He sighed. "You test my patience."

"I'm sorry, but it must be like this. I'm still new to the coven...and to my wolf."

"I hate that you have to go away and be intimate with another man!"

"Please, darling, you have my heart, not him. I have loved you since we were children. Another six months and we can announce our engagement."

"Promise?"

Viktor stepped out of the shadows and coughed, unable to listen to any more. Alina and Ioan stepped away from each other.

"Lord Bacau," said Alina.

"Lady Alina, are you all right?"

"I'm fine. This is Lord Ioan Getzi."

"Lord Getzi," acknowledged Viktor. Alina's beloved was tall, lean, with a thick head of ebony hair and eyes as blue as the Black Sea. He was attractive in a dark, brooding sort of way that almost reminded him of Nasguard. Unspoken tension thickened the air.

"May I escort you to your room, Lady Alina?" Viktor asked.

"All right, Lord Bacau." She paused and reached for Ioan's hand, whispering something to him. Reluctance flashed in the tall lord's eyes, but he acquiesced to Alina's wishes.

Viktor made sure Alina was beside him before they walked down the hall. Silence remained between them until Alina paused in front of her door.

"This is my room."

"Where's your attendant?" he asked.

"It's late. I snuck out to meet Ioan."

"Invite me into your room."

Her mouth dropped open, but she quickly recovered. "I will not."

"Why?"

"For the same reason I refused Ioan. It is inappropriate for me to take a lover into my room during this meeting of the nobles. I am my father's heir. How would that look? Besides, Viktor, I made it very clear to you how I feel about Ioan. I love him. You have a wife. It is not wise for us to share intimacies outside of our relationship as wolf and witch."

He stood there, straightening his back, letting her words sink in. She was right, of course. He loved Sonia. His body had clearly responded to the close proximity of Alina, giving way to his more feral urges. He was a man right now, not a wolf, and he was in control. So why did it feel like his precious control was so close to spiraling off the edge of a cliff?

He backed away. "You're right, of course. I overstepped my bounds. I apologize."

Her face softened. "Viktor, you must try harder to rein in your urges or everyone here will realize there's something between us that shouldn't be. We don't want our secrets to come out."

He pursed his lips. "All right."

"Good night, Viktor."

"Good night, Alina."

She opened the door and went inside. Viktor made his way back to his room, deeply disturbed by his lack of control in his human form. Why was it getting harder to rein in his desires?

~ * ~

Mihai sat at the table beside Radu Brancoveanu. Next to him sat his daughter, Alina. Viktor sat on the other side of Mihai.

Iancu Getzi from Transylvania and his sons sat across from them. Iancu was the count; Sorin the heir. Iancu was a little older than Radu with hair that was balding. His sons were around Mihai's age.

Mircea from Carpathia sat with an advisor who took notes. The noon meal was being served. This was their last meeting.

"I'd like to review the provisions we've discussed in previous talks and affirm everyone's assent," said Mircea.

"Go ahead," said Mihai. He liked Mircea. The monarch was in his late twenties and had a young daughter named Edwina.

Mircea glanced at his notes. "Since Carpathia and Moldavia are the bigger and more sound principalities, it is agreed upon that our families will enter the unification marriage. I already have a daughter. If Mihai has a son, our children will wed when they are eighteen. Six weeks after the wedding, we, as the nobles of Romanian principalities, will come together and pledge our allegiance to them, uniting us as the Kingdom of Romania."

"Yes, it's agreed," said Radu.

"What if Mihai doesn't have a son?" asked Iancu.

"I suggest we revisit this provision in five years' time here in Bucharest. By then our families should be established and we can best decide then who can enter into the unification marriage," said Mihai.

"That's a good idea," said Radu. "I'd be honored to host another conference."

"Now, Wallachia will be compensated by having the capital of the new nation as Bucharest," said Mircea.

"Agreed," said Iancu.

"And Transylvania will receive monetary compensation and the building of a railroad from Bucharest to Targu Mures and Suceava," continued Mircea.

"I agree," said Mihai.

"Carpathia and Moldavia will each pay for forty-five percent of the railroad. Wallachia will pay ten percent."

Mihai looked around. "And if any of us should pass, our heirs are committed to the agreement we made here today."

"I will honor it," said Sorin.

"As will I," said Alina.

"Excellent," said Mircea. "My advisor has drafted this agreement in four copies. I'll pass them around. We'll all sign and keep one copy."

Mihai signed the papers. Although he had enjoyed spending time with the other Romanian nobles, he was ready to leave, but he had to talk to Lady Alina before he left.

~ * ~

"Argh!"

Theresa rushed to Sonia's side as her sister-in-law doubled over, clutching the backrest on the sofa. They were in the library. Sonia usually did her knitting there while Theresa worked on her painting.

Mrs. Nocesti helped Theresa carry Sonia to the couch. She lay on her side, grabbing her distended womb.

"Where does it hurt?" asked Mrs. Nocesti.

"Here," Sonia grunted. She pointed to her side, near the rib cage.

Theresa wrung her hands together, worried. Sonia was in her eighth month and her baby was nice and round. Sonia reminded Theresa of when Victoria had given birth. She hoped that wasn't happening now.

"She's not going to have the baby, is she?" asked Theresa.

"No, the pain is in the wrong place. I'm going to get Dr. Stanza and the willow bark pills."

"Hurry."

"I will." Mrs. Nocesti rushed out the door.

Theresa knelt next to Sonia, rubbing her hand over Sonia's hair. "This is so sudden. Did the baby kick?"

"I don't know...Theresa...am I bleeding?"

Theresa shivered at the thought, but visually checked Sonia's dress. "I don't see any blood staining your dress."

"Thank God. Theresa, it hurts."

"I'm sorry. I wish I could do something."

"Hold my hand."

Theresa offered Sonia her hand. Sonia gripped it so tightly, Theresa's knuckles turned white. Her own pulse accelerated. Spots appeared before her eyes. Theresa's breathing grew rapid. She saw the baby in the womb, kicking the area of Sonia's discomfort. The baby struck the blood barrier. It was weak, and because of that, was causing Sonia pain.

"Baby, no, don't kick your mother there. You're hurting her. Please, don't kick. Turn around, please, turn around," Theresa said, gasping for air as sweat trickled down her brow. The baby turned. It was a boy.

Sonia let go. Theresa's link with the baby disappeared.

"What did you do?" whispered Sonia.

"I...I don't know."

"Theresa, you made it stop. How did you do that?" Sonia gasped.

"I don't know."

"I felt your energy – it pulsed through me."

"Oh." Theresa's mind reeled in confusion. She stumbled and reached for the couch.

Mrs. Nocesti and Dr. Stanza rushed in.

"Sonia!" cried Dr. Stanza.

"The Queen!" exclaimed Mrs. Nocesti.

Theresa knelt, one hand clutching the couch, the other her womb. She wasn't as round as Sonia. Theresa took a deep breath. She couldn't explain what had just happened, but it had rocked her to the core of her being. No human should have the type of experience she just had. She felt Sonia's baby. She felt Sonia's pain. She learned Sonia's baby was a boy. The baby must be a witch. That's what Theresa felt.

"Your Majesty, are you all right?" Mrs. Nocesti rubbed a cool cloth over Theresa's brow.

"I'm fine, I just..."

"Are you hurt?"

"No, I was holding Sonia's hand. That's all I was doing – holding her hand."

Mrs. Nocesti quickly examined Theresa. "You appear fine, Your Majesty."

Theresa nodded, straightening her shoulders. "How's Sonia?"

Dr. Stanza gave Sonia a pill that she swallowed with tea. She and her sister-in-law exchanged a knowing, secret look, each aware of the fact it was due to Theresa's efforts that Sonia's pain had stopped.

"The pain is over, Theresa. There's a dull ache there now." Sonia paused and looked at the doctor. "Do you know what's wrong?"

"It might be best if you are restricted to bed rest until you deliver. Mrs. Nocesti, I'd like your thoughts."

"Yes, Doctor."

Theresa bit her lower lip. Could she tell the doctor what she saw? Sonia's life was in danger because the blood barrier between her and the baby was weak. How could she explain it to the doctor? She had to find a way. She feared for her sister's-in-law's life.

~ * ~

Mihai watched as Viktor rode away on his horse from Curtea Veche. Mulfaltar was closer to Constanta than Bucharest. Quickly, he walked back into the castle, intent on finding Lady Brancoveanu. The castle bustled with activity as visiting servants rushed about, preparing to leave.

Just as he was about to ascend the stairs, Lady Alina, dressed in traveling clothes, descended.

"Lady Alina, may I have a minute of your time?"

"I don't have much. My escort is waiting for me in the livery."

"I'll join you so we can talk. You're on the way to the pack house, aren't you?"

She flashed him a look, confirming his statement.

"Why didn't you leave with Viktor? He's your wolf, right?"

"It would look inappropriate. No one will realize I've gone if I leave by myself."

"Ah, I understand."

They walked out of the castle.

"May I ask how Viktor is with you?" asked Mihai.

She paused. "Viktor is well liked in the pack and by the witches, but I am a little concerned."

"How so?"

"He asked to be intimate with me outside of the confines

of our relationship as wolf and witch."

Mihai stopped. "Intimate?" She said the word so coolly, as if it was just a task or a chore. God, Viktor was betraying Sonia with this woman. He realized he had been warned of that all along, but right now he had to fully acknowledge it.

"Your Majesty, I provide Viktor what he needs. My heart cares for him, but I don't love him."

"How can you be intimate with him if you don't love him? My God, my sister is his wife."

"Even in his human form, Viktor is stronger, quicker, and has more stamina than us combined. Be grateful that what I do for him allows him to be a man and a husband to her when the moon isn't full."

Mihai took a breath, calming himself. She was right, of course. "I'm sorry. How did you become his witch?"

"The von Krackens asked, and my father owed them. My service is paying off the debt."

"I understand. So, why are you concerned about his request?"

"A wolf and witch can be lovers outside of the full moon, but my heart belongs to another man. I don't want Viktor to confuse what he needs and what he wants."

"Do you want me to say something to him?"

"Consult the von Krackens. They'll know what to do. I must take my leave, Your Majesty, I'm sorry. I have to arrive at the pack house by sunset."

"Of course."

Alina approached a waiting carriage with just a driver, no footmen. She entered and the carriage, offered Mihai a slight wave of her hand then gestured for the driver to set off.

Mihai pursed his lips. Why would Viktor want to be intimate with Alina unless he was developing strong feelings for her? Worry seeped into his bones, and he prayed that Viktor's actions would not upset his sister – just when she needed all her strength and courage to have his baby.

~ * ~

Viktor watched Alina's carriage pull into the stables. She was late in arriving, but he understood why. The meeting of the nobles was very productive and Viktor was proud to have worked on it.

Timon walked into the main room from the hall. "Viktor should take the kill tonight."

Viktor turned away from the window and faced Timon. He had yet to make the initial first kill for the pack. The thought of doing it repulsed him to the core of his being.

Nasguard and Gascon sat on the bench, rolling weed. Bane finished stoking the fireplace and looked up.

"I'll take the kill," said Nasguard.

Timon crossed his arms and a smug expression crept over his face. "I think Viktor should have it. Especially if he's going to lead the pack soon. He must show us he can kill."

"I'm not afraid to kill."

Bane stood. "Then it's settled. Viktor will kill first tonight."

Viktor walked away from the window and joined Gascon at the table. The sun would set soon – within the hour. He was prepared to kill someone to prove his worth, but the thought did not set well with him. He was not a killer or violent by nature. He did what he had to at the pack house to get by. Still, he wasn't going to back down from Timon's challenge. Viktor wasn't sure how he was going to feel or how he was going to react, but he was glad Alina was here. He needed her.

~ * ~

The night air was humid. Viktor's fur bristled. His heart beat faster in nervous anticipation. Being summer, more gypsies braved the darkness, making them easy targets for the wolves.

The wolves came to the edge of the woods next to the road. On the other side was a clearing where a wagon rested. There were three men and one woman. She was cooking, two men were drinking, and the last man was playing a guitar.

Viktor stood where the forest met the road, studying the gypsies. He would attack the ones who drank.

"Hurry." Timon's thoughts rang out.

Viktor closed his eyes, prayed for his soul, and pounced.

~ * ~

Viktor felt heat blast his face from the fireplace, and he looked up from the floor where he lay. A blanket covered him. Despite the warmth, his body lightly shook. Alina bent down.

"Are you all right?"

He didn't feel right. His body was an odd combination of disgust and exhilaration. She helped Viktor to his feet and sat him in the bed, covering him with the blanket.

She handed him a chalice. "It's a combination of brandy, honey, and brooklime powder."

"What will it do?"

"Calm you down."

"Why is my body shaking?" Viktor sipped from the chalice.

"You had the first kill and the most blood. Your body's not used to it."

He closed his eyes, pained. "I killed."

"I know," she said, softly. "It's not pleasant."

He gave her the chalice and hung his face in his hands, shame washing over him. "I didn't want to kill, Alina, but Timon... I couldn't look weak...I had to."

She wrapped her arms around him. "I understand, Viktor. We all do."

He jerked his head up and stared into her eyes. "It was the most thrilling experience I ever had. There is a part deep inside me that enjoyed it very much, and because of that, I'm ashamed."

"Let me feel what you feel."

He jerked his hands away from her. "No, I don't want you to know this feeling. It's wonderful – and miserable, and..."

She stroked his face with her delicate fingers, and his anguish lightened. He tried to push her away, wanting to spare her, but she clung to him, never giving up. She cared for him – deeply. Viktor grabbed her wrists as his emotions soared, shame replaced by lust. Alina understood his shame, the secret exhilaration and did not judge him. He twisted so she was underneath him. Most of the turmoil had dissipated, but one small part of it niggled away at the back of his mind. Guilt. Guilt haunted him. He pushed it away. He had to in order to keep his sanity.

"Alina, I want you..."

"No, you need me."

"I know you don't judge me. You accept me as I am."

A tear rolled down her cheek and he cupped her face.

She nodded her consent, and he kissed her, lust fueling his urges now.

Chapter Twenty-One

Early September

Theresa stood next to the window in the library, arms crossed, looking onto the royal gardens. Her canvas was only half completed. She'd been deeply troubled since she had made a connection to Sonia's baby days earlier. While she had managed to stop the baby from hurting Sonia, her sister-in-law continued to show physical discomfort due to the baby's size.

Theresa pinched the bridge of her nose in an effort to deal with her own inner turmoil. She could not be human. She had to be a witch, too. How else could she have talked to the baby? She thought about it – the baby didn't reach out to her, she had reached out to the child.

Sonia had only mentioned the encounter once, but they had been interrupted. Theresa wasn't ready to tell her husband she thought she was a witch. How could it even be? And her family? She didn't want to deal with them right now. Mihai had been very busy with Parliament and the railroad. She didn't want to weigh down what little time they had together with such a confession. While she accepted Mihai as a witch, would he be so accepting of her? Why wouldn't he be? Why did she struggle with this?

The door opened. Theresa turned around, torn away from her weighty thoughts. Sonia walked in.

Theresa smiled. "Hello, Sonia. Where's Mrs. Nocesti?"

"I asked her to give me some time alone with you."

Theresa approached Sonia and they awkwardly hugged, due to their size. Theresa gestured toward the couch and Sonia sat down. Theresa joined her.

Worry lined Sonia's face. "Can you talk to the baby?"

Theresa made a fist and covered her mouth. What could she say? She didn't want to lie, that would do no good.

"I don't know. I didn't do it consciously. I was so scared for you; I just channeled my thoughts and energy through our hands."

"Channeled thoughts and energy?"

Theresa nodded. "That's how I would explain it."

"Witches channel energy."

"I know."

Sonia drew in a deep breath. Theresa spied a conflicted look on Sonia's expression.

"I think I'm a witch."

"Have you told Mihai what you believe?" Sonia asked.

"No, I'm not prepared to tell him just yet. I need to know more."

Sonia reached for Theresa's hand and squeezed it. "There's no more hiding now, but you should consider telling Mihai. He loves you."

"Hiding what?"

"It's not my place to say."

"Am I a witch?" Theresa asked.

"Search your heart."

Theresa pursed her lips. "I believe I am a witch."

"I can offer no more." Sonia then pulled Theresa into a warm embrace. The women just held each other in silence for several minutes.

Finally, Sonia pulled away and looked into Theresa's eyes. "Do you know what's wrong? Is it the baby or me?"

"The baby appeared fine. He felt fine—"

"He?"

"You're having a boy."

"Oh, Theresa!" Sonia hugged her again. Theresa placed her hands on Sonia's arms and looked at her. "The baby is small, but appears all right. There is a blood barrier between you and the baby. It is weak and getting weaker as the baby grows in size."

"How can that be? Since changing my diet, I've felt so much better."

"As I sensed it, the diet change has helped manage the symptoms better, but the problem is still there."

"What can I do?"

"I'm not sure. Rest. Don't exert yourself. I fear you'll give birth early – the baby will get so big your weak blood barrier will bleed out." Theresa's voice shook with fear.

Sonia nodded.

The door opened. Mrs. Nocesti and Dr. Stanza walked in. Viktor and Mihai followed behind. Dr. Stanza carried a leather-bound book. Theresa saw apprehension and worry etched into Viktor's expression. Viktor sat down next to Sonia, taking her hand in his. Mihai stood behind the couch and gently placed his hands on Theresa's shoulders. Turmoil and deep concern for his sister surged through him.

"Dr. Stanza has something to tell us," said Mihai.

The doctor sat down in a chair across from the sofa and Mrs. Nocesti stood next to him.

"I've very concerned for Princess Sonia and I want to share my conclusions."

Viktor glanced at Sonia. His nostrils flared, betraying his anxiety. Theresa swallowed. Viktor was deeply troubled and Theresa sensed it – like she would sense Mihai's emotions. She clenched her fists. She'd never felt Viktor's emotions before, or more accurately, she was now *aware* of Viktor's emotions. She pushed back her own apprehension. Theresa would worry about Viktor later.

"What conclusions?" asked Viktor.

Dr. Stanza patted the leather book and looked at Mihai before speaking. "The king was the one who came to me recently asking about his mother's confinements. I was younger at the time and made notes in this journal. Her confinements appear similar to the Princess. The symptoms are a bit different, but Sonia's mother also suffered from headaches and had difficulties gaining weight."

Theresa's heart spiked with unease. Mihai's emotions tensed. He was scared of losing his sister. Viktor's emotions were even more violent. It felt like a vicious wind whipping off him laced with cold, angry fear. Theresa crossed her arms and rubbed her hands up and down them to ward off the chill.

"What can I do?" asked Sonia.

"You are a month from your due date, which escalates the danger. From now on, I want you to rest. Conserve your energy and strength. Do not exert yourself. You must have your wits about you and you must be able to help me when labor begins."

Sonia nodded. "I will."

"Good."

"Now your mother's labors were quick with high blood loss, but I was able to control it. I believe if Sonia is similar, we can manage the birth."

Viktor nodded his head. "What does 'rest' mean?"

"No outside walks. Stay in bed. Read books. Knit. You must be idle."

Sonia grimaced.

"You must do it, darling. I can't bear to lose you or the baby," said Viktor.

She let out a long breath, full of resignation. "I'll do as the doctor requests."

"I'll be with you as often as I can. I even have a deck of cards to help the boredom," said Mrs. Nocesti.

Sonia gave her a small smile.

"How about the queen? Is Theresa...in danger?" asked Mihai.

Dr. Stanza looked at Theresa. "She's had a good confinement with no reported problems. I don't anticipate any issues with her delivery."

"Could she have the baby now?" asked Mihai.

"She would be early. The baby would be small, but with the proper care, should live."

Mihai's relief washed over Theresa like a wave.

Dr. Stanza stood. "Mrs. Nocesti and I will leave you alone. If you have any other concerns, please let me know."

Both Sonia and Viktor nodded.

Theresa watched Dr. Stanza and Mrs. Nocesti leave.

"Theresa, let's give Viktor and Sonia a moment. Will you join me in my study?"

Theresa stood up and smiled at her husband. He returned her smile and offered his arm to her. She took it, and they walked out.

~ * ~

Viktor was solely focused on Sonia. The doctor's voice had been grave, his expression grim. Viktor drew his wife into an embrace, mindful to use a gentle touch. Her body initially tensed, but then relaxed as she became comfortable next to him.

He closed his eyes and recalled their first spontaneous, yet delightful, kiss. Sonia's lips had been light and playful, igniting a passion inside him he'd never experienced before. Viktor had loved touching her, caressing her, branding her. He couldn't lose her. He would go mad from the grief.

"You're tense," said Sonia.

He opened his eyes. "I have much on my mind."

"What were you thinking about?"

"How we fell in love."

A hint of a smile crossed her lips. "It was the most wonderful time of my life."

"And mine." He paused. "I hate what happened to us,

but I am grateful that you stayed with me."

"I love you, despite what occurred."

"And I love you. You must do what the doctor says. This is a bad time for me to go to the pack house, but the full moon is two days away."

"I will, I promise." Sadness laced the tone of her voice.

"I know this confinement has been hard for you, and I know you miss being a nurse. When the baby is born, I'm going to make sure we have the best nannies so you can go back to the hospital if you want."

"Thank you, Viktor." She kept her voice quiet. "I will master my lessons so you no longer have to go to your pack house."

"I would like that. It's been a rough year." He kissed her temple. He couldn't lose her. She held his heart – his humanity. He feared what would happen to his soul if Sonia died.

~ * ~

Mihai shut the door to the study and embraced Theresa. She rested her cheek against his chest and they stayed there, in each other's arms, for several minutes.

Theresa sensed Mihai's emotions had settled a bit, but worry still thrummed within him.

"Let's sit on the couch," said Theresa.

Mihai smiled at her and took her hand, leading her to the sofa. She sat down next to him.

"I'm worried for Sonia, too," she said, finally.

"I've done everything I can. Now I must trust in Dr. Stanza and Mrs. Nocesti."

"I think the doctor did the right thing by ordering her to rest."

"So do I. I'm just glad your confinement has gone well."

She placed her hand over his and rested her head on his shoulder. She felt concern for her deep in his bones.

"I'm going to send Mr. Tybeski to inspect the railroad

construction while Viktor is gone. I want to stay here."

"I think that's wise. You should be close in case Sonia needs you."

"I agree. Have you given the nursery much thought?"

"Some. There's a crib in a store near Parliament that I like."

"I'll purchase it tomorrow."

"How efficient you are."

"If we have a son, his colors should be red and gold – for the crown prince."

"Are there colors for a girl?" she asked.

"I believe the colors are red and silver, but if you want something else..."

"That's fine. I would like to have the nursery close to our apartments with a window overlooking the gardens and a rocking chair to hold the baby."

"I know just the room. While Viktor is gone, I'll have the nursery completed."

"Make it big enough for both babies," said Theresa.

"I will. I'll get two cribs."

"Good."

There was an awkward silence.

"Theresa?"

"Yes."

"I do love you, and I'm glad you've been able to manage this confinement. I couldn't bear to lose you."

"I'll be fine, Mihai." Her voice offered reassurance. Gently he ran his fingers over her hair, and she basked in warm feelings that intermingled between them. The moment had passed for Theresa to bring up her suspicions regarding her own heritage with Mihai. For now, she would enjoy the warmth and when she felt the time was right, she would talk to her husband about her belief that she was, indeed, a witch, herself.

Chapter Twenty-Two

A week later
13 September 1866

A sunbeam filtered in from the window, casting a bright light over Mihai's desk. He stopped reviewing his paperwork and rubbed his eyes with his fingers before relaxing.

The past week had been rewarding. The nursery was upstairs, near his apartments, full of furniture and clothes for both babies, ready for their arrival. He secretly delighted in preparing the room, knowing that his son or daughter would soon be born.

He had enjoyed staying at the castle this week and not rushing between the railroad and Parliament. Sonia followed Dr. Stanza's orders, remaining in her room, only venturing out for breakfast, evening meals, and to the library to pick out a book. Mihai even played a few games of cards with his sister. Theresa would also sit with her. She'd read to Sonia or Sonia would embroider while Theresa painted. Mihai also found time to study the spells and books that Beatrice had left with him.

Viktor returned from the pack house moodier than ever. Mihai sensed a feeling of disgust resided in him that he couldn't vanquish. Disgust over what, Mihai didn't know. He tried to get Viktor to talk about his time away, but his friend refused. And that troubled Mihai. Since becoming a wolf, the friendly conversations that they often shared were now practically non-existent. Viktor held a tight rein on his emotions. Mihai's steadfast, warm-hearted friend had been replaced by a quiet, brooding man he hardly knew.

Mihai placed his hands on the edge of his desk, his eyes drifting to the slender middle drawer. He recently put a hunting pistol there, loaded with silver bullets.

Just in case.

There was a knock on the door and Viktor walked in holding several papers.

"Good morning, Mihai."

"Good morning, Viktor. What do you have there?"

"Mr. Kazha delivered some of the children's drawings for Theresa and Sonia." Viktor paused and presented Mihai with the pictures. "He also wanted us to know that the teachers were hired and the children start classes on Wednesday."

"That's wonderful." Mihai went through the papers. A smile graced his lips at the children's efforts. Most were of him, Theresa, and the baby. He couldn't wait to show his wife.

A blood-curdling scream ripped through the study. Mihai looked at Viktor.

"What was that?" asked Viktor.

"Let's pray it's not Sonia," replied Mihai.

They sprinted out of the room and down the hall. The scream had come from the library. God, he hoped it wasn't Theresa, either. Mihai glanced at Viktor. Panic and fear braced his expression.

Dr. Stanza and Mrs. Nocesti ran down the hall from the opposite direction, meeting Mihai at the library door. Dr. Stanza pushed the door open and rushed in.

"Sonia!" yelled Viktor.

Fear raced down Mihai's spine. Sonia lay on the floor, clutching her belly, panting, her face contorted in pain as blood pooled between her legs.

Damn! Why wasn't she in her room?

"We need to get Sonia to a room with a bed," said Dr. Stanza.

"Go to the guest rooms across the hall two doors down," said Mihai. He clasped his hands together, trying to control his anxiety. He hated seeing his sister like this.

"We need to move now," said Dr. Stanza.

Sonia screamed.

Fear rolled off Viktor in violent waves, but he bent down and picked Sonia up in his arms, following Dr. Stanza and Mihai to the guest rooms.

"Mihai! Is Sonia all right?" Theresa raced along the length of the second story hall from their apartments toward the staircase.

Mihai paused at the bottom of the steps. Panic shone in his wife's eyes.

"Theresa, slow down when you approach the staircase!"

Another gut-wrenching scream came from the guest room. Theresa missed the first step of the staircase. She lost her balance, fell, tried to brace the fall with her hands, but went tumbling head first down the steps. Mihai's heartbeat spiked.

"Theresa!"

His breath caught in his throat and his blood rushed through his veins. Theresa landed in a crumpled mess right at his feet. He collapsed next to her, wrapping his arms around her chest. Her body shook uncontrollably. Her sharp hazel eyes glazed over.

Mihai raked his gaze over her body. She stirred and a loud wail escaped from her lips. A red stain marred the dress between her legs.

"Help me!" yelled Mihai.

"The baby..." she gasped. Her stomach tightened.

Mihai put his hands over the baby and then jerked them back. Her womb was as hard as a diamond. The tightness left and pain racked her face. She screamed.

"Theresa, oh, Theresa, please be all right." He ran his hands through her hair. "I need a doctor!"

Dr. Stanza peered out of the doorway. "What happened to the queen? Princess Sonia's condition is very grave. She's lost a lot of blood. I must attend her."

"Theresa fell down the stairs."

Theresa rocked back and forth in his arms, whimpering, sweating profusely. Her fear threatened to overwhelm him, but he stiffened his spine and resolve. He had to be strong for her now.

Dr. Stanza's grimace revealed his desperation. "Mrs. Nocesti! Go with the king and queen. Take her up to her room and deliver the baby. She's had a good confinement and the delivery should not be as difficult as Princess Sonia's. I'll stay here."

"Yes, Sir."

Dr. Stanza looked back into the room. "Viktor, find two women who have some experience in birthing. Send one to help Mrs. Nocesti and one to me. Do it now."

Viktor ran past him toward the kitchen.

Mrs. Nocesti knelt down next to Mihai and they exchanged worried looks.

"Help her," said Mihai.

Mrs. Nocesti lifted Theresa's dress. After assessing his wife's condition, Mrs. Nocesti stood.

"Can you carry her to her room?"

"Yes." Mihai scooped Theresa into his arms and walked up the steps. She screamed.

"Can you give her something for the pain? Some laudanum?" His knowledge of roots failed him.

Mrs. Nocesti opened the door to their apartments. "I don't know."

"You don't know? She's in pain." Mihai put her down on the bed.

Mrs. Nocesti ran her hand over Theresa's head and stopped next to her ear. She motioned for Mihai to feel.

"That's a bump. She has a head bruise. It isn't wise for

the queen to lose consciousness right now. I need her help to push the baby out and she must have her wits about her. Not only that, if she goes to sleep so soon after receiving such a bruise, she might not wake up." She paused for breath.

"Argh!" cried Theresa.

"She might die?" His voice shook with fear.

Mrs. Nocesti undid the laces of the dress. "Yes, she could die. We must be careful."

Just then, Tatiana, a girl from the kitchen, appeared in the doorway.

"I was told to help you," said Tatiana.

Mrs. Nocesti rolled the sleeves of her shirt up her arms. "Get me several bowls of warm fresh water and lots of towels. Then go to my room and bring up my brown bag. My birthing tools are in there. Do it quickly."

Mihai held Theresa's hand. Fear coiled around his limbs. His whole world would fall apart if he lost her.

Tatiana returned with the bowls of water and towels before departing again for the brown bag. Mrs. Nocesti removed Theresa's clothes, but covered her in a large towel to preserve her modesty.

"Mihai, our baby..." Theresa's voice dropped off.

"You're going to deliver." He made his voice strong for her.

"I'm early. Save the baby."

"The baby will be small, but should be healthy, Your Majesty," said Mrs. Nocesti. She wet a rag.

Theresa screamed. Terror played havoc with Mihai's psyche as he watched his wife's womb tighten again. If only Beatrice or Victoria were here.

Mrs. Nocesti thrust the rag at him. "Run this over her forehead. Talk to her. Don't let her lose consciousness during the birth. She must stay awake."

Mihai nodded.

His wife groaned in agony. Mrs. Nocesti spread her legs.

"Push, Your Majesty."

Theresa grunted, but bore down. Mihai wished he could take the pain away. Tatiana returned with the birthing tools.

"Push again, Your Majesty."

Sweat beaded Theresa's brow. Her eyes had a distant expression. Mihai wiped her forehead.

"Theresa, be strong. Push. Darling, please." Mihai squeezed her hand.

"One more push. I feel the head!"

Theresa pushed.

"That's it...that's it..."

Mihai heard a pop. The baby was out.

Tatiana's hands went to her cheeks. "The cord is choking the baby!"

Sheer panic filled Mihai.

"Give me the scissors from my bag," said Mrs. Nocesti.

Tatiana handed the instrument to Mrs. Nocesti, who cut the baby's cord.

Theresa's head rolled onto the side of the pillow. Mihai caressed her cheek. "Stay awake, Theresa."

Mrs. Nocesti washed the baby. After an initial wait, the baby took deep, but awkward breaths.

Mihai looked at Mrs. Nocesti. "How is the child?"

"Congratulations, Your Majesty. You have a boy."

"But his breathing—"

"He's early, but he's breathing on his own. He'll catch his rhythm, you'll see."

"A son," Mihai whispered with awe. "Theresa, we have a son."

His wife's breathing was shallow. She could hardly focus her eyes. He was more worried about Theresa than the baby. He had to trust the midwife.

"Take the baby to the nursery," said Mrs. Nocesti,

looking at Tatiana. "I must still attend the queen."

"Show me the prince," said Mihai.

Tatiana wrapped the boy in blankets and held him next to Mihai. All he could see was the boy's face and neck. His son had a full head of ebony hair and blue eyes. He also had bruising around his neck.

"Put the prince in the red and gold blankets when you get to the nursery," said Mihai. His son appeared fine, but his deep breathing unnerved him.

Mrs. Nocesti looked into Theresa's eyes. "Her pupils are normal now. That's good."

"Will she live?" Mihai asked.

"I believe so. She's needs to rest. I'm confident now she'll awaken once she does. I'm going to give her a very small dose of laudanum to help her. You may go, Your Majesty. I'll stay with her."

"I am not leaving my wife."

Mrs. Nocesti nodded and gave Theresa the elixir. Theresa coughed and closed her eyes. Her breathing grew normal.

Mihai raked a hand through his hair and then squeezed Theresa's hand. He loved her! She was his world and the thought of losing her chilled him to the depths of his being.

A sharp, piercing cry ripped through the castle. Sonia! Oh, God, he prayed his sister would not die.

~ * ~

After finding two women in the kitchen to assist Dr. Stanza and Mrs. Nocesti, Viktor raced back to the room Sonia was in. She lay on the bed, her head cocked to one side, sweat covering her face.

Dr. Stanza was trying frantically to deliver the child.

Viktor rushed to Sonia's side and grabbed her hand. Fear wrapped its icy tendrils around his bones. His wife was dying.

Maria appeared at the door.

"Get me clean water and rags now!" yelled Dr. Stanza.

Viktor kept his gaze on Sonia. He had smelled human blood before – he'd even killed a man, but this was different. He couldn't stand to look at her blood.

"I need you to push, Sonia. I know you're weak, but push," said Dr. Stanza.

Sonia grimaced, her push was fragile. Viktor shoved a strand of his wife's hair out of her weary face.

"Darling, why were you in the library?" he asked.

"I was bored...wanted a book to read..."

"Push, Sonia," Dr. Stanza ordered.

She grunted and screamed.

"I love you, Sonia," said Viktor, desperation in his voice.

Sonia tried to focus her eyes on him. "I love you, Viktor. I'm in so much pain..." Her voice dropped to a whisper.

"Sonia, you have to be a mother to this baby."

"One more push..." said Dr. Stanza.

"Viktor...make Mihai and Theresa the baby's godparents. They will help you care for him."

"Yes, of course, whatever you want..."

"I have the baby!"

Sonia cried out, lifting her head, and then she collapsed onto the pillow. Her eyes grew unfocused, and her breathing became irregular.

"It's a boy!" shouted Maria.

Viktor sat there numb. In this moment, he knew Sonia was dying. His reason to stay human was gone.

"Get me the scissors, girl! The baby is choking!"

The doctor's voice sounded distant, as if echoing through a fog. Viktor rubbed his face with his hands. He loved this woman. He went to that damn pack house and became a beast so he could return to this castle and be human for her. He glanced at Dr. Stanza.

Maria's hands trembled as she gave him the scissors. The doctor cut the cord. The baby was small, with a full head of ebony hair – just like Sonia's. He gasped for breath, and had bruising from the cord around his neck.

The doctor slapped the baby on the bottom. The infant coughed, but started breathing on his own.

"Wash him off, and if he stops breathing, hit him on the bottom like I did," said Dr. Stanza.

"Yes, Doctor."

Viktor released Sonia's limp hand. Ice spread through his limbs, as he felt an acute sense of loss. Viktor knew in his soul that Sonia had passed. He wanted to be human for Sonia – for their baby.

"I have to try and save Sonia," said Dr. Stanza. "Her condition is very critical. She's losing too much blood! Take the baby to the nursery and wait for me there. Maria, stay here and help me."

"I know you are doing your best," said Viktor, quietly. "Let me have my son."

Maria wrapped the boy in blankets and gave him to Viktor. The boy was tiny, but had incredible blue eyes. This baby was his only reason for living – for remaining human – but his breathing was very shallow. Viktor had to try – for Sonia's sake.

Viktor quietly stepped into the hallway. The castle seemed unnaturally silent. Were the servants hiding? He took the steps two at a time to the second floor, but as he reached the top step, the baby stopped breathing again. Viktor frantically slapped his son on his bottom the way the doctor had, trying to revive him. He pushed gently on his chest and listened for a heartbeat. He rested an ear against his son's nose, straining to hear a breath but he knew his son was dead.

Viktor collapsed onto the step, tears streaming down his face. He'd lost his wife and son. His soul fell into an unfathomable pool of pain and despair. He couldn't take anymore. With the death of his son, he'd lost his reason to retain his humanity. He was no longer a husband or a father, he was only a beast. He had nothing to live for.

Viktor stood and took long strides to the nursery and went inside. He sat down on the floor against the door with his dead son in his arms and gave vent to his own deep pain. He should slash his wrists and join Sonia.

A baby cried. Surprised, Viktor got to his knees, his shirt stained in tears, and looked at the nearest crib. Resting in a red and gold blanket was a baby.

Mihai and Theresa's baby.

He hadn't noticed Tatiana sitting nearby. She looked surprised and a little afraid. He cleared his throat.

"I'm sorry. I didn't know you were here," he said, quietly. "Dr. Stanza instructed me to bring the baby up here."

Tatiana nodded.

Viktor suddenly had a thought. "Tatiana, would you please assist Dr. Stanza? My wife might die and he could use the help. I can stay with the babies."

Tatiana nodded again and quickly left the room.

Once she had left Viktor went to the crib and unwrapped the baby – a boy. The baby was breathing steadily and had a slight discoloration around the neck, but in a different place than the baby in his arms. They shared the same ebony hair and blue eyes. Uncanny! Well, why wouldn't they look similar? Mihai and Sonia were siblings.

Viktor's jaw tightened so fiercely, he thought it would snap. The baby in the crib was his reason for living – for acting human. It would give him what he needed to stay alive, and he owed that to Sonia. Her death would not be in vain. Their son would live.

He knew he was running out of time before Dr. Stanza might arrive. Without giving it further thought he took Mihai's child out of its blankets and put his baby in them. Then he wrapped the living child in his blankets. No one would know he switched the babies. He would make Mihai and Theresa godparents like Sonia requested and Theresa would have an active role in raising the child since Sonia was dead. Theresa would still essentially be the baby's mother.

Viktor took a deep breath to push away a little sliver of guilt that niggled in the back of his mind. Yes, this was wrong, but he had done a lot of wrong things – even killing a man. He had to do this to keep the humanity in his soul.

Viktor put his fist to his mouth and grimaced. He cared for Mihai as a brother. How could he do this to him? Mihai had treated him better than Fedir ever had.

He had to find a reason. A reason. A reason. His mind raced. Mihai ignored Theresa when it came to the orphanage. Yes, that's it – Mihai ignored Theresa often.

He swallowed and stared at the crib. The baby in his arms wiggled. He wasn't sure he could carry out such a deception.

The door creaked open. Mihai entered.

"Viktor!"

"Mihai, I have bad news." Viktor steeled his spine. He felt wooden – like a toy soldier.

Mihai crossed his arms. "Sonia? My sister?"

"She's dead."

Mihai cupped his face in his hands. His body shook. Deep sadness emanated from him. Finally, he looked up, his eyes moist. "I'm sorry."

"I know you loved her very much," said Viktor.

"I...yes, I loved Sonia, but you..." his voice trailed off. "You've lost your wife."

Viktor swallowed. "Yes. I'm numb."

Mihai paused, then continued. "Theresa is awake now. I was so afraid she would die. She wants to see our baby."

Viktor sensed a wide chasm of anguish clashing with joy within Mihai. Interesting. He'd never consciously felt

Mihai's emotions, but it made sense. Mihai was a witch.

Viktor held up a hand. "There's more."

"What?"

"I came up to the nursery with my child and found yours dead." Viktor's jaw involuntarily twitched at the lie.

"What?" Mihai's voice thundered throughout the room. "That's impossible! He was breathing!"

Mihai ran to the crib and threw open the blanket.

"No!" screamed Mihai. "Not Sonia and not my son!"

Mihai turned around and lunged toward the bureau, pushing the items onto the floor. He snatched the colored Easter egg off a shelf and flung it at the wall. Anger raged in his body, rolling through him like a fierce winter storm.

Viktor's jaw twitched again.

Mihai went back to the crib. He ran his fingers over the baby and then collapsed to the floor.

"It can't be! It can't be my son who is dead! And Sonia...poor Sonia...!"

Viktor stood over Mihai and clamped a hand on his shoulder, firm in his resolve to carry out his lie. He was convinced now that he'd done the right thing. Mihai let his emotions guide his decisions now. His friend was consumed in deep pain. Mihai was weak and the child needed a strong father.

Mihai got to his feet, looking at the crib. "How could the prince have died? I saw him. He was breathing."

"Theresa did fall down the stairs. I don't suppose the birth was easy."

Mihai hung his head, cupping his face in his hands. His body shuddered, wracked with pain. He was pathetic to watch. Finally, he raised his head and looked at Viktor. "Where are your tears for Sonia?"

"I've already shed my tears for her. I have to be strong for my son now."

The gentle whimpers of the living child in his arms

caught both of the men's attention. Viktor and Mihai looked at the baby. The baby's mouth puckered. He must be hungry.

"Mihai, my son must be fed, and the only one here to do it is Theresa," said Viktor.

Mihai fisted his hands. Viktor felt unfathomable anguish coming from within him.

"How can I tell my wife that her son is dead, but she must provide for yours?"

Viktor swallowed. He hadn't thought about that. He hadn't given Theresa's feelings much thought, considering she would be the baby's mother in Sonia's place.

"You must have this baby fed or he'll die," said Viktor, stonily.

Mihai unclenched his fists. The door opened and Mrs. Nocesti walked in. She glanced at both men.

"Is something wrong, Your Majesty?"

"The prince is dead," said Mihai. A tear rolled down his cheek.

Viktor's jaw twitched again.

Mrs. Nocesti raced to the crib and looked inside. She examined the baby carefully and then looked at Mihai. "I don't understand. I thought the prince would live."

Viktor snarled. "I am sorry over the loss of the prince, but Theresa must feed my son."

"It might take a day or two to find a wet nurse, Your Majesty. We didn't anticipate the babies would come so soon. We need to have the queen feed the child."

Mihai hung his head. Viktor sensed anguish, guilt, and shame.

"Compose yourself, Mihai. You are a king and you cannot show weakness outside of this room in front of your servants. You must be strong in front of Theresa when you ask her to feed your sister's child," said Viktor. He realized he began to feel disgust at Mihai's behavior.

Mihai drew a handkerchief from his pocket and dried his face. He took deep breaths. Viktor sensed the gesture calmed Mihai. His friend walked to the crib and grabbed the rails, stiffening his back.

"What's your son's name?" asked Mihai.

Viktor's jaw twitched again. Damn his own lies, but Mihai was far too trusting. Alexandra had made a fool out of him. Viktor would have thought that Mihai, as a witch, might have been able to see through the switch, but he let grief cloud his intellect. Viktor realized he couldn't tell a soul about the switch – not even Alina.

"In her dying breaths Sonia said she wanted you and Theresa to be the child's godparents, and I agree. I'm going to name him Michael after you and Gregory after Theresa's father. I think that's only right considering the role you'll play in the baby's life."

Mihai looked up. "Follow me. Bring the baby."

Viktor followed Mihai out of the room. Mihai straightened his chin. Sadness etched the lines of Mrs. Nocesti's face. She accompanied them across the hall. Mihai paused, took another deep breath and knocked on the door before opening it.

Theresa sat in the bed, her back against the headboard. She wore a modest gown.

Mihai's faint expression was laced with sadness. He was an open book to Viktor, his friend's emotions raw and close to the surface.

"What's wrong?" asked Theresa.

Mihai sat next to the bed. "I have bad news."

Her expression stilled and grew serious. "Sonia?"

"She...died."

"Oh, Mihai!"

"Our baby...didn't make it, either."

"Our son is dead?"

"Yes."

Theresa grabbed his shirt, curling her fingers into the fabric. "How could that be? Was it the fall? Me?"

"The fall was an accident. When you gave birth, our son was alive, but when I went to check on him, he was dead." Mihai's eyes grew moist and he collapsed against her breast.

"No!" Theresa pushed him away and struggled to get out of the bed. Mihai grabbed her wrists and held her down. Anger and denial surged within her.

Viktor's eyes narrowed. Had he just sensed Theresa's emotions? Anger? Denial? Pain? It couldn't be!

He peered at Mrs. Nocesti. He saw sadness in the nurse's eyes, but he didn't sense her emotions.

He turned toward Theresa again. Fury danced in her eyes and washed over her like a raging river.

Theresa was a witch! And she wasn't as trusting or as foolish as Mihai.

Viktor recalled how Theresa could always make him smile – even laugh in an easy, unpretentious manner. He now realized her emotional state was reacting to him, relieving the tension and anxiety he always carried within him. Theresa put him at ease much in the same fashion Alina did.

"I want my baby!" Tears streamed down Theresa's cheeks. Mihai restrained her wrists until the fight went out of her. Exhausted, she looked at Viktor.

"What's Viktor doing here?"

"Sonia's baby is alive and hungry. You are the only one who can feed him," said Mihai.

Theresa brought a fist up to her mouth.

Mihai cupped her chin. "Viktor has named the boy Michael after me and Gregory after your father. We are going to be the boy's godparents, and with Sonia gone, you will be his mother in all the ways that count."

"I lose one son and gain another?" She covered her face

with her hands.

Viktor sensed slow acceptance within her. He stepped forward. "Theresa, please, feed the baby."

Theresa glanced up, acknowledging the concern in Viktor's voice. Did she sense the hunger in the baby? Her true maternal connection? Viktor shivered at the thought.

"Mrs. Nocesti, show me what to do," said Theresa.

Mrs. Nocesti looked at Mihai and Viktor. "The queen and I require privacy."

Viktor glanced at Mihai and they walked out. Now that he knew Theresa was a witch, Viktor felt like he had just received a second chance on his life – and his humanity.

Chapter Twenty-Three

Mihai paused in front of his apartment's door to steel his courage. It was several hours later and Mrs. Nocesti had been wonderful seeing to Theresa's needs. The nurse had also put out a call for a wet nurse and would interview candidates tomorrow.

He needed to see his wife. He had to know Theresa would be fine. Mihai took a deep breath, knocked on the door, and went inside.

"Theresa?"

"Mihai."

She leaned against the headboard. He sat down in a chair next to the bed and she closed the book she was reading. It was about tarot. Her skin was pale, but her sweet hazel eyes were sharp and alert. Her auburn hair fell past her shoulders in neat waves.

He reached out for her hand and she took it. "Darling, we must talk."

Her eyes darkened with sadness. "I'm sorry to hear about Sonia. I loved her like a sister. She had a wonderful heart full of kindness. I'm going to miss her."

"Thank you. I'm going to miss her very much." Mihai paused. After they left Theresa with Mrs. Nocesti, Mihai and Viktor found Dr. Stanza with Sonia. He had raised a blanket over Sonia's body. Observing the gesture tore a deep hole in Mihai's heart.

"Do you or Viktor have plans for her funeral?"

"Viktor and I have talked, but your input is important to me as well."

"Oh?"

"I want our son and Sonia buried next to my father."

Theresa cupped her chin, a wave of incredible anguish crested inside her. She nodded. After a moment, she composed herself and lowered her hand. "I think that would be fine. Sonia adored children. She liked going to the orphanage with me."

"Darling, we need to talk about our son. We have to give him a name."

A look of tired sadness passed over her features. "I'd like him to have a unique name."

"My middle name is Hadrian. Would that be acceptable to you?"

"Yes, that's fine." She paused. "I'm sorry, this isn't easy for me."

"I can sense that. The sadness is deep inside you."

She let out a long breath and closed her eyes briefly. "Perhaps Hadrian Leopold? I always liked Leopold."

"Hadrian Leopold it is."

"What now?" she asked.

"You'll be bedridden for several days, so I'll plan the funeral for ten days from now. I'm sending a message to your family so they can come."

"Thank you."

Mihai squeezed her hand. "There's something I want to tell you."

"Mihai, I understand. I sense your sadness; it's just as deep as mine. You don't have to talk about it."

"This is important to me."

"All right."

"When I saw you fall down those stairs, my life flashed before my eyes. I might have lost you. The thought terrified me."

"Mihai—"

He held up a hand. "Love is more than passion and intimacy. It's trust. It's faith. It's respect. My love for you is all this and more. "

"Mihai—"

"You make me complete." His voice was soft and he cupped her cheek, gently stroking her jaw with his thumb.

She placed her hand over his and closed her eyes. A sense of joy grew within her, and while the sadness lingered, he knew the words brought her happiness.

She opened her eyes. "I love you, too."

The moment was quiet, but just being with her had shined a light into his heart.

"The railroad is almost done, and when you are well, perhaps we can try again for a baby."

"I would like that."

Slowly, Mihai stood. "I have much to do, but if you want, I'll come back to say good night."

"Please." Her lashes dropped a little and she yawned.

"I'll be back soon."

Theresa flashed him a small smile, lay down, and closed her eyes.

Mihai quietly shut the door behind him. The castle was quiet. He knew that the deaths of both Sonia and the Prince had also stunned many of the servants, and they had laid wreaths, candles, and flowers in the garden, near the gazebo. This was their way of expressing their grief.

Mihai entered his study and stared out the window. Viktor sat near the wreaths, his head in his hands. Viktor was an odd mix of sadness and...confidence. That bothered Mihai. What did Viktor have to be confident about? It was an odd emotion to feel right now. Mihai would go talk to him after he talked to the von Krackens. He went to his desk, laid out his runes, and channeled as much energy as he could muster.

"Georg von Kracken."

After a long minute, the older man's face shimmered weakly into view.

"What's wrong? Something's happened."

Mihai's initial despair was gone, only to be replaced by a numbing pain that reminded him he was alive. "Sonia died in childbirth. Theresa also went into labor. Our baby died."

His mouth dropped open. "What? How could that be?"

"Theresa accidentally fell down the stairs."

"By Dalca! I'm coming with Beatrice and Edward immediately."

"Thank you."

"And the wolf? How is he taking this?"

"I sense a deep sadness within him. Even now, he's out by the wreaths in the garden placed there as a memorial to my sister."

"Watch him carefully. Do you sense anything else?"

"Confidence."

Georg's faced wrinkled in concern. "What does he have to be confident about?"

"I'm at a loss. I can barely think myself."

"Expect us in two days."

Mihai nodded.

"Keep my daughter away from the wolf. She's very vulnerable right now."

"I will."

"Mihai, I'm deeply sorry for your loss. Your sister was a good woman. What did you name my grandson?"

"Hadrian Leopold."

"The news of his passing wounds all of us. Do not grieve too deeply. Do not allow Theresa to grieve too deeply."

"Thank you, Georg. Goodbye."

"Goodbye."

Mihai sat down in the chair behind his desk. A small tear escaped from the corner of his eye and trailed down his cheek. He wiped it away and sat there, lamenting the losses of his son and sister.

~ * ~

Theresa stood next to Mihai, before the royal vaults. She

held his hand, her eyes painfully dry and exhausted from crying. She had no more tears to shed. The royalty of Moldavia were buried on the grounds of St. Mikhail's Church in the vaults close to the rear of the church. Father Gregori blessed the vaults – one for Sonia and one for Theresa's infant son, Prince Hadrian Leopold Sigmaringen.

The funeral had been private. Mihai had invited the prime minister and several important members of Parliament. Viktor was in attendance, and thankfully, her father, Edward, and Beatrice had come. She missed Victoria, but her father said she was needed at home – one of her children was ill. Seeing her family, especially Beatrice, revitalized her.

Mihai had been very tender and his attention had been exactly what her aching heart needed. He was hurting just as deeply as she was, but she had confidence they would overcome. Just this past week, he took his meals with her in their room. He massaged her shoulders, which helped take away some of the physical pain. He talked to her about the railroad, which was close to completion. He had wonderful ideas for them and Michael come Christmas.

Theresa swallowed, pushing back a small wave of happiness that made her feel a tad guilty. Her godson was a beautiful ray of light in all this tragedy. While he was small, he was perfect. He rarely cried and she missed him when she had to give him to the wet nurse. He had thick black hair, similar to her husband's, and blue eyes as bright as the sky. She took time out of her day to rock him in the rocking chair and sing him lullabies. Being with him made her heart hurt less.

Viktor had also been kind. He visited her at least once a day. At first they talked about Sonia, and Theresa came to understand that Viktor had loved Sonia deeply. Eventually, he talked about her less, and just yesterday, he brought her cards and flowers from the children at the orphanage who missed her. He instinctively seemed to know what would put her at ease, and a part of her was uneasy with the growing, but seemingly natural, rapport between them.

Father Gregori made the Sign of the Orthodox Cross, going to his right shoulder first. "In the name of the Father, Son, and Holy Ghost. Amen."

Mihai squeezed her hand. Beatrice approached and presented her with a red rose. Theresa nodded her thanks and placed the rose on the infant coffin.

The pallbearers lifted both the coffins and slid them into the vault next to Mihai's parents.

Theresa wrapped her arms around Mihai's waist. He held her close.

"May the Lord watch over both of them," said Mihai, quietly. His inner strength permeated her body, infusing her with the will to continue.

Father Gregori dismissed those in attendance.

"Theresa."

She turned around. Beatrice held out her arms, and Theresa hugged her sister. Viktor stood near the gate, his hands clasped in front of him. He appeared dignified, but she sensed a strange restlessness just underneath – a restlessness he hid with his staunch composure. Edward put his hand on her shoulder. Just as she turned away to embrace her brother, Viktor's lip gave a strange, almost involuntary twitch.

Something was wrong with him. Did Sonia's death affect him deeper than she thought? She couldn't worry about Viktor right now.

Edward hugged her, distracting her for the moment.

~ * ~

The next day, Theresa stood in front of the window in the library, her arms crossed in front of her. She watched as Miss Pompeli laid a small wreath near the gazebo. All felt the loss of Sonia and the Crown Prince. At least now, she was stronger – physically. She still felt a deep sense of loss over Hadrian. At times it would consume her and she would wallow in despair like she'd never known before. Thank God for Michael. She loved to hold him in her arms.

Theresa wanted more children.

When she first met Mihai, she knew she wanted him to be the father of her children, but she didn't expect Hadrian to be conceived so soon. She wanted to settle into her marriage and get used to being Mihai's wife, but she couldn't deny she enjoyed being pregnant, despite the aches and pains. Her growing desire to have another child overwhelmed her at times and she feared because of the accident she might not be able to have any more.

It was an irrational fear. Dr. Stanza told her and Mihai they could try when they were ready, but she was insecure over his reassurances. He hadn't been able to save Sonia.

She had to wait before they tried again, but the desire to try immediately raged through her. And the insecurity that she might not be able to have another baby waged war with her intellect. It was an impossible place to be. She had to focus on other matters right now – namely, how to tell Mihai she believed she was a witch.

Perhaps she should consult the tarot for guidance. Yes, she would do that. She'd been studying tarot all summer long with Mihai and was confident in her ability to read the cards.

The door opened and Beatrice walked in carrying a tray of tea and scones. "I thought I'd find you here."

Theresa gave her sister a gentle smile. "I'm glad you came, Bea."

"We're all deeply saddened by the loss of Sonia and Hadrian."

"Thank you."

Theresa joined Beatrice on the couch and steeped her

tea.

Beatrice glanced at Theresa. "Time will dull the ache. It's never easy to lose those we love."

Theresa nodded. "How long can you stay?"

"Father wants me to leave tomorrow, but I'm trying to talk him into letting me stay at least a week."

"I'll talk to him. I'd like you to stay."

"I'm sure if you ask, he'll let me stay. You always had him tied around your finger."

"Really, Bea."

"You did."

The door opened and Viktor walked in carrying Michael. He was loosely wrapped in his blanket and a bit fussy.

Theresa stood. "Viktor."

"The wet nurse just finished with him, but I can't get a burp from him."

Theresa walked over to Viktor and raised her hands, taking the baby from him. The infant calmed, and Theresa put him on her shoulder, lightly patting his back. Michael felt perfect in her arms.

"You are amazing with him," said Viktor.

Theresa smiled, his compliment warming her heart. Viktor returned her smile with one of his own.

"How cozy you two look," said Beatrice.

Theresa turned to face her sister. Beatrice's eyes narrowed, full of suspicion.

"What do you mean, Bea?"

Beatrice clapped her hands. "It's obvious Viktor appreciates you."

The baby burped, and Theresa felt the tension drain away from his little body. She held the infant up to her face and he curved his little lips into a smile.

Viktor stood behind Theresa and placed a hand on her shoulder. "Of course I appreciate Theresa. She's going to be Michael's godmother." Defensiveness laced his voice.

Deeper suspicion grew in Beatrice's eyes. "And when is the baptism?"

"Next week – before the full moon," said Viktor.

"Really, Bea. I love Michael like I would love my own child."

Beatrice crossed her arms.

The door opened and Mihai walked in. "Theresa! There you are."

Viktor took several steps away from her.

"Hello, Mihai." She held the baby in her arms and he snuggled comfortably against her. While the infant settled in, Theresa sensed high tension in the room – especially coming from Viktor.

"Ah, Viktor. Beatrice. It's nice to find you here as well," said Mihai.

Viktor stepped beside Theresa. "Hello, Mihai."

Mihai smiled at the baby in Theresa's arms. "How's Michael?"

"He's doing well. The wet nurse just finished with him," said Viktor.

Mihai glanced at Viktor. "I just received a telegraph from Herr Wursteg. They'll be ready to drive the golden stake in about ten days. It will be near Poarta Alba."

"That's wonderful news," said Viktor.

"Come, Viktor, let's give Mihai and Theresa a minute alone," said Beatrice. Her look was firm.

Viktor said nothing, but took Michael from Theresa. Beatrice stayed close to Viktor as they walked out.

Theresa was curious. Why did her sister almost bite Viktor's head off with her clipped replies and harsh voice? Didn't she know Viktor was hurting, too?

Mihai gestured toward the couch. Theresa took a seat next to him. She sensed sadness in her husband, but it wasn't as overwhelming or overpowering as it was in her. No, satisfaction surged within him.

"I missed you today." He took her hand in his.

"How was Parliament?"

"The docks are becoming run down. Parliament wants to propose an import tax, but I'm concerned they'll make the tax too high. The Prime Minister and I have been debating the tax rule."

"It sounds complicated."

"The only complication is our inability to compromise." He paused. "Herr Wursteg wants me there when they drive in the last stake. I told him I would attend."

"Ah, is that what the golden stake is?"

"Yes."

"When is it?"

"During the full moon."

"Viktor will miss it."

"I suppose he will, but he's missed several events. Why do you bring it up?"

"He's worked hard on the project. He deserves to be there."

"We all understand that he has to go away."

Theresa shrugged. "Yes, of course I do."

Mihai cocked his head. "Viktor hasn't acted inappropriately with you, has he?"

"No. I just know he's worked hard – as hard as you. It's a shame he has to miss it."

"Yes, it's a shame." He paused. "How do you feel?"

"I'm slowly getting my strength back."

"I sense the sadness is still deep inside you."

"It is. I'm trying to overcome it."

He cupped her cheek. "After this final visit to the railroad, I don't intend to leave you."

"No?"

"No. I want to take you out on the yacht for a day, and if weather permitting, perhaps another lunch at the winery. I'd like to invite some children from the orphanage to tour the castle."

Her heart sparked. "I would love that."

"Maybe we can take the train to Bucharest and go shopping at the Christmas markets when Advent comes."

"Or maybe we can travel to Austria? The Christmas markets in Vienna are beautiful," she said.

"I'd like to do that with you." He leaned forward, kissing her, his lips warm and moist, full of longing and love. She broke the embrace, afraid of letting it grow. She wasn't ready for more, but she did want to feel him – body and soul. She needed physical reassurance of his love. Theresa pressed against him, burying her face against his throat. He ran his fingers gently through her hair.

"This has been so trying for us. So much has happened since you came last winter. I love you, Theresa."

"Oh, Mihai." Her heart soared.

He kissed her temple. "I want to have another child with you. I want to fill the castle with children."

She closed her eyes, wanting the same thing.

Chapter Twenty-Four

Several days later, Viktor found himself in front of the altar in Saint Mikhail's Church, a sleeping Michael in his arms. Mihai and Theresa stood on each side of him. Theresa's disapproving sister, Beatrice, sat in the pew behind them. He sensed Beatrice didn't care for him, but it wasn't her opinion that mattered – it was Theresa's.

Theresa had been very attentive to Michael since he was born. The baby brought her great happiness and he liked being near her when Michael was with her. It made him feel almost human. But now he found the more he was around Theresa, the more he wanted to be around her.

Father Gregori lit two candles from the tall white one next to the altar and approached. Viktor wore a jacket, vest, white linen shirt, and trousers. The cravat around his neck felt constricting. Mihai wore the navy blue uniform of the king complete with medals and aiguillettes. Theresa wore a red gown with a gold sash, and a small diamond tiara.

Father Gregori gave one candle to Mihai, one to Theresa.

Viktor couldn't stop staring at Theresa. She was beautiful with her thick auburn hair tumbling down her back. Her dress accentuated her curves.

Father Gregori made the Sign of the Orthodox Cross, going to his right shoulder first, then he looked at Viktor.

"Who have you chosen to help guide this child on his spiritual journey?"

"King Mihai to be his godfather and Queen Theresa to be his godmother."

"King Mihai, Queen Theresa, are you prepared to take the baptismal promises for the child?"

"I am," they both replied.

Viktor's lip twitched. Unease grew in his limbs. He couldn't help but think that Mihai would be a weak example of a man in his son's life.

"Do you reject Satan?" asked Father Gregori of them.

"Yes," said Mihai and Theresa loudly. Viktor was silent.

"And all his works?"

"Yes."

"And all his empty promises?"

"Yes."

"And do you believe in God, the Father Almighty, Creator of Heaven and Earth?"

"Yes."

"Do you believe in Jesus Christ, born of the Virgin Mary, who was crucified, died, was buried and who rose from the dead?"

"Yes."

"Do you believe in the Orthodox Faith and promise to raise him in accordance with our beliefs?"

"Yes."

"King Mihai and Queen Theresa, pray the creed of our faith over this child and confess your true beliefs."

Together, Mihai, Viktor, and Theresa prayed the Nicene Creed of the Orthodox Faith. "What name have you chosen to give this child?" asked Father Gregori.

"Michael Gregory Bacau," said Viktor.

Two altar boys approached and took the candles from Mihai and Theresa. Father Gregori gestured toward the font, and Viktor brought his son forward. He turned toward Theresa who helped him undress the baby. Michael was completely naked. With a tap to the buttocks, Theresa woke the sleeping baby. Michael squirmed.

"In the Orthodox Faith, the infant shall be completely immersed in the baptismal font three times. This is to symbolize the three days Christ spent in the tomb and his rising to a new life in three persons, the Father, Son, and Holy Ghost," said Father Gregori.

Viktor held Michael in his arms and immersed his son's body into the font. Michael cried as soon as he was lifted out. Mihai did the same, followed by Theresa. Michael cried each time. After the third time, Viktor held Michael while Father Gregori anointed the baby with oil on his hands, feet, and forehead.

The altar servers approached with a clean white garment. Michael cried as Theresa assisted Viktor in putting the gown on him. After he was dressed, Theresa took the baby into her arms, gently rocking him. Theresa's natural mothering instincts impressed Viktor.

Michael settled into her arms. The baby adored Theresa. It was obvious in his shining eyes. Viktor's jaw tightened. He couldn't deny he wanted Theresa as a mate. Bane had Hecuba. Viktor wanted Theresa. He knew she was perfect for him. She was a witch. As for Alina, he couldn't see her acting as a mother to Michael. Alina made it clear she didn't want to be with him outside the wolf/witch relationship. Viktor knew it was wrong to desire Theresa, but he had decided he would do whatever it took to make her his. He would have to wait, bide his time, but soon the perfect opportunity would present itself – he was sure of it.

~ * ~

Theresa's gaze skimmed over the books on the shelf. She drew in a breath to help ease her restlessness. It didn't work. Yesterday she had stood as godmother to Michael and felt a deep connection to the baby. The feeling unsettled her. Sonia had been his mother, not her, yet she calmed him. Her presence made the baby happy. She didn't know what to make of that.

Michael slept now. Mihai was at Parliament. He felt the Prime Minister was wavering on the amount that he wanted to impose for the dock tax. Mihai wanted to ensure the success of his compromise. Theresa was glad just to have him home.

The door opened and Beatrice walked in. “Hello, Theresa.”

Theresa smiled. “Hello, Bea.”

“Looking for a book?”

“Yes. Unfortunately, I can’t find one that interests me.”

“Why don’t you finish your painting of the winery?” asked Bea.

“I don’t have the heart yet.”

Beatrice motioned toward the sofa and sat down. Theresa joined her.

“You’re still very sad, aren’t you?”

“Yes.” Theresa paused. “Bea, is it wrong of me to want another child?”

Beatrice raised an eyebrow. “So soon?”

“Yes.”

“Well, I think it’s natural to want another child, but perhaps your desire is a bit impulsive. You should wait a little longer, I think.”

“Why?”

“Get over the hurt of losing Hadrian. Let your emotions settle. Don’t let this sadness guide your decision.”

“Mihai wants another child, too.”

Beatrice took Theresa’s hands and squeezed. “Please, listen to my advice. It’s not given lightly.”

Theresa nodded, not really excited to hear Beatrice’s advice, but she knew her sister’s words had always been sound.

“I came to tell you I have to leave for Bucharest for a day or two.”

“Bucharest? Really? Why?”

“Father has business dealings with the Brancoveanus. He wants me to make sure they’re happy.”

“When will you leave?”

"Immediately. If I leave now, I can be there by nightfall."

"When will you return?"

Beatrice wrinkled her brow. "I hope to be back after the full moon."

"Oh, that's not long."

"No, not at all. Will you be all right?"

"I'll be fine."

"Are you sure?"

"I'll try to pick up my paint brush."

Beatrice stood. "All right, then. I'll see you in a couple of days."

Theresa got to her feet as well and hugged her sister. As soon as Beatrice left, Theresa's curiosity spiked. The visit to the Brancoveanus seemed rather sudden.

She sat down and rubbed her hand over her eyes, trying to dispel the sudden loneliness of her sister's departure.

Out of the corner of her eye she spied her tarot book resting on the table next to the window. Tarot. The cards would have answers for her. Unable to resist, she stood up and walked to Mihai's study. The tarot cards lay on his desk. She picked them up and returned to the library.

Once she was comfortable on the couch, she began to shuffle the cards. A restless energy grew within her. Theresa embraced it, as she shuffled them, letting her energy flow over them.

"I can do this. I am a witch. I can read the cards," she whispered.

Confident, she shuffled the cards and laid them face down in the pattern of a Celtic Cross on the table before her.

"Will Mihai and I have more children?"

Slowly, she turned over the cards. Most of them were upside down. Her heart sank.

The fool was upside down. Her life's journey was not going as expected. There would be obstacles – almost insurmountable.

Three children surrounded her life. Three losses. Pain.

She would have three children with Mihai and lose them all.

"No!" she cried.

Theresa raced to the window, and crossed her arms, tears flowing down her cheeks.

"I can't have children." Her voice hitched.

The emotional pain drained her strength. She collapsed to the floor.

The door opened. Theresa didn't move, and she didn't have to look at who was coming in. She knew from his earthy, pine scent it was Viktor.

He raced to her side and knelt before her. "What's wrong?"

Concern laced his dyed blue eyes. She was unwilling to face him, but she couldn't look away. Viktor would understand her pain. He knew what that type of heartbreaking pain felt like.

"Theresa, talk to me."

"I'm a witch."

He said nothing, only slowly nodding his head in acceptance.

"You believe me?" she asked, surprised he would embrace the statement so quickly.

"I've suspected it for several days now. As a wolf, I sense emotion, and I've felt deep sadness within you. It's understandable."

She pinched the bridge of her nose.

"Let me help you to the couch."

"No."

He raised an eyebrow. "Why not?"

"I don't want to go back there and look at the cards."

"What cards?"

"I read my tarot."

"I see. Did it tell you bad news?"

"I can't have children, Viktor."

He pursed his lips. "Really?"

She hung her head in shame. Viktor curved his fingers around her chin, lifting her head back up. "You want more children?"

"Yes."

His lip twitched and an intense, hungry expression crossed his face. "I have a suggestion."

"What?"

"I know a witch who can give you your heart's desire. She's my leader's witch."

"Leader? What are you talking about?" She could barely comprehend what he was saying, the grief was so deep inside her.

"Bane is the leader of my pack. Hecuba is his witch. If you want, I'm sure she can work the magic necessary to give you what you want – a child." His voice was cool, yet with subtle undercurrents. Of what? Desire?

"Say it plainly, Viktor." A small bubble of hope welled up inside her, despite the mention of Hecuba. Theresa had no doubts that Hecuba was dedicated to committing evil – after all, she was the witch who had killed Mihai's mother.

"If you curse yourself to become a werewolf, Hecuba can work the magic to give you the child you want."

"Become a werewolf? Like you?" Horror tore down her spine.

"Or you could curse the child. I can't imagine you would want to do that to a child though."

"How revolting!"

He shrugged his shoulders. "I only offered you a solution to your problems. It's your choice to make."

Theresa scrambled to her feet. "Get out!"

"Really, Theresa, think about it. Why don't you use your magic to help yourself? I can contact Bane and make the arrangements. The full moon is two days away." Viktor stood.

She glared at him. "Leave!"

His expression turned calculating. "Think about it. You have time."

"Damn it, go!"

He turned around and walked out. How dare he make such an unreasonable suggestion! Theresa clenched her fists. And yet, she had to admit it was a suggestion she dared to entertain. Her emotions were raw – on edge – driven by a need to sate the powerful desire within her.

Should she tell Mihai about the reading? Have him read the cards? She shivered and crossed her arms, rubbing her hands up and down. It would break Mihai's heart to learn they couldn't have children. She couldn't do that to him. Theresa needed more information. When she had picked up the tarot cards, there was a book about witchcraft on his desk. Maybe she could find answers there.

Moving with firm determination, she left the library and went to Mihai's study. The book was still on his desk. She sat down and opened it. Theresa flipped the pages slowly, yet fluidly, her eyes hunting for certain words – magic, curses, and werewolves.

Time passed. Deep into the book, she found her answers.

A person can be cursed into becoming a werewolf. A promise is made in blood between the binding parties. Dark magic is used to curse the individual. If it was found out the witch entered into a curse, it could mean death.

She closed her eyes. This was hopeless. Why was she entertaining such a foolish notion? Because she wanted a child. Could a curse be broken?

Theresa kept reading. Powerful, good magic could break a curse. What was powerful? Theresa's fingers skimmed the words. Love. The act of making love, to the one the cursed loved, could break the curse. If they make love to a person they are not in love with, then the curse will never be broken. This must be done by the eighteenth birthday or the curse will take effect regardless.

Theresa leaned back in the chair and closed her eyes. Could she do it? Curse the child she and Mihai would conceive just to give him an heir? Could she control that child's life, watch over him or her, and ensure that he or she made love to the one they were in love with? Could she hide this from Mihai? She had to.

She hung her head in her hands. Why was she even contemplating this foul action? Because she loved Mihai. He loved her. They were entitled to happiness.

She lifted her head and closed the book. Theresa had much to think about and little time to make a decision.

Chapter Twenty-Five

Mihai entered the nursery expecting to find Theresa. Instead, Viktor was there watching the wet nurse burp the baby.

His stomach tightened. Theresa hadn't been in her room or the library.

Viktor's lips twitched as he turned to face Mihai. Odd that Mihai hadn't noticed it before, but he realized Viktor had been doing that since Sonia's death.

"Hello, Mihai."

"Viktor, have you seen Theresa?"

"The last time I saw her was in the library."

Mihai crossed his arms. Where was she? He knew one more place he could check.

"Did you and the Prime Minister come to a compromise?" asked Viktor.

"Yes. I'm very pleased, but I wish it hadn't taken so long. Can you make arrangements to have the children from the orphanage come for a tour next week? I think that might cheer Theresa up."

"Of course. After the full moon."

"Yes." Mihai paused. Michael burped. The wet nurse smiled at the baby.

"How's Michael today?" asked Mihai.

"He's fine," said Viktor, quickly.

"Will you be joining us for the dinner meal?" asked Mihai.

"Yes, of course."

"I'll see you then," said Mihai.

Viktor nodded and Mihai left. He walked down the hallway into the empty apartments and opened the wooden door that blended into the wall. He stepped into the secret staircase that would take him to the tower.

Nervous energy pulsed through him. The tower was their special place, but they hadn't been here in weeks. Why would Theresa go there now?

He opened the door. Theresa sat at the table next to the telescope. His wife's hurt and longing lay naked in her eyes, but there was more. Her eyes were red. Had she been crying? He sensed tension within her – tension that was frighteningly intense.

"What's wrong?" he asked.

"I'm fine now."

He crossed the distance between them and knelt before her, taking her hands in his. "Something's upset you."

"I'm fine," she repeated.

"Why did you come here?"

"I wanted to think. I wanted to remember..." her voice trailed off.

"When we conceived our son?"

She bit her lower lip. "Yes."

He squeezed her hands. "We will have more children, darling."

She held her head up high, proudly. "Yes, we'll have more children."

He stood up and drew her into his arms. Why did he sense resignation?

"Darling, I have to leave for Poarta Alba tomorrow. They're putting the last stake into the rail line. Do you want to come with me?"

She pushed back and looked into his eyes. "No, I'll stay."

"Are you sure?"

"Michael needs me."

He cupped her cheek. "I understand."

"Mihai, there's something I want to tell you."

"Oh, what?"

"I think I'm a witch."

He withdrew, raking his gaze over her. "Why do you believe this?"

"I sensed the baby in Sonia's womb. He was hurting her and I told him to stop. He did."

Mihai's eyes widened. He paused as he considered his options, but happiness seeped into his bones. He could finally talk to her about being a witch without betraying her father's trust. "Is Beatrice here? We need to talk."

"Bea? No, she left for Bucharest. Why do you ask?"

"She's a witch, too, Theresa." Mihai paused again, unsure if he should tell her the truth. No doubt her father would be upset with him, but Theresa was Mihai's wife, and he was through hiding the truth from her.

"In fact, your entire family is a witching family," he continued.

Theresa raised her hand to her mouth as shock filled her eyes. "Everyone? Bea? Ed? Victoria?"

"Yes. They're good witches – I've learned much from them, especially Beatrice."

"But...they didn't tell me?"

"No. Your father's dreams told him he shouldn't."

"And you kept their secret?"

"Your father asked me to."

"I'm your wife!" Anger surged within her, and she pounded her fists on his chest.

"Theresa, stop hitting me!" He grabbed her wrists and pulled her roughly, almost violently, toward him so the length of her body pressed against his.

"You love me! How could you not tell me?"

He stared into her wide hazel eyes. "I honored your father's request, but I won't any longer. You are my wife, and I do love you. It's not fair to you anymore, especially if you already believe you are a witch."

She softened against him. He locked his hand on her spine and kissed her with savage intensity. Her lips were hard at first, but she finally relented, kissing him back, threading her fingers over his shoulders and into his hair.

God, he loved this woman.

Mihai broke the kiss and looked into her eyes. "When Beatrice returns, we'll talk."

She nodded.

"I know this is an emotional subject. We're expected downstairs for dinner. Do you feel like eating right now?"

Theresa sighed, then nodded. Mihai took her hand. His wife's emotions had calmed a bit, but he still sensed resignation, apprehension, and a hint of fear. He had no idea how to lessen her hurt, but he knew he had to find a way.

~ * ~

Viktor arrived at the pack house around three in the afternoon. He secured his horse and with determined strides walked inside. He couldn't help but smile. Theresa had approached him before he left, after Mihai departed for Poarta Alba. She wanted Viktor to arrange what he had suggested – she wanted to be cursed so she could conceive a child.

"Viktor, why are you smiling?" asked Bane. The tall, lanky wolf stood next to the wooden table. Nasguard, Timon, and Gascon rolled weed.

"Theresa Sigmaringen has requested a favor."

"Oh. Who is this woman?"

Hecuba and Diana walked into the room from the hallway. Hecuba's eyes betrayed her fatigue.

Diana wrinkled her brow, thoughtful. "Isn't she the new Queen of Moldavia?"

"Yes," said Viktor.

Hecuba cackled. "Isn't this precious? And what does she want?"

"She wants to conceive a child – and she's willing to curse herself to have it done."

"How ironic! Esmeralda's brat has grown into a man and has a witch for a wife who needs a favor from me."

Timon's eyes blazed with disgust. "This woman is a fool."

Viktor shot both of them a look. "She's who I want."

"Want? What about Alina?" asked Bane.

"She cannot give me her heart."

"Yet you think the Queen of Moldavia can?" asked Bane.

"Yes. She is my child's godmother."

Bane turned toward Hecuba. "Can you do the magic?"

"Yes, but I need to confirm her wishes and it's late in the day."

"It's an hour and a half on horseback," said Viktor.

"I can't make that journey in this old body," said Hecuba.

Bane glanced at Diana. "Travel to the castle and confirm the queen's wishes. If she agrees, escort her here. We'll be waiting for you in the clearing to the rear of the pack house."

Diana nodded.

Hecuba coughed. "Where are Maria and Alina?"

"They should be here soon," said Gascon.

Hecuba held out a gnarled old finger and pointed at Viktor. "Let me make this plain to you – the magic assumes the child will be cursed. She must ask to take the curse on herself."

Viktor frowned, but nodded his acknowledgement.

Timon grunted. "Diana, come with me for a minute."

She followed him into the hallway. Viktor watched him with narrow eyes. Timon didn't factor into tonight. After the magic was done, Alina could be free to marry her Ioan and Theresa would belong to him. He just needed a plan. He shrugged his shoulders. What could he tell Mihai to make him leave Theresa? How about the truth? She cursed her own child.

~ * ~

Theresa lay Michael down in his crib. She had rocked him to sleep. It was one of the many activities she enjoyed. Restless, she walked to the window and crossed her arms, looking down onto the courtyard. What was going to happen now? Would Viktor come and take her to his pack house?

She raked a nervous hand through her hair. She couldn't believe she was contemplating this, but both she and Mihai desired another child and the tarot said she couldn't have any. She had to be strong. According to the book, the cursed child could break it if he fell in love. Theresa would watch over the child, guide its course, do everything in her power to see that he or she would break the curse when the time came. She was a witch, after all. And she would move Heaven and Hell to save her only child.

A woman on horseback wearing a brown cloak approached. Theresa didn't recognize her. The soldiers on guard at the entrance stopped the woman.

Who was it? Anxiety pulsed through Theresa like a rapidly beating drum.

There was a knock on the door.

"Come in."

Mr. Tybeski walked in. "Your Majesty, there's a young lady to see you. She said Lord Bacau sent her."

This was it. Theresa acknowledged Mr. Tybeski with a slight nod of her head and followed him down the stairs to one of the reception rooms next to the entrance hallway.

As Theresa opened the door, she paused and looked at Mr. Tybeski. "Can you wait outside the door?"

"Yes, Your Majesty."

Theresa entered the room and closed the door behind her. The woman wore a long brown cape, the hood draped over her shoulders. She was thin, but her expression spoke of great inner strength. The woman had light brown eyes and long walnut-brown hair.

"I am Diana Melchior," she began. "I was sent by Viktor Bacau and by the leader of our pack, Bane Bacau."

Theresa raised an eyebrow, intrigued by the names. "I am Theresa Sigmaringen."

"You are the Queen of Moldavia?"

"Yes."

"I am a witch," said Diana.

"So am I," said Theresa, proudly.

"Do you want our high witch to work her dark magic in order for you to conceive?'

"Yes."

"I sense much turmoil in you. Do you doubt this decision?"

"No." She swallowed, determined to be resolved, but unsure and doubting at the same time.

Diana drew in a deep breath. "The magic assumes you will curse the child – you know that?"

"Yes."

Diana paused, her expression softening. "This is not a wise choice."

"This is the only choice left to me."

"Go and eat. You'll need your strength. I'll escort you to the pack house after nightfall. Can you depart without being noticed?"

"Probably not."

"I have anast dust – to help those who see us forget."

"All right."

Diana sat down on a chair. "I'll wait here until you are ready."

"I'll have some tea and scones brought in."

"Thank you."

Theresa walked to the door and put her hand on the knob. She paused. Even now she doubted herself, but she knew she was a witch and was determined to help her child overcome the curse that would conceive him or her.

~ * ~

Mihai looked at the growing clouds. An uneasy chill raced down his spine. Something didn't feel right.

Workmen pounded on the remaining stakes. Sergeant Ceseanu from his royal guard stood close by. The sun dipped closer to the horizon. Mihai should be excited to see the final stake driven in. Several reporters from Bucharest and Constanta were in attendance.

So why didn't he feel excited?

He missed Theresa. And he knew he had to do more to shake her out of the lingering despair she felt since the death of their son.

"Your Majesty!"

Sergeant Ceseanu approached with Herr Wursteg. The German held a golden stake. The workmen stopped and watched.

"We are ready. Do you want to drive the stake in yourself?" asked Herr Wursteg.

"I'd be honored."

Herr Wursteg presented Mihai with the stake. Mihai walked over to the last tie. A workman set the stake and Herr Wursteg gave Mihai a thick sledgehammer. Mihai raised it high over his head and brought it down. The stake went in, but only a little. Mihai continued pounding. The stake went in deeper each time. Camera lights flashed in his eyes, but Mihai ignored them. It felt good to release his pent-up aggression.

With one last swing, the hammer connected with the stake and Mihai knew it was snug in the tie. He looked up and smiled. Several flashes went off.

"A word, Your Majesty," said a reporter.

Mihai nodded. Sergeant Ceseanu took the sledgehammer from him.

"When will the first trains run?" asked another reporter.

"I believe we want to do a couple of test runs. Once Herr Wursteg gives me the word, I'll contact Count Brancoveanu. I would anticipate the first run within a week or two."

"Very well."

Mihai gestured to Herr Wursteg. "Do you mind answering the rest of the questions? It's getting late and I want to go home."

"Yes, Your Majesty."

Mihai put his hand on Herr Wursteg's shoulder and looked out at the crowd. "Herr Wursteg will answer the remainder of your questions. I just want to say that this railroad brings us closer to Romanian unification and I look forward to the day the Romanian principalities are united."

Applause rang out. Mihai departed, Sergeant Ceseanu at his side.

"Your Majesty, we have a room reserved for you at a local inn."

Mihai paused. "For the night?"

"Yes."

He rubbed his hand across his mouth. He didn't want to stay overnight.

"I'll stop by the inn for dinner, but after I eat, we'll travel to Constanta."

"It will take us several hours and the route will be dark."

"I have the best guards." Mihai paused, smiling. "Pay the innkeeper for the night and thank him for preparing the room."

Sergeant Ceseanu nodded, opening the door to the carriage. Mihai stepped inside. Theresa needed him, and from now on, he was determined that his wife would be involved in everything he did. The carriage ambled off.

~ * ~

Theresa wore a simple gown covered by a dark cloak, much in the same fashion Diana did. A full moon lit up the sky, but it was early, only an hour after nightfall. Diana took Theresa to a log cabin, but when she found it empty, escorted Theresa to a clearing. Tiny beads of sweat formed on her temples.

Knots twisted in Theresa's stomach. Fear gnawed at her limbs, but she pushed it aside. She told herself she was doing the right thing, and she trusted in her abilities as a witch to save the child she would conceive.

In the clearing, Theresa spied an old woman dressed in a silver robe next to a small wooden table with a bag, a cup, and a knife. Two younger women, their faces partially obscured by their hoods, stood behind the old lady. A fire burned in the shape of a pentagram next to her. A wolf stood beside the old woman. On the far side several wolves gathered. Theresa glanced at the wolves quickly, trying to discern which one was Viktor, but found it difficult to tell.

Theresa clenched her fists in an effort to push down her rising fear. Diana continued to stand next to her, and surprisingly, the witch's presence calmed her a little.

The wolf approached, shifting into a man. He was tall, but thin, with beady yellow eyes similar to Viktor's.

"Take off your hood," said the old woman.

Theresa pushed the covering away from her face. Her hands shook.

The naked man stopped before Theresa. "I am Bane." He paused and gestured toward the old woman. "She is Hecuba, my witch. Viktor tells me you want a favor."

"Yes."

"In exchange for Hecuba's magic, you agree to curse the child. When your child turns eighteen, he will transform into a wolf and become a member of my pack."

"Yes, but I want assurances."

The wolf laughed. "Assurances? There are no assurances, just my rules."

Theresa steeled her spine. "I want reassurances that should the child fall in love before their eighteenth birthday, this curse goes away."

Hecuba stepped forward. "Love can break this."

Bane held up his hand. "I know the power of love, witch." He paused, turning his head to look at Theresa. "I also know it is the physical act of the child making love to the one he loves that will free him of the curse."

"I understand," said Theresa.

"These conditions are near impossible to meet. I mean, what young man entering his teenage years doesn't want to sample what's around him?"

"Perhaps, but I want assurance that if these conditions are met, the curse will be broken."

"Should the conditions be met, the curse will be broken."

"Good."

"Step forward to the table," said Bane.

Theresa followed his instructions, stopping before the old woman.

Bane looked at the wolves. "I require blood from a member of the pack."

A dark-haired wolf shoved the wolf next to him, causing that wolf to stumble. The dark haired wolf with the wild eyes trotted forward.

Bane pointed to the pentagram. "Walk through the fire."

The wolf did so, changing into a man. He was the same height as Bane with thick dark brown hair. Theresa's nose twitched from the stench of him.

Bane picked up a cup from the table. "I require blood from both of you. Hold out your palms."

Theresa did as instructed. Hecuba slashed Theresa's flesh with the blade. Theresa flinched upon being cut. Then she did the same to the man. Theresa noticed he didn't move when the knife pierced his skin. Their blood dripped into the cup below.

Theresa looked at the man before her. "What's your name?"

"Timon."

Hecuba raised her hands to the moon and began chanting. Blue light shaped like a lightning bolt came out of the sky and struck her. She placed her hands on the cup and then collapsed.

Bane thrust the cup at Theresa. "Drink!"

She swallowed a taste of the coppery liquid, fighting back her gag reflex. Timon took the cup from her and finished off the contents.

Bane put the cup on the table, dropped to his knees and pushed Hecuba's shoulders. She lay face down in the dirt. "Get up, witch."

She didn't move.

"Witch, I'm talking to you!" Bane's voice cracked with apprehension.

"Is she dead?" asked Timon.

Diana ran forward and knelt next to Bane, examining Hecuba. Finally, she looked up. "This last use of dark magic has killed her."

Theresa took a step backward. She didn't want to be here anymore. She found the violence abhorrent and the scent of the blood filled her with nausea.

"No!" cried Bane. He leapt to his feet and grabbed the knife off the table. What was he going to do?

He turned the blade on himself and drove it into his heart. His body collapsed over Hecuba's.

"Bane!" cried Timon. The wolves howled.

Panic coursed through Theresa's limbs. She turned around, intent on running back to her horse.

Timon grabbed her wrist. Their eyes met. "I will come for your child on its eighteenth birthday if he is not a wolf before."

"You cannot have him."

"Then pray you make me a worthy adversary." Timon let go of Theresa's hand.

"Go, Queen! Leave!" shouted Diana. The wolves' howls excited the other nocturnal creatures around them.

Theresa turned around and ran out of the clearing.

Chapter Twenty-Six

Viktor's lupine eyes widened with shock. Everything had gone wrong! He scraped his paw against the dirt, trying to ease the swelling anxiety and disgust that filled him.

He'd meant to give the blood Bane needed for the curse, but Timon was a second faster and shoved him aside. It was Timon who walked through the pentagram of fire and became a man. It was Timon who gave his blood for the curse! Theresa's child owed his life to Timon, and Timon would go after him or her with a vengeance.

And Theresa! She was supposed to curse herself, not the child. She wasn't fit to be Michael's mother. No, that selfish bitch had ruined Viktor's last chance at happiness. She would pay dearly for what she did tonight.

Nasguard brushed against him, baring his wolverine teeth. *"By Dalca!"*

Viktor turned to face him. *"What's wrong?"*

"Hecuba and Bane are dead. This wasn't supposed to happen."

Viktor snarled. *"Let them rot. Let's go to the cabin."*

"We follow Timon now. He's human when he shouldn't be. He's the leader!" said Gascon.

"But I thought I would be."

"No, you aren't. You didn't walk through the fire. You aren't human now," said Nasguard.

Viktor's insides grew cold with betrayal.

"Wolves! Witches!" cried Timon.

Viktor glared at Timon. He stood next to the pentagram, arms outstretched. Diana knelt next to the bodies of Hecuba and Bane's.

"We go to the pack house," said Timon.

"What about the bodies?" asked Diana.

"Leave them. We'll come tomorrow to bury them."

Diana joined Alina and Maria. Apprehension filled their eyes, but they walked toward the pack house.

"Come, guard the witches," said Nasguard.

Viktor followed him and they trotted next to the women.

Timon stepped away from the pentagram and shifted as effortlessly as Bane would have into a wolf. They raced home. Viktor's disgust grew until it permeated every bone of his lupine body.

No, Theresa wasn't worthy to be a mother. He couldn't forgive her. She would pay for betraying him.

~ * ~

Viktor woke up in the main room of the pack house next to the fireplace. He stood, his joints in incredible pain.

"Alina!"

No answer. He stumbled down the hall to his room. Alina was asleep in the bed. He pushed her shoulder. "Wake up."

Alina stirred. "What's wrong, Viktor?"

"Everything."

"Viktor, get out here now!" Timon's voice was cold and calculating.

Alina frowned. Viktor sensed raw fear in her.

"Timon. You must go. He's our leader now."

Viktor clenched his fists. "I've had enough of Timon. I won't answer to him."

"Viktor!" cried Timon again.

"Go," said Alina.

"Fine. Get dressed and bring the other witches to the main room. I'm going to end this between Timon and me right now."

Alina nodded. Viktor marched out of the room and went to the main hall. Timon stood next to the long wooden table dressed only in trousers. Nasguard and Gascon sat on the couch. Timon pointed to a bowl on the table. Viktor stopped next to the couch, ready to pounce on Timon.

"What do you want?" asked Viktor.

"Your loyalty."

Viktor sneered, revealing his elongated incisors. "Never."

"Have it your way. I will let you leave the pack if you eat these mushrooms."

Viktor flexed his fingers. "Mushrooms? Surely, you're mad."

"Don't do it, Viktor," said Gascon.

"They're dangerous. You'll go crazy," said Nasguard.

Alina and the witches entered the room.

"The only way we'll be free of Timon is to eat the mushrooms," said Diana.

"I will," said Viktor.

"You know they are dangerous!" said Maria. "You'll go insane."

Diana turned to Maria. "Yes, they are very dangerous. I picked them myself, but they are the only way."

Viktor glanced at the witches. Diana palmed a glass vial into the sleeve of her dress. What did it mean? He didn't care. His joints trembled. His heart ached. Sharp pain raced through his spine.

"Give me your damn mushrooms," said Viktor.

"I'll eat, too," said Diana. She gestured toward Maria and Alina. "As will they."

Alina turned pale. She reeked of fear, yet she did not protest.

Timon's snarl of pleasure dropped a little. "And what you, Nasguard? Gascon?"

Nasguard stood. "I'll eat."

"As will I," said Gascon.

"By Dalca! May he curse the lot of you."

"Timon, once the last person eats, no one in this house

will be bound to you. You must leave here and never return," said Diana.

"You presume to dictate to me?"

"We all hate you, Timon. What's to stop Viktor or Nasguard from killing you?" asked Diana.

"I'll do as you say and leave. I'll start a new pack – you can all fend for yourselves!"

Viktor stepped forward. "Give me a mushroom."

Timon held out the bowl. Viktor grabbed a mushroom and shoved it into his mouth. Diana, Nasguard, Alina, Gascon, and finally Maria did the same.

Viktor fell to the ground, his limbs shaking. He choked. Fire spiked through him.

Timon stood next to the door and laughed wildly as everyone in the room collapsed onto the floor.

"May you all rot in Hell!" Timon slammed the door behind him as he left.

The blood froze in Viktor's veins; then in a wild rush, pumped again. Colors danced before his eyes. Theresa. He envisioned taking the baby from her arms and slashing his nails across her cheek. She collapsed in a pool of her own blood. He turned around, satisfied Theresa would bleed to death. He was going to kill her now.

Viktor stumbled to his feet and raced out the door, intent on making Theresa pay for her betrayal.

As he closed the door, a woman calling his name echoed in his ears. He ignored her.

~ * ~

Diana placed a vial to Alina's lips and tipped it down her throat. Alina felt the liquid coat her insides, soothing the rush of anxiety caused by the mushroom. Breathing deeply, Alina sat up. Diana poured a vial of liquid down Gascon's mouth, then Maria's.

Nasguard put his hand on Alina's shoulder. "Are you all right?"

"Yes, I believe so. What happened?"

"Diana gave us an antidote," said Nasguard.

"Viktor!" cried Diana.

Alina glanced over and saw Viktor pull the door open and he raced outside.

"Viktor, come back!" cried Diana. She ran to the door and flung it open. "Damn, he's gone."

"Did he have the antidote?" asked Alina.

"No, not yet. He'll go mad."

"Mad? You mean insane?" asked Alina.

"Yes." Diana paused. "Maria, bring us all a drink of water. It will help cleanse our systems."

"What just happened, Diana?" asked Nasguard.

Diana sat down on the wooden bench and raked a hand through her hair. "Timon suspected something important would happen last night. He knew how sick Hecuba was, and doubted she had enough strength to do the magic requested of her. He told me to pick the mushrooms. I knew what they were capable of, so I used a little of the juices to make an antidote for everyone while waiting at the castle. If he gave it to us, the antidote would save us. It has to be administered within the first thirty minutes of eating the mushroom. I fear Viktor will go crazy."

Anxiety knotted inside Alina. She crossed her arms. "I sensed deep anger and resentment inside him when he woke me up this morning."

"Diana, let me ask you this – are we free?" questioned Nasguard.

Maria entered carrying mugs filled with water and began distributing them.

"Yes, we are free. We can go our own ways," said Diana.

"Well, I, for one, am glad. I've had enough of obligations," said Gascon.

"You will still need help to get through the full moon," said Diana.

"Maria, will you come with me?" asked Gascon. He held out his hand.

She placed her hand in his. "Yes."

"I intend to claim my estates in Carpathia. I was well-off once. Perhaps I can get my old life back," said Nasguard.

"I wish you the best," said Diana.

"Would you want to come with me, Diana? At least for a little bit, until you decide what you want to do?"

"Thank you, Nasguard." Diana drew in a deep breath. Her brow wrinkled in thought. "I would like that."

"What about you, Alina?" asked Gascon.

Alina rubbed her hands together. "I must go to the Sigmaringens and warn them of the danger Viktor presents. Then I'll go home to my father."

"I wish you all well," said Diana.

Alina went to her room. She gathered her cloak and satchel, glad her duties and obligations were finally over. She could go home and marry Ioan, but first she had to travel to Constanta with due haste. She feared what would happen if Viktor confronted the Sigmaringens.

Chapter Twenty-Seven

Mihai arrived at Delfin Castle shortly after midnight. He was bone-tired from the trip, so he knew his men were, too. After instructing Sergeant Ceseanu to retire the men after the horses were taken care of, he went inside.

An eerie quiet surrounded the castle. Mihai checked the nursery. Michael, his wet nurse, and the nanny were asleep. Satisfied, he closed the door behind him and went to Theresa's room.

Light from the full moon filtered in through the window. Theresa lay on the bed in her nightgown, her hair spread out over her pillow. He sat down in the chair next to the bed. Her chest rose and fell in a rhythmic fashion. He leaned over and placed a hand gently on her exposed shoulder.

He sensed her sleep was light and a disturbance would easily awaken her. He also sensed deep anxiety within her. Was it preventing a heavier sleep? An earthy scent caught his nose. He glanced over at the chair in front of the dresser. A cloak rested there. Had she been out earlier?

Gently, he rubbed his thumb over the soft flesh of her shoulder.

"Theresa, darling, I love you," he whispered. "I'll talk to your father. I want him to acknowledge that you are a witch." He paused. "I'll do everything in my power to help you overcome your heartache."

He leaned back in the chair, stretched out his long legs, and closed his eyes.

~ * ~

Beatrice entered the library. The sun had just risen. Her

sister was probably just getting up herself. Beatrice had arrived at the castle late last night, close to eleven. She stayed a little longer than she anticipated with Count Brancoveanu. The Count was an engaging man, and if he had been twenty years younger, Beatrice might have entertained having an affair with him.

She chuckled at the thought. She still might.

Beatrice sat down at the couch. Before her on the table was a tarot spread. Curious.

Tatiana walked in with a tea service and a breakfast plate. Beatrice thanked her and the maid left.

Beatrice steeped her tea and looked at the cards. Who would have laid them out? It was a perfect Celtic cross. She drew in a breath. Only two people in the castle could have done this – Mihai or Theresa.

She prayed it was Mihai. Beatrice sipped her tea as she examined the cross with a careful eye.

What she saw caused her to nibble anxiously on her lower lip. The cards were clear. Three children would be had, three children would be lost.

Beatrice rubbed her hands on her arms. The message on the face of the cards was not comforting. Beatrice looked deeper. Six children would be had in all.

The door opened. Beatrice looked up. Mihai.

"There you are! I've been looking for you everywhere," he said.

Beatrice patted the spot next to her. "Come. Sit. We have to talk."

"I agree."

"Where's Theresa?"

"Upstairs with Michael. She'll join us shortly." He sat down next to Beatrice.

She pointed to the spread. "Did you do this?"

"No." He paused, then peered at her. "Theresa knows she's a witch. She probably did this."

"What? How did she find out?"

"She made the deduction herself. I didn't tell her, only confirmed it for her."

Beatrice pursed her lips disapprovingly. "You confirmed it?"

"I also told her that all her family members are witches – including you."

"By Dalca!" Beatrice rubbed her hand across her mouth, dread racing through her body. "My father is going to give me the boils for a month!"

"The boils?"

"Let's just say the boils are unpleasant. This is not good."

"I expect you to be honest with her."

"Of course I will. She's my sister. Our father will have to accept her secret is out. No doubt he'll be displeased, but we have a more pressing matter."

"Oh?" He raised an eyebrow.

"How knowledgeable is Theresa in tarot?"

"She knows the cards."

"Look at the spread and tell me what you see."

Mihai ran his eyes over the cards. They danced with unease. "Three children are had, three are lost."

"Look deeper."

Mihai studied the cards, then sat back. "Six children are had in all."

"Good. However, the deeper interpretation is lost if you don't look carefully enough."

He wrung his hands together. "We've already lost one child. I can't imagine losing two more."

She placed a hand over his and transferred her calming thoughts. He relaxed a little. "You must be strong and remember the deep love you have for my sister. That will get you through the heartache."

Mihai nodded.

"Damn. I hope this doesn't make Theresa a practicing witch. It might mean her death," said Beatrice.

"If your father asks, tell him I did it."

"Lie?"

"Yes. I love Theresa."

Beatrice frowned.

"I'll see to it she never practices, I promise."

Beatrice rubbed her arms with her hands. "All right I'll do it."

There was a knock at the door.

"Come in," said Mihai.

The door opened. Sergeant Ceseanu stepped in. "There's a noblewoman here to see you, Your Majesty."

Mihai got to his feet. "Who?"

"Lady Brancoveanu from Wallachia."

Beatrice's heart rate jumped. This could not be good. She placed her hand on Mihai's arm. "Something is wrong," she whispered.

"Show Lady Brancoveanu in."

Sergeant Ceseanu departed. Within a minute, he escorted Alina Brancoveanu into the room.

"Lady Alina, would you like some tea? Have you had breakfast?"

"Thank you. Perhaps some tea and a little food would be nice."

Mihai spoke to Sergeant Ceseanu, then he joined Beatrice and Alina.

"What's wrong?" asked Beatrice.

Alina glanced nervously at Mihai, then to Beatrice. "Hecuba and Bane died last night. She was performing a dark magic spell and her body just gave out."

Mihai held up a hand. "Hecuba?"

"Yes," said Alina.

Deep emotion welled in his eyes. "She's the witch who killed my mother."

"She's dead now – along with the wolf who was her mate," said Alina.

"Who took over the pack?" asked Beatrice.

"Timon."

"Timon?" questioned Beatrice.

"Yes. To extract our loyalty, he threatened us with psychoblin mushrooms. Diana, however, had prepared an antidote. We took the mushrooms, freeing our ties to Timon."

"And Viktor? Did he take the antidote?" asked Mihai.

"No. He departed before Diana could give it to him. I fear he's coming here to do you harm, Your Majesty," said Alina.

The door opened and a maid brought in a breakfast tray. Beatrice collected the tarot spread so there was room for the tea tray. Alina ate.

"What did these mushrooms do to Viktor?" asked Mihai.

Beatrice frowned. "They'll make him mad. He's wild now – more animal than man."

"Alina, does he intend to harm me? Theresa?"

"I believe so. I sensed deep anger and resentment coming from him last night."

Apprehension threaded through Beatrice like a snake. "Damn. Just what my father feared. The wolf would either turn his attention on you or Theresa."

"My bond with Viktor is broken," said Alina.

"How can I protect Theresa?" asked Mihai.

"You have to kill him," said Beatrice.

"Kill him? He's the father of my nephew."

"He's no longer the man you knew, but a feral beast. You must be prepared to kill him." Beatrice's voice was firm. She knew the only way they'd be safe now is for Viktor to die.

Alina sipped her tea. "I'm sorry I had to bring you such bad news. Thank you for breakfast, but I should leave for

Bucharest now."

"How are you traveling?" asked Mihai. Concern laced his voice.

"I'm alone on horseback."

"That won't do. There is danger for you," said Beatrice.

"I'll have Sergeant Ceseanu prepare a carriage. One soldier will drive, one will act as the footman," said Mihai.

"Thank you."

Mihai left to talk to his sergeant.

Beatrice walked to the window. A sudden chill ripped down her spine. She wrapped her arms around herself. Something was wrong, but she couldn't put her finger on it.

Mihai returned as Alina finished her meal.

"The carriage is ready," he said.

Alina smiled. "Thank you."

Beatrice placed her hand on Alina's elbow. "Send me a message through the runes so I know you arrived safely."

"I will."

Mihai and Beatrice escorted Alina to the door. They watched her enter the carriage. It ambled off.

"Your Majesty!"

Mihai spun around. At the top of the staircase, Sergeant Ceseanu held Mr. Tybeski. Blood trickled down the right side of his face and his right eye was swollen.

"What happened?" Mihai ran up the stairs, Beatrice right behind him. Bone-numbing fear ran down her back.

"It was...Lord Bacau...he went to the nursery..." Mr. Tybeski said out of breath.

Beatrice grabbed Mihai's arm. "Theresa?"

"The Queen tried to stop him...but he took the baby...she's hurt..."

"Sergeant, take Mr. Tybeski to Dr. Stanza, then send him to the nursery."

"Yes, Your Majesty."

Beatrice raced after Mihai. The wet nurse lay on her bed, unconscious, a bruise on her temple. Theresa lay at the foot of the crib. Across her cheek were four deep fingernails slashes. Blood trailed down her face onto the floor. Mihai ran to her and cradled her in his arms.

"Theresa, what happened? Can you hear me?" he asked.

Beatrice grabbed a baby blanket and placed it against Theresa's cheek. She stirred. Beatrice sensed shame within her sister. Why? Because she didn't stop Viktor? The shame was deep. Was there another cause?

"It was Viktor. He took the baby."

Beatrice locked eyes with Mihai. Hatred flared within him.

"Can you help her before the doctor arrives?"

"Yes, hold the blanket."

Mihai did as Beatrice instructed. She pulled a small bag out of her dress pocket and removed a vial of brooklime root powder. She raced to the table next to the crib and poured water from a craft into the vial. Capping it, she shook the vial, mixing the powder and water. Satisfied, she knelt down next to her sister and pushed Mihai's hand away. She poured the mix over the scratch marks. The bleeding stopped and the wounds dried over.

Theresa clenched her fingers on Beatrice's arm. "Stop the pain."

"I will."

"How can I help?" asked Mihai.

"Go after Viktor. Now. He can't be far."

Mihai stood. He stiffened his shoulders. "I'll shut down Constanta if I have to."

Sergeant Ceseanu appeared at the door. "Your Majesty, I have news."

"What is it?

"A stable hand saw Lord Bacau get into the carriage we prepared for Lady Brancoveanu – with a baby."

Mihai turned to face Beatrice. "Do everything in your power to help Theresa."

"I will, of course."

"Sergeant Ceseanu, come with me. Take the platoon of soldiers here at the castle down to Constanta. We're going to lock down the city. Don't let that carriage out of the city limits. I'll search every inch of Constanta to find my godson."

"Mihai—"

"What, Beatrice?"

"Remember everything I taught you. You'll need it to defeat him."

"I will."

He paused and knelt before Theresa. She looked at him with pain-filled eyes.

"I love you," he said.

"I love you, too." Her voice was weak and shaky.

Mihai marched out the door. Beatrice turned her attention to Theresa's face. The slash marks were deep, but the brooklime was setting in. The blood was caking over and would soon flake off, revealing unbroken skin.

"Bea..."

"Hush, don't talk. Just let the mix do its work." Beatrice reached into her satchel and gave her sister a willow bark pill. Then she glanced toward the window and said a silent prayer. *May Dalca's strength be with you, Mihai.*

Chapter Twenty-Eight

Alina opened the door to the carriage and was immediately bombarded with negative emotions – fear, hate, and loathing.

"Get in and act normal," Viktor said in a harsh, raw voice.

Alina swallowed back her own fear and glared at the baby in Viktor's arms for courage. Quietly, she entered the carriage and knocked against the driver's wall. The carriage ambled off.

"Good. From now on it is just us."

She raised an eyebrow. "Us?"

"You are Michael's mother now." He thrust the baby into Alina's arms. Michael fussed and cried.

"Calm him down," said Viktor, sneering.

Alina ran her fingers over the baby's face, thinking gentle thoughts. Michael stopped fussing, almost intuitively responding to her. Curious. He wanted warmth – caring. She pursed her lips. How was she able to sense him? Why wouldn't she be able to sense him? The baby had witch's blood in him – after all, Viktor's wife was a witch.

Alina peered at Viktor. "You took the baby without permission?"

"I am his father. He is mine to take." Viktor's lip twitched.

"You should take him back. You are mad and I am not his mother."

Viktor lunged out and grabbed Alina's hair. "You will be loyal to me or I will kill you and find another witch who can."

Sheer fright spiked within her. Foul creature! Fear glittered in Michael's eyes. His tiny fingers curled around the fabric of her dress, making his knuckles white. What damage had the wolf inflicted? Alina had to remain calm and find a way out of this danger.

The carriage rattled down the dirt road. Alina continued to stroke Michael's cheek, soothing him. Viktor sat in the seat opposite her, his lower lip twitching in a haphazard rhythm. His eyes jumped from side to side. Damn! There was no humanity left in his lupine gaze. For now, though, she would obey him. He was extremely powerful, and she didn't doubt he would carry out his threat to kill her if she defied him. She had to stay alive and protect the baby.

The coach ambled onto the cobblestone streets of Constanta. Alina snuggled Michael against her breast and peered out the window. Chimneys spilled smoke into the air. People walked the streets, some casually, some quickly. A squad of cavalry soldiers rode down the road. Viktor leaned over and looked out the window. The soldiers posted themselves throughout the area. King Mihai rode by on his horse, accompanied by his personal guard. His face was consumed with fury. Praise Dalca! There was hope.

"Mihai thinks to find the child. You see to it he doesn't," said Viktor.

Alina pursed her lips. Viktor's hatred for King Mihai raged through every pore of his body. The carriage stopped. Viktor glared at her. There was a knock on the window and the driver opened the door.

"My Lady, Constanta's being locked down. We can't leave the city right now. I've parked us in front of an inn if you want to get a room."

"I think that's wise."

Viktor's nostrils flared. "We need to leave."

"Enough! We have to wait this out or you will be discovered for sure." Alina narrowed her eyes, determined to have her way. If they left the city, then she and Michael were doomed.

Viktor grabbed her wrist. "Fine, we'll wait this out, but you will be loyal to me."

"My Lad—" said the driver. He looked confused and concerned.

"I'm fine. Lord Bacau and I will get a room here."

The driver nodded his acknowledgement and helped Alina out of the carriage. *"The Wolf's Tavern"* loomed before them. Alina suppressed an ironic laugh. The roughshod exterior and shoddy wooden façade sent a shiver down her spine. The tavern smelled of cigarettes and stale beer. She hoped the rooms weren't as vulgar.

"Follow me." Viktor marched toward the door.

Alina exchanged a worried look with the driver. "Find King Mihai," she mouthed. He nodded.

"Alina!" Viktor waited for her by the door arms crossed. She joined him, Michael in her arms, and they walked inside.

Viktor spoke to the proprietor and obtained a room on the second floor. They ascended the creaky steps in stony silence. Michael snuggled closer to her.

Viktor found the room, opened the door, and walked to the bed, collapsing on it. His body shook.

"I need another mushroom."

Dalca! The last thing he needed was another mushroom. Thankfully, she didn't have any. Ignoring him for the moment, she surveyed the room. The bed was dirty. A light layer of soot covered the window overlooking the street. The furniture was worn. She took off her cloak and bunched it up, placing it on the table. She placed Michael on the makeshift bed.

"Alina, I want another mushroom."

"I don't have any. If you're in pain, I can give you some laudanum."

"Fine. Give me the laudanum."

Alina bent over Michael and whispered. "Just a minute, I must take care of your father."

Michael scrunched up his face in disapproval.

Alina withdrew her satchel from her dress pocket and removed a small flask. She walked over to Viktor. He leaned up on his elbows and she poured the contents of the vial down his throat. His eyes glazed over and he fell asleep. She spied his sapphire pendant around his neck. A sapphire protected against poisoning. Deciding against removing it for now, she paused. Dare she pry into his soul? She sensed a tremendous amount of blackness within, but she had to know what she was up against. Despite her better judgment, she laced her fingers with his and probed his soul.

She pulled away with a quick jolt. Viktor's pain was deep. Every good emotion he ever had had been tangled into knots around his heart. They were twisted, thorn-ridden, and diseased. The sensitive person he had been was now gone, replaced with this hateful being consumed with revenge.

Alina rubbed her hand over her mouth. He wanted revenge on the Queen, and Alina could guess why after witnessing the events of last night.

Michael whimpered. Alina walked away from Viktor. She took Michael into her arms and brushed her lips against his cheek.

"Momma."

Alina jerked away. Yes, this boy was a witch – and with the promise of being a powerful one.

She put him down on the table and splayed her fingers over his face. "Show me your birth."

Images of his mother tumbling down the stairs flooded his mind. His mother was hurt. His father carried her up the stairs. He was early, so he must fight, but he knew he had enough power to survive. Queen Theresa filled his images. Mother.

"Show me your father."

King Mihai.

Alina withdrew her hand, confused. Weren't Viktor and his wife, Sonia, this baby's parents?

She lunged for her satchel and withdrew buckthorn for its truth-telling properties. She removed her athame and pricked Viktor's finger. It bled. She placed buckthorn on the blood. It turned purple.

Alina went to Michael and pricked his heel, sprinkling buckthorn on his blood. It turned yellow.

Shock coursed through her veins. Viktor was not this baby's father! No, his true parents were King Mihai and Queen Theresa. Alina put her fist to her mouth. How could she tell the King and Queen the truth? She didn't doubt they would believe her, but there were other factors involved. The von Krackens were a powerful witching family. No, they would be delighted the boy was returned to Theresa. Alina would then have to explain why Viktor went mad. It would come out the Queen cursed her future child to become a wolf. Alina should have spoken up. The von Krackens might punish Alina for her lack of action, but they would also be forced to execute the queen. She swallowed down a lump of fear. The law was death to a witch who cursed her child. Even though Hecuba had performed the curse, Alina had stood by and allowed it to happen. The von Krackens would be forced to uphold the law and execute the queen before the child was born.

Alina couldn't do it. If she told the truth, she gave the queen a death sentence – and herself. If Alina and Michael lived, the Sigmaringens were Michael's godparents, and they would raise him in the absence of his "true" parents. Alina knew she had no choice. She had to keep silent. And when the cursed child was born, Alina would offer her services to Queen Theresa in the hopes of saving the child from the curse.

Chapter Twenty-Nine

With Sergeant Ceseanu at his side, Mihai locked down Constanta using the platoon of cavalry soldiers that was detailed for security at Delfin Castle. Before he left, he secured his revolver with the silver bullets to his person. He also carried his athame and anise power. He had every intention of searching each alley and dark corner for Alina, Michael, and Viktor.

Viktor. It pained him that his best friend couldn't overcome the nature of the beast. If only Sonia hadn't died! Viktor hadn't been the same since her death. And Mihai knew Viktor could never be the man he used to know.

Mihai was confident he'd shut the city down in time. He rode Aladdin down one of the streets near the docks. A man dressed as a coach driver approached. Sergeant Ceseanu appeared to recognize him. He pulled the reins of his horse and stopped. Mihai did so as well.

Sergeant Ceseanu glanced at Mihai. "That's the man I assigned to drive Lady Brancoveanu's carriage."

Determination revitalized Mihai.

The man waved. "Your Majesty! Sergeant Ceseanu!"

"What do you know, Ciprian?" asked the sergeant.

"A man took Lady Brancoveanu to *"The Wolf's Tavern"*. She looked reluctant to go. I believe it was Lord Bacau."

"Did she have a baby?" asked Mihai.

"Yes."

Mihai couldn't hesitate; he had to strike. "Sergeant, gather a squad of men and surround the tavern. If Viktor should try to leave, shoot him on sight. I'm going inside to find Lady Brancoveanu."

"Yes, Your Majesty." Sergeant Ceseanu rode off.

"Take me to the tavern," said Mihai.

Ciprian walked to the corner and pointed to the left. Mihai nodded his acknowledgment and dismounted his horse, hitching Aladdin up to a nearby post. Once his horse was secure, he surveyed the façade. Nine slender windows overlooked the street. In one of them, he thought he spied a woman. Alina?

He marched into the tavern. A small entrance opened up into a bar area. There were only a handful of customers. The proprietor stepped out from behind the bar. "Your Majesty."

"I have no quarrel with you. What room is the noblewoman in?"

"Second floor, third room on the left facing the street."

"The man with her is a criminal. I would suggest you all leave now."

Those in the bar scurried out the door. Mihai took the steps two at a time to the second floor. When he got to the top, he checked his belt. His gun hung on his right hip, his athame on the left. In the utility pouches were his anise powder and several darts.

He imposed an iron will of control over his body. Nothing was more important than saving Michael and Alina.

He knocked on the door.

"Who is it?" came Alina's voice.

"King Mihai! Open up, Lady Brancoveanu!"

Wood snapped. A baby cried. Mihai couldn't wait. A kick to the door weakened the hinges. With another kick, the door snapped open. Mihai rushed in, gun drawn. Viktor had a knife to Alina's neck. Michael was in her arms.

"Come to kill me, Mihai?" Viktor's voice was cold, devoid of emotion.

Mihai froze near the door. He didn't have a good shot of Viktor with Alina next to him. His shirt was open showing a glistening stone around his neck. A sapphire. Damn. The thing would protect him against poisoning and Mihai was counting on using his silver bullets.

"If I have to."

Viktor's eerie laugh stabbed at Mihai's heart. "I'm your friend – your sister's husband. You wouldn't kill me. Now put the gun down."

"Let Alina and Michael go."

"Drop the gun."

Mihai stooped, placing the gun on the ground. Alina's gaze darted to the table. There were several powders and vials spread out haphazardly. Did she mean for him to use them? He sensed fear rising within her.

"I have no intention of letting them go. Now, you're going to let me walk out of here."

Mihai pursed his lips. Alina's gaze once again went to the table. She must want him to use the powder.

Viktor pushed Alina forward. Michael cried.

"Stay where you are, Mihai." Viktor turned to look at his companion. "Alina, shut the baby up."

That was the split-second Mihai needed. He lunged, grabbed a handful of the powder, and flung it at Viktor. It stung Alina's eyes as well. They both coughed and wheezed. Viktor released her. She grabbed the sapphire around his neck and yanked on the chain. The stone fell to the floor. Alina collapsed, falling to her knees, holding Michael still, and looked at Viktor. Mihai felt a rush of energy fly past them.

"Wisps of buckthorn speak true,
blind the beast, his heart impure,
bring sight to the man
whose aim is just and right and good."

A spell! Viktor dropped the knife. Mihai grabbed Viktor's wrists. This was his chance now that the pendant was off.

"King Mihai!"

Mihai glanced at the door, taking his attention off Viktor. Sergeant Ceseanu.

"Take Alina and Michael to safety! Now!" Mihai yelled.

Sergeant Ceseanu rushed to Alina's side, helped her to her feet, and pushed her out the door, Michael clung to her.

Viktor shoved Mihai against the wall of the room. Damn, he was strong! Mihai did not have Viktor's strength, but he did have his wits.

"You're weak, Mihai."

Mihai brought his leg up, striking Viktor near his groin. Viktor tumbled backward. His former friend may be strong, but Mihai could channel energy.

Viktor caught his balance and lunged at Mihai again, tackling him. They fell to the floor, tumbling over each other. Viktor's fist connected with Mihai's ribs. Pain seared through him. Mihai had to end this – and quickly.

Mihai channeled a rush of energy out of his hand, "Get away!" Viktor blasted from Mihai and struck the bed. Mihai looked at the gun and held out his hand.

"Come to me!"

The gun flew into his hand. He pointed it at Viktor's heart.

"Think to shoot me? Try. Your bullets won't harm me." Viktor wiped his hand over a spot of blood on his lower lip.

Mihai hesitated. Viktor had been his friend. He'd been a brother to him.

Viktor drew in a breath. "Your wife is a witch, Mihai."

"I know."

"She's done something quite awful."

Disgust tore through Mihai. He would not listen to the lies coming from Viktor's lips. "Shut up!"

"Theresa can't have children. She—"

Mihai pulled the trigger. Viktor must have seen the spread, but it didn't matter. Theresa would have children.

The tarot said so!

Viktor collapsed to the floor, his face registering shock. "You did it. You really pulled the trigger."

"Did you doubt me?"

Viktor sneered. "Yes."

Mihai dropped to his knees as Viktor's body jerked in place. "I loved you, Viktor! I loved you like a brother."

Viktor's lips twitched. His skin turned pasty silver and his joints locked in place. Viktor was dead.

His heart wept for the tragedy that had befallen his friend, Sonia, and Michael.

Sergeant Ceseanu rushed into the room. "Are you all right, Your Majesty?"

"Yes. How is Lady Brancoveanu? Michael?"

"They're safe."

Mihai grimaced from the pain in his torso as he got to his feet. "Take Lord Bacau's body and burn it."

Sergeant Ceseanu summoned several soldiers and removed the body. Once they were gone, Mihai hung his head and stood on the spot where Viktor's body had been. His friend had been born a man, but died a beast. A sunbeam filtered into the window, striking his face. His body warmed. Mihai would go home to his family – Theresa and Michael. He'd lost much this year, but gained much as well. He was king, a father to his godson, a witch, and a husband – and he would be the best he could be.

Epilogue

August, 1867

Theresa lay in her bed, her newborn son sleeping in her arms. Roses, carnations, daffodils, and even lilies filled her room.

Her son's birth had been easier than Hadrian's. Her new baby was perfect with ten fingers, ten toes, and sensitive blue-hazel eyes. He had Mihai's thick ebony hair. The boy would be as handsome as his father. Unfortunately, there was an unusual birthmark on his shoulder. A crescent moon. And according to Alina, that was proof the child had been cursed. Alina had told her that much when she had returned Michael to the castle.

Theresa closed her eyes and shivered, painfully regretting her actions. Beatrice had told her she'd misread the cards. She would have six children, three would live, three would be lost to her. She didn't need to resort to a curse to conceive the child in her arms. In her grief, in her confusion, she did something foolish. She could never tell Mihai or Beatrice. Beatrice must never see her son's birthmark. The only one who knew was Alina. With Alina's help, Theresa was confident she could help her son break the curse he was now under.

The door opened and Mihai walked in holding their eleven-month-old godson in his arms. Her husband wore a white linen shirt neatly tucked into his trousers. Michael was a sweet boy with a gentle disposition. He crawled everywhere and had just recently started walking along the furniture. He explored everything. Sonia would have been proud of him.

"I was told you were up." Mihai sat on the edge of her bed, surveying his new son with pride.

"He's as handsome as his father."

Mihai's emerald eyes sparkled. Michael wiggled in Mihai's arms. He placed the child on the bed. Michael got on his knees and peered at the baby.

Mihai put his hand on Michael's shoulder and looked at Theresa. "Michael will always know he is Sonia's son, but we'll raise the boys to be brothers in their hearts."

"I think that's wise. Mihai?"

"Yes."

"Do you sense Michael's emotions?"

Mihai smiled. "I do. I just didn't think I'd sense them so early."

Theresa nodded.

Mihai paused before speaking. "Do you like the flowers?"

"They're beautiful."

"Did you hear the gun salute that rang out in front of the Parliament building earlier?"

"It spooked me at first."

"I'm sorry, but it's how we mark the birth of the Crown Prince in Moldavia."

"What should we name him?" asked Theresa.

"Do you have a suggestion?"

"I want him to have a unique name. I don't want him named after anyone."

"All right."

"What do you think of Stefan?" asked Theresa.

Michael smiled and gently rubbed the baby's blanket.

Mihai laughed. "I think Michael approves. What do you think of Sebastian for his middle name?"

"Stefan Sebastian Sigmaringen? I think it's a mouthful, Mihai."

"He is the Crown Prince of Moldavia and the future king of Romania. His name should be a mouthful."

Theresa laughed. "Fine. I agree to the name."

Mihai grew silent, a thoughtful look in his eyes.

"Mihai, is something wrong?"

"It's just a poignant moment for me. My future lies with you and the boys, but I will never forget those who touched my life – my mother's goodness, my father's determination, my sister's perseverance, and I will never forget what Viktor meant to me."

Theresa reached for his hand and squeezed. "We will honor all their memories."

He leaned over and kissed her.

The End

Coming Soon

Twilight Over Moldavia

Moldavia Moon – Book Two

Romanian unification is on the horizon and the spirited Crown Princess of Carpathia, Caroline, would prefer to ride horses and archery to embroidery and dancing. Complicating her life is her recent discovery that she's a witch.

Prince Stefan Sigmaringen travels to Carpathia to meet Caroline. He discovers he has much in common with her. He also learns that a strange man, Timon, has an unnatural interest in him.

Upon Stefan's engagement, he overhears his mother confessing to a horrible secret – she cursed him in order to conceive him and Stefan will become a werewolf when he turns eighteen. There is a condition to overcome the curse, but it will require Stefan to draw on all his inner strength and Caroline, her courage. Can they break the foul enchantment and secure their future or will Stefan give himself over to the lupine curse that haunts his family?

Sunrise Over Brasov

Moldavia Moon – Book Three

Rosa Getzi lives a life of intrigue at Poiana Brasov with Clement, a werewolf, and Cassandra, the witch. Her past doesn't matter to her – until she discovers what it holds.

Prince Michael Sigmaringen joins his sister-in-law, Caroline, and the vampire prince, Darius, in a daring rescue, igniting Rosa's desire to find her family. However, all is not as it appears. Rickard, Rosa's friend, escapes with her. Clement will go to any lengths to get Rosa and Rickard back.

At Darius' fortress, Michael soon discovers Rickard is a new breed of werewolf – one who can control the change, and Clement hopes to exploit Rickard's abilities.

Michael's courage, strengths, and convictions will be tested like never before. Can Michael and Rosa find true happiness and the rid the lupine haunting of the Sigmaringens once and for all?

Reviews for:

The Wolf's Torment

Moldavia Moon – Book One

5 Stars, Queen Tutt, Rhonda Tutt

Perfect Paranormal/Fantasy with a Twist!

Wow! I absolutely loved this book. The secret lives of witches and were-wolves fill this story with a captivating romance and a twisted drama. I was totally glued to the pages and wanted it to last forever and wishing I had their magical spells to transport myself into their time period. The writing is beautifully smooth and visionary.

The characters are brilliantly built and their chemistry will melt your heart. I loved Prince Mihai, he is heir to be King one day and comes home from school to live a destiny his father has planned – yes an arranged marriage to a women he has never met (Theresa). I loved his passion and dedication to his father and sister. His resistance towards his intended is short lived and he soon finds himself madly in love. The author did a beautiful job showing the family closeness between them as they worked together as a unit.

Mihai is a witch, and he knows it, but he has never practiced or even learned what talents he could obtain. He inherited his witch blood from his mother and the author's details of his mother's demise is tragic but is one of the first things that drew me into the story line, I couldn't put the book down – totally spellbinding.

Lady Theresa is a doll, she is so innocent and sweet, one would call her a daddy's girl even though she has older brother and sisters. She is very educated and naive of the witch and were-wolf world that surrounds her. Her family is head of the witch coven and they have kept this secret from her due to her father having the future sight in dreams and how her life would end if she ever practiced it. But Theresa has a little insight about Mihai due to the fact she has been dreaming of him since she was a little girl, she just never realized how much better he'd be once she finally got to meet him. Yes, love at first sight. Their passion was magical – heat rating 3 Flames. With one heartache after another, with all the drama that goes on, my heart sank at what happens with her baby and her sister-in-law's baby – I actually yelled "NO!"

The witches amazed me. There are two types of witches as we all know – a good witch and a bad witch. Mihai and Theresa's family are good witches and they find themselves at a constant state of preparing and guarding against evil. I loved all the potions, herbs, and healing abilities that were described – made me want to plant some myself – LOL

The were-wolf pack is totally wicked; I loved the culture the author built around them. Their rituals and methods of being a part of the pack is mind blowing. This is the first time I didn't like the were-wolves in a book. On a full moon we know wolves have to change and hunt but the only way they can have their needs met and satisfied is through sexual relationships with a witch for only a witch can handle their roughness and calm them down with their powers.

Viktor was Mihai's best friend from school and came home with him to become his right-hand man. I fell for him quick when he fell in love with Mihai's sister and they got married. But a twist of faith reeks habit as Viktor is bitten by an ancestral were-wolf from his bloodline to become the new leader of the wolf pack. The tragedies and the twisted revenge gripped my heart and turned me against him. I couldn't believe what I was reading, it was shocking – I had a WTF moment.

The story's plot line is perfect, and the climax unraveled all at once as Theresa realizes she is a witch, Viktor goes crazy becoming conniving, deceitful, and revengeful with his wolf blood, and Mihai grows into his witch gift with the help of Theresa's family so he can protect the woman of his life and their future of uniting Romania with the other smaller kingdoms.

The happy ever after leaves you happy with Mihai saving the day but filled with questions of the wolf curse that Theresa has bestowed upon her 2nd child and whether Mihai and the rest of their family will ever find out about it and when they do what will happen to Theresa then – will she be hanged as her father's dreams foresaw? This was an amazing story and I highly recommend this to all paranormal romance lovers. Excellent Read!

4.5 Books, Book Bling, Elizabeth Alsobrooks

I love historical fiction, vampires, werewolves, witches, suspense, exotic settings, royal intrigue and romance. What's my point? This book has it all! What a treat.

There is also one other thing I look for in excellent fiction, and that is an opening hook that lets me know what I'm in for, and an action-filled plot that lives up to my expectations. Stephanie did not let me down. The background information that is essential to the plot line is deftly woven into story, such as a careening carriage chase wherein we learn the secret truth about the hero's mother. Ah...the plot thickens.

The prince is mouthwatering delicious and as if that weren't fun enough, his best friend, equally awe inspiring, falls for his kid sister and then promptly gets turning into a werewolf! Delightful, you say? You bet!

It's not all fun though. Yes, there are nonstop games, but the teams are good and evil. Laced with twists and turns, this was a plot I could really sink my teeth into—if only I could live that long. If you like the pagan elements of Reign, the thinly veiled diabolic revenge and greed of Game of Thrones, or the outright dark magic the good guys must face throughout the espionage of the Hobbit, this book will not let you down. And the happy ending required of all romance reads will put a smile on your face.

5 Stars, The Crafty Cauldron

I was pleasantly surprised by *The Wolf's Torment.* It was brilliantly written, the visuals were awesome. This is a dark, paranormal fantasy at its best. It amazes me when an author can take a subject/plot that has been written to death and make it new. I loved her take on vampires/werewolves. She was extremely adept at getting the torment and passion behind the characters. I am a HUGE paranormal fan, and I was totally wrapped up in this book. I think even if you aren't a paranormal fan, you will like this book. 5 stars for me. It totally kept my attention.

About Stephanie Burkhart

Stephanie Burkhart was born in Manchester, New Hampshire. She served in the U.S. Army from 1986-1997 in the Military Police Corps, spending over seven years overseas in Germany and a deployment to Hungary. Her highest military award is the Army Commendation Medal (3x). In 1995, she received a Bachelor of Science degree in Political Science from California Baptist University, graduating magna cum laude. Currently, she lives in Castaic, California and works for LAPD as a 911 Dispatcher.

Read more about Stephanie at
http://stephanieburkhart.com

www.ingramcontent.com/pod-product-compliance
Lightning Source LLC
LaVergne TN
LVHW090549110826
845146LV00001B/75

9798989144846